Book Five

INCARNATIONS
OF IMMORTALITY

*Being a
Green
Mother*

PIERS ANTHONY

A DEL REY BOOK
BALLANTINE BOOKS · NEW YORK

A Del Rey Book
Published by Ballantine Books

Library of Congress Cataloging-in-Publication Data
Anthony, Piers.
  Being a green mother.

  (Incarnations of immortality ; book 5)
  "A Del Rey book."
  I. Title.   II. Series: Anthony, Piers.
Incarnations of immortality ; bk. 5.
PS3551.N73B43   1987   813'.54   87-47742
ISBN 0-345-32222-3

Manufactured in the United States of America

First Edition: December 1987

10 9 8 7 6 5 4 3 2 1

CONTENTS

1. SONG OF THE MORNING / 1
2. HAMADRYAD / 11
3. TINKA / 26
4. QUEST / 45
5. MYM / 60
6. ORLENE / 75
7. LIVIN' SLUDGE / 88
8. JONAH / 107
9. LLANO / 133
10. NATASHA / 161
11. SONG OF DAY / 177
12. SONG OF EVENING / 198
13. GREEN MOTHER / 219
14. FORBIDDEN SONG / 235
15. CHAOS / 257
16. WEDDING / 288
AUTHOR'S NOTE / 302

–1–

SONG OF THE MORNING

She was just a child, but in the dream she was a woman, beautiful, in a bridal gown, walking down a long aisle on the arm of a man she couldn't quite see.

But the dream was split-screen, and the other part showed the great globe of the world. That was her, too, in the strange way the dream had of making it seem real. But the world was mostly dead; no human beings remained on it.

Somehow she knew that these were two aspects of her future, and that one of them would come to pass. Marriage—or destruction. But which one? Why? It wasn't frightening, just mysterious.

Then music swelled. It was a lovely, mysterious melody. She woke, afraid it would fade away along with the rest of the dream, but it remained, coming from outside.

She scrambled out of bed, leaving her sister Luna sleeping. Well, Luna wasn't exactly her sister, but it was complicated to fathom, so that was good enough. Let her sleep for the moment; this shouldn't take long.

She shoved her toes into her slippers and scurried across the floor in her nightie. Lured by the melody, she scrambled down the stairs, along the hall, and reached the door. She put both hands up on the solid knob and turned it, and after a brief struggle got the door open.

The summer dawn was cool but not cold. Orb hurried out, intent on the melody, not caring what time or temperature it was. The landscape seemed preternaturally bright, better than real life; this was fun!

She paused before the house, reorienting on the sound. The farm backed onto a forest, and the sound was from the forest. She ran across the field, scattering chickens, and reached the edge of the wood, panting. She was four years old, and this was a good-sized trek for her to accomplish alone. She wasn't supposed to come here without an adult, and that gave her a bad twinge of unease, but the music was fading, and she knew she had to catch it right away.

The forest loomed thick and dark, and it was girt with monstrous spider webs and mean brambles and other awful things, so she scouted along the edge, hoping for a way through. The music was becoming quite faint, making her desperate.

She found a path! She ran down it, into the depths of the wood. But the music was now fading out entirely, to her horror. She stopped to listen for it, but it was gone.

Except—there was another sound, not the same, but possessed of its own melody. Maybe that would do. It was ahead and, as she continued along the path, it grew louder.

The path debouched at the river. Orb had encountered the river before, but not at this spot. Here it was trippling merrily over rocks, making its music. She strained to hear the tune of it behind the rushing noise of water, and it came clearer, but imperfect.

She made her way along its irregular bank, guided more by her ears than her eyes. Now she heard another sound, neither the first melody nor the second, but a kind of tittering laughter. It was coming from a swirling pool a little downstream.

Then she spied the source of the mirth. Girls were playing in the pool! Lovely, lithe, bare girls with long tresses. They were swimming and splashing and diving and having a terrific amount of fun, and their trilling laughter made the last melody she had heard.

One of the nymphs spied Orb and called out to her. "Hello, child of man! Come join us!" The others laughed anew at this.

—2—

Orb pondered briefly, then decided to do it. She drew off her nightie and stepped out of her slippers. Naked, she went down to the pool.

"She heard me!" the nymph exclaimed, astonished.

Orb paused. "Did I do something wrong?"

The nymphs looked at each other. "You see us, child of man?"

"Yes. Don't you want me to splash with you?"

Again they exchanged glances. "Of course we do!" the first nymph said. "But do you know how to swim?"

"No."

"But then you might drown!"

Orb hadn't thought of that. She was sure that drowning would be very uncomfortable. "Then why did you ask me to join you?"

"We didn't think you would hear us," the nymph explained.

"Or see us," another added. "We were only teasing, the way we do."

"Why?"

"Because we are water sprites," a third said. "The children of men aren't usually aware of us."

Orb was perplexed. "Why?"

Several sprites shrugged. "We don't exactly know. It just is so."

There was an instant flowering of laughter. "Oh, you rhymed!" another cried.

The others splashed wildly at the one who had rhymed, giggling. Orb really wanted to join in, but she realized that she would have to learn to swim first.

"Why didn't I hear you or see you when I saw the river before?" she asked.

The sprites looked at each other, perplexed. "Why *didn't* she?" one repeated. "We have seen her before, and she was oblivious."

Orb didn't know what the big word meant, but judged that it meant what it was supposed to. "Yes, why?"

"Maybe she changed," one suggested. "Did you change recently, little girl?"

"This morning I head a song I never heard before. It woke me up. I was looking for it."

Again the sprites exchanged glances. "She changed," they agreed. "Now she can join us."

"How?" Orb asked, eager to participate.

"There's an inner tube someone's forgotten," one of the sprites informed her, perceiving her dilemma.

"Oh, I can float in that!" Orb agreed. "Bring it to me!"

The nymph shook her head. "Alas, we can not," she said sadly.

"Why?"

"We can not touch the things of the children of man. At least, not to affect them. Only mortal creatures can do that."

Orb accepted that. "Then tell me where it is, and I'll fetch it myself."

"Gladly!" The sprite led her downstream a short distance. There, hung up on a dead branch, was an inflated inner tube.

Orb waded into the shallow water, her legs tingling with the chill of it, and hauled on the tube. "Oh, it's heavy," she complained. "Can't you help me?"

"I don't think so," the sprite said sadly. "I really can't touch you or it." She demonstrated by reaching out to touch Orb, and her hand passed through Orb's arm without sensation.

"Oh, you're a ghost!" Orb exclaimed, not certain whether to be pleased or frightened.

"No, just a sprite. I can touch natural things like water, but not unnatural things like the children of man."

Orb decided it was time for introductions. "I'm Orb," she announced. "Who are you?"

"I'm—" The sprite paused, concentrating. "Oh, I don't think I have a name! I never realized."

"Oh, that's very sad!" Orb said. "I must give you a name."

"Oh, would you?" the sprite asked, pleased.

Orb concentrated, trying to think of a name. Beads of water trailed down the tube as she continued to tug at it. "Waterbead!" she exclaimed.

The sprite clapped her little hands. She was not much larger than Orb, though formed as an adult or nearly adult woman. "Oh, thank you!" Then, focusing on the tube: "Maybe if you lifted it a little, instead of just pulling . . . "

Orb lifted—and abruptly the tube came free. She clambered into it, and in a moment was floating.

"If you paddle with your hands . . . " Waterbead suggested.

Orb paddled, and the tube began to move. Soon she was out in the pool, moving splashily. The sprites laughed and splashed back at her. The droplets of water did touch her; they were natural. This was indeed fun, despite the cold.

Waterbead swam out ahead, making little whirlpools in the water. Then the other sprites joined in, fashioning a larger whirlpool. Orb's tube spun around in it, making her laugh giddily. Oh, yes, this was fun!

They were now at the lower side of the pool, and the current was picking up, carrying Orb on down the river. "Maybe you should paddle upstream," Waterbead said.

"Why?" Orb was enjoying the ride.

The sprites suffered one of their little pauses. "We can't go too far that way," one explained. "The water goes bad."

Orb didn't like bad water, so she paddled. But now the current was too strong for her. She made no headway, and soon her arms were tired, and the tube picked up speed downstream.

"We can't follow!" a sprite cried. One by one they dropped back, returning to the quieter pool, until only Waterbead remained.

"Maybe you should go to shore," Waterbead suggested.

"Why?"

"Because the bad sprites are downstream. If you go to the shore, you can stop before you reach them."

Orb tried to paddle for shore, but the current fought her, and she could not reach it.

"Oh, I must go back!" Waterbead cried. Indeed, she looked distressed, her hair turning lank and her skin clouding up. "Get out of the bad water as soon as you can, Orb!" Then she stroked swiftly upstream, leaving Orb alone.

The tube spun about, bouncing through the rapids, and Orb had to cling on for dear life. Then the river smoothed out in a kind of lake, with a factory beside it. A huge pipe poured dark fluid into the water.

Indeed, the water was bad, here; it was discolored and cloudy, so that she could no longer see to the bottom, and it stank of something rotten. Orb did as Waterbead had advised and paddled for the shore away from the factory.

But now more sprites appeared. These were of similar size to the first ones, but their bodies were twisted and their hair tangled. "What's this? A child of man!" one cried.

"Drown her!" the others chorused.

"But aren't you sprites?" Orb asked, alarmed.

"She sees us!" the twisted creatures cried as if horrified.

"Of course I see you and hear you, too," Orb said.

The hostile sprites ringed her, staring. "We can still drown her," one said, scowling. Her eyes were cloudy, as if there was disturbed weather inside her head.

"Not while she's in that tube!" another pointed out.

"Then get her out of the tube!"

They splashed at her, not playfully as the others had, but roughly, so that the water stung her face. "Hey, stop that!" she cried.

They did not. One rushed at her, making a horrible face. "Out! Out! Out!" the mean sprite screamed.

Orb got angry. "Yah!" she screamed back and struck at the sprite with her fist. She missed, but made a bad splash of her own. Then she whipped her arm back and forth, throwing up water so that it flew all over, and screamed so hard that her face heated.

The nymphs were daunted. Evidently they had never seen a temper tantrum before. It was a thing Orb was good at; sometimes she even frothed at the mouth, alarming everyone. Luna almost never got mad, but Orb made up for both of them when something set her off.

The sprites withdrew to a safe distance. "We can't touch her," one said.

"We don't have to," another answered. "There's more than one way to drown a mortal. Start a swirl."

"A swirl!" the others agreed.

They swam in a circle, stirring up the water, forming a great whirlpool. The nice sprites upriver had made fun swirls, but this was an ugly maw. Orb's tube was sucked into it. Faster she moved, as the sprites accelerated the water. The tube tilted as the center of the whirlpool dropped low. Orb was afraid she would topple over. Then she would have to let go, because her head would be under the foul water. Her anger was replaced by fright. What could she do now?

"A boat!" a sprite screamed angrily.

"It can't see us," another said.

"Yes it can!"

Abruptly the sprites left the whirlpool and dived under the murky water. The swirl eased, and Orb was able to see the boat. "Daddy!" she cried.

In a moment her father Pace was there, lifting her out of the tube and into the canoe and wrapping a blanket around her shivering body. She hugged him, crying, her relief causing her to let go of all the anger and fear.

But she was young, and in a moment the siege of emotion passed. Now her curiosity returned. "Daddy, I saw the sprites!" she exclaimed.

"You saw them?" he asked, repeating her statement in the way that adults tended to do. He seemed pleased.

"Nice ones in the pool, but mean ones here. Why is that, Daddy?"

"Because this water is polluted," he said. "The factory pours its wastes into the water, and that ruins it, and the sprites who live here become twisted. It is a sad thing."

"Why?"

He did not chide her for her "Why's." Daddy understood her. "Because the factory can make more money if it dumps its wastes out instead of paying someone to haul them away. We have tried to get the factory to stop, but it has a lot of money and it uses it to prevent us from stopping it."

"But the sprites—"

"It is said about them," Pace agreed. "But very few people can see them, so there is no clientele." He paused, realizing that he had gone beyond her vocabulary. "No one to try to help the sprites."

"Oh. That's very sad, Daddy. Even if they are real mean."

"Yes, it is. Perhaps when you grow up, you can do something about it. Then this colony of sprites won't be mean anymore."

That was too complicated to grasp fully, because Orb wasn't sure how anything could be other than it was now, so she asked another question. "How come nobody can see the sprites?"

Pace shook his head. "Some folk just seem to have more magic than others," he said. "Just as some are taller than others, or more mischievous. Or have worse tempers." He gave her a little squeeze. He didn't even mind her tantrums, which was one of the perplexing things about him. "Magic has run in my family, and that's part of it."

"What's the other part?" They were at the shore now, and he was lifting her out.

"Why, you know that, Eyeball," he said with mock reproval.

Orb considered. Then she smiled. "Your music, Daddy!"

He nodded. "My uncle had it. My cousin had it. I have it. And maybe you do, too, pumpkin."

"I heard a song," Orb confessed, knowing that her father would soon get around to inquiring why she was out in the lake. "When I woke up, I just had to find it. And I couldn't. It just went. Then I heard the river, and it was singing, too, only not the same, and the sprites called, and—are you going to tell Mommy?"

"Will you promise me not to do it again?"

Again Orb considered. "Daddy, I've just got to reach that song!"

"Dumpling, you just can't reach that song."

"Why?"

"Because it is the Song of the Morning. It fades out when dawn ends."

"But—"

"It will return tomorrow at dawn. I'll take you out to listen to it. Now will you promise?"

"Okay, Daddy."

"Then I won't have to tell your mother."

"Okay, Daddy!" she repeated, hugging him. Then: "But why aren't you mad?"

"Daddies don't get mad at little girls—"

"Oh, Daddy, you fibbed!"

"When they turn up with magic talents," he concluded.

Orb sobered. "I don't think I can make music like you."

"You heard the Song of the Morning. And the Song of the River. You saw the sprites. Those are signals of our family magic. It is just manifesting now. I was older than you are now when I first heard the music, and older yet when I learned to make it. Give it time, peanut."

"Okay, Daddy." She could tell how pleased he was about her hearing the Song. That was her luck, for she knew she had gotten herself into a lot of trouble, almost drowning in the river. Then, just in case he might reconsider, she changed the subject. "How am I related to Luna?"

Piers Anthony

She knew by his reaction that she wasn't deceiving him, but he answered anyway. "You are her aunt, technically."

"But I'm the same age!"

"Age doesn't matter. Niobe and I are your parents together and Luna's grandparents separately, and you are the half sister of each of her parents."

"I know!" she exclaimed. "A half and a half is a whole! I'm a whole sister!"

But he shook his head. "Half sister to her father the Magician, and half sister to her mother Blenda. Because you share one parent with each. Two halves. But either qualifies you as Luna's aunt."

Orb shook her head. "That's too mixed up for me, Daddy."

They were approaching the house. "I could draw you a chart, but I don't think you could read the names."

"I'll learn, Daddy!" she exclaimed.

So when they got inside, and Orb had been washed and cleaned by her mother, who did not ask questions after receiving a warning look from her father, Pace made a chart for her.

```
Cedric = Niobe = Pacian = Blanche
   |         |          |
   |        Orb         |
Magician ======== Blenda
              |
            Luna
```

Then he went over it with the two girls, because by this time Luna was up and curious, too. "My cousin Cedric Kaftan married Niobe, back way long, long ago," he explained. "Their son became the Magician. Meanwhile, I married Blanche, and our daughter was Blenda. The Magician married Blenda, who was his second cousin, and they had you, Luna." He tweaked a strand of her clover-honey hair, and she smiled. The two girls had been born only days apart and had trouble remembering who had been first.

—9—

"Cedric died young," Pacian continued, "and later Blanche died. That was when Niobe and I got together, and had you, Orb. So you are the Magician's half sister through Niobe, and Blenda's half sister through me. The two of you are of different generations, even though you are the same age and look like twins."

"Why are you so much older than Niobe?" Luna asked.

Pace smiled. "I'm actually eleven years younger than Niobe," he said. "She was the most beautiful woman of her generation, and she kept her youth."

The two girls looked at each other, the clover-honey blonde and the buckwheat-honey blonde, and shook their heads. They suspected they were being teased. It was obvious that Pace was much older than Niobe!

"Which relates to the prophecy concerning the two of you," Pace continued.

"What?" Orb asked.

"A prediction, a divination, a telling of the future," he explained. "What will happen. I think it is time for you to know it."

"Yes!" they agreed together, for this had the smell of mystery.

"It was a complex prophecy and it caused the Magician to lay a geis on you both, that no further prophecy can be made for you. It started with your fathers, when we were young, before we ever married. It was that each of us would marry the most beautiful woman of her generation and have a daughter."

"And you did!" Luna exclaimed. "Our mothers are—"

"Yes. That is part of it. But the rest of it is this: that one daughter might marry Death, and the other might marry Evil."

"But we're too young to marry anyone!" Orb protested.

"So you are—at the moment. But when you both grow up and are as beautiful as your mothers, remember that prophecy and be careful. No one knows exactly what it means."

"We will!" they chorused, not taking it seriously, for they never really expected to be other than they were right now. In later years, however, they were to remember, and Orb would wonder: did this relate to her vision? A wedding—and a dead world?

– 2 –

HAMADRYAD

Two years later both Orb and Luna could see the sprites and other magical creatures, and Orb could hear the music of natural things, while Luna could see their auras. It was a secret from their mothers but not from their fathers, because Pace could relate to the magic of nature and the Magician, Luna's father, knew everything about magic. The mothers were virtual twins in beauty, though they were, like the girls, of different generations. But they had no such perceptions and seemed too busy with practical matters to be concerned with them. Luna's mother Blenda spent most of her time assisting the Magician, who was doing ever more obscure research in magic, while Orb's mother Niobe did the laundry and shopping and meals and reading stories. Luna came to regard Niobe as virtually her mother, for Luna spent more of her time here than at her own home.

Luna tried in vain to show Orb the auras she perceived, which she said manifested as shimmering glows around and through all living things, while Orb had the same frustration when trying to have Luna hear the songs of nature. "It's the Song of the Morning!" she would exclaim at dawn. "Can't you hear it, Motheaten?"

"Look, Eyeball—if you can't see the auras as plain as day—!"

But the other magic Pace had promised Orb had not materialized. She could hear the music, but could not make it. Oh, she could sing, and with fair effect considering her age, but there was no magic. She was glad that her father had not told her mother about her misadventure with the sprites of the river—at least not about the cause of it, which was her ability to hear the Song of the Morning. She heard that song every morning now, if she was awake, and it was always lovely, changing a little with the nature of the land and the season, so that there was always a refreshing novelty about it. If only she could make music like that!

"Daddy . . . " she pleaded one day.

"Maybe the hamadryad can help you," Pace said.

"The what?"

"She taught the Magician his first magic," he explained. "She's a tree-nymph, like a sprite for a tree, and she befriended the Magician when he was a baby. We used to take him there to visit her for an afternoon, when he lived with us. They seldom deal much with our kind, but Luna's the Magician's daughter, and you are very like her, so maybe she will meet you. I know your mother will be glad to take you there, just for a visit."

"Oh goody!" Orb exclaimed, hugging him.

So they went for a day to the cabin near the swamp that they maintained as a vacation house. Niobe made sure that both girls were wearing their polished moonstone amulets, for the Magician had given them these for protection, and there could be dangers in the swamp.

The swamp was impressive. The trees expanded their bases near the water as if to embrace as much of it as possible, and magic surrounded them. Luna kept exclaiming as she saw the interactions of their auras, and Orb as she heard their separate yet interactive melodies. Niobe evidently perceived neither, but realized that the girls were not teasing her.

They came to the giant water oak. "Hamadryad!" Niobe called. "Do you remember me? You trained my son, the Magician."

The dryad appeared, perched on a stout lateral branch. She smiled cautiously; she remembered.

At that moment Orb suffered a recurrence of her vision-dream. She was walking down the aisle with the strange man, and the globe was turning, dead. Who was the man, and what had happened to the world, and how did she get involved with either? She tried to turn her head to see the man and managed a little, catching a fleeting glimpse of his profile. He was no one she knew now. And the world—she was responsible, in some fashion. She knew, and was horrified.

"I have brought the Magician's daughter—and mine," Niobe said, jolting Orb out of her vision. "Will you meet with them?"

The dryad peered down at the two girls. Luna and Orb, coached on this, smiled like twin moons.

The hamadryad nodded. She would meet.

"I will return in two hours," Niobe said.

Orb turned on her in alarm. "You are leaving us here?"

"The dryad will not approach an adult," Niobe explained. "Only a child. But you are safe here; she will not harm you, or let you harm yourselves, if you do what she says."

Uncertainly, the girls watched Niobe retreat. They knew she would not put them in any danger; she was extremely fussy about that sort of thing, and her definitions of risk could be pretty annoying. Such as eating too much candy, or playing in deep mud. Still, the swamp seemed awfully big and dank.

When Niobe was gone, the hamadryad came down the tree. She did not exactly climb down, she walked down. It was as if her feet were glued to the trunk, allowing her to walk at a right angle to it. That was impressive.

In a moment the dryad stood before them. She was no taller than they were, but was more finely proportioned, more like the sprites. Her hair was green and leafy, and her body, though unclothed, had ridges resembling bark. She was pretty in the way a tree was pretty, and in the way of a woman, too.

"Hello," the dryad said tentatively, as if not expecting any favorable response. She was poised for instant retreat.

"Hello," Orb responded.

The hamadryad responded with a smile so brilliant it was like a shaft of sunlight reaching down to touch her. "You *are* his child!" she exclaimed.

"Uh, no, not exactly," Orb said. "That's Luna. I'm Niobe's child."

"What?" Luna asked, perplexed.

"She got us confused, that's all," Orb said.

"How do you know?" Luna asked.

"You heard her! She called me the Magician's child."

"But she didn't say anything!" Luna protested.

"What?" Orb asked, in her turn.

"She did not hear me," the hamadryad said sadly.

Orb turned to Luna. "You didn't hear her?"

"Hear what? She only moved her mouth."

Now Orb realized. "It's like the music! I can hear it and you can't."

"Well, you can't see the auras, smarty!" Luna retorted.

"She sees auras?" the hamadryad asked.

"Oh, sure," Orb said. "I hear things, she sees things. Mommy can't do either. But Daddy can hear the music, so he said we should come see you."

"Who is your father?" the hamadryad asked.

"He's Pacian Kaftan. He makes magic music."

"Yes. So did Cedric, his cousin. The first time I heard it, I almost fell out of my Tree!"

Orb pictured the dryad falling out of the tree and she started to laugh. The dryad laughed, too.

"What's so funny?" Luna demanded.

Orb realized that she would have to translate, or there would be trouble. Usually she was the one who got mad and threw a fit, but Luna could do it, too, when she tried. "She says when she heard Grandpa Cedric's magic music, she almost fell out of the tree!"

Luna giggled. That *was* funny!

"But then he died," the hamadryad said. "It was so sad. The Magician was right here with me, just a baby then."

"A baby?" Luna asked when Orb translated. "My father?"

"Yes. He could hear the music and see the auras, but he couldn't make them. But he was very smart and he wanted to learn, so I taught him the natural magic."

"Can you teach us?" Orb asked. "Daddy can make such wonderful music, and he says maybe I can, but I can't!"

"Come into my Tree," the hamadryad said. "Perhaps I can teach you."

"Oooo, goody!" Orb cried, clapping her hands.

They scrambled up into the spreading branches of the tree, unable to walk the trunk in the manner of the hamadryad. Orb scraped a knee a little, but she was used to that.

Above, the leaf foliage closed in about them, forming a pleasant bower. The branches twisted this way and that and had knots and boles that were like chairs, and they sat on these. Speckles of sunlight came through, making it pretty.

"Ooo," Luna exclaimed. "The aura brightens where the sun strikes!"

"That's because the light is the life of my Tree," the hamadryad said. "Light and water and soil and air—four mundane elements."

Luna's brow furrowed as Orb translated. "I thought there were five elements."

"Yes. We call the important one spirit, or magic."

"That's why my father studied magic!" Luna exclaimed. "'Cause you told him that!"

"Yes. He wanted to help the natural things, as Cedric did. We dryads are magic, but we don't have much power over unnatural things, so I thought maybe if he learned . . ."

"I guess he's still learning," Luna said. "He and Mommy spend all their time with it."

"Let's see what we can do with your own magic," the hamadryad said, diverting the subject to safer territory. Orb was still relaying her words to Luna, who could not hear them. "Can you do this?" She made a gesture in the air with her right hand.

Luna stared at the space defined by the gesture, though Orb saw nothing. "Ooo, lovely!" she exclaimed.

"Try it yourself," the dryad said.

Luna made a similar gesture. "It's not working," she said, pouting.

"But the hand is only part of it! You must emote, too."

"What?"

"You must *feel*! Become one with the natural aura, shape it to your desire. Try it again."

Luna concentrated, gesturing again. Orb saw nothing, but the hamadryad smiled. "See? There's a little!"

Luna had scrunched up her eyes in her concentration. Now she looked. "Ooo, uck!" she exclaimed with distaste.

"But it's aura!" the dryad insisted. "You did it!"

Luna considered, as Orb relayed this endorsement. The truth was, Orb was tiring of this exchange. "I guess I did."

"But you must practice," the dryad cautioned her. "Art is not mastered in a day. It takes years to be good."

"Years!" Luna exclaimed impatiently. "I want to do it now!"

"Most people can't do it at all," the dryad reminded her. "But you, when you learn, will be able to read the auras of people and to know whether they are good or evil, because you will know the types of auras. A person may tell you a lie with a straight face, but his aura can never deceive you. That was why I knew the Magician was good, even when he was a baby, and that he had greatness in him, though there was a dark side. Because of his magnificent aura."

"Dark side?" Luna asked when all this reached her.

"He was good, but he had the capacity to relate to evil. Sometimes I still fear for him. If Satan turned him to evil—"

"Satan?" This was Orb's query.

"Oh, maybe I shouldn't have mentioned that," the dryad said. "Satan isn't nice."

Orb was bored with these proceedings, as they did not involve her, and words like "capacity" strained her resources. "What about *my* magic?" she asked.

The dryad turned to her. "Oh, you have been so helpful, Orb, I didn't realize I was neglecting you. Yes, we must see about your own magic. Tell your sister to practice her aura-painting while I work with you."

Orb, pleased with the compliment and the attention, decided not to quibble about the hamadryad's error. Luna was her niece, not her sister. She relayed the word, and Luna was satisfied to face away and make her gestures of nothing.

"Do you sing?" the dryad asked Orb.

"Yes, but not the way Daddy does."

"You, too, must emote. You must put your feeling into it. Magic involves the whole of a person's desire. That may be why most people don't have magic; they don't really *want* it. Not as part of them.''

"But Mommy doesn't have magic!" Orb protested, thinking that refuted the statement.

"Niobe had more magic than anyone, and gave it up to marry your father," the hamadryad said. "Now try to emote."

Orb concentrated as she hummed a tune, but nothing happened. "It's not working!" she said, aggrieved. "Why should it work for Luna and not for me?"

Before the dryad could answer, there was music from below. All three of them turned to look, peering down below the tree.

The music was approaching down the path, getting louder. It was a violin playing, and the man playing it was dressed in a bright, light blouse and dark trousers. He had glossy long hair falling across his shoulders and piercing black eyes. Beside him danced a woman in a glaringly red skirt and green kerchief about her hair, and no shirt at all. There were many rings on her fingers and long earrings dangling by her bare breasts, so that she flashed constantly as she moved.

Behind them came others, similarly garbed. Some played mandolins and some played instruments that Orb could not define at all, and all were dancing in their way. They came to the foot of the tree and drew up in a circle about it. There were perhaps a dozen of them, including a number of children.

An old woman stepped forward. "There!" she said, pointing directly at Orb and Luna. "Two magic children!"

"Gypsies!" the hamadryad exclaimed. "I have heard of them. Beware—they steal children!"

The man who had played the violin stepped up. "The seer knows," he said. "Come down from there, children. We wish to see your magic."

"Go away, you ruffians!" the dryad cried. "These children are not for you!"

"Oho!" the man said. "A tree-nymph! Well, this is not your business, oak-spirit. All we want are the children."

"You can't have them," the dryad said.

"Be quiet, dryad, or we'll chop down your tree," the man threatened. The hamadryad made a little squeal of outrage and pain, appalled by the threat.

"How come *he* can hear her when *I* can't?" Luna asked somewhat querulously.

"Get up there and bring them down," the man said. Immediately two husky young men ran up and scrambled up the tree. In moments they were in the branches and reaching for the girls, who were frozen in shock.

But as the hands of the men reached for Orb and Luna, and touched them, both men froze. Their hands never closed; they merely remained touching.

"Get on with it," the man called from below. "We don't want to tarry long here."

"We can't," one of the young men gasped, not moving.

"What do you mean, you can't?" the leader demanded. "They're only children!"

"They've got amulets," the other said.

"Oho! I should have known that children as valuable as this would be protected. Well, there are other ways. Drop back down."

The two young men did that literally, dropping from the big branches to the ground and landing lithely.

The leader smiled up at the girls. "We are the Raggle-Taggle Gypsies," he announced. "We like children and we have wonderful times. Magic children have a fine life with us—the best of all. Come and join us."

But Orb and Luna, heeding the hamadryad's warning, balked. They simply stared down, unmoving.

"We'll show you!" the Gypsy said. He snapped his fingers. Immediately the others brought out the instruments and resumed their music. The women danced, and the children cavorted acrobatically.

"Ooo, that does look like fun," Luna said.

The music intensified, and now Orb heard a suggestion of the magic melodies of nature. The Gypsies knew that music!

"Don't go!" the hamadryad cried. But in vain; the two girls, fascinated by the fun the Gypsies were having, just had to go down and join it. In a moment they were on the ground. The Gypsy children took their hands and formed a circle, and they danced, kicking out their legs with sheer abandon.

After a bit, the music stilled. "It's not exactly the Llano," the

Gypsie leader said. "But we do enjoy it. It's yours, if you join us."

At the sound of the word "Llano" Orb's pulse did a minor leap. Something about that word thrilled her. A suggestion of her dream-vision flashed by the backs of her eyes.

"We can't join them!" Luna protested in a sharp whisper. "Your mother would be furious!"

But Orb was distracted by the word. "The 'Yano—" she started, unable to pronounce it the way the Gypsy had.

"Oh, the Llano!" he exclaimed. "You have rare taste in music, child! But no one possesses the Llano, though many seek it. We Gypsies come as close to it as any, but all we ever capture is some trifling fragment. Come with us, child, and we shall search for the Llano together! Our seer says one of you can see auras, and the other can hear the songs of nature. With your help, perhaps we can find the ultimate song!"

"Oh, yes!" Orb exclaimed, clapping her hands.

"No!" the hamadryad cried from the branches of the oak. "The Llano is a delusion and a cheat! Mortals who quest too close to it only sicken and die. Don't trust these people!"

"Chop down her tree!" the Gypsy leader snapped.

Immediately his husky youths brought out axes and approached the tree. The hamadryad screamed and seemed about to faint.

This was too much for Orb. Her temper had never been moderate, and now she exploded. "Leave her tree alone!" she cried fiercely.

The Gypsy leader glanced down at her, amused. "Or what?"

"Or we won't go look for the 'Yano!" Orb said, striding toward the trunk.

The first youth was lifting his axe high, about to make the first chop. Orb charged right into him, trying to reach the axe. She was prepared to climb right up him and bite his arm if she had to. Luna followed her lead and grabbed the other youth.

Both youths froze, their will departing.

"Got to get rid of those amulets!" the Gypsy leader muttered angrily.

That gave the hamadryad her cue. "The Magician made those amulets!" the cried.

"Of course he did," the leader agreed. "He makes them and

−19−

sells them; that's how he earns his living. We trade in them, too. But people can be separated from their amulets.'' Then, to the youths: "Put away those axes; I was only fooling.''

The girls let go of the youths, and the youths retreated. Now the Gypsy leader addressed Orb. ''That is a very fine amulet you have. May I look at it?''

Flattered, Orb reached for hers, ready to remove it.

"Don't take it off!'' the dryad screamed. ''That's your only protection from evil!''

But the leader evidently had another idea. ''It's no protection at all,'' he said, gesturing to an old woman. ''See, it's changed into a giant squiggly worm!''

The old woman threw powder toward the girls and gesticulated weirdly and uttered strange words. Orb felt something wriggling at her neck. Luna screamed—and sure enough, her amulet had changed into a grotesque worm.

The two girls tore at the chains about their necks, trying to get rid of the horrible creatures.

"No, no!'' the hamadryad cried. ''It's just illusion! Don't take them off!'' But the children, horrified, were beyond reason. In a moment both amulets were off and flung away.

Now the Gypsies pounced on Orb and Luna. ''Got you now, my little treasures!'' the leader exclaimed. ''Your talents will add a pretty penny to the pot, once we get you broken in. You'll learn to beg and steal and dance—you'll soon be perfect Gypsies!''

The girls, now thoroughly disenchanted, began to cry.

But the hamadryad wasn't finished. ''Fie on you, vile creatures!'' she screamed. ''Turn loose those girls this instant!''

"Or what?'' the leader inquired, exactly as he had before.

"Or I'll tell my neighbor dryad what you have done, and she'll tell her neighbor, and so on till the news reaches the tree by the Magician's house!''

The Gypsy leader laughed. ''Forget it, nymph! The Magician doesn't watch out for every stupid client of his merchandise! There are thousands of these amulets about.''

"He watches out for these ones!'' the dryad said. ''One's his daughter, the other his sister.''

All the Gypsies froze. ''Uh-oh,'' the old seer said. ''She speaks the truth. I didn't think to check for that before!''

"We'll be far gone from here before the Magician comes," the leader said.

The woman shook her head. "Give it up, Raggle. We want no quarrel with him. He's not just an enchanter of stone. He's the most potent sorcerer in Ireland and some distance beyond, and getting stronger every day. He will destroy us; we can't hide from him."

The leader blanched. "You're sure, Taggle?"

"I'm sure."

He sighed. "Then so must it be." He turned to the girls. "We'll leave you now, children; sorry we couldn't have you with us, but that's the way it goes."

The troupe began to move out.

"No, you don't!" the hamadryad screamed. "You have wronged these poor girls! You must make amends!"

"Don't push your luck, nymph!" the leader growled. "The Magician doesn't protect *you*. Our axes can still—"

But again the old seer was cautioning him. "I see it now, as I should have before. The Magician loves this dryad. She it was who trained him in natural magic when he was a tot. If anything hurt her or her tree—"

"Damn it, woman!" the leader exclaimed, furious. "Why didn't you tell me before?"

"We all make mistakes," she said. "I was so intent on the prize to be won, I forgot to look beyond."

"What a mistake!" he groaned. "How are we to get out of this?"

"You'll make amends!" the hamadryad called. "That's what you'll do, you scoundrels!"

The leader sighed. "It seems we must." He turned again to the girls, who had picked up their amulets, which no longer squiggled. "I hereby abjectly apologize to the two of you. But let me explain. We are not bad folk, we are Gypsies, and we follow the Gypsy way. We are always kind to our children, including those we adopt; not one of them would trade our way for that of the settled kind. I was stolen and adopted myself, and I bless my fortune! We are free folk, as free as any on earth. We sing and dance the day long and we are happy in what we do. We meant no harm to you; we merely wanted you to join us, because we appreciate both music and magic as no other folk do. You would have liked our life. It is not every child we choose; only those with true talents. Our approach to you was a compliment, not a threat."

The girls were six years old and were learning how to be vulnerable to flattery. But the hamadryad was several hundred years old and of a less forgiving nature. "Forget the blarney!" the called. "Get to the amends!"

"I was coming to that, wood-sprite," the leader said, firing a dark glance in her direction. Then he smiled graciously. He could be completely charming when he tried. "To make amends for our misunderstanding, we shall give you an invaluable gift: a True Telling of your fortunes, at no charge."

Orb glanced at the tree, and the dryad nodded affirmatively. This was a suitable amend. "Yes," Orb said, and Luna agreed.

The old woman came forth again. "Give me your hands," she said.

The girls extended their hands as if for an inspection before a meal, and the seer took one of each. She closed her eyes. "Let us look into your futures," she intoned.

A shadow of the vision touched Orb.

The woman shuddered and dropped the hands. "It's barred!" she exclaimed. "I cannot read their lives!"

"A likely story!" the hamadryad called.

"No, 'tis true!" the seer protested. "A counterspell has been laid on these two, rendering their futures opaque. I doubt that the Horned One himself could penetrate these lives! Certainly I can not, nor any Gypsy."

Luna looked at Orb. "Daddy," she said.

That made sense. The Magician had evidently protected them with more than the amulets. Maybe there was some threat in having their futures told, so he had prevented it.

"You're trying to renege!" the dryad cried, outraged.

"We must offer something else," the Gypsy leader said quickly. "We always keep our deals."

The dryad snorted at this, but the man was serious. Orb was quick enough to grasp her opportunity. "Maybe the 'Yano?" she inquired.

The leader shook his head. "Child, I can not give you that! No mortal person can. The Llano can only be found for one's self.

My playing is but the poorest suggestion of it, anyway; I have never been able to approach it closely."

"But I really want it!" Orb said.

Luna's curiosity had been roused. "Maybe if you just tell us about it," she suggested.

"Even that is little enough," the man said. "Our whole band together hardly knows—"

"Yes, tell us!" Orb said. "It is like the Song of the Morning?"

The leader pursed his lips. "You hear that? You are a rare child indeed! Yes, it is said to be like that, only much, much more. The Song of the Morning is just one of the five major Songs of Nature, or perhaps one aspect of the whole, while the Llano *is* the whole. It is the ultimate in music, the song for which all Gypsies long, and from which all Gypsies take their inspiration, however poorly they understand it. When we die, we hope to join the province of the Llano and listen to it and play it for eternity." He glanced around. "What do the rest of you know?"

A young woman, a dancer, spoke up. "I heard a tale of the Llano, I know not if it be true, but I think it is. It is of a young woman, a Gypsy like me, who loved a mundane prince, but he would pay her no mind at all unless she gave up her band and her wandering and settled forever in his castle, and that would have killed her, for no Gypsy can survive such confinement. But she knew she would die, too, if she did not possess him. So she went to his castle and stood outside the turret where he stood, and she sang him a piece of the Llano. And he came down from that tower, mounted his fine horse, rode out, picked her up, and rode to her band, and he married her and joined the Gypsies, and their love was forever, because of the Llano."

Orb listened, entranced. What a song that must be, if just a little piece of it could do that!

Now an old man spoke. "I know a tale of the Llano. A Gypsy man like me was caught by the mundanes and sentenced to be hanged for stealing, when he had only pursued his normal way of life. Seeing that they refused to understand that he had taken the bread only to feed himself and his family, and knowing that no help was close by, he gave himself up for lost. But then he remembered a bit of the Llano he had heard once years ago, and now the melody returned to him clearly. And as they laid the noose about his neck, he sang that fragment. And they took away the noose, unbound his hands, set him free, and gave him money, too, because of the Llano.''

Orb liked that story, too. She wondered if the Llano could enable her to escape punishment when she did something wrong. In a way it had already, when she had avoided trouble by explaining about the Song of the Morning to her father.

A child spoke. ''I know a tale of the Llano, too. A child like me was out in the forest gathering berries, and a big old wild beast, I don't know what it was, maybe a wolf or a mountain lion or a dragon or something, it came and was going to eat him up 'cause it was hungry, and the boy was scared stiff, but he remembered a bit of the Llano and he sang it, and that beast calmed right down and became his pet instead, because of the Llano.''

Taming a wild beast with a song? Orb liked that, too.

The Gypsy leader looked around the group, but no other person spoke. ''It seems that's as much as we know about the Llano,'' he said. ''It is very little, I know, but if we knew how to find it, we would be seeking it for ourselves and not dallying here in the swamp. Maybe you, if you can hear the Song of the Morning, will someday hear the rest of it. We know of these Songs of Nature, but few of us can actually hear them. I was adopted by the Raggle-Taggle tribe because I could hear the voices and songs of the natural ones.''

''I guess it's enough,'' Orb said, mollified. The hamadryad was silent, so the Gypsies moved away. In a moment the entire band was gone.

''But is any of that true?'' Luna inquired when they were back in the tree. ''Maybe they made it all up.''

''They adapted it,'' the dryad said, and Orb translated, as Luna still could not hear her. ''The originals may not have been Gypsies, but probably the episodes happened. The Llano is said to be the ultimate in music. I did not believe in it, but maybe I was wrong. If only we hamadryads knew it, we could protect our trees from the depredations of man.''

They worked some more on Orb's music, but in only a moment, it seemed, Niobe was back, and the session was over. By common consent, the girls did not tell Niobe of the adventure with the Gypsies, knowing that only mischief could come of this. They came many times thereafter to the hamadryad's tree, and slowly Orb learned to make the music of the kind her father made, and Luna learned to paint with the aura.

But of the Llano Orb could learn no more. She didn't ask her folks, because then she would have had to tell them where she had learned of it, and that could have gotten awkward. Anyway, she doubted they knew. The Magician surely knew, but he was unapproachable; even Luna, his daughter, didn't dare bother him when he was deep in magic research, which was all the time. So Orb endured with private longing. One day, some day, she would go out herself in quest of the Llano!

-3-

TINKA

Orb stood at the wake, feeling cold. Blenda, Luna's mother, was dead, and there was nothing she could do about it. Technically Blenda had been Orb's half sister, for both of them were the daughters of Pacian, but she had been easier to think of as an aunt. Blenda had been the most beautiful woman of her generation, but she had aged rapidly in the past few years. Whatever researches the Magician had been doing had taken the life-strength from both himself and his wife; now she was dead, and he was old. It was hard to believe that he was Niobe's son!

Orb and Luna were seventeen, going on eighteen, supposedly at the prime of maidenhood. It was said by others that they were beautiful, though not as much as their mothers had been. That was hard to appreciate in this hour of bereavement. What was the point of beauty, when a person still had to age and die?

Abruptly the Magician crossed to Orb. "We must have music for the wake," he said.

Orb quailed. "Oh, I couldn't—" For though she had never been truly close to Luna's mother—and Luna herself had not been as close as both of them were to Niobe—the grief of this termination was on her.

"She liked your music," the Magician said. "She will not hear it hereafter."

Orb glanced wildly about, seeking some escape from this duty, and caught Niobe's gaze. Niobe nodded. Orb would have to do it.

She fetched her harp. She had been given this when she was twelve; it was from the Hall of the Mountain King. It was magic, and it amplified her talent enormously. Her father's music embraced the listener when he touched; hers extended beyond touch. She had not realized that Blenda was even aware of it.

She played on the instrument, then sang. She had intended a sad song, but it came out happy, to her dismay; it seemed that something other than her own will was guiding her. In the old days, she understood, wakes had been happy affairs, all-night parties, but now they were more somber, and certainly she did not feel festive. But she found herself singing a song of light and joy, and the Magician was smiling, and somehow, amazingly, it seemed right.

Then Luna painted a picture of her mother, in her youthful beauty, and it was the loveliest of portraits. This would go with Blenda, in such manner as it could. She would travel to Heaven with treasured things.

After the wake and burial were done, things did not return to normal. The Magician decided to move to America, and of course Luna would go with him. This hardly cheered Orb; Luna had been her closest companion all her life. But what was to be, was to be. The two girls had a tearful parting, and then Luna and her father were gone. Oh, they had promised to keep in touch, and to visit back and forth, but Orb still felt bereft.

There did not seem to be much point in staying home, now. Orb's father Pacian was over seventy and was slowing down; she rather feared that he would be next and she hardly cared to witness that. So she approached Niobe about the possibility of traveling, apprehensive about her mother's response, but to her surprise it was positive. "By all means, dear," Niobe said. "It is important for a girl to get some experience of the world, before she has to settle down. Just be careful."

Now perversely, Orb had a second thought. "But you, Mother—can you manage without me? I mean—"

Niobe hugged her. "I love you Orb, but I can manage. Here, the Magician left something for you."

It turned out to be a carpet: a beautiful small silken one that nevertheless supported her weight lightly enough. "Oh, it's absolutely lovely!" Orb breathed ecstatically. "But that means—"

"That he knew you would be going," Niobe finished. "He cares for you, Orb, as he does for Luna; he just doesn't show it often. He told me where to take the two of you to obtain your instruments. I think his neglect as a baby caused him to lose facility for the expression of love, but he feels it."

Orb did not comment. Niobe was the Magician's mother; if she had neglected him, she must have had good reason. "I will use it to visit him and Luna!" she exclaimed.

"You will not!" Niobe snapped. "This is not intercontinental tapestry! You would perish in some storm far from land. No, this is strictly a local transport, close to ground. You'll have to take a scientific airplane to cross the ocean. But you don't need to visit them so soon anyway; go about your business and see what you can find."

Orb nodded. She had never spoken to her mother of her longing for the Llano, but evidently Niobe knew. So she flung her arms about the older woman and just hugged her, and that was enough.

But Niobe was not done. She had a gift of her own: a cloak that would garb Orb in whatever manner she required, so that she would not need to tote a suitcase of clothing. "Return when you are ready, dear, and I will be here." Perhaps significantly, she did not mention Pacian.

Orb hugged her again and shed another tear. Then she packed some food and her little harp, took a good map of Eire, and settled herself on the carpet. It lifted with her thought, being one of the refined modern ones that responded only to the owner and needed no spoken commands.

She hovered for a moment, blowing a kiss to her mother. Then she was off, sailing up to treetop level, the wind taking her cloak but not threatening her. She was on her way.

She was looking for the Raggle-Taggle Gypsies that she had met as a child. They had told her what they knew of her real objective, the Llano, but perhaps they could now tell her where to look for it.

First she went to the swamp where the old water-oak stood, to consult with the hamadryad. She and Luna had visited often in the summers when they were young, but seldom in the later years. Nevertheless the dryad welcomed her immediately, even coming down from the tree to hug her as she got off the carpet.

"But I'm adult now," Orb protested, pleased. "How can you approach me?"

"You are still an innocent," the dryad said. "Besides, I know you. There is no music like yours."

Orb elected to ignore the slight about her experience, for the dryad had been a precious friend. "What I really want is to find that song, the Llano," she confessed. "So I'm looking for those Gypsies, because perhaps they can tell me where to look."

The hamadryad frowned, not liking the Gypsies who had threatened to chop down her tree. A threat of that nature was never forgiven by her kind. But she recognized Orb's need, so she helped. "We have watched that tribe, my sisters and I. It is now south, in Cork."

Orb thanked her and resumed her journey, after a parting almost as poignant as the one with Niobe. The flight was long, and night was coming, so she ate sparingly from her stores, then lay down on the carpet and slept while it continued its travel. Her cloak kept her warm, and she knew no one would bother a solitary flying carpet; they were, after all, common enough. This really solved the problem of nights, for she was as safe here as she could be anywhere—at least when there was no storm.

In the morning she found herself hovering over one of the enchanted forests of Cork: the trees that magic enabled this county to grow for their marvelous bark, providing employment and income for many residents. She circled until she spied a park that had good water and facilities; then she landed and refreshed herself. Her food was running low; she had money and would have to buy more soon, but right now she was too eager to locate the Gypsies.

Back aloft, she searched for signs of their presence and soon spied a motley collection of tents. As she approached she saw the women with their pots, and the men with their horses and cattle, and the children playing, all of them wearing bright bits of color. These were they!

She landed, rolled up her rug, and fitted it into her knapsack along with her harp. The combined load was fairly heavy, but she didn't want to leave anything of value untended in this vicinity. Her prior experience with the Gypsies had taught her this caution.

As she walked up, the Gypsy children flocked to her. "You want nice cloth?" one cried. "My mother has the best!"

"You want fortune told?" another inquired. "My big sister knows all!"

Then a Gypsy man strode toward her. His hair was midnight black and his eyes the same, making his dark skin seem light in comparison. With a wave of his arm he scattered the children. "Welcome, beautiful woman!" he exclaimed. "Come let me show you the wonders of perfect love!"

"Just take me to your leader," Orb said, somewhat daunted by this approach.

"I am the leader," he proclaimed, putting his arm around her. Because the knapsack was high on her back, his hand fell low. He squeezed.

Orb leaped and whirled on him, her face flaming, and perhaps her bottom, too. "How dare you?" she demanded.

The man laughed. "A woman of spirit!" he said. "What a joy to bed you!" His dark gaze seemed to transfix her, and somehow it seemed that the decision about her action had already been made.

Orb put her left hand on the amulet hanging at her neck, drawing power from it. She knew the Gypsy couldn't hurt her. Not physically. But his lewd words and behavior appalled her. She just wanted to get away from him and get about her business.

The man, pressing what he perceived to be his advantage, reached for her again. But this time the power of the amulet manifested, and as his hand touched her, his volition drained away. These amulets had protected Luna and Orb throughout, the only exception being when they had invaded the Hall of the Mountain King, whose power was supreme within his own demesnes. But she had no onus against the Mountain King; he was a good man, if man he was, and his magic harp had vastly enhanced her life.

Why hadn't the amulet protected her from the man's familiarity before? Because she hadn't known it was coming, and he hadn't known it would offend her. Now she did know, and so did he, and the protective magic was operating. A matter of interpretation, perhaps, but it made all the difference.

Now that she had him helpless, she had a better idea. "You're not the leader, are you?" she said.

"No," he agreed. "I just told you that so you would like me."

"Perhaps you can help me anyway," she continued. "I am looking for the Llano. What can you tell me?"

"The Llano!" he exclaimed, and his hand fell away from her. At that point he recovered his volition. "What did you do to me, woman?"

"I overwhelmed you with my personality," she said sweetly. "Are you going to answer my question?"

He whistled. "Lady, I think I had better! But all I can tell you is that we don't know where to find the Llano. I don't think any of us can, here. I think you would have to ask at the source of the Gypsies."

"And where is that?"

He looked embarrassed. "We don't know that either. We think we came up out of Egypt, through Spain; that is how we derive our name, E-Gypt-sy. But that may be just a story."

Orb considered. It struck her as an excellent story. "Why then I suppose I'll just have to go to Spain and inquire there," she said.

The Gypsy fidgeted. "That may not be wise."

"Why not?"

"Look, lady—you can't just walk into a Gypsy camp and start asking questions. You'll wind up in somebody's tent, and—" He paused, evidently remembering her power of resistance. "Well, maybe not. But the Gypsies of Spain are more—well, they wouldn't let you get off as easily as I am, and your magic may not protect you there. We're just a primitive band, but there they know more of the old lore. You would run a risk."

His words had the ring of sincerity. Orb leaned forward and kissed him lightly. "I thank you. I shall take care." She turned away.

"Wait, lady!" he protested.

She turned back. "Haven't you had enough of me?"

"I think I will never have enough of you, lady! But I recognize your power. Please, a boon—the others have seen me talking to you, and if you just go away they will know I failed with you. If you would stay a little longer, let me show you around, be your guide, they would think—"

"Why should I care what they think?" she snapped. "You tried to—to handle me!"

"I know, and I apologize. But this is the way of a man with a beautiful woman—the Gypsy way. I would have been the shame of my tribe if I didn't try! And now—my reputation—"

Orb tried to remain objective, but the repeated compliments about her appearance were getting to her. Perhaps the Gypsy had a case. Her temper, quick to fray, was also quick to mend. "I have no intention of—"

"I understand!" he said quickly. "Obviously a woman of your quality has no interest in riffraff like me! But if you could just appear to be—I would be so grateful, and if there is any favor I could do in return—"

He wanted to avoid being shamed before his folk. She could appreciate that. She melted, some. "Well, I do need to obtain some food, to travel with—"

"Yes, yes!" he agreed avidly. "I will guide you to the best we have! The best prices, no cheating! If only—" he made a partial gesture with his arm.

Orb decided that she was in command of the situation, and the man might indeed be useful. "Yes, you may touch me—but no squeezing. And nothing more—there is nothing beyond this."

"Yes! But there will *seem* to be more."

She nodded. The Gypsy put his arm about her waist, below the knapsack, and he did not even touch her rear, let alone squeeze. The other Gypsies glanced and nodded appreciatively; the man was scoring again.

In due course Orb resumed her journey, stocked with excellent food. The man had been as good as his word and had indeed been useful. He had asked only that he be allowed to walk her through the forest, out of sight of the others, so that they would draw their conclusions. She did, and the Gypsies surely did, and that was all. "But if you ever *do* want a man for other purposes—" he said at the end.

"I will know where to find you," she agreed. Indeed, he seemed not a bad sort, once reined, and she had learned—or relearned— that the word of a Gypsy, once honestly given, was good.

Still, as she left him, Orb suffered a tinge of regret, not for anything that might have passed between them, but because she felt she had lost a portion of her innocence.

Orb took an airplane to Spain, heeding her mother's advice. Indeed, as she looked out the window and saw the mass of clouds below, she realized that it would have been foolish for her to attempt this trip on her carpet. Any trifling storm could have dumped her, and even the fog of harmless clouds could have caused her to get lost. Magic was grand, but science had its place, too; they were complementary mechanisms of accomplishment.

The plane landed at Granada. Orb made discreet inquiries and learned that the Gypsy quarter was the Albaicin, on the hill facing the Alhambra. This was in the larger region of Andalusia, familiar to her by reputation because Luna's father had imported special stones from here for his enchantments, called anadalusite. They changed color with the light, being green at times and orange at other times—and more than that, after enchantment. Thus she was glad to make the acquaintance of this country, on whatever pretext.

"But don't go there alone," the travel agent warned her. "A tourist can get into trouble. Hire a guide who knows the language."

"The language?"

"The Gypsies speak their own language among themselves. They will cheat you, or worse, if you go alone."

She thanked him. Then she went to a private place, changed the aspect of her cloak to male apparel, bound up her hair, and rubbed a little dirt into her cheeks and chin to simulate the first shadow of a beard. She intended to avoid the peril of being a lone woman by passing for a man. She unrolled her carpet, rode it to the Albaicin, and landed out of sight of the Gypsies. She rolled up her carpet and packed it away.

She stepped out toward the Gypsy quarter. The hill was dotted with holes, and it was apparent that the Gypsies lived in these holes, for music emanated from them. That was one thing about these folk; wherever they were, there was music. No one who really liked music could be all bad!

She started up the hill. Immediately an old woman approached her, carrying flowers, speaking in Spanish. Orb shook her head. "I do not speak that language," she said gruffly, walking on. She hoped she sounded like a man.

The old woman faded back, and a young one appeared. "Ah, you are from England," she said.

"Ireland," Orb replied shortly, keeping her voice gruff.

"I would adore being your guide," the young Gypsy said, unconcerned by the distinction. "There is an ancient Moorish castle close by—"

"I am looking for music," Orb said.

"Music! Why it just happens that the finest Gitano guitarist is my best friend!"

"Gitano?"

She smiled. "This is our name for ourselves. A man is a Gitano, a woman a Gitana. I will tell you all about it—"

Orb concluded that this Gypsy woman did not have the information she desired. "No, thank you." She moved on.

The young woman brought herself up straight, inhaling to make her breasts stand out. She caught Orb by the shoulders and turned her around so that she could stare into her face. "Señor, are you a hundred years old? Do you not see how I am longing for you? For years I have been waiting for a man like you! How can you deny me so cruelly!"

Orb, caught completely off guard, burst out laughing. She had forgotten for the moment that she was masquerading as a man.

The Gypsy girl, thinking she was being mocked, reacted with fury. A knife appeared in her hand.

"No, wait!" Orb cried. "Can't you see that I am a woman, like yourself? I didn't want to come alone—"

The Gitana's mood reversed as quickly again. Abruptly she was laughing, too. "Ah, now I understand! You fear the Gitanos!" The knife was gone.

"I just want to locate the source of Gypsy music."

"I can take you to an old woman who knows songs that have been long forgotten!"

That sounded promising. "Very well."

"For just a few pesetas . . ."

Oh. Of course the girl wanted money. Orb didn't have the local currency, but tried a small Irish coin, and the girl accepted that. Then they were off to see the woman who knew the forgotten songs.

But when Orb mentioned the Llano, the old woman shook her head. "If I knew that, I would be there myself!" she exclaimed. "Only at the source of the Gypsies can that information be found!"

"But where is that?"

"That, too, I can not tell you. We came from Egypt, but that may not be the source. Perhaps the Gypsies of the Pyrenees . . ."

This was Basque country. The Pyrenees marched to the water of the Bay of Biscay, and the Basques were on either side of the border between Spain and France, speaking their own language. Orb made no progress here, speaking none of the three tongues. She knew the Gypsies were here, but they were hidden from her, keeping their nature secret.

She refused to give up. She rented a room in a village house and went out daily to talk with the people, asking about the Gypsies. No one professed to know anything about them.

Finally she became desperate. She went to the center of the village square, brought out her harp, and began to play. In a moment people appeared, listening, as she had known they would. No true Gypsy could remain aloof from magic music, and hers was special. Soon virtually all the village was present, the folk standing in a great circle around her.

She stopped, put away her harp, and walked though the crowd, back to her room.

It was not long before there was a knock on her door. Orb answered, hoping that her ploy had been successful.

A dark urchin stood there, dressed in bright rags. "Nicolai bids you come," the child said.

This smelled like victory. Orb did not question the message; she wrapped her cloak about her and stepped out.

"With your music," the child added.

Orb smiled. She fetched her harp, then accompanied the child out and down the street, to a hidden hovel fashioned from refuse.

She was appalled to think that anyone should live in a place like this, but so it was.

Inside was an old man. She knew immediately that he was a Gypsy; his whole appearance and manner spoke of it. He sat on a decrepit wooden chair and held an ancient fiddle.

The man stared at her for a long moment. At last he spoke. "Teach my child your music," he said.

Startled, Orb glanced around for the urchin, but the urchin was gone. "I can not do that," she protested. "I only want to know—"

Nicolai stilled her with an impatient gesture. "Tinka!" he called.

A buxom young woman appeared, her dark hair bound under a colorful kerchief. This was evidently his daughter.

But there was something odd about the way Tinka looked about. Her gaze was random, her eyes not focusing. Orb realized that the girl was blind.

Nicolai lifted his fiddle and played. The hut seemed suddenly to come alive, animated by his evocative music. It was as if the walls became transparent, and the world outside was tinged with gold. The instrument sang of wonders barely beyond vision.

Abruptly he stopped. "But Tinka—see," he said. He reached out and took his daughter's left hand and brought it up. She looked away, but did not resist.

Orb gasped. The hand was shorn of the ends of all its fingers. Only the first joints after the knuckles remained, and the thumb. The girl had suffered some terrible accident in childhood.

"She cannot play," the man said gruffly. "She cannot dance." He glanced down at the girl's feet, and Orb saw that they were twisted. "Fifteen, and unmarried, and no children. Yet she is comely. Teach her your music."

"But—" Orb did not know how to get hold of this situation. "I—what I do, it can't be taught—"

"Take her hand," Nicolai said.

Fighting against her own repulsion, Orb reached out and took Tinka's mutilated hand. As she touched it, she heard a faint sound, as of a distant orchestra.

Tinka had the magic!

-36-

"I can't teach her," Nicolai said. "My music is all in my fiddle. But you can."

Sorrow, sympathy, and surmise played through Orb's emotion. "Perhaps I can," she agreed.

"Take her," he said.

Numbed by this prospect, Orb obeyed. She led the girl by the hand from the hut, and out to the street.

People were all around, but they went about their business with studied unconcern. No one seemed to look directly at Orb as she led Tinka to her apartment, yet all were aware.

Orb had sought the Llano. Instead she had found a student. Somehow she knew that this was her rite of passage. If she taught the girl, the Gypsies would cooperate.

Tinka was shy, volunteering nothing, merely shrugging when Orb questioned her. Her clothing was ragged, her shoes falling apart. Orb realized that it would be pointless to try to teach her anything in her present state. First she had to win the girl's confidence, and before that she had to get her presentable.

"Come on, Tinka," she said briskly. "We're going shopping."

The girl stared blankly past her.

"For clothing, shoes, whatever," Orb said. "You're a pretty girl, if—"

Tinka continued to look blank. Orb suddenly realized that she had not heard the girl speak. Was she dumb as well? No, for she had answered to her father's call, and a person who could hear, could speak. If she wanted to.

All in good time, she decided. Surely the girl could sing, or her father would not have sought Orb's instruction for her.

Yet why was she so unresponsive? "You do understand me, don't you?" Orb asked.

Tinka shrugged. Now it was evident that she did not. She had responded only to the inflection of questioning.

Orb sighed. "Well, come anyway," she said. She took the girl's hand and led her out. Tinka followed docilely.

They went to a store that sold clothing. "I want this girl properly dressed," Orb told the proprietor. Because this store catered to the tourist trade, English was understood here. "Dress, shoes—and gloves, I think. With—you'll have to do something for the fingers. But not like a tourist—like a proper village girl, a pretty one. You'll have to choose the colors; she can't see. Can you handle it?''

The man brought out his fat wife. They spoke in what Orb assumed was Basque. The wife took Tinka away. Orb began haggling about payment; she was learning how to manage, here. She had enough money to cover any reasonable contingency, but those who spent too freely were not held in high esteem. Even so, the storekeeper was asking too much; Orb's bargaining became serious.

It took some time, but when the wife brought Tinka back she was stunning. She was clean, and her hair had been brushed out and fastened back with nylon combs, and she wore a bright print dress, white blouse, flowery shawl, and slippers that made her feet look almost normal. Sturdy gloves on her hands masked the missing fingers. She was, indeed, a pretty girl.

The wife stood Tinka before the mirror. Orb thought that was a mistake, but it wasn't; the woman was verifying the hang of the dress, making final adjustments.

"Lovely!" the storekeeper exclaimed, and his voice rang with a sincerity not entirely inspired by the money he had made on this transaction.

Tinka heard. For the first time she spoke—but her words were unintelligible to Orb.

"What language is that?" Orb asked quietly.

"Calo," the storekeeper said. "She's a Gypsy wench. I thought you knew."

"But I don't know Calo!"

"Why would you want to? Teacher her English."

Orb took the girl back to her apartment. Again the villagers affected not to notice, but Orb knew they were watching more closely than before. Apparel could make a significant change in the appearance of any woman, but Tinka's transformation was remarkable. The girl even held her chin higher and walked with more confidence, as if conscious of the impression she was making.

Orb fixed something for them both to eat, not certain whether Tinka was conversant with civilized food, but the girl had no trouble.

At last Orb tackled the problem of teaching. "Can you sing?" she asked, and when the girl did not react, Orb brought out her harp and sang a brief song.

Tinka smiled. In a moment she was humming along, picking up the melody immediately. Her pitch was perfect, her voice good. She could sing, certainly.

But that was not what Nicolai wanted from Orb. He wanted the magic.

Orb put her hand on Tinka's arm. Then she sang, using the magic. She knew that the girl heard the sound of the hidden orchestra.

Indeed she did. She spoke a veritable torrent in the Gypsy language. She wanted to learn this.

"But I can't understand your words," Orb said. "It would really be better if we understood each other."

Tinka, having heard the magic, was eager to cooperate. She was not a stupid girl, and soon she was meeting Orb more than half way. She pointed to herself and said her name, then touched her new dress and said a word for it, and a shoe with its word. She was telling Orb her language.

Orb considered only briefly. It occurred to her that if she wanted to get real information from the Gypsies, it would help to speak their language. It should be as easy to learn Calo as to teach Tinka English.

There was a great deal more to it, but that was the point of decision. Orb proceeded to learn the Gypsy language, and Tinka learned to invoke the magic orchestra. They went at both projects with almost total immersion, so that in a day Orb knew a few basic words and some of the syntax, and Tinka had succeeded in making the orchestra respond in a minor way. In a week they were communicating freely with each other on both the verbal and musical levels, though with far to go on each.

Orb discovered that the Gypsy language had no words for what in her own were rendered as "duty" and "possession." This was because these concepts were foreign to the Gypsy nature. Gypsies felt something like duty only in the manner they honored their own culture, and they owned only what they wore and used. They had no vested property, no estates, no mortgages; they acceded to such things only in deference to the demands of the other cultures with which they interacted.

This explained a lot. Others might call the Gypsies thieves—but how could there be theft, when there was no ownership? Others thought them shiftless—but that only meant that the Gypsies felt no need to do anything other than survive. To hold a regular job, to serve in a nation's armed forces—this sort of thing simply did not relate to the Gypsy nature. The bad qualities the Gypsies were judged to have were mostly the misunderstandings of outsiders. Gypsies did have values, and these, when understood, did honor to them. Music, joy, sharing, love, loyalty to one's own—the Gypsies were like one huge, scattered family, and Orb related to that. She had always wanted to belong—to something.

Tinka stayed with Orb, at Orb's expense. It was obvious that the Gypsies had no money; this was the only way it could be done. Orb didn't mind; she had never dreamed she would be in such a situation, but she felt really fulfilled when she worked with the Gypsy girl, making steady progress. The quest for the Llano could wait long enough for this.

One day the urchin showed up again. "Nicolai says come to the dance."

"Dance?" Orb asked blankly.

But Tinka came alive. "We must go," she said in Calo. "I know where."

Satisfied with that, the urchin departed. Now Tinka became the instructor, getting Orb properly dressed for the occasion. This was a special challenge, as Orb had no wardrobe of her own, only the magic cloak. The girl had to describe the necessary costume, and Orb asked questions about detail, and finally they got it right. Orb now looked very much like a Gypsy woman, and the mirror told her that this guise became her.

They went out, as evening closed. Tinka led the way, but was guided by Orb's cautions about steps, buildings, and traffic.

Hundreds of people were gathered at the central village square, dancing in pairs, snapping their fingers with marvelous precision. The beat was so accurate that Orb suspected that some of her own magic ran in the blood of the Gypsies—for indeed, these were Gypsies, revealing themselves to her at last. She realized that Tinka was her pass; she had come with the blind girl, and the girl was obviously in good health and spirit. Perhaps Nicolai had spread the word—or perhaps it had been enough just to be seen with Tinka, on those prior days. Certainly it was no liability to be seen with Tinka now; the girl was radiant, a stunning beauty.

Soon a young man came for Tinka. Orb didn't know whether the girl could dance, but let her be her own judge of that. It turned out that she could, and quite well, when guided by a competent partner.

Orb, gazing about the throng, caught the eye of Nicolai. He was playing his fiddle along with other Gypsies, and their music was lively and wonderful, but he was evidently not totally taken up by it. When he had Orb's attention, he nodded, slowly. Then she knew how pleased he was to see his daughter dancing. Tinka had the skill, but she had probably not been much in demand, before. Tonight she glowed, and in the dance it was hard to tell that she was blind.

A young man came to ask Orb herself to dance, but she demurred. "I really don't know this kind of dance," she explained. "I would rather just watch."

He left, not pushing it. But soon another came, and she turned him down, too, as politely as she could. She just didn't want to get in over her head.

Then old Nicolai came, handsome even in his age in his worn but elegant dress-up clothing. "If you would be a Gypsy, you must learn the Gypsy ways," he said, and held out his hand to her.

Orb could not refuse. She could tell by the reactions of the others that this was a signal honor. So she danced with him, and Nicolai was a veteran dancer and made it easy for her, though she did not know the nuances of this one.

"Tonight there is only one more lovely than my child," the old man murmured. Orb smiled; it seemed to her that none of the other women present looked better than Tinka, but she was not going to debate the matter.

Before long they stopped, and Nicolai returned to his playing. Tinka returned, breathless with constant dancing; her feet really were not up to it, and she had to rest. "They say my father danced with you," she said in Calo. '"He has not danced in years, not in public. Only when he taught me."

"I know he is pleased with you," Orb said.

"He is pleased with *you*!" Tinka said. "Because you have helped me. He has given you the mark of favor."

"You have helped me, too," Orb said warmly. "You are teaching me your language."

The girl found her hand and squeezed it joyously.

"He mentioned that there was one here more lovely than you, but I did not see her," Orb said, curious.

Tinka turned her face to Orb, astonished. She laughed.

"I don't understand," Orb said, nettled.

"Since my mother died, no one has ever been lovelier than me, in my father's eyes," Tinka said. "Until now. He meant you."

Orb found herself blushing. She had missed the import entirely!

Then the pattern of the dancing changed. The music was similar, but the motions and style were completely different. Man and woman glanced sidelong at each other, and their bodies assumed provocative postures. The erotic suggestion was infinite; it was as if they were indulging in a prolonged sexual act in public. Orb felt her face flushing for a new reason.

"That dance," she whispered. "What is it?"

Tinka of course could not see it, but she knew. "It is the *tanana*," she said. "Few outsiders are allowed to see it."

Orb watched, fascinated despite her revulsion. She had never been exposed to such raw invitation, yet it had beauty, too. The man desired the woman, as men did; but the woman desired the man, too, and was aggressively leading him on, assuming postures calculated to inflame his passion. The whole was stylized, and each couple was coordinated; it was indeed an established dance. Watching it, Orb could understand why the typical Gypsy girl was sexually active before menarche, and a mother in her early teens. For children were dancing, too, exchanging the same suggestive stares. She saw girls no older than six flaunting their hips and showing their thighs. It could have been a joke, but was not; every motion was choreographed, just so, even the most lascivious. Orb could appreciate how a man could be excited by the youngest of such girls, and she herself experienced a rush of desire as she watched the men.

Flustered, Orb wished she could leave before her embarrassment was evident. But she knew she could not—and a deeper countercurrent in her didn't want to go. Her own appetite was stirring, and part of her wanted to participate, flinging away caution and indulging in the passion of the moment with complete abandon.

She spent the rest of the occasion in a kind of fog; it was Tinka who got her safely home. She slept—and in the morning was disgusted. "Any man could have done anything he wanted with me!" she exclaimed, appalled in retrospect. She spoke in Calo, imperfectly, but the feeling was there.

"No," Tinka said. "My father decreed that you are not to be molested."

"I mean that I would have welcomed it!" She spoke as freely as her command of the language permitted, for though her association with the Gypsy girl had not been long, it had been intense, and they were becoming confidantes. Three years separated them, but the Gypsy girl's knowledge of sexual matters was greater than Orb's.

"No shame in that!" Tinka exclaimed, laughing. "For five years I have longed for a man, any man, but few would touch me, because of my faults."

Faults: her blindness and her mutilated hands and deformed feet. But Orb was aware now that the restriction was not because men found Tinka unattractive, but because they deemed her to be unable to perform the role of a Gypsy wife and mother. Sex was much on a Gypsy man's mind, but it was not untempered by practical considerations. "Few?"

"My father got some to come. But I knew . . ." She shrugged.

Paid love. What girl of any age wanted that? In Tinka's case it was evidently more than dating, but the principle remained. Tinka wanted to be truly accepted and to captivate the love of a man by her own resources. "I think they are more interested now."

"Yes. Three asked me to the bush last night, but I wouldn't go."

"Three!" But Orb had seen how much in demand the girl had been for dancing, and of course the line between dancing and complete sex could be fuzzy, as the *tanana* showed. Orb set aside her own reservations, knowing that the strictures of her culture did not apply here. "Why not?"

"Because they were riffraff. After I learn what you are teaching me, I can get a noble."

She had a point.

The work continued, though it was a pleasure. Before she knew it, months had passed, and Orb had not only learned the language, she had learned much about the Gypsy culture. Tinka taught her the *tanana*, though Orb had no intention of ever doing the suggestive dance in public, and other nuances of the culture. Meanwhile Tinka progressed on the evocation of her latent magic and was able to generate the orchestra at will. Orb noted with interest that for the girl it was a Gypsy orchestra, not a conventional one. But its power was as great.

It ended with seeming suddenness. The Gypsies were a traveling people, and the population of the village was constantly changing. They did not have wealth, as that was not a Gypsy objective, but some families were in better regard than others. Tinka encountered a handsome, talented, clever Gypsy man, danced the *tanana* with him, and touched him constantly, and Orb knew she was playing the magic music for him. This was the one she wanted, and it seemed that it required only five minutes for her to captivate the man entirely. The man was not concerned about her blindness or her hands; he recognized her music as a treasure beyond such matters. Her beauty hardly hurt, however. Before the evening was done, they had agreed to marry.

Orb was sorry to see her relationship with Tinka end, but she knew it was time for her to move on. She had learned as much as she could here and now was far better equipped to pursue her quest for the Llano. The Gypsies of this region did not know where it was, but agreed that the source of Gypsies was the place to look. They were not sure where that was; perhaps the Gypsies of Northern France would know . . .

—4—

QUEST

Orb no longer had to ask about to locate the Gypsies of the region she traveled. Now she knew the signals of their presence and could find them directly. Because she now spoke their language as well as many of them did—most were bilingual, speaking the local language often at the expense of their own—she was accepted by them. In fact, her knowledge of Calo enabled her to get along at times when English didn't, because it crossed national boundaries as freely and existed where English didn't.

In northern France they told her another story of the Llano. She sat among the several wives of the local chief—known to outsiders as his wife's sisters, because polygamy was not an approved family style here—and listened. The women had heard this tale before, of course, but enjoyed it again. It seemed that once in the past a tribe like theirs had been trapped by soldiers of the hostile government, in one of the periodic persecutions of the Gypsies. Outsiders didn't understand about things like stealing food or deceiving the gullible with fortunetelling or entertaining men for money with erotic dancing. Orb herself had become more tolerant in such respects than she would have believed a few months ago.

"But today is the day my love and I are to be married," a young man protested as the cordon tightened.

"We are trapped and outnumbered and out of bullets," the chief said. "Most of our men have already been killed. In an hour we may all be dead. How can you think of marriage?"

"I love her! I may have no other chance to marry her."

"We have no food, no wine for the celebration."

"Her lips are wine enough for me!"

The chief realized that he had a point. "You speak like a true Gypsy," he said. "We shall have the wedding!"

They gathered in a circle for the occasion. But their musical instruments had been destroyed by the pursuing soldiers, and they had no bright clothing to wear for the dancing. The soldiers were approaching; shots sounded, and bullets struck the trees beside their camp. They couldn't wait.

One old man among them knew a piece of the Llano. His voice was weak and cracked, but he began to sing, and the young couple danced the *tanana* to that song. The rags they wore seemed to become bright and new; the tarnished buttons on his jacket took on a glow as of fine gold, and her dull earrings and bracelets seemed to catch fire. The circle of Gypsy women snapped their fingers to the music, and the old man's voice became stronger. Now it seemed to fill the glade and intensify the day; all of them were garbed in color. The bride had been of passable feature and figure; as the song suffused her she because beautiful and provocative, holding all eyes as if magnetized.

The soldiers closed in, firing their guns. Bullets smacked into the bonfire, throwing up embers. But the Gypsies, mesmerized, kept snapping their fingers, and the couple danced with utter abandon. The song expanded to touch the soldiers. They stared, amazed that the Gypsies should be ignoring them.

Then a Gypsy girl stepped out of the circle, took a soldier by the hand, and brought him in to the center to dance. The song overpowered his will, and he set down his gun, followed her, and took her in his arms and danced. Another girl took another soldier, and a third did the same, while the song continued. Soon all the soldiers were in the circle, their mission forgotten.

All night they danced. When the morning came, and the old man's voice gave out, and the dancers were too tired to continue, the soldiers looked about, dazed. Each had a lovely Gypsy girl on his arm, and the last thing he wished to do was harm her. How would they explain this to their commandant?

They conferred and decided that there was no way to explain it. They would be executed themselves if they returned. So they decided to remain with the Gypsies and marry the girls they had danced with. The tribe survived, stronger than before, because of the Llano.

"So it may be that the blood of a soldier runs in my veins," the chief concluded. "I do not begrudge it."

But he did not know the Llano itself, or the source of the Gypsies. "But perhaps the Gypsies of Germany can help you," he suggested.

In Germany they had a problem. Consumption had taken out a chief, and the officials had buried his body in a pauper's grave and driven the wives out of town. The women were bedraggled and absolutely filthy. "But I can get you water!" Orb exclaimed.

As one, the three women shook their heads in negation. "We may not wash or touch water until his body has disintegrated completely in the earth," one explained.

So it was that Orb learned of the Cult of the Dead. All Gypsies followed it, including those of France and Spain; there had been no death in the vicinity when Orb was there, so she had not encountered this then. When a Gypsy died, all his scant possessions were burned along with his corpse; in that manner his women were freed of their geis and could be clean again. But when the authorities interfered, their plight was severe. "We can not even feed the grave," they said. For it was the custom to set food on the grave, so that the spirit of the deceased would not go hungry.

Orb stayed the night with them in their tent, though the smell was thick. But no sooner had she fallen asleep when she was awakened by a commotion outside. She scrambled up with the woman and peeked out.

There stood a bedraggled man, dirt sifting from his beard. "Faithless wives!" he cried loudly. "Why have you not brought me food? Are you trying to starve me?"

It was the ghost of the dead man. The women fell down in terror, crying. The ghost advanced angrily on them, making as if to strike. Orb stepped out, acting before she knew it. "It is not their fault, Gypsy!" she cried in Calo. "The townsmen won't let them near the grave!"

The ghost turned on her. "Who are you?" he demanded.

"Just a woman in quest of the Llano," Orb said bravely. How could she be debating with a ghost?

"Impossible!" he said. "Even I do not know the Llano! How can you, an outsider, seek it?" He took another step toward the fallen women.

Orb did not know what else to do, so she sang. She started a Gypsy tune, projecting her magic with it.

The ghost paused again, evidently daunted. He did not move till Orb stopped singing.

"There was a man like me, who died," he said then. "His family could not burn him or his horse, because it was raining and they had no fire. But one among them knew a fragment of the Llano, and she sang it, and the pyre heated and steamed and finally burst into flames, and destroyed it all, and he rested in peace, and his wives were clean." Then he faded out.

The women scrambled up. "You saved us!" they exclaimed.

"Only for tonight," Orb said, troubled. "Will the ghost really hurt you?"

"Oh, yes, he was always an angry man in life, and death has not sweetened him. We must feed his grave!"

"Or better yet, burn his body," Orb said.

"Yes! But how can we do this? The police—"

Orb feared that she would get them all arrested, including herself, but she had to try. "Perhaps he has told us how. I will try to help you. Can you burn his body if you are given access to the graveyard?"

"If the police let us. But they will not."

"Perhaps they will. We'll try it tomorrow night."

On the following night they drove the Gypsy wagon to the town, making as little commotion as possible. They parked at the edge of the graveyard. The family members set to work digging at the gravesite, while Orb settled herself with her little harp and waited.

The police were alert. Within the half hour they arrived in force. Burly policemen charged up to the graveyard.

Orb began to sing, accompanying herself on the harp. Her magic flung out, touching the moving men.

The men stopped, listening. They stood about her, doing nothing else. The Gypsies, beyond the range of her full magic, continued working.

Orb sang song after song, keeping the policemen mesmerized. In due course the corpse was out, and the pyre built. The fire started, and then blazed high, and the stench of burning meat wafted out.

The ghost appeared. "That's more like it!" he exclaimed. Then, as his body crumbled into ash, he faded out.

Orb stopped singing and playing. She rejoined the Gypsies as their wagon pulled out. The police still stood, bemused, looking at the open gravesite and the pile of embers.

They went to the nearby river, and the women stripped and plunged in, desperate to get clean again. Then they set about washing their clothes.

Finally, shivering, naked, they wrapped themselves in blankets from the wagon. "You did it!" one exclaimed. "If that was not the Llano, it was akin!"

"It was not the Llano," Orb said. But she was quite pleased with herself.

Hungary was the land of Gypsy music. World renowned composers and musicians were here, and Gypsy orchestras toured the country. Historically, the top composers of Europe had drawn upon Gypsy music, popularizing it as their own. Schubert, Brahms—the beauty of their music owed its share to melodies the Gypsies had possessed before them. The Hungarian pianist Liszt had transcribed Gypsy music as the Hungarian Rhapsodies.

Here the Gypsies were known as Tziganes. They had been here before the Magyar conquest, and the Magyars sought to profit by mingling Tzigane blood with their own. When the Tziganes resisted, laws were passed requiring Tziganes to become Christians and to marry only Magyars. This drove many Tziganes out of the country, into Russia and Poland and Germany and France, in one of their great historical diasporas. Many did pretend to accept Christianity, decorating their wagons liberally with crosses, but at heart they believed in no religion but their own. They were required to settle in houses and desert their own language; this caused another exodus, for no true Gypsy could be anchored in one place long. They were accused of cannibalism and severely persecuted for it, their denials being taken as confirmation of the charge.

Still they survived, and their facility with metal and wood

greatly benefited the sedentary culture around them, and their music shaped that culture. It seemed that every blacksmith was a Gypsy, and every musician a Gypsy, too. The greatest of contemporary Tzigane musicians was Csihari, a violinist who was said to be able to charm the souls of the living and the dead.

So it was to this Gypsy Orb went. But no Gypsy of the region would tell where to find him. She was an outsider they termed "Ungar," or "stranger," not to be trusted. She realized with flattered bemusement that they took her for a Gypsy; her command of the language and customs had enabled her almost to pass as one of them, despite her honey hair. Perhaps they took her for a crossbreed, as Gypsies frequently married outside their culture. Yet it seemed that they held foreign Gypsies in greater contempt than they did the mundanes.

She came to a village where the Tziganes were especially surly—an extremely unusual state for this normally happy people. "What is the matter?" she asked.

"Csinka defiled the water!" she was informed gruffly.

"What?" Orb asked, startled by the similarity of that name to that of her friend Tinka.

"She walked over the underground pipe that brings our water," the woman explained indignantly, taking Orb's exclamation as outrage. "Now we have to forage at great range for our needs. It's a terrible inconvenience."

Orb sought out Csinka. The woman was almost suicidal in her chagrin. "I lost my way—I had a big package to carry and I didn't see where I was going, and before I knew it I had stumbled over it," she confessed tearfully.

In the Gypsy culture, in some regions, women were fundamentally unclean; Orb had learned this along with the language, but had not encountered it before. The onus was worst at the time of childbearing; the woman's clothing of the time would be burned. But her nether region could be suspect at any time. Thus she could not step over copperware without defiling it, and the same evidently applied to buried water pipes. No one here would drink the water that Csinka had defiled by her passage over the pipe.

Orb knew better than to argue the merit of such a custom. Such things varied from tribe to tribe and from region to region, but were honored tenaciously where they held. But by her definition

Csinka was innocent, and she wanted to help. "I once helped a woman to burn her husband's body," she said. "Perhaps I can help you, too."

For an instant Csinka's eyes lighted. Then despair resumed. "There is no way. We cannot lay a new pipe."

"But if I can banish the defilement on the present pipe—"

"Are you a sorceress?" Csinka asked with interest.

"No, only a musician, of a sort. I came to meet Csihari, but they will not let me see him."

"Nobody sees Csihari!" Csinka said. "He sees whom he will, and only whom he will."

So Orb had gathered. "Perhaps if I sing him a song, he will come."

Csinka shrugged. "He might. But how can this remove the defilement from the pipe?"

"It is my hope that the music will do that."

Csinka shook her head, not understanding. But Orb made her show the place where she had inadvertently stepped over the pipe. Then, in the middle of the day, Orb set up a chair at that spot, sat on it, and began to play her harp.

She sang a song of water: of mountain springs, clear flowing streams, shining ponds, and deep pure lakes. She spread her magic out, not to an audience, but to the water in the pipe below her, willing it to respond, to assume the purity of the water of which she sang.

An audience formed, as was always the case when Orb sang. Gypsy men, women, and children, the Tziganes, standing and listening. She continued singing, songs of clean water, rendering them as well as she could in Calo. The audience continued to grow, until it filled the street.

When Orb first touched the water with her magic, she had felt the defilement of it; anyone who drank it would be sickened, and clothes washed in it would remain unclean. The soul of the water reeked of its special pollution. But as she sang, interacting with it, it clarified, until it became as clean as the water she sang about. She had not suspected she could do this until the need arose and had not been sure until she actually felt the response of the water, but now it was certain. The magic of her music had this power.

She paused and gazed across the audience. "The water is un-defiled," she said. "Who will drink it now?"

They merely stood, not accepting this. After all, she was sitting right over the pipe, continuously defiling it herself.

"I touched it with my song, and it is clean," she said, "It will not hurt you. Drink of it and see."

"I will drink of it!" Csinka exclaimed. She went to the tap on the pipe that rose from the main line and filled her cup and drank.

She stood and was not harmed. The water had not sickened her.

"She is not harmed because she defiled it!" a man said. The others nodded; it was no test.

"But *I* am over it now," Orb pointed out.

Point well taken. They glanced at each other, uncertain.

"You need this water," Orb said. "I am a woman; my body defiles it. But my music counters the ill, and this water is pure. Who else will drink of it?"

But no one trusted this. No one volunteered to try.

Was her effort to fail, even though the water had been restored? Orb did not know what else to do. Reluctantly she got up and put away her harp.

"I will try the water," a man said from the edge of the crowd.

Heads turned. There was a murmur of awe as a handsome, well-dressed middle-aged Gypsy marched forward to the tap. He turned it on, put his cupped hands under, and drank from them. Then he let the remaining water fall, turned off the tap, stood untouched. "It is good water," he said.

Then the others came and tried it, too, and agreed that the water was good. The curse was off it, and they could return to their normal existence.

"Oh, my lady, thank you!" Csinka cried, tears of gratitude flowing.

"Thank this man," Orb said. "He believed when the others did not. He made them accept it."

"Because I knew," the man said. "I heard the music, like none before."

"Thank you," Orb said. "May I know your name?"

"You did not know?" Csinka asked, amazed. "He is Csihari!"

Orb's jaw dropped. "But you would not meet me!" she exclaimed to the man.

"I had not heard you play." He put out his elbow. "Come to my wagon, and I will play for you."

Orb took the arm. They walked down the street, the others giving way before them, until they reached the musician's wagon. There he brought out his violin and played an extemporaneous theme, and it was the most beautiful music Orb had heard. Again an audience gathered, but it did not matter; Orb had ears only for the singing violin. How well justified was this Gypsy's reputation!

When he paused, Orb glanced at her own harp. "May I?"

Csihari made a gesture of acquiescence and started another melody. Orb settled herself on the ground, set up her harp, and played it, making counterpoint to his theme.

The magic spread out, animating the faces of the listeners in a widening circle. Violin, harp, and the hidden orchestra: a duet with a mighty accompaniment. Not a person moved; all were enraptured.

Then Csihari stopped and set down his violin. "Enough," he said gruffly. He gestured at the audience. "Leave us."

In an instant, it seemed, the crowd had dissipated, and the two of them were alone. "You are not Tzigane," the musician said. "What did you want of me?"

"I seek the Llano."

"Ah, the Llano!" he breathed. "I should have known!"

"I am told that I may find it at the source of the Gypsies," Orb continued. "But I am having trouble finding that source. I thought you might know it."

"I know the source, but not the Llano. I fear that even there you will not find what you seek."

"But if it is Gypsy music—"

He shook his head. "The Llano is not ours. We only dream of it, no closer than any other. We long for it as our salvation, but it is denied to us."

"I don't understand."

"You have not then heard the Story of the Nail."

"Nail?"

"It is only a story," he said depreciatingly.

"But it relates?"

"Perhaps."

"Then may I hear it?"

"You know that the Tzigane are only nominally Christian, just as Gypsies in Moslem lands are only nominally devotees of Mohammed. We truly honor no belief but our own."

"I understand," Orb said. In this, too, she had learned tolerance.

"When the Romans set out to crucify Yeshua ben Miriam, whom others now know as Jesus, they required four stout nails for his hands and feet. In those days nails were scarce and valuable and had to be crafted individualy for the occasion. So they sent out two soldiers with eighty pennies in the currency of that day, to purchase the nails from a local blacksmith. But the soldiers, being indolent, stopped at an inn and spent half the coppers drinking the foul wine of Jerusalem. It was late in the day before they emerged, having spent half the money. They were due back with the nails by dusk and they were half drunk, so they hurried to the nearest blacksmith and demanded that he make the four nails. But the man had seen Jesus, and refused to forge the nails to crucify him. Angry, the soldiers set his beard on fire, but he remained adamant. They had to go elsewhere for the nails.

"The soldiers were half-drunk, but they had the sense not to mention the name of the victim to the next blacksmith. They simply told him to make four nails for the forty pennies they had. He protested that he could make only four small nails for that price. They threatened to run him through with their lances if he did not get to work. Suspicious, he refused. Enraged, the soldiers made good their threat, and killed him, and went on to a third blacksmith.

"This one they gave no choice: he would make the nails immediately, or they would kill him. Frightened, he went to his forge—but then the voice of the dead blacksmith seemed to cry out, telling him that these nails were to crucify an innocent man, and he threw down his tools and refused to work. So the drunken soldiers struck him down and hurried on to a fourth blacksmith.

"This one was a Gypsy, who was just passing through and knew nothing of the local politics. He was glad to take the money and make the nails. As he made each one, the soldiers took it and put it in a bag. But as he forged the fourth nail, the soldiers said that these were to be used to crucify Jesus. At those words, the voices of the other blacksmiths sounded, pleading with the Gypsy not to make the final nail. Frightened by this manifestation, the soldiers fled with the three nails they already had.

The Gypsy finished the fourth nail and tried to cool it, but the water went up in steam and the nail continued to glow. Alarmed, he packed away his tent and equipment and fled, leaving the hot nail behind. But when he sought to pitch his tent at another place, that glowing nail appeared, still sizzling. He fled again—but wherever he stopped, that hot nail was there.

"But an Arab had a wheel that needed patching. So the Gypsy blacksmith took the hot nail and used it to patch the iron hoop. When the Arab left, the wheel carried the nail away. But months later the blacksmith was brought a sword to repair, and its hilt began to glow. It had been forged from the iron nail in the wheel and returned to haunt him.

"He fled, but the nail reappeared wherever he went. All his life that dread nail pursued him and when he died it haunted his descendants. Jesus had been crucified with only three nails, his feet pierced by one instead of two, and the fourth one pursued the members of the tribe who had forged them. So it has been to this day, and it is supposed to be the reason that we must constantly travel, so that it will not catch up. It is also said amongst us that only the grace of the Llano can cool that nail and give us peace, for the Llano is the universal absolver. But I doubt it; I suspect that the Llano is but an illusion sent to tempt us, like the Grail of the Christians, having no tangible reality. How could a mere song abate the crime of making such a nail?"

Universal absolver? That was interesting! "But why weren't the Romans haunted for doing the deed?" Orb asked.

"How do we know they were not? Where is the Roman Empire today?"

Orb nodded. "Maybe they did pay. But I think it is time for the nail to be put to rest. I will keep looking for the Llano."

"I think you have as much of the Llano as any mortal person can have. Woman, give up this chase and marry me."

Orb stared at him, uncertain whether he was joking.

"You have magic in your music. With you by my side, I can achieve a closer semblance of the art I crave. Besides, you are beautiful."

He was serious! Orb had no interest in such a marriage, but realized that it would not be politic to turn such a man down arbitrarily. "I am not certain this is wise," she said. "Perhaps you had better have a seer pronounce on such a union."

"By all means!" Csihari snapped his fingers, and a Gypsy boy ran up. "Fetch a seer, the best," he said.

Soon an old woman arrived. "I mean to marry this woman," Csihari said. "What are the auspices?"

"Give me your hands," the seer said.

Orb presented her hand, and the musician did likewise. The old woman closed her eyes, peering into the future. But in a moment, as Orb had known would be the case, the seer broke off the effort. "It is blank," she said.

"How can it be blank?" Csihari demanded.

"I look, but I see nothing. There is interference."

Csihari looked at Orb. "This is something you know of?"

"My half brother is a magician. He protects my future. I think I am not meant to marry, yet."

"It must be so," the seer said. "Only the hand of the most potent of magicians could balk my vision. I think he means to see that nothing turns aside this woman's quest."

Csihari sighed. "I should have known that this was too good a prospect to be true. It seems I cannot marry you, fair maiden."

"I feared that this would be the case," Orb confessed. The musician was being so polite about it that she was almost sorry that the marriage had fallen through.

"Go to Macedonia," Csihari said. "This I believe is the source of the Gypsies of Europe. Perhaps you will have your answer there."

In Macedonia she found more Gypsies than anywhere else; it seemed that every second person in the nation had some Gypsy blood. The Calo they spoke was, by all accounts, the purest version of the Gypsy language extant. The Gypsies had, she was informed, been brought to this region by Alexander the Great, for he had recognized their competence in metalworking and desired to enhance the battle prowess of his army by that knowledge. The Gypsies had not come as slaves, but as honored guests, and they had been well treated, and the abilities they taught Alexander's people had contributed substantially to Macedonia's surge toward greatness.

Then Rome had risen, and the Macedonian empire had crumbled. Gypsies had been hauled away to teach the Romans. The golden age had passed. Gypsies spread out, hiding in the mountains, fleeing to other lands, clutching their freedom. But most remained to serve the new masters. This was, after all, their home.

But was it their source? Orb doubted it and in time she learned more of the story. Where had Alexander found the Gypsies? Not in Egypt, despite the derivation of their popular name from that land; they were not truly E-Gypt-sies. No, he had brought them from beyond the Persian empire, from the land of Hind. That was their most ancient home.

And Hind, Orb knew, was India, or part of it. That was where she had to go.

She took another scientific airplane, her route proceeding from Macedonia, across Anatolia and to the coast of Asia Minor for a change of planes. The next was routed across Arabia and on to the Kingdoms of India. Orb relaxed, knowing it was a long flight; she might as well sleep.

But fickle Fate interfered. Men appeared on the plane, bearing weapons. One spoke in a language she did not understand, and several other passengers reacted with horror. Then another man spoke in English: "This is a hijacking. We are going to Persia."

"But Persia is at war!" another passenger protested. "We'll be shot down!"

"No," the hijacker replied. "They know we're coming. This plane is now the property of Persia. Now we are going to record your names and nations, so that we can obtain ransoms for you. Anyone who does not cooperate will be conscripted into the Persian army."

"But my family is poor!" a third passenger cried. "We can not afford ransom!"

The hijacker smiled grimly. "Then welcome to the Persian army! I'm sure you'll like it on the front line."

Orb quailed. This was no good for any of them! The war between Persia and Babylon had been dragging on with internecine vigor, and both sides were desperate but refused to make peace. Neither honored international conventions with anything much beyond lip service. Now it seemed they were recruiting personnel and money by sending agents out to steal entire airplanes.

The listing proceeded, as each passenger in turn gave his or her name and nation, knowing no way to resist. The plane flew east toward Persia.

But the hijackers had miscalculated, or perhaps the pilot had deceived them. Another airplane appeared, bearing the markings of Babylon. Orders were barked on the radio, obviously directions to land in Babylon or be shot down.

"We'll die first!" the hijackers exclaimed defiantly.

There was a warning shot, of the Babylonian type. It put a hole in the left wing. The plane began to wobble.

Orb knew they would all die if someone didn't do something immediately—and there seemed to be no one who could. Except herself, by default. She was no hero, but she valued her life. She wished she had avoided science and stayed with her tried and true magic carpet. She had the carpet with her, of course—but in the baggage compartment.

"Go up and tell the pilot to resume course when I distract the hijackers," she said to the woman beside her.

"But they will kill you—and me!"

"Perhaps not." Then Orb took out her harp and began to play.

"Hey!" the English-speaking hijacker said, swinging his gun about. But he paused as Orb began to sing.

She spread her magic out, pacifying all those in the airplane. She nudged her seat companion, who stirred herself and made her way up toward the cockpit. She continued playing and singing, knowing that the moment she stopped, the hijackers would resume their mischief.

But the Babylonian plane wasn't affected by her singing. Another shot was fired, putting another hole in the wing.

Orb broke off her singing for a moment. "Tell them we're landing!" she called, then resumed her song before the hijackers could revert.

"That's no good!" the pilot called back. "Babylonia is just as bad as Persia!"

"Then lock on the radio!" Orb cried. "I'll sing to them, too!"

In that time, one of the hijackers lifted his gun and aimed it. But before he fired, Orb's song resumed, and he remained as he was, listening, the gun pointing but not firing.

Now she concentrated on the occupants of the Babylonian plane. Could she move them, too, by her singing? The radio would carry her voice there, but they were not before her; she could not see them, and they could not see her. How much of the magic effect was from proximity? She didn't know. But she concentrated her mind on that other plane, singing to its operators, hoping that the magic would carry.

Her own airplane shifted course. At first her heart leaped; she feared it was going down because of the damage to the wing. Then she realized that the pilot was doing it, turning away from the direction dictated by the hijackers. It was also away from the Babylonian airport. If her music was not pacifying the other plane . . .

No third shot came. The airplane proceeded south to an emergency landing in Arabia. Orb was able at last to rest. Fortunately the authorities were embarrassed by the lapse in airplane security and did not publicize the event, so Orb was not besieged by reporters. In due course another passenger airplane arrived, and they were carried on to India, albeit somewhat delayed.

There she had another disappointment. India was huge and fragmented into many kingdoms, each with its own language or dialect, none of which she understood. There seemed to be no Gypsies here. She understood they had come from northern India, perhaps being the inhabitants before conquest imposed the caste system and made them pariahs, made them flee for their freedom. It was said that their language was very similar to Sanskrit. Perhaps there had been many waves of Gypsies as new oppressions occurred in India. But until they departed, they were not Gypsies; they were natives. The source might be here, but not the song.

Well, she would look through all of India, if she had to, until she found some clue. She would simply tour each kingdom, asking the natives. Somewhere, someone would know something about the Llano. She had to believe that.

She started in Calcutta. She knew better than to travel alone through such a vast and varied land, so she joined a road show that was passing through. She had only to audition for the master of the show, and he hired her on the spot for a fee she knew was too low. But her purpose was not money, but company, and the show promised to wend its way through much of India in the coming year. She was satisfied. Her quest continued.

– 5 –

MYM

Orb fit right in with the show. This was partly because of her recent experience with the Gypsies; she had learned to adapt to other ways with grace, and this group was Gypsylike in a fashion, though a purely commercial venture. She knew it was principally her music that won the others over.

The master introduced her to those others. "This is Orb from Ireland," he said. "She will travel with us, and she will be the main attraction and have the best wagon. Listen to her."

The others stared stonily at her, angry that an outsider should so abruptly find favor. Then Orb put her fingers to her harp and sang. The music and the magic reached out and embraced them, and they melted, as the master had known they would.

She completed her song. "How many rupees do you figure she'll bring in?" the master asked.

Orb saw them nod. The mermaid in her tank of water, the harpy on her perch, the exotic snake dancer, the illusionist magician, the assistants and handymen and animal trainers—all of them recognized that her act would make money for them all, and that was the point of this show. Anything could be forgiven if it profited the group.

Still, Orb intended to get to know each of them personally and to avoid assuming any airs. She was not in it for the money, and she needed to foster no private resentments.

The show moved out of Calcutta. The wagons were hauled by elephants, who were guided by mahouts. At first Orb sat in front, fascinated by this mode of travel, but soon lost interest. Most of what there was to see was the enormous rump of the elephant. So she rode inside her wagon, which was like a cramped house, with chairs, a bed, and a hotplate to cook on, and tried to read a book. But the road was bumpy, and she had read the book before, so she could not escape boredom that way. She craved human company.

She jumped down from the slow-moving wagon and waited for the following vehicle to pass. This happened to be the one containing the mermaid's tank. "May I join you?" Orb called.

A hand appeared, beckoning her. Orb jumped onto the wagon and got next to the huge tank. The mermaid lifted her head from the water, and the water in her lungs spewed out as she cleared them for air. This was startling, but Orb realized it was natural; the creature had to adapt to the element she was in at the moment.

"I realize you don't talk," Orb said. "But you do understand, don't you? I am lonely, and I would appreciate company, if you don't mind."

The creature gazed at her. Her head was that of a human woman a bit beyond the flush of youth, and her hair was greenish and somewhat straggly when out of the water, but her breasts were quite well formed. The scales commenced at about the level of the waist, and thickened below, providing a completely decent covering for her nether portion. Her tail was strong and healthy, and it swept slowly through the water, keeping her aloft. There were gill slits along her neck where it merged with her torso, and some farther down along her sides; water still flowed from these.

"Forgive me if I am being impolite," Orb said. "I have never met a mermaid before. The closest I have come was in childhood, with river sprites. But they were human in form—I mean they had legs."

The mermaid only looked at her. "A curse on me!" Orb muttered in Calo. "I'm only affronting her!"

The mermaid smiled. "You speak the tongue!" she exclaimed in the same language.

Orb gaped. "I thought you didn't—"

"I speak—when I choose," the mermaid said. "But few are worth speaking to."

"But how—I thought you were a creature of the sea!"

"But my father was a man," the mermaid said. "He annoyed a magician by luring away his wife. Gypsies are like that. So the magician put him under a curse that made human women resemble fish in his eyes, and vice versa. Thus he found romantic solace thereafter only in the water. My mother was unable to care for me, because I can't endure the pressure of the deeps, so my father cared for me as well as he could on land. Finally he sold me to this show, and I have been earning back my stake. It is not a bad life; I meet interesting creatures." Her gills, finally clear of the draining water, closed up, becoming unobtrusive lines; the portion of her above the water now looked completely human.

Orb recovered her composure. "But you are being touted as—forgive me—as a freak. A creature who kisses men for a fee."

"I like kissing men," the mermaid said. "And more, on occasion. They are so warm, so dry, so lusty."

"More?" Orb hoped she misunderstood.

"My scales are only external; I am mammalian inside. I can be with a man if he likes it in the water. The mahouts know."

She had not misunderstood. "But—why?"

"Why not? I get bored and lonely, too."

Orb nodded, her tolerance advancing another stage. How bored would she herself get, if confined to a tank of water all her life? The company of anyone, on any basis, might become increasingly attractive.

"I—would you like me to read to you? Or do you already read?"

"Men have not shown interest in teaching me to read," the mermaid said. She gave her torso a little shake, suggesting the aspect of her in which men showed interest.

"I—I could teach you, if you would like—but my books are in English—"

"I know a little English," the mermaid said. "I don't speak it because they say my pronunciation is fishy."

"Someone is teasing you!" Orb snapped. "That's cruel."

The mermaid shrugged. "The freaks learn to accept such things."

"You're not a freak, you're a person!" Orb cried.

The mermaid smiled. "Don't tell anyone; I would lose my livelihood."

Another notion occurred. "The harpy—is she—?"

"Much the same," the mermaid agreed. "If she stopped cursing people, they would not pay to see her."

"I mean—an enchantment?"

"I think so. It is a favored vengeance of magicians. They are not concerned about the offspring. A crossbreed could get bitter, if she pondered overlong on the matter."

"I should imagine so! But I wonder—would the harpy also like to learn to read? There is a whole world of entertainment and education in books. No need to—to be with men unless—unless a person really wanted to."

"Ask her. Perhaps we could have a class."

Orb made her way to the harpy's wagon. "What do you want, you simpering slut?" the harpy screeched.

"I—the mermaid—we thought that if you cared to learn to read in English, I could teach you—"

The creature considered. "You're not putting me on?"

"No. It just seemed—I mean, I get bored myself, with all this travel, and—"

"When's it start?"

"Why, anytime. Now, if—"

"Well, come on, woman!" The harpy opened her cage by shoving at the gate with a claw, jumped out, spread her wings, and flapped heavily out of the wagon.

Orb followed. Soon they were at the mermaid's tank, and Orb had her book. The lesson began.

Word spread, and next day a mahout joined the class. Before long there were half a dozen members. They met for an hour every morning and another every afternoon, while traveling. Progress was slow, but they had time.

Thus it was that the months passed as they crossed the great continent of India. Orb once again had found herself in a role she had never anticipated, but again it made sense, for she liked helping people. She hardly noticed the kingdoms they toured; one was much like another, the crowds as gawky in each, the thrown coins the only recompense for the performances. No one seemed to know anything tangible of the Llano, but this life seemed worthwhile for itself.

A man came to Orb's wagon one evening after a performance. He was not impressive. He was short, and his face was swathed in bandages so that only his eyes, nose, and mouth showed. He wore a dirty gray shawl. She took him for a laborer, for he wore the mark of the Sudra caste, the servant class, though his color and mein could have suggested a higher classification.

Orb suffered a feeling of *déjà vu*, but could not place it. There was something about this person.

"Yes?" she inquired. She wasn't afraid; few spectators intended mischief, and the members of the troupe kept alert for each other; if the man threatened her, there would quickly be several workers and perhaps a mahout with his elephant on the spot. What was it about him that nagged her?

The man opened his mouth, but did not speak. Instead he gestured, as if helpless.

"I am sorry," she said. "I can see that you have been injured, but I do not speak the local dialect. Do you know English?"

The man tried again. His mouth worked, and finally the sounds came out. "Ah–ah–ah–I do," he said.

She glanced sharply at him, tilting her head. "You are shy?" she inquired, her sympathy manifesting. "There is no need to be. What is it that you wish?"

The man struggled again to speak. "N–n–n–not sh–sh–shy," he said. "I st–st–stu–stu–stutter."

A stutterer! She should have realized. Now her sympathy took over entirely. "Come inside."

They sat facing each other. The man did not speak, and she realized that she had to carry it. "I have not before talked directly with a person with your problem. Forgive me if I am clumsy; I don't quite know how to help you."

He struggled, and she had the wit not to interrupt him or try to complete words for him, though his effort of communication was laborious and almost painful. What he wanted, it turned out, was help to leave the kingdom. He was not, he claimed, a criminal; he merely needed anonymity.

What should she do? The man seemed sincere, but of course a criminal would do his best to deceive a potential helper. Then she remembered one of the special qualities of her harp. It could not be stolen from her, because it would not suffer the touch of a dishonest person, and a thief would be dishonest. If this man could touch it, then she could believe him.

She explained this. Without hesitation the man reached out and touched the harp with his finger. There was no reaction.

Orb smiled with relief. "Now let us be introduced," she said. "I am Orb Kaftan, and as you may have heard, I sing."

"I—must not tell you my identity," the man said haltingly. "I am not injured; I wear the bandage to conceal my face."

"Oh—you mean you are a political refugee?"

"Ap-ap-ap-aprox-i-i-mately," he said. His stuttering had been alleviating slightly as he relaxed, but that word was difficult.

An indirect answer. But the harp had vindicated him, so she accepted it. "May I see your face?"

He unwound the bandage. His face was clear and handsome, almost aristocratic, in the fashion of the people of India. Again Orb experienced that feeling of familiarity, as if she had known him before. She had not, of course. "But I must not show it openly," he said.

Orb considered. The show was chronically in need of animal tenders and menials. If he were willing to—

He was. She fetched him a clown mask so that he would not have to wear the bandages, explaining that most of the entertainers were also workers, every person earning his keep, so it would not seem unusual for a clown to be seen cleaning an animal cage. In fact, those who cleaned out the dragon manure generally did wear clown suits, because the dragon was less surly when entertained. The master was glad to have another hand, since the pay for this level was only board and room—a bowl to share the main pot at meals, and a spot on a wagon. Thus the stranger joined the troupe, and Orb was pleased that she had been able to help another person.

A few days later, he came to her again: he thought he could

perform. "My mouth may be handicapped, but not my body," he explained haltingly.

She took him to the tour master, who was large and fat and no-nonsense. "Strut your stuff," the master said. "I have no time to waste on would-be stars."

The clown amazed Orb by doing a front flip, a back flip, and standing on his hands. He was an acrobat!

At the master's behest, he repeated the performance on top of the horizontal branch of a tree.

"What else?" the master asked, affecting to be unimpressed. That was significant; usually the affectation was unnecessary.

The clown juggled five sharp knives.

"What else?"

The clown had evidently prepared for this. He went into a mime act, doing a clever imitation of a warrior whose sword kept getting in his way. He had no costume and no sword, but it came across clearly. When he managed to spear his own foot, the master smiled. When he tried to sheathe the blade rapidly and passed it through his crotch instead, the master laughed.

"You got it, mime! Work up a complete act; I'll put you on pay. We'll call you—um, let's see." The master stroked his chin. "The Mime. No, Mym. Mym the Mime! You've got a talent, boy. Wish I'd known before."

Orb was as impressed as the tour master. Who was this man, who had accepted such lowly status, yet had such talents? She went about her business as usual, but now she was aware of Mym, her fellow performer.

When they came to the huge city of Ahmadabad, Orb decided to go shopping. The tour master insisted that she have protection. Thus Mym, wearing an artificial beard and a nondescript tunic, accompanied her.

She was delighted with the wares, proceeding from stall to stall. Such fine material! Such lovely trinkets! But all too soon Mym caught her arm, signaling that they should depart. Reluctantly she concluded her purchase and started back with him.

He seemed nervous. He guided her into an alley. Then she realized what had been bothering him, as five brutish men closed in on them. Thuggees—the local cutthroats!

"Hide!" Mym told her beside some old wooden crates. She

hastened to obey, knowing that she could do nothing to help. He took a board and faced the ugly men. It seemed a pitiful weapon against a single man, let alone five. Orb was very much afraid that the two of them were in for a robbery and beating and perhaps worse.

Her amulet! Could it protect them both? No, it could not protect even one in a case like this, because while she nullified one thug by touching him, the others could strike with their swords.

She heard the men exclaiming, laughing at Mym. Oh, if only she could *do* something! Perhaps if she sang!

Then there was an abrupt commotion.

In a moment Mym was back, bearing his silk handkerchief. He required her to be veiled, so she could not see. He guided her out of the crates and out of the alley. Then he unveiled her, and they resumed their walk back to the caravan. The thuggees were gone. Evidently he had somehow frightened them off.

Orb was relieved to make it back safely. She had been really worried for a moment! Now she understood the tour master's concern about safety in the big city. The delight of shopping in the bazaar was not worth the danger.

A few days later the tour master came to talk with her. "What do you know about thuggees?" he asked.

"Very little," Orb said. "Mym and I were broached by some in the city, but he persuaded them not to molest us. Your concern was well taken."

"He persuaded them?" the master asked, wrinkling his brow. "What did he say to them?"

"Well, he didn't really talk to them. He—he has difficulty talking, you know."

"Did he signal them in some way? Give them money? What?"

"I really didn't see," she confessed. "I was hiding, at his behest. Then he blindfolded me and brought me out. I think that was so I wouldn't see the thuggees. Perhaps it was part of the agreement, so I couldn't identify them." But that made little sense to her as she said it, because she had seen the thuggees before.

"You saw nothing," the master said, as if making a point.

"Nothing. Why, is something wrong?"

"I hope not," the master said, and departed, leaving her perplexed.

On the next reading session, Orb took a moment to inquire about this matter. "The tour master was questioning me about thuggees," she said. "Is there something I should know about?"

"You haven't heard?" the harpy screeched, flapping her wings with excitement. "Five thuggees were found in town, hacked into pieces. Blood splattered all over, and—"

"Watch it, birdbrain!" the mermaid snapped.

"Dead?" Orb asked, stunned.

"Probably they went after a berserker and got wiped out," the mermaid said. "After they left you."

"A berserker?"

"You don't know about berserkers?" the harpy cried. "One taste of blood, and they go absolutely wild and just start killing, like sharks, and nothing stops them! They just cut and hack and—"

"Finally get killed themselves," the mermaid said firmly, again cutting off the harpy's joyful description. "So whatever happened, it's over now, because the only peaceful berserker is a dead berserker."

"That's horrible," Orb said, shuddering. "I'm glad we didn't encounter a berserker!"

The harpy fluttered her wings. "Well, I think—"

"Let's get on with the reading," the mermaid said, with a fierce warning glance at the harpy.

Orb proceeded with the lesson, but she was ill at ease. There seemed to be something they weren't telling her.

Later, she asked Mym about it. "Did you know that those thuggees we encountered were found slaughtered? How do you suppose that happened?"

"A berserker," he said, stuttering so badly that she decided to spare him further talking for a while. Evidently the matter had come to his attention, too, and disturbed him as it did her.

They were in her wagon, suffering through a long wait while a downpour of the monsoon season inundated the landscape. Some wagons leaked, but Orb's was tight, and it was an excellent place to be. "I think we should get to know each other better," she said. "We're—well, we're fellow performers now, and—" She shrugged, finding herself unable to say directly that she very much enjoyed his company. Mym, so unprepossessing at first, was a handsome, talented, and decent man, and the mystery of his origin made him intriguing.

He nodded, agreeable to whatever she wished. That was another thing about him—he was a gentleman. The mermaid had hinted to Orb that Mym was quite interested in her, and Pythea the snake charmer had said the same. Both confessed to having offered Mym entertainment of the intimate kind, but he had declined because his interest was elsewhere. Orb had blushed, then found herself flattered, and was developing more than an idle interest in Mym herself. She knew he would never force on her any attention she did not want; she felt safe with him and comfortable, and that counted for a lot.

She told him of her history, such as it was: her youth in Ireland; the acquisition of her magic harp from the Mountain King; and her quest for the Llano. He listened closely and, when she came to the song, he said he had heard of it.

"You have?" she asked, excited.

He told her a variant of one of the stories she had heard before—how a young woman had loved an esteemed warrior and captured his love by singing the Llano, even though she was of lesser birth than he, and not beautiful.

Orb smiled, glad to have this confirmation. "Of course it couldn't happen in real life," she said.

"It could happen," he said haltingly.

She looked at him, understanding that what the girls had told her was true. The rain beat down, making the wagon seem more protected and intimate. She wished she could—what? Embrace him? She had never done that with a man, in the romantic sense. "But of course you're not a prince. Not that it matters, Mym. I—have been growing very fond of you, even—"

"I-I-I-I—" He was unable to get the words out at all.

She put her hand on his. "It doesn't matter, Mym. You don't need to speak to me in words." But she knew it did matter, to him.

Then she had a bright notion. "I have heard that sometimes—Mym, can you sing?"

"S-s-s-sing?" he asked blankly.

"It invokes a different portion of the brain, as I understand it. So some stutterers can sing clearly, even though they can't talk. Come, try it; sing with me." And she launched into one of her Irish songs: "O Danny boy, the pipes, the pipes are calling, / From glen to glen, and down the mountain side."

Doubtfully, he joined her: "And from the trees, the leaves, the leaves are falling, / 'Tis you, 'tis you must go and I must bide."

They both paused, astonished. He had not only managed to sing it without stuttering, he had sung it clearly and well.

"You could make it as a singer!" she exclaimed.

"I-I-I-I could!" he agreed, awed.

"No—sing it," she urged him. "You don't need a song; just hold the note, any note."

"I can!" he sang in a level note.

"Now you can say anything you want to!" she exclaimed. "Oh, Mym, I'm so pleased!" And she flung her arms about his neck and kissed him.

For a moment he responded. Then he withdrew. "I must not," he sang.

"Not?" Orb tried not to feel rejected.

Freed of his incapacity in this miraculous way, Mym became far more expressive. "I am not what I seem," he sang. "I *am* a prince." He went on to explain how his name was Pride of the Kingdom, and he was the second son of the Rajah of Gujarat. He had been confined to the palace because his father did not want his speech impediment to embarrass the family. He had been trained in every royal art, particularly that of combat, just in case anything should happen to his brother. Ashamed, Mym had fled the palace and hidden from his family, aided by a magic charm he possessed. Until he had attended the show and heard Orb sing. Then—

He shrugged. It was obvious that he had been captivated by her from the outset; now he had confessed it. Her heart went out to him. Then she remembered the other mystery. "Those thuggees—"

Then he confessed to that, too. As a prince, he hated such vermin, and when they had threatened her, he had drawn upon his devastating combat skills and slaughtered them all. "I blindfolded you," he sang, "so that you would not see their bodies."

Orb turned away, crushed. Her worst concern had been confirmed. Mym was a killer, perhaps close to a berserker. How could she associate with him?

When she looked again, he was gone. He had known how this news hurt her. She saw now that the mermaid had suspected and protected her from this revelation. Orb was at heart an innocent girl.

She threw herself on her bunk and sobbed.

But as the night passed, and the next day, and the rain abated and allowed them to proceed to their next station, her horror ameliorated. The mermaid was helpful, reminding her of her probable fate had Mym not acted as he had against the thuggees. "No man who goes beserk at the thought of a threat to the woman he loves can be called evil," she said. The others in the class agreed, even the harpy. "I'd love to have a man mangle bodies for me!" she screeched.

So it was that Orb's horror metamorphosed to an opposite emotion of similar intensity, and she realized that she loved Mym. She nerved herself and went to him to apologize.

"Forgiven!" he sang immediately.

She flung her arms around him and kissed him.

After an enchanted moment he drew back. "I am a prince," he reminded her in his new singsong.

She hardly cared about that; royalty meant little to her. "I will remain with you here in India, if I need to," she said.

"No, no!" he sang. "You must continue your quest for the Llano! I would not deny you your dream!"

"But I think I have found my dream, in you," she said. Her heart, so long her own, seemed to be inflamed, but it was a wonderful feeling. She had never known such love before.

"Only part of it, only part," he demurred. "And that part you can have without sacrificing the other. I will go with you, wherever your quest leads."

She smiled. "You are truly the most wonderful of men." Then she kissed him again, savoring the amazing new emotion.

She drew back her head to look at him, struck by something. "Turn your head," she said abruptly.

He obliged, uncertain of her intent.

"Yes!" she exclaimed. "You are he! That's why you looked familiar!"

"Who?" he sang.

"The man of my dream! I really *have* found you!"

He shook his head, perplexed. Then she explained about her childhood vision of walking down an aisle on the arm of a man she could never quite see, except for a glimpse of his profile. "You are that man!"

"I should be glad to be in your dreams," he sang. "But I am not certain how I entered that one!"

"It was a dream of marriage," she said. "Don't desert it."

"I shall try not to," he agreed.

That night Mym moved into her wagon. The news of their romance had spread across the troupe at a velocity that left light somewhat behind, and Mym's belongings had traveled here before he knew of it.

They lay together, not making love, just simply holding each other. Mym had, he confessed, known many women in sexual detail; it was expected of a prince, and concubines were a rupee a dozen. But he had never been in love. Orb admitted she had no experience in either love or sex, and had never felt the lack, until now.

"The touch of your hand is melody to me," he told her.

"That's just my magic!" she reproved him. He laughed, and they kissed and kissed again.

On other nights they did make love, many times and with abandon, but it was only an affirmation of their love, not an end in itself. She just wanted to be with him as closely as she could.

Meanwhile, the show went on, and the months passed. They traversed India and crossed the Indus River. The end of Orb's tour with the carnival was approaching, and she had not found the Llano, but she didn't care; she had found Mym instead.

But at the outskirts of Karachi, disaster came riding on horseback. An officer of Gujarat, Mym's kingdom, appeared. "Prince, we have come for you!" he called. "The Prince, your brother, is dead. You will return with us."

Orb came out. "You must go," she said. "Your Kingdom needs you."

"Damn my Kingdom!" he sang.

"I will go with you, my love." She had no need of any royal life, only to be with him. She was sure she could handle it.

"No," the officer said firmly. "The Prince alone must come. He will marry a princess of the Rajah's choosing."

Orb felt the clutch of horror on her heart. Was she to be separated from him?

"N-n-n-never!" Mym cried.

"We are instructed to pay the woman an adequate sum," the officer said. "She will not be in want. But she is not to see the Prince again, by order of the Rajah."

"An adequate sum!" Orb exclaimed indignantly. How could any monetary payment make up for the outrage and anguish of such a parting?

"It is here," the officer said, proffering her a small package. Orb was hardly aware of accepting it; she was numbed by the awfulness of the situation.

She looked at Mym. He was standing as if dazed, his eyes staring ahead. A trace of blood showed on his lip.

The officer kneeled before him, proffering the hilt of his sword. "If it pleases you, Prince, strike off my head first, and any others you wish. We shall not take arms against our Prince. But you will return to the Kingdom."

Blood at Mym's mouth. The berserkers went wild at the taste of blood. . . .

"Mym!" Orb screamed, understanding. "They are only doing their duty! You must go with them!"

He heard her. He turned his head to the side and spat out the blood. It was evident that he could berserk, and the officer knew it, but that he had it under control. He took the sword, reversed it, and returned it to the officer.

Then Mym turned to Orb. "I will return to you," he sang. "Until that time, I give you this." He brought out a ring that was in the form of a tiny green snake.

"But what is it?" It was as if they were two actors on a stage, and she was watching from an audience; she could hardly believe that this was happening.

"Wear it, and it will answer any question. One squeeze for yes, two for no, three if neither applies. It will also protect you." And in his hand the ring came to life, the little snake slithering across from his palm to hers, rearing up and hissing as if to bite. Then it coiled around one of her fingers and became cold metal again.

"Until you return," she said, his face blurring as her tears sprang forth.

He embraced her and kissed her deeply. Then he went with the officer. He mounted a fine horse that had been brought for him, paused to wave to Orb and to the others of the troupe who had befriended him, and rode away.

Orb gazed after him until no sight of her beloved remained. Then she swooned.

She woke in her wagon, with Pythea tending her. "Oh, I'm so sorry!" Orb explained. "I am distraught, but it's not like me to—"

The snake charmer put out a hand to restrain her. "Orb, it isn't that. I know the signs."

"What?"

"My dear, you are with child."

Orb fainted again.

-6-

ORLENE

The members of the show rallied around her with the warmest support. Orb realized that for now her best course was to continue as she had been, doing her part of the show, concealing her condition from outsiders. It would be some time before her pregnancy became obvious. Perhaps Mym would return before then.

It was several days before she thought to open the bag the officer had given her. She was amazed; it was filled with the most precious of stones—emeralds, rubies, sapphires, opals, and diamonds, all of large size and perfect nature. She took it to the tour master for an appraisal, and his eyes threatened to bulge from his head. "I would offer to buy them," he said, "but there is not money enough in my lifetime to purchase the least of these. You are an excruciatingly rich woman, Orb."

"But I have no need of wealth!" she said. "All I want is Mym!"

"I cast no aspersion on your desire. But if his love were for sale, this would cover it. They have not cheated you, materially."

"Take the gems," she said disconsolately. "I can not abide any price for my love."

"Orb, I would gladly cheat a stranger, but never one of my own, and you are the best of mine. You have a baby to consider; save this wealth for that child, if for nothing else."

He was making sense. "Then take one of these and sell it, and use the money for the benefit of the good people of this show," she said.

"You really want to do this?"

"I do."

He took a blue sapphire. "It will take a while to sell this, for it must be done privately, without attracting the attention of the thuggees to us. Hide the others; let no one know you possess them. I will report soon."

The wagon was unconscionably lonely. She had become accustomed to sleeping in her lover's arms; now she could not stand to be alone. But there was no one she could share with; Pythea had to sleep with her big snake, lest it stray, and the mermaid was confined to her tank.

Then she remembered her ring. It was supposed to answer questions. Did it work?

"Ring," she said, addressing it. "Is it true that you can talk to me by squeezes?"

The ring squeezed her finger, once.

"Can you anticipate the future?"

The little snake squeezed three times.

"Sometimes you can?"

One squeeze.

She took the plunge. "When will Mym return to me?"

The ring squeezed her finger three times.

She said the word she dreaded. "Never?"

Three squeezes.

"Never as—as my lover or husband?"

One squeeze.

There it was; somehow she had known it would be so. Yet she tried again, unable to let go of her dream of joy so readily. "I'll never touch him again?"

Two squeezes.

Foolish hope! "I *will* see him again?"

Squeeze.

"But not—as we were?"

Squeeze.

She had done it clumsily, but had learned all that she needed to know. Why torment herself with advance information about how she would encounter Mym when he was Prince, with some lovely wealthy princess on his arm, hopelessly married? Even if he still loved Orb, he would not kiss her or even encourage her then; she knew him and his iron honor. Oh, surely he would not willingly marry elsewhere, but if it was necessary for the good of his kingdom he would do it, and then be true to it.

Her romance with Mym was through. Instead of hopelessly suffering, she should turn her face forward to the future. At least he wasn't dead! And she did have something of him—his baby.

What was she going to do with a baby? Certainly she could not go home to have it; nothing like this had ever happened in her family. How could she take care of it and raise it? Her situation was impossible!

Well, not entirely. She had all the money she would ever need, in the form of the gems. She could buy herself some private house and hire a trustworthy servant for the shopping and all. She could get through, economically.

But socially—what of that? She had always been a creature of companionship, first with Luna, then with Tinka, then with Mym. Now she realized that part of what had made her restless at home was Luna's absence; she needed someone compatible to be with, to share herself with. How well Mym had filled that need!

She felt her grief surging forward again and quelled it as well as she could. She would simply have to see about getting herself some company. Someone she liked. Maybe—

She paused in her thoughts, taking stock. She had liked Tinka, the blind Gypsy girl. Of course Tinka was married now, but Gypsy women went out as a matter of course to earn money in any way they could. Could she hire Tinka?

She held up the snake ring. "Could I?" she asked.

Squeeze.

She felt a wash of relief and gratitude. Now she had a notion where to go.

The sapphire brought an amount of money that surprised Orb; the tour master had done well in the sale. He issued a quite handsome bonus to all the members of the tour and had the wagons repaired, starting with the leaky roofs. Orb had asked him not to identify the source of the money, but they knew anyway. When the time came for her to leave the show, they surprised her with a farewell party that was intended to be cheerful, but where much crying was accomplished instead. They did not know of her pregnancy; Pythea had kept her mouth shut, and so had the mermaid, whose eye for the signals was also keen. Were it not for the impossibility of birthing and caring for a baby on the road, Orb would have felt inclined to remain with the show.

So she left and took an airplane to the Pyrenees. There she garbed herself appropriately; the cloak Niobe had given her changed into whatever apparel she needed with so little thought that she tended to forget its nature. Then she unfurled her little carpet and set out in search of Tinka.

It did not take long, because the Gypsies of this region were more sedentary than most. Tinka was in a village near the one she had lived in before, hiring herself out as a singer for the tourists. It was sometime work, as the tourist season waxed and waned, and the girl's opportunities were limited because of her blindness. Her ideal marriage was under a certain amount of strain because she had not conceived despite her husband's best efforts.

Orb approached her at her home, where she cooked alone; her husband was out on a business trip whose nature was best not inquired into; it could involve smuggling. "Tinka," Orb said in Calo. "Do you remember me?"

"Orb!" the girl cried, instantly recognizing the voice. She came to Orb and hugged her.

It was the simplest thing to arrange. Tinka was, she admitted privately, somewhat lonely, and would love to have regular work. Her husband would be pleased by the income. She advised Orb on the best house to rent and the best places to shop. It seemed only a moment before two weeks had passed, and Orb was comfortably situated with a full-time maid and companion. All she had to do now was get on with the baby.

But that took time; it could not be hurried. In the interim, she talked Calo with Tinka, and they sang. Orb had to confess, when Tinka inquired, that she had not made significant progress in finding the Llano, but had gotten the baby instead. "I would take the baby instead," Tinka said wistfully.

That made Orb consider her future with the baby. What was

she to do with it? She had always known she could not keep it—but how could she let it go?

She asked the ring. "Should I give the baby to Tinka?"

Squeeze, squeeze.

"Why not?"

Squeeze, squeeze, squeeze.

"Is she likely to be a bad mother?"

Squeeze, squeeze.

"A good mother?"

Squeeze.

"But not right for this?"

Squeeze.

"Then who *is* right?"

Squeeze, squeeze, squeeze.

Orb explained the situation to Tinka. "My magic charm tells me that you would be a good mother, but that I am not to give my baby to you. I don't know to whom to give it."

Tinka was disappointed, but accepted it. "There is still time for me to have my own baby," she said.

"Indeed there is!" Orb agreed warmly. "You are three years younger than I am!"

They concentrated on music, for Tinka was still perfecting her talent, and her status as servant was only nominal; she was a friend. It was delight to sing together. Tinka also encouraged Orb to practice the *tanana*, though at first Orb felt deliciously wicked. Even when it was being done by two women, and one of them only pantomiming the glances, it was the most suggestive thing conceivable.

"But I can't imagine when I would ever want to do this for a man," Orb said. "It's positively lascivious!"

"And think how much more so, if you sing your magic, too," Tinka said.

Orb had to laugh, though her face was burning. "I would never be so wanton!"

"You must have been a little bit wanton, to get that baby," Tinka remarked.

Orb remembered Mym and dissolved into tears.

"I'm sorry," the Gypsy girl said immediately. "I did not mean—"

"He's a prince," Orb said, forcing herself to talk about it, to share the burden with one who would understand. "But he had to marry one of his own, and they took him away. He never knew . . . " She patted her belly, which was filling out.

She shared the whole story with her friend, and it did help. Tinka agreed that there had been no alternative for Mym. "Just as there was none for us, when the conqueror came," she said. "You are now an exile, like the Gypsies."

Oddly enough, that made Orb feel better. The Gypsies understood about being excluded from society; they had been persecuted in many places, across many centuries.

The telling reminded her that the magic ring had informed her that she would see Mym again, though not as a lover. How could the ring know, if her future was opaque to divination?

She asked it, having learned how to evoke meaningful responses from it. "My future can not be read, can it? By any ordinary means?"

Squeeze.

"But you can read it?"

Squeeze, squeeze.

"Then how do you know I will see Mym again?"

Squeeze, squeeze, squeeze.

"Caught you in a contradiction, didn't I!"

Squeeze, squeeze.

"You can't read my future—"

Squeeze.

"But you just *read* my future!"

Squeeze, squeeze.

She was enjoying this, perversely. She knew the snake would come up with an explanation; she just had to ask the right questions. "*Not* my future?"

Squeeze.

"Whose future, then?"

Squeeze, squeeze, squeeze.

"Mym's?"

Squeeze.

There it was. The ring had looked into Mym's future and seen him encountering her; therefore she encountered him, too. Probably the ring also knew in what connection they met, but Orb could find no way to evoke that information from it. She simply could not guess the correct questions.

Because it could look into Tinka's future, and Tinka was with Orb, the ring could tell Orb her future needs. It was evident that Orb was safe enough in this house and would birth a healthy baby; after that she would leave, and Tinka would care for the baby—

"What? You said she could not adopt—"

Squeeze.

"Oh. She is only caring for it, not adopting it."

Squeeze.

"Why do I keep saying 'it'? Is it a boy?"

Squeeze, squeeze.

"A girl."

Squeeze.

"I did suspect it would be one or the other. But I have no intention of just running off and leaving my baby behind! At least I'll put it—*her!*—up for adoption myself."

Squeeze, squeeze.

"Ring, you must be wrong! It just isn't my way!"

But the ring was adamant. Orb would depart suddenly, and the baby would not see her again.

She dropped this line of investigation, as it did not appeal. She would find out in due course.

Orb tried to tune Mym out of her consciousness, to forget him, but the presence of his child within her made this impossible. Even in sleep she did not necessarily get relief, for Mym came into her dreams. There had been a time, before they realized that he could sing his words without stuttering, when he had teased her to marvelous effect. She had been singing, accompanying herself on her harp, practicing a new song, and he had begun to mimic her.

Now she saw him again, doing an impromptu but graceful dance—his stutter had not extended to his feet!—while he mouthed the words she sang. Soon he was properly into it, pausing dramatically in time to the song, emoting with rare conviction as the key passages occurred, his feet striking the floor as the harp's notes sounded. Others came to watch, and Mym's emulation was so perfect that it really did seem as though her voice were issuing from his throat. Orb herself began to suffer the illusion, feeling as though *she* were mouthing *him*. But soon laughter overcame her and burst out, ending the song—and so apt was he that he even emulated her laughter. That set off the entire audience. The tour master wanted to make it part of the show, but Mym demurred; he did not want to be seen in public without his costume.

Orb woke laughing—but as she realized where she was, her mirth turned to tears. Never again, those happy days!

Yet even this experience seemed to help her, as if a little more of her grief had been wrung out, and she was less depressed thereafter. After all, her memories were all she had of Mym now, and so were worth treasuring.

Orb had to remain in the house increasingly as her term advanced, for she didn't want her condition generally known. This was awkward for Tinka, who was not apt at shopping alone. Finally they arranged to have groceries delivered, unusual as this was for this village. Orb preferred to be viewed as an eccentric, rather than to have her situation clarified.

But as the time of birthing drew near, she knew there were limits to secrets. The ring informed her that she was likely to need a midwife. Tinka made the arrangement and used the money Orb gave her to swear the old Gypsy woman to secrecy, and the midwife took care of the rest.

But as the contractions came, there was pain. Orb had decided to birth her baby the natural way, taking no medication, but realized that this was impractical; the pain was too much. So the midwife gave her medicine—and it had no effect. The midwife tried alternative medicine—with no better result.

"What's the matter?" Orb asked the ring. She did not actually speak; she had learned to direct her questions subvocally. "Is there something wrong with the medicine?"

Squeeze, squeeze.

"Wrong with me?"

Squeeze, squeeze.

"Wrong with the situation?"

Squeeze, squeeze, squeeze.

Then she realized. "My protective amulet! It's protecting me from the medication! Because that stuff could be dangerous."

Squeeze.

"Should I remove the amulet?"

Squeeze, squeeze.

"Then how shall I bear the pain?"

Squeeze, squeeze, squeeze.

"There is a way?"

Squeeze.

"Something in lieu of medicine?"

Squeeze.

"A spell?"

Squeeze.

Orb asked the midwife for a spell to take her mind off the pain. The Gypsy woman obliged with a Spell of Analogy.

Orb found herself outside, in the mountain. Rather, she *was* the mountain, the air about it, the vegetation on it, and the water running through it.

But the mountain was in distress. A boulder had formed within it and was blocking the egress of a deep spring-fed river. Pressure was building up, and this was the focus of pain. That boulder had to be gotten out before the pressure cracked open the mountain.

"This is ridiculous!" Orb exclaimed. "I'm not a mountain!"

But the vision persisted, and after a time she gave herself up to it. She became the landscape and labored with its problem. She heaved—and slowly the boulder moved, squeezing down the channel, wedging past the constriction. She heaved again, and it nudged through, first a part of it, then the breadth of it, the riverbed straining and scratching but not breaking. A third great heave, and at last it cleared, and the water burst out and spattered down the slope, free.

She emerged from the vision. Her baby was out, and she was panting, her pain abating. The spell had gotten her through.

It was female, as the ring had foreseen, and in perfect health. Tinka put the baby girl in her arms. "I'll name her after me," Orb murmured, distracted by the wonder of this new life. "No, they'll call her eyeball! Make it Orlene instead."

Then she realized that she was being short-sighted. "I can't keep her! I have no right to name her!"

"Name her anyway," Tinka said.

The logic appealed.

Orlene was a delight. Orb nursed her and burped her and changed her diaper and joyed in being a mother. She wished she could remain here forever with the baby. And why not? The gems from Mym's kingdom represented a virtually inexhaustible fount of money.

But she realized in a moment that it remained impossible. Orlene would not remain a baby forever; she would become a little girl, and then a young woman. What kind of a life would it be for her, with no father, no family, no freedom? She needed legitimacy, a family, friends, school, a social life—everything that Orb herself had had, and could not pass on. The kindest thing she could do for her daughter was to relinquish her.

Then, abruptly, the ring squeezed her. She hadn't asked it a question; it was trying to get her attention. "Something the matter?" she asked.

Squeeze.

Orb's dread returned. "I have to leave now?"

Squeeze.

"But why? Surely a few more days with my child—"

Squeeze, squeeze.

"Where am I supposed to go?" Orb stood and pointed her finger, turning slowly, and when she came to the proper direction, the ring squeezed.

The direction was north. "Home?"

Squeeze.

"I'm needed at home?"

Squeeze.

"Something has happened?"

Squeeze, squeeze.

"*Will* happen?"

Squeeze.

Then suddenly she knew. "Daddy!"

Squeeze.

Her father was old and had been slowly failing. This could only mean that he was dying.

"But I could go home, then return here—"

Squeeze, squeeze.

The ring had always been right. She had tested it many times, idly. She believed it. It was better to make a clean break now and do what she had to do.

"Tinka, the time has come," she said. "I must leave Orlene with you, but you cannot keep her. You must give her for adoption to some well-to-do tourist family who will be able to care for her properly."

"But I would not know who—" Tinka protested. "I can not even speak their language!" For they were speaking Calo.

Orb removed the magic ring. "Wear this. It will guide you: one squeeze for yes, two squeezes for no. When it tells you the family is right, give them the baby."

The ring came to life, and the little snake raised its head and looked at her.

"Something else to tell me?" Orb put a finger down, and the snake coiled about it. "What am I forgetting? Something else I must tell Tinka?"

Squeeze.

"To help Orlene?"

Squeeze.

"My amulet! I'll put it on her, to protect her!"

Squeeze, squeeze.

"Then—?"

Squeeze.

"Then you? Give her you?"

Squeeze.

Suddenly it made sense. "You will remain with Orlene and guide her throughout her life?"

Squeeze, squeeze, squeeze.

"Or at least until she grows up and can make her own decisions?"

Squeeze.

"Yes, of course. I know you will do what is right."

Squeeze.

Then she removed the ring again and gave it to Tinka. "When you find the right family, put this ring on Orlene's finger. It will fit."

The girl nodded.

"And for you, for the time when you have your own baby—" Orb brought out her ruby. "This will make you rich. Your husband is an honorable man? I mean, he wouldn't cheat you?"

Tinka nodded again.

"Then get his help when you need to market this." Orb put the gem into the girl's hand, then impulsively hugged her. "I fear I will never see you again. I love you, Tinka."

Then the Gypsy girl began to cry, and Orb wept with her. But what had to be had to be, and in due course Orb departed, riding her carpet to the nearest airport, where she took an airplane home.

Pacian was indeed dying. Niobe greeted her tearfully. "Oh, Orb, I'm so glad you came home now! How did you know?"

"I had a ring that advised me," Orb explained. "It couldn't see my future, but it could see those who associate with me. I'm sorry I stayed away so long—"

"You're adult now; you have your own life. But this—"

It was bad, but Orb was glad she had come home. It would have been so much worse if her father had died in her absence. The ring had warned her truly.

She put her hand on his arm, and sent him her music, and felt his own rise in response. "Remember when you told me of the Song of the Morning," she said.

"Go find your song, Orb," he replied. Then they held hands and the music intensified, until he lost power and had to sleep.

Two days later he died. Orb handled most of the arrangements, sparing her mother that.

But after the wake and burial, Orb had no inclination to remain. Niobe was able to handle the tree farm, and Orb did indeed have her own life to make. It wasn't that she didn't love her mother, for she did; it was that the happy years of their family existence, with Luna really a part of it, were over, and that was all too obvious.

"Perhaps you should go visit Luna," Niobe said, as if reading her thoughts. "You could go on tour in America. . . . " For of course Orb had written home often, advising her family of her location. She had omitted a certain key detail of her past year, not from any desire to deceive her mother, but because she simply hadn't known how to cope with the fact of an illegitimate baby. One day she would tell her mother, but not right now, not when there was grief enough already.

"I will visit Luna, and see about an American tour," she agreed. Indeed, the notion appealed to her, for Luna was her closest companion and friend.

But first she visited her old friend the hamadryad. She approached the old oak tree in the swamp and called out, but the dryad would not come down.

"But it's me, Orb!" she cried. "Don't you know me?"

"You have lost your innocence," the dryad called from the branches.

Orb realized it was true. She had loved a man, and borne a child, and given it away; what innocence remained to her? Suddenly she was overwhelmed by that loss, not realizing how she had valued it until this moment. She sank down to the ground and wept.

Then the hamadryad came down and touched her momentarily. "It is the fate of mortal women," she said. "My kind can never know it."

Orb looked up, and the dryad was crying, too, for the loss she could never sustain. Orb reached out to her, but there seemed to be a barrier between them, and they were unable to touch.

"But can't we still be friends?" Orb asked.

"From a distance," the dryad agreed.

That seemed to be the best that could be salvaged from a mixed situation. Orb blew her friend a kiss and returned to her own kind. The things of wild magic seemed inevitably to retreat as a person became older and more experienced. That was indeed something worth crying about.

— 7 —

LIVIN' SLUDGE

Actually it was some time, a year or more, before she made the trip to America. She had wanted to go immediately, but had not felt free to desert her mother right after Pace's death, and then there had been requests for her music locally, and one thing led to another, the time frittering away. Then news had come of the Magician's death, and that shocked her into action, so that she completed her commitments in good order and made the trip at last. Perhaps, she thought, she simply hadn't wanted to let go of the last hope that her old life could be restored.

Luna lived in Kilvarough, the town that had imported the famous Irish ghost, Molly Malone. Orb mostly tuned out the journey across the wide sea, trying to focus on the future to avoid focusing on the past, and not succeeding any better than she usually did. Mym, Tinka, Orlene, Niobe, the hamadryad—all of these memories were painful because she knew she could never again know them as she had experienced them before.

But as she drew near, the thought of reuniting with Luna cheered her increasingly. With Luna, she knew, she could truly share, because of their closeness and the mutual spells of protection and immunity to having their futures read. The Magician, Luna's father, had gone to a lot of trouble to cloud their futures;

now she wondered why. She also wondered about the news that Luna was dating Thanatos, the Incarnation of Death; that sounded grim indeed, and perhaps was one of the considerations that had contributed to Orb's delay. No, that dating had begun after the Magician's death; she was getting things confused.

Still, she remembered the old prophecy, dating from before their births: that Luna might marry Death, and Orb might marry Evil. Nonsense, of course; surely a Gypsy fortune telling, and though the Gypsies, as she well knew, could prophecy with the best, they tended to slough off when the matter was not important. Probably someone had made up something dramatic for the benefit of what she took to be a gullible tourist, and later the Magician, annoyed by that, had banned any further predictions. Certainly Orb had never had any truck with evil, and never would! Still, if Luna was actually doing it . . .

Luna met her at the airport. At first Orb didn't recognize her. Then, shocked, she exclaimed: "Luna! What have you done with your hair?" For Luna's clover-honey tresses had changed to chestnut brown, completely transforming her appearance. She was still beautiful, but different.

"Father made me do it," Luna said. "He wouldn't say why. But this is the way it must be for the rest of my life."

"What an odd thing! And is it true that you are—?"

"Taking up with Death?" Luna laughed. She was obviously in excellent health, not likely to die at all soon. "Yes, it is true; you'll meet him soon enough."

They took a taxi carpet to Luna's residence, which was an elegant mini-estate, fenced in, guarded by two lean and hungry griffins. They charged up as the carpet drew close, half-spreading their wings, but relaxed when they recognized Luna. She paid the carpeter, and the two of them entered the iron gate.

Orb was a bit nervous about the griffins, but Luna merely introduced her to them, and that was sufficient. It was evident that they attacked only strangers.

The interior of the house was very nice. "Oh, you are painting again!" Orb exclaimed, recognizing the pictures on the walls.

"It's one way of easing the loneliness since my father died," Luna said.

"How—if I may ask—?"

"He arranged it so that Thanatos would have to collect him personally, and then he offered me to Thanatos."

"He *what*?"

"He wanted me to be friends with the Incarnation of Death," Luna said, as if this were routine. "I didn't understand at first, but later I did. It seems that I am to have an important role in a confrontation between God and Satan about twenty years hence, so Satan naturally wishes to eliminate me before then, and only Thanatos can protect me."

"But what a cynical—what a horror!"

Luna shook her head. "No. Thanatos is a decent man. I have asked him to visit later today, so you can meet him."

"So you—you are satisfied to associate with Death?" Orb asked, accepting this with difficulty.

"I think I would marry him, if that were feasible. But it seems not to be, so we merely associate."

Orb decided not to question that further. She had known Luna well, but wasn't sure how well she knew her now.

"And you," Luna said warmly. "What have you been up to these past three years?"

Orb told her. She found herself hesitant to mention the baby, but also unable to refrain.

"A baby!" Luna exclaimed. "How wonderful!"

"Illegitimate," Orb reminded her. "Given away for adoption."

"A baby!" Luna repeated, as if this were the greatest possible accomplishment!

"Niobe doesn't know."

"I'll say nothing. But how wonderful to have had the experience!"

Orb realized that Luna faced slight prospect of having a family. Viewed that way, it was indeed a lucky thing to have done. Pressed by Luna, Orb described the baby in detail, and it did seem to make the burden of the loss easier to live with.

They had a meal, still talking, catching up on things, and it was generally wonderful. They had been so close for so many years, almost like twins, and it was good to be close now. Every so often they laughed for inadequate reason, cried for similar reason, and hugged each other, girls again.

Then Thanatos arrived. He was a black-cloaked figure whose

face was a skull and whose hands were bones. Orb was awed—
but then he laid back his grim hood and manifested as an ordinary
young man, quite flesh and blood. "But he really is the Incarnation of Death," Luna reminded her. "He collects souls and
guides them to their proper destinations, in the difficult cases."

Orb had no comment to make. Thanatos filled in with a question
of his own. "I understand you are musical, Orb. Do you plan to
perform here?"

"I'm really looking for the Llano," Orb said, still reticent in
the presence of this odd figure. "I suppose I might perform, too."

"Perhaps you could travel with a group, as you did in India,"
Luna said. "One that goes where you want to go."

"I suppose I should," Orb agreed vaguely.

"I encountered a group that might use a competent addition,"
he said.

"Oh?" Orb found herself interested. Certainly she had to
travel, and certainly she didn't want to do it alone. "What
group?"

"They call themselves the Livin' Sludge. They started in
Miami, but now they accept engagements elsewhere and seem to
want to go on a tour, but have some difficulty obtaining suitable
bookings."

"No wonder, with a name like that!" Orb exclaimed.

"Groups run to names like that here," Luna advised her gently.

Orb shrugged. "Are they good musicians?"

"I am not a proper judge," Thanatos said. "But when they did
a command performance for me, assisted by a girl from a neighboring choir, it was a considerable production. I suspect they wish
to duplicate that experience, but are not sure how. They seem
competent as performers, but it is magic they seek, and that is
harder to achieve."

"I have magic," Orb said.

"So I understand. It is possible that you could be the element
they need for the type of success they seek. I should warn you
that they have some problems with drugs, which they are trying
to eliminate."

"Through music?"

"Would this piece you mention—I am not familiar with it—
would it help them?"

"The Llano? I think it would, if they could find it. The Gypsies call it the universal absolver. But if I knew how to find it, I would do so forthwith."

"Then perhaps you could search for it together."

"Perhaps we could!" Orb agreed, abruptly liking the notion. To be with a group that was searching for the same thing she was—that could be wonderful! "Can you put me in touch with them?"

"I can take you to them, if you wish."

Orb had an abrupt second thought. "You say they are addicts? Of what?"

"What they call 'H,' enchanted for greater potency. It isn't really the same kind of thing that is historically known, but a designer drug that emulates heroin, extraordinarily addictive. They believe that the right music can relieve them of the craving. They do not appear to be bad people, merely ones who have fallen into unfortunate habits."

"But heroin! What real hope for reform can there be?"

Thanatos shrugged. "My own balance of evil approached fifty per cent when I attempted suicide, but my new mission has given me strength. I think reform is possible, given the right motivation and circumstance."

"My own evil threatened to overwhelm me," Luna said. "Yet it seems that I am fated to play a key role in the salvation of mankind. I, too, find it necessary to believe that salvation is possible for anyone who really makes the attempt."

Orb had another thought. "You can judge the amount of evil in a person? I mean, not a dead soul?"

"I can," Thanatos agreed.

"I—" Now she found herself shy. "Could you—would you—?"

"Read your balance?" he finished. "This I can do. But I regard it as a private matter. Are you sure you wish it?"

"I have no secrets from Luna. Can you do it here, now?"

"He can," Luna said.

"I'd really like to know."

"As you wish." Thanatos reached into a fold of his cloak and brought forth two cabochons—polished, half-rounded stones. One was light, the other dark.

He brought the light one near Orb, passing it along her body from head to foot at a distance of a few centimeters. It flickered as it moved. With each flicker it became brighter, until at last it shone like a little moon.

Then he used the dark one in the same manner. It, too, flickered, but it became darker as it did so, until it was completely dull, with no shine at all.

Thanatos set the two stones together, and they merged, forming a ball. The flat planes of their bottom sides seemed to curve, forming a yin-yang shape.

He let the ball go. It floated upward, until it threatened to rise out of reach. He reached up and caught it. "Your balance is positive," he said. "But there is a significant amount of evil on your soul. You have done something you should not have."

Luna was silent, not divulging Orb's secret. But Orb decided to reveal it herself. "I had an affair," she said.

Thanatos nodded. "That is evil, by the current definition."

"And I had a baby. Illegitimate."

"That is greater evil. But I think not enough to account for the amount you show."

"I did not tell my mother."

"That accounts for it," he said.

"Do you condemn me for that?" she asked, somehow wanting his acceptance.

"No. I killed my own mother, and Luna deceived her father. We understand these things. But the definitions of good and evil were set up before our time, and they are the ones that prevail. It is not necessary for Incarnations to agree with the prevailing rules; it is only necessary for us to implement them. By the old definitions, you have sinned grievously, and your soul is weighted accordingly; by my definition you have sinned only if you caused unnecessary pain to an innocent person. Did you do that?"

"I caused my lover pain, because he had to separate from me."

"Were you the agent of that separation?"

"No."

"Then that sin is not yours, by definition. But my definition is meaningless; I do not make the rules."

"Still, I feel reassured."

"It is reassuring to know Thanatos and to understand him," Luna said.

"Yes. I am coming to understand that." For the man who held the office of Death was evidently a decent person, one it could be possible to love—and Luna did love him. That portion of the prophecy seemed to be true: Luna might marry Death. But the other, that Orb might marry Evil—could this be the start of the shifting of her balance toward total evil? She shuddered.

But perhaps if she found the Llano first, she would be able to avert that horror. That made the search more urgent. "Let's go see the Livin' Sludge," she said abruptly.

"Take her," Luna said to Thanatos.

He nodded. "Mortis is outside."

"Who?" Orb asked.

"His steed," Luna explained. "You'll like Mortis." She seemed amused.

"Oh—a horse." Orb was relieved.

She followed Thanatos out. Evidently Luna was not coming along. Maybe the horse could carry double but not triple. What had Luna found so funny?

A pale sedan was parked nearby. The two griffins lay beside it, almost as if guarding it, unless they liked the company of such machines. Thanatos went to this. He opened the door.

"This car? But Luna said—" Orb was confused.

"This is Mortis."

"But—"

Thanatos had drawn his cowl back over his head. The skull-face grinned. "Show her, Mortis."

The car changed. Its wheels stretched down, its hood stretched up, and its body reconvoluted. In a moment the vehicle had become a handsome pale horse.

Orb stared. Then she laughed. No wonder Luna had been amused! She had known about this.

Like all girls and most women, Orb loved horses. She approached the handsome animal, extending her hand so he could sniff it. "Hello, Mortis," she said. "May I pet you?"

Mortis' ears perked forward. That meant a favorable reaction. She reached up slowly and petted him on the neck, on the side away from the mane. Then, unable to restrain herself, she stepped in close and hugged his neck. A horse was almost as wonderful as a baby!

Then Thanatos mounted and extended his skeletal hand to her. She took it, putting her left foot up into the available stirrup, and swung herself into the saddle ahead of him. It was an awkward maneuver, but she had learned it young. His arms came around her, but she trusted Luna to know her man, and knew that there would be no trouble.

Thanatos held her steady and spoke to Mortis. There were no reins. The horse took a step forward, paced by the two now-friendly griffins, and then leaped into the air, again paced by the griffins. The griffins had huge, beautiful wings, and the horse did not—yet all three were flying readily. Rather, the horse was galloping through the air, as if his hooves found purchase in it.

They charged upward into the sky. The griffins cried out in parting and turned to descend back toward the residence. It was evident that they would have loved to travel with the horse forever, but had guard duty to honor. Had Luna come, they could have come, too. Well, perhaps another time.

They moved above the occasional clouds, traveling generally south. Orb saw an airplane passing to the side. The horse seemed to be outdistancing it, yet no wind ruffled Orb's hair.

"How is it that we can travel so high and fast, yet feel no wind or cold?" she asked. "When I ride on my carpet I have to wear warm clothing." Of course her magic cloak took care of that, but the point was valid.

"The magic of the Incarnations is of a different order than that of mortal folk," Thanatos replied.

So it seemed! "And how is it that you are willing to perform such a mundane task as taking a mortal woman to see a mortal musical group?"

"It is not every woman who would love the minion of Death," he said. "Your cousin Luna is one."

And for Luna he would do anything. Perhaps it made sense. She concluded that it was best not to pry into that relationship.

"She says that there is no other like you for music." Thanatos continued after a pause.

"I don't know whether that is true, but I do have a talent," she said.

"I hope you find the group compatible."

"Thank you, Thanatos," she said, touched.

Then Mortis started down, and the great city of Miami spread out beneath them.

"How is it that no one stares at us?" Orb asked.

"Few people care to observe the approach of Death."

Answer enough! They dropped down to the streets, and the horse's hooves touched the pavement.

Then, abruptly, the two of them were sitting in the car. Mortis had changed form and was now driving along the street, in traffic.

They drew up at a slummish area of town. Thanatos opened the door and they got out. Orb heard music from a practice hall. Guitar, drum, electric organ—that seemed to be the extent of it, by the sound.

Several shaggy teenagers glanced up as they entered the hall. "Uh-oh," the drummer said. "He's here again!"

"Is your singer recovered?" Thanatos inquired.

The drummer shook his head. "She's out of it. And we can't get decent bookings without her." He glanced sidelong at Thanatos. "You comin' for one of us this time?"

"No. I come to bring you a new member, perhaps."

The teenagers relaxed. "You know, that black chick—she was something! We never did a hymn before, but—" The drummer shook his head. "If you gave us her . . . "

"No. This is the one I bring." He indicated Orb.

They focused on Orb. "Whatcha play?" the drummer asked, noting Orb's container.

"A small harp."

"A what?"

Orb turned to Thanatos. "I'm not sure this is right. Maybe that black girl they mentioned would be better for them."

Thanatos considered. "I will inquire. Meanwhile, play for them."

Orb shrugged. She brought out her harp, set it up, settled herself on the floor, and started a song of Ireland. She let the magic spread out, touching them. But she noticed that Thanatos was walking out of the hall on his errand, evidently not touched. Of course he was an Incarnation, not subject to mortal effects; still, she was disappointed.

The members of the Livin' Sludge listened, entranced. When Orb concluded her song, they closed in about her. "Sheesh, woman!" the drummer said. "You're a pro! You want to join *us*?"

"I want to seek the Llano," she said.

"The what?"

"A magic song," she explained. "It is said to accomplish miraculous things, when properly sung."

"Like what?"

She told them some of the stories of the Llano she had heard. They listened attentively.

"This song," the drummer asked finally. "Do you think it could get a man off the shi—the stuff?"

"The stuff?"

"Spelled H," he said.

"Are you referring to a drug?" Of course Thanatos had explained this, but she felt it was better to get the news directly from them, so that there was no question of a violation of confidence.

"*The* drug," he agreed.

"I don't know. But I think so."

"Then we want the Llano!" he said.

"I don't know where to find it," Orb said. "I expect to have to travel."

The drummer glanced at the others. "We'll travel!"

"But we ain't in her class," the guitarist said.

Orb suspected that was an accurate assessment. But she did want to search for the song, and if these folk had a similar ambition, she wanted to consider the matter fairly. "Perhaps we should find out how we are together," she suggested.

"Sure, let's try it," the drummer said eagerly. He glanced about again. "You guys pick up on her tune?"

The organist touched his keyboard. The theme Orb had played sprang forth. The guitarist joined in. The drummer settled down to his drums, sounding a beat.

Orb nodded. These kids looked like the sludge they called themselves, but they were apt with their instruments. She began to play and sing herself.

The magic spread out, as before—but this time it touched the hands of the musicians, and amplified, and now it seemed that all of them had it. Just as the harp increased Orb's own magic, the instruments of the Livin' Sludge were providing magic for them. Orb had never noted this effect before—but of course she had never played with other instruments before. She was surprised and gratified.

The song ended. "Geez," the drummer said. "Like it was before!"

"I think we could—how do you put it—make it," Orb said, impressed.

"That's not exactly how we put it," the drummer said. "But for sure, we could be one hot sound!"

Their eyes were attracted to the entrance as Thanatos reappeared. The black girl was with him. She was young, perhaps sixteen, thin and pretty. "This is Lou-Mae," he said. "She sang with you once before."

"She sure did!" the drummer exclaimed, getting up to approach the girl.

"I—" the girl faltered. "I sure would like to—I never sang that kind before, but ever since, all I can remember is how it felt—"

"We know," the drummer said.

"When the preacher saw Death, he told me right off to go with him," the girl continued. "He knew I couldn't stay with the choir no more. But—" She looked at Orb. "You already got a singer?"

"Is there a limit?" Orb asked.

"Naw," the drummer said quickly. "If it flows with her, it flows. Let's give it a try."

They gave it a try. The girl did not know the Irish song, so they found one she did know, which Orb also knew, and tried it as a group.

It worked. The magic embraced the instruments and the voice of Lou-Mae, and an ordinary song became miraculous. Orb's voice had a different tonal quality from that of Lou-Mae, and the two fused in an intense harmony buttressed by the instruments.

It ended, after seeming timelessness. Thanatos nodded. "It seems you integrate," he said.

Lou-Mae looked toward the door. An old black preacher stood there. "You go with them, girl," he said. "You got the callin'. I know God wants it that way. I'll square it with departed.

"I guess we've got a group," the drumme chicks want to travel with us, it sure—"

"Chicks?" Orb asked. "Baby birds?"

The three boys and Lou-Mae laughed. "Close enough," the drummer said. "But you know, we've got to get a gig, or it's nothing. We—you know, our rep isn't exactly what you'd call—"

"I will get you a performance," Thanatos said.

"Like before? In the street? That wasn't—"

"A regular engagement. I am sure Luna could arrange it."

"Who?"

"My cousin," Orb said. She and Luna seldom bothered to clarify the precise relationship between them, and "cousin" was a reasonable approximation. She turned to Thanatos. "But why should we impose on her? She isn't obliged to—"

"She asked me to."

So Luna was out to help Orb in a substantial way. Orb nodded to herself. She would have done the same for Luna.

Thanatos addressed the others. "If you will collect your instruments, I have transportation outside."

The drummer was startled. "Transport? Are we going somewhere?"

"To Kilvarough."

"But—"

Thanatos gazed directly at the drummer. The drummer paled. "Yeh, sure. We're going."

They trooped out to the street, where Mortis waited in automobile form. The drums and guitars and electric organ and electronic equipment were stacked in the trunk, which had ample room for them all, even though it hardly seemed large enough. Then the three youths got on the rear seat, and Orb and Lou-Mae took the middle seat, and Thanatos took the driver's seat.

Orb had not realized that the car had three seats, or that it was sized to carry six or more people in comfort. But of course she had not been paying attention to the vehicular aspect of Mortis.

The car moved out into traffic. "Ooops," Thanatos said. "I

ee I have a collection that should not wait. If you will excuse me, this will not take long.''

No one objected. What could he mean by a "collection"?

The view outside the windows blurred. They seemed to be speeding through the countryside at a suicidal rate.

"Geez," one of the Sludge exclaimed. "We're goin' *through* stuff!"

So it seemed; trees, buildings, even a mountain passed in cut-away section as the car zoomed along on an even keel. Orb and Lou-Mae stared as raptly as did the boys. Orb saw the black girl cross herself.

As abruptly as it had begun, the blurring ended. The car was now proceeding along a country road. The scenery had changed completely.

"Say, where are we?" the guitarist asked, amazed.

"Portland," Thanatos replied.

"Geez! All the way to Maine, just like that?"

"Oregon," Thanatos said, perhaps smiling.

"Must be magic!"

"True."

The vehicle slowed, then stopped. An old woman was slumped over a table in the front yard of an isolated house. Thanatos got out, went to her, and put his hand into her body. He drew something out. It was invisible, but they all knew he was not pantomiming. He put the thing into a small bag he carried. Then he returned to the car.

"Heart attack," Thanatos said. "It wasn't right to let her suffer long."

"You mean she wasn't dead?" Lou-Mae asked.

"Not until I took her soul."

"You mean you have to take every soul of everybody who dies?"

"Only those in balance. Those who can not readily either rise or sink."

"Geez," the drummer said. "Guess we don't need to worry 'bout that. We know where we're goin'. Straight down."

"Not necessarily," Thanatos said.

"He can read your balance of good and evil," Orb said.

"Then he knows," the drummer said flatly.

The car was phasing cross-country again. "No," Thanatos said. "Only if I read you, and I do not do that gratuitously."

"You can tell if we're going to be saved?" Lou-Mae asked.

"No. I can only read the present balance. Your salvation depends on yourself."

"Would—would you read me?" she asked. "I know I've sinned—"

Thanatos turned in his seat, ignoring the driving, but the car seemed to know its own way. He brought out his two stones and passed them near her. The light one flashed often and glowed brightly; the dark one flashed only seldom and hardly darkened at all. "You are about ninety-five per cent good. You would have to sin continuously for some time before being in danger of Hell."

"But I get these real bad thoughts sometimes, and I just know—"

The drummer laughed. "Sister, if thoughts could do it, I'd be a cinder now! It only counts if you *do* it!"

"True," Thanatos said.

"But—"

"Read me," the drummer said. "I'll show you what black is!"

Thanatos oriented the stones on the drummer. Both the light and dark ones flashed. When he put them together, the ball slowly sank. "Your balance is negative, but not strongly so; right living can rectify it soon enough."

"But I'm into H!" the drummer protested. "Spelled H! We all are! That's damnation right there!"

"There is no absolute damnation," Thanatos said. "You must have redeeming qualities. I believe one of them showed when you helped Lou-Mae to find her place, when she sang with you the first time."

"Well I had to," the drummer protested. "She's a good girl! It wasn't right to mess her up."

"And so you appreciated good, and you did good. Thoughts don't count when they are not acted upon, but motive counts when you do take action. You helped her, from altruistic motive. You want to do right, and you do do it when you have opportunity. That goes far to mitigate the evil of your lifestyle."

The drummer was amazed. "But I didn't do it because of my

balance! I just—I mean, sometimes you just gotta do what's right. There's no choice in it, it's just the way it is."

"That is why it counts," Thanatos said, and turned back to the front.

"I don't get it," the drummer said. "If I had no choice, how can it count?"

"I think he means that another person might see it another way," Orb said. "Another might not choose to do what was right, or perhaps might not even see what was right. Your conscience gave you no choice, and *that* counted."

"Precisely," Thanatos said.

"Geez," the drummer said thoughtfully.

Now the vehicle was slowing again. It stopped—and there was Luna's estate.

They got out, and the Sludge unloaded their instruments. Orb had kept her harp with her, as she always did.

Then Mortis reverted to equine form and started grazing on the lush lawn.

The Sludge stared. "We were in a horse?" the drummer asked.

"In the rear of the horse," Lou-Mae said, stifling a laugh. Then her face straightened. "Oh, I shouldn't have said that; it's not nice."

"Chalk up one smidgeon of evil to your soul," the drummer said, laughing himself. "At that rate, you'll be damned in only three centuries!"

They trooped into the house, paced by the two griffins.

Luna took over. "I think you will want to clean up," she said. "And perhaps some new clothing. The facilities are that way." In a moment she had bustled the three boys off. The Livin' Sludge had struck Orb as a fairly ornery group, but the combination of Thanatos' office and Luna's certainty and their own desire for great music had rendered them docile. Probably it was their passion for music that accounted for the greater part of the good on their souls; that was sincere.

"And you," Luna said to Lou-Mae. "I believe I can put together a suitable outfit for you. This way." She led the girl away.

Orb was left with Thanatos. "How can she be so sure this will work, when she hasn't even heard us sing as a group?" she asked.

"She told me to bring them back only if it was good," Thanatos said. "She has connections; she will get an audition."

An hour later the group reassembled. The three boys were clean and in new clothing, their hair combed; they looked amazingly presentable. Lou-Mae was stunning in a bright red dress, and a sparkling ruby in her hair.

"Oh, I forgot you," Luna said to Orb. "You can wear one of mine; we always wear the same size."

"Not any more, I fear," Orb said. She had forgotten to mention the magic cloak and didn't want to do it in public.

Sure enough, Orb's pregnancy had amplified her bosom somewhat. But Luna was ready to do some quick stitching on an elegant green dress, until Orb explained about the cloak, and duplicated it without stitching. Luna gave Orb an emerald for her hair, to match the color. Gems were one thing Luna had in quantity, both enchanted and mundane; she had inherited the Magician's collection. They were enchanted to return to her when their use was over, so she had no concern about loss or theft.

"Now find a suitable piece," Luna said, setting them up in a larger room. "I will see about the audition."

They discussed it, discovering to no one's surprise that they had few if any musical tastes in common. The boys knew modern acid, Lou-Mae knew black spirituals, and Orb knew Old World folk songs. "You mean to say that none of you know "Londonderry Air?" she asked in frustration. She had sung that with Mym, so now it had special meaning for her; she thought everyone in the world knew it.

"Never heard of it," the drummer said. "Maybe if you play a few bars . . . "

Orb did so. "Oh, 'Danny Boy'!" the drummer said. "I've heard that!"

"So have I," Lou-Mae said.

"Well, then . . . ?" Orb asked.

So they played with it and worked out an arrangement that suited them all. They practiced it, experimenting with harmonies. Orb sat with her harp, and Lou-Mae stood beside her, their dresses and gems brightly complementing each other.

"You know," the drummer said, "I heard once that it wasn't

a chick saying good-bye to her man, but his older father. That sort of changes it.''

''It is open to interpretation, of course,'' Orb said. ''I always preferred to think of it as a farewell by a lady friend as Danny went off to war, a conscript. But I believe you are correct. Yet unless we had a male singer—''

''No, 'sokay,'' he said quickly. ''But you know, if we could sort of act it out a little—''

They tried it. The drummer set aside his drums and posed as the young man, and Orb confined herself to her harp, not singing, leaving that to Lou-Mae.

The two remaining Sludge and Orb played a preamble; then the drummer and Lou-Mae walked into the center. They paused there, facing each other, and Lou-Mae began to sing.

> ''Oh, Danny Boy, the pipes, the pipes are calling
> From glen to glen, and down the mountain side.
> And from the trees, the leaves, the leaves are falling;
> 'Tis you, 'tis you must go, and I must bide.''

There seemed to be an electricity as the song progressed and the magic took hold. The drummer and Lou-Mae were staring at each other as if genuinely loath to part. Mountains seemed to form, and the sound of the pipes that the organist made seemed to echo across them. A breeze stirred the imagined trees, and leaves tumbled down, for it was autumn. The same breeze stirred Lou-Mae's dress and hair, and she was lovely.

As the song ended, something snapped. The drummer stepped forward, and Lou-Mae met him halfway, and they embraced as if drawn together by irresistible magnetism, and kissed, long and deep. Then he hauled himself away, dramatically reluctant, and stumbled down the hill, while she watched, sobbing. They knew they would never be together again.

The music ended, and they came out of it. ''Geez,'' the guitarist said. ''I'd a sworn you two was in love!''

''I guess I thought I was, for a moment,'' the drummer said, reappearing from the next room. He looked at Lou-Mae. ''*Am,* maybe.''

She dropped her gaze shyly. "Maybe," she agreed, wiping away her tears. She was evidently shaken.

"I will check her schedule," a new voice said.

Startled, they looked. There stood Luna and an older man. "This is the director of the Kilvarough Arts Center," Luna said. "I asked him to come here to audit you, and we decided not to interrupt."

"We definitely want you," the director said. "I believe there is an open date in two months. We are a public service organization, so we can not afford more than a nominal gratuity, but the exposure is excellent. If your group is amenable—"

"They are amenable," Luna said.

"I shall be in touch shortly," the director said. Luna escorted him out.

"Arts Center?" the organist asked.

"That would be a most prestigious engagement," Orb said. "After a successful performance there, it should be possible to get bookings almost anywhere else."

"That's great!" the organist said. "But all we got is one song! How we gonna do a full show?"

"I think we shall have to work out other pieces," Orb said. "Perhaps some solo renditions, interspersing the group efforts."

"I guess," the organist said. He looked at the drummer for agreement, but the drummer was locked in a gaze with Lou-Mae, oblivious.

"I think we have started something," Orb remarked.

"But we got a gig!" the guitarist said gleefully.

"Let's see to it that we are ready for it."

"But you know, we gotta stay somewhere—I mean, a month—"

"I suspect my cousin will arrange something."

Her confidence was justified. Luna found lodging for them all. They practiced diligently, working out new songs and new skits, fashioning a variety program from parts that had just one thing in common—magic. As they worked together, they came to know each other and to respect one another's qualities. The drummer and Lou-Mae were definitely a couple, but Orb made it plain that however much she might respect the music they were creating, she had no interest in any romantic attachment with any of the boys.

When the time of the performance came, the audience chamber was only a quarter full. "This is typical," the director confided. "There is not any great support for the arts today, alas."

"It's still a damn sight bigger than anything we've seen before," the drummer said. Then, embarrassed: "Delete that; I mean we never had a big crowd."

They started their performance. The audience seemed not particularly impressed—until the first note sounded, and the magic spread out. Then the people were rapt. All coughing ceased, all motion; it was as if statues sat in every chair.

After the intermission, there were substantially more people attending, and more filtered in, until at the end the hall was better than half filled. "That has never happened before," the director confided.

Next morning the reviews appeared. It seemed that several of the city's critics had hastened to the hall and taken in at least part of the performance. Orb read, and felt dizzy. "Can this be us?" she asked.

"It's the wildest praise any local performance has ever had," Luna assured her. "They felt the magic; mere expertise would never have moved them like this."

In the afternoon the offers started coming in. Cities all over the country were asking for the Livin' Sludge, and offering fees that left the boys' mouths hanging open.

The group was on its way.

– 8 –

JONAH

Luna was in touch with sundry professionals, and set the new group up with a bookkeeper who would stay in touch and handle their bookings and records. She was Mrs. Glotch, a grandmotherly woman of unquestioned competence and integrity. She refused to travel, but would be on constant call, and would update them whenever they called in. If an emergency arose, she would search them out; Luna gave Orb a stone that would serve as a beacon, so that Mrs. Glotch could always locate her geographically.

But how would they travel? The boys had blithely assumed that they would rent a bus and fit it out with beds and a kitchen, so they could live on the road. "No way I get in that bus!" Lou-Mae declared. "I'm a good girl!"

Orb was less concerned about her morals or safety, because of her amulet, but shared the girl's disinclination for this type of travel. "Why not use commercial transport and hotels?" she asked.

"You know what they *cost?*" the drummer demanded.

"And I won't trust my organ to shipping," the organist added. "It'd arrive broken, in the wrong city."

"It sure would!" the guitarist exclaimed, and he and the drummer broke into crude laughter, while the organist looked nettled.

Orb exchanged a glance with Lou-Mae. Had they missed something? Then Orb realized that there was more than one meaning of the word "organ," and caught the point.

They did seem to have a case. Money should be no problem, with the bookings they could now get, but the problems of shipping were notorious. They needed their own transportation.

They considered renting a railway car, but the ones they were shown were ancient and bug-ridden, and the tracks did not go to many cities, and schedules were erratic. They considered a private airplane, but the cost was horrendous, and the chambers crowded; in addition, the guitarist was afraid to fly. They considered a mobile home, but Lou-Mae declared that to be little more than a mobile bedroom and would have no part of it.

Luna hated to admit it, but the boys' original notion of a revamped bus seemed to be the only feasible mode. But Lou-Mae remained adamant; she had a thing against buses, somehow believing that she would be confined to the rear if not actually molested. "But I'll see that no one bothers you," the drummer assured her. "You're the one I'm afraid of, Danny-Boy!" she retorted. Then she kissed him.

The others nodded. Lou-Mae had liked the drummer ever since that first song together and had dubbed him Danny-Boy after their success with Londonderry Air. But she regarded it a sin to be intimate with a man outside of marriage, and a lesser sin to have the opportunity for such intimacy, even if it was scrupulously avoided. She was, perhaps, afraid of herself. She represented an ideal standard, and the boys respected that without quite understanding it. The bus was out. But what else offered?

"There is magic," Luna said. "A big carpet—"

"Not on your life!" the guitarist exclaimed. "We'd be blown off!" His fear of flying seemed worse with the prospect of an open carpet.

"Or a dragon-drawn wagon—"

"Can't trust a dragon," the organist asserted. "Those reptiles are only waiting their chance to turn and toast you. Half of 'em hid out in Hell when magic was banned, and the evil never did get out of 'em. Sure, the drivers use safety spells, but spells can glitch.''

"Perhaps unicorns, then."

"They can't be controlled," the drummer said. "'Cept by a—" He paused, his eye turning on Lou-Mae. "Then again—"

"I always adored unicorns," the black girl confessed.

"Yeah, but if she—if something happened to—where'd we be then?" the organist demanded, looking sternly at the drummer. "Way out nowhere with a pair of enraged unicorns!"

"What do you mean, *if something happened*?" Lou-Mae exclaimed angrily. "I tell you, nothing could—" But then she looked at the drummer, who was trying to stifle a blush. "I mean, nothing *would*—well, not likely, anyway." Now she seemed to be attempting her own blush, though her dark skin protected her. "Maybe we'd better pass on the unicorns."

"Maybe I'd better consult with the local Gypsies," Orb said. "They surely know how to travel with baggage."

"You're a Gypsy?" the guitarist inquired. "I always thought it would be nice to live in wagons and rip off the—I mean—"

Orb smiled. "Gypsies do what they have to, to survive. They aren't bad people, but they don't like to be tied down."

"I know the feelin'," he said.

"Come with me, if you want, and we'll see what they have to say."

"Well, sure, okay!" he agreed, pleased.

Orb's carpet would hold two in a pinch, but there was no way the guitarist would get on it, so they took a taxi to the next township, where a band of Gypsies was passing. They decided to take their instruments along, because Gypsies always responded to music.

It was a disappointment. These Gypsies wore ragged but conventional clothes and drove battered cars. On top of that, they were surly and suspicious of strangers. "Get away from here, woman," one snapped. "We've got trouble enough."

"But I have lived among you, in Europe!" she said. "I speak the language!"

"Yeah? Speak the language."

"I am looking for good transportation," she said in Calo.

They looked blankly at her. Then one old woman nodded. "It's the old tongue," she said. "But we've almost forgotten it, here, and the young ones never learned it."

"Oh." Orb tried to mask her disappointment. "But perhaps you can help me anyway. All I want is information on—"

"You can't use a car or carpet?"

"We have a group of five, with instruments. One won't ride a bus, and one won't fly. We'd prefer to travel together, if we can agree on how to do it."

"You know Gypsy ways?"

"As I said, in Europe—"

"Can you dance?"

Oh. "I know the *tanana*," Orb said guardedly. "But—"

The woman laughed. "But you can't *dance* it! You'd die of shame. Because you're not a Gypsy, just an observer."

"That's right. But I do respect the Gypsy ways, though they are not mine. Can you help me?"

"Maybe, girl, maybe. You know of Jonah?"

"Who?"

"The fish that swallowed Jonah."

"Oh, you mean the whale? In the Bible?"

"The *fish*. He was damned for that, but not in Hell. Damned to swim the air and earth, but never the water, until the Llano sets him free of his guilt."

"The Llano! You know of it?"

"Of it. Not much more. You seek it?"

"Yes!"

"Then you're in luck. Jonah may help you. He's sleeping in Clover Mountain. Call him out, do the dance, and if he likes you he'll swim for you. Most of the time."

"A *fish*? I don't—"

"He's what you want, if you can win him over. We tried to get him, but we're not pure Gypsies anymore, and—"

"Move!" a man called. "They're comin'!"

Instantly the gypsies, men, women, and children, piled into their cars, and the cars cranked up, sputtered, and got moving. As this occurred, three trucks roared in, filled with men. They had shotguns, and looked angry.

"Get *outta* here, girl!" the old gypsy woman screamed at Orb as her car squealed away.

Two of the trucks careened after the fleeing Gypsies, the shot-guns firing. The third skewed toward Orb and the guitarist.

"Run!" Orb cried, realizing the danger they were in.

They ran. They cut across a ragged field, but the truck pursued, bumping across ruts and churning up turf. "There's two!" a man yelled.

"Kill 'em!"

"Naw! One's a slut! Lay 'er first!"

They crossed a gully, then a ridge, and half-slid down the other side. The truck screamed to a halt, balked by the terrain. "Catch 'em afoot!" a man yelled. "They can't cross th' rapids!"

The rapids? Now Orb heard the sound of spuming water. Already her breath was rasping, and her side was developing a stitch. She stumbled, and the guitarist caught her and helped her along. "How'd we get into this?" he gasped.

"They must," she gasped, "have stolen a horse or a girl. Now they're scattering. But we—"

"Behind the eight-ball!" he finished. "But we're not Gypsies!"

"I think one of us will get raped and the other killed before they find out," she puffed. She was not at all certain that her amulet would protect her from this; it had never been tested against more than one person at a time.

He heaved out a laugh. "Wonder which'll get which?"

Then they came up against the rapids. The water charged past like an express train, throwing out spray. The bank dropped steeply to it, beset by rocks and boulders. There was no safe way across.

"The carpet!" Orb cried, wriggling out of her knapsack and dumping it on the ground. The little carpet unrolled immediately. "Get on!"

"I can't get on that!" he protested. "I can't fly!"

Now the pursuing men crested the hill. "There they are!"

The guitarist stood frozen, petrified by both alternatives. The men charged down the slope.

Orb grabbed her companion by the shoulders and shoved him onto the carpet. "Sit down!" she cried in his ear.

Numbed, he obeyed, holding his cased guitar in his arms before him. She jumped on behind him, spreading her legs to circle his body, putting her arms around him. She willed the carpet aloft.

It lifted as the first man arrived. "Hey!" the man cried as the carpet with its burden almost banged into him. Then he grabbed for it.

Orb swung out with her left arm, cracking him on the neck. She did it without thinking and was appalled at herself even as the shock ran up her arm. Then she willed the carpet out toward the river, gaining effective elevation in a hurry as the land dropped away.

The guitarist stared down. "Geez!" he exclaimed, and tried to scramble off the carpet.

"Stop it!" Orb hissed into the back of his head. "You'll overbalance it!" Indeed, the carpet, overloaded, was already tilting scarily.

The guitarist tried to shrink into himself. "Worse'n a bad trip!" He shuddered.

"Just shut your eyes and keep still!" Now they were over the turbulent water, sinking slowly. The carpet was doing its best, but double weight was too much for it.

"Don't let 'em get away!" a man cried.

Orb didn't dare look back. She urged the carpet on across. It obeyed unsteadily.

There was a bang. They were shooting! Orb did what she had to do—she guided the carpet slightly down and forward, so that it could gain velocity in the descent.

"Aaaahh!" the guitarist cried as the bottom seemed to drop out. "Geez Keerist!"

Orb clapped her hands over his eyes, as if shielding a baby from a bright light. "Relax, it's all right, relax," she said. She felt moisture on her fingers: he was crying. Then she hugged him.

It worked. He relaxed slightly, feeling somewhat secure in her embrace.

Another shot sounded. Then the carpet cut through the spume at the water's verge, seemed virtually to skip the surface, and plowed into the far bank. They tumbled off, brought up short by the slope.

A third shot sounded, and there was the thud of something striking the bank nearby. At least they weren't good marksmen!

"Go there!" Orb cried, hauling on the man, shoving him in the right direction. He scrambled as directed, and they dived behind a great spray of water from a boulder in the river, finding cover from the party on the other side. They were safe for the moment. The guitarist stared at the river. "You should have left me," he husked. "I almost got you killed."

"I couldn't do that!" Orb exclaimed indignantly.

"You know I'm worthless, hooked on H. Wouldn't have been much loss."

"Now stop that!" she snapped. "You—" But there wasn't much encouragement she could make, because he really did not have much to recommend him. "You're a fine musician."

"I'm a zilch musician! Only time I play well is when you're spreading your magic. That's *you*, not me." He pondered a moment. "But I'll make it up to you somehow, I swear! What little I am, I owe to you, and my life, too."

"I'll be satisfied if you just get off the H."

He rolled over and put his face in the ground. "God! If only I could!"

"You can't just stop?"

"You don't know what it's like!"

"You're right, I don't. If I wanted to stop a thing, I would simply stop it, I think."

He lifted his face to stare at her. Dirt crusted it; he looked almost like a zombie. Then, with a convulsive movement, he reached into a pocket and brought out a packet. "Then take it! It's all I've got! Don't let me have it!"

Orb took the packet with a certain revulsion. "Your life is ruined for this?"

"You got it, sister."

Orb tucked the packet away. "Then I will hold it for you. I will be pleased if you never ask for it back."

He did not reply. He simply set his face back in the dirt.

After a time the pursuers gave up, as they were unable to cross the river. Orb heard their truck departing. However, she had not spent time with the gypsies without learning a trick or two. "I think we had better not cross back," she said. "Someone could be lurking."

"Right," the guitarist said, relieved. He did not want to be airborne again. He recovered his instrument and shouldered the strap.

Orb considered. "I think I might climb this bank, but I would prefer to use my carpet. If you prefer to climb—"

"Gotcha," he said, and began to scramble up.

Orb settled on the carpet with her harp and his guitar and willed herself aloft. Now the carpet responded alertly, having recovered from its prior overload. Soon she was at the top, watching the guitarist catch up.

"Now I am not sure just where we are," she said. "But it would be foolhardy to try to return to our taxi, even if it weren't for the river, and I rather suspect that the nearby town would not be safe for us either. I think we would do best to go in an unexpected direction."

"Like what?"

"Like Clover Mountain. It must be near here. To find the fish."

"I'm game," he said.

"Why don't I continue carrying your guitar on the carpet, leaving you free to walk?" she suggested.

He was glad to agree; he did not want to get on the carpet again. He dusted himself off, and she floated up to about head height. "The mountain, slowly," she said to the carpet, speaking aloud for the guitarist's benefit.

The carpet quivered, reorienting. Then it set off roughly north. Orb was relieved that this was not toward the river.

"It knows?" the guitarist asked. "Just like that?"

"It can follow simple directives, yes," she said. "I don't know where the Clover Mountain is, but it can zero in on any identified location. It's very handy that way."

"Magic is nice," he agreed.

She floated at a walking pace, and he walked. The terrain was uneven but not rugged, now that they were away from the river. They made decent progress and in an hour reached the foot of the mountain. It was now late afternoon; there would be time to verify whether the fish was here. Orb really did not know what to expect.

"I suppose I should just call him," she said. "Then, if he appears, I'll have to, er, dance."

"What's so bad about dancing?"

"It is a rather special sort of dance." She nerved herself, then put her hands to her mouth and called "Jonah!"

There was a vibration in the mountain. For a moment Orb was afraid that a tremor or earthquake was starting. Then something brownish and monstrous swam out of the slope and into the air.

The two of them stared. It was a giant fish—swimming through rock and air as if both were water. The Gypsy woman had spoken truly!

The fish slowly circled in the air, then came to hover before Orb. It waited.

Orb was suddenly abashed. "I never really thought—what can I do now?"

"Dance," the guitarist said, his voice rough.

She looked at him—and was surprised. He looked haggard. "What happened to you? If I had realized the walk was so hard on you—"

"'Snot that. I'm outta condition, but—" he shrugged.

She caught on. "The H! You're suffering withdrawal!"

"You got it, sister."

"You look awful!"

"I feel awful. But there's no way to do it but to do it. You better get dancing before that fish gets mad."

"Oh. Yes. But—"

"You need music," he said. "And you can't play your harp, 'cause you're dancing. That's where I come in." He was taking out his guitar.

He started to play, but his hands were trembling so badly that the notes were horrors of discordance. He concentrated, but still could not do it. His face was ashen.

"How can you be so far gone, so quickly?" Orb asked, appalled.

"S-spelled H is fast," he said, his teeth chattering.

It sounded like a stutter, and that did something to Orb. She had loved a stutterer! "Take it!" she cried, flinging the packet at him. Her endurance had been less than his, and she hadn't even been the one experiencing it!

He pounced on it. "Geez, I tried, I tried!" he muttered. "But H just don't let go!" He took a pinch of the powder in the packet and brought it to his nose and sniffed.

The effect was remarkable. In a few seconds his countenance

cleared, and his breathing subsided. He took up the guitar and strummed, and the chord was perfect. "What song?"

"Any song," Orb said. "What I'm about to do is almost as hard for me as staying off the H was for you."

"Yeh." He played, and the sound was good, though not with the magic Orb had.

Yet she needed magic! She knew that she had to do a dance that would convince the big fish she was a Gypsy, and her natural resistance to the appalling suggestiveness of the dance would destroy the effect, for true Gypsies were uninhibited about sexual matters. Magic could enable her to do it.

"Magic!" she said urgently to the guitarist.

He shook his head. "I told you, I'm nothing by myself. When you're singing and playing, it comes, but—"

"Let it come!" she hissed, taking hold of his shoulder and shaking it.

Suddenly there was magic in his playing. Her touch had done it. The notes of the guitar made the very ground resonate, and the grass of the slope and the leaves of the nearby trees swayed to the beat. The monstrous body of the fish quivered, responding to it.

She removed her hand. There seemed almost to be a band of electricity connecting them, and the magic continued. Only one guitar was playing, physically, but it seemed like a thousand. "Geez," the guitarist murmured under his breath.

The fish still hovered, watching. Orb arranged her clothing, hitching up her skirt and tightening her blouse, making her body more salacious than she cared to. But this was the way of the *tanana*, and she had to do it.

Then she went into the dance, treating the fish as a partner, imagining it to be a dark Gypsy man who matched her moves with his own. She expected to be stiff, for she was tired and this was a dance she had never expected to do before any audience whatever, but the rhythm of it caught her up, and she found herself performing. She was a Gypsy lass, dancing to provoke a man to passion!

She thrust out her hip, turned, and shot a sidelong glance at him, inhaled, whirled, and moved her hips again. Body and glance, leap and pose, breast and buttock and whirling hair—the *tanana* was taking her where it would, inciting the erotic response. She had never before felt so completely wanton, not even when in the act of love itself; the suggestion was more potent than the reality. She became shameless, inviting, lascivious, assuming poses that would have completely alienated her if performed by another. It was the *tanana*!

At last, exhausted and exilarated, she finished. She had done her best and her worst; let the fish make of it what it might. The guitarist let the last note fade, his eyes locked on Orb, his jaw slack; he seemed mesmerized.

"And we want to find the Llano," she gasped as she stopped.

The fish considered. Then it descended slowly to the level of the ground, and slightly below it, so that its mouth was flush with the earth. Its body overlapped without seeming resistance; there seemed to be no reality of soil for it, just the psychic water in which it swam.

It opened its mouth. Its throat was a vast long cave, dry and bright.

"We're supposed—to go in?" Orb asked, amazed. "To be swallowed by the fish?"

Jonah merely waited. "Better do it," the guitarist said. "The thing could snap us up quickly enough any time it wanted to." He seemed much less affected by this than by the spectacle of the dance.

They entered the monstrous mouth, carrying their instruments and the carpet. They walked down the cave.

Deep within, it opened into a lighted chamber. There were projections that resembled chairs and tables and even couches.

The guitarist plumped down in one. "Home, James!" he said.

The fish moved. Orb hastily took a seat by the wall. The scales here were translucent; she could see out.

The landscape outside was moving. Rather, Jonah was moving, swimming through air, smoothly traversing the route.

"We're flying," Orb said. "Doesn't that bother you?"

"We're *swimming*," the guitarist said. "That doesn't bother me. I feel safe, here."

Surprisingly quickly, they arrived at the city. Orb peered out, looking at the people, but the people seemed to be unaware of the huge fish. As with Mortis the horse, it was in effect invisible to ordinary folk.

Jonah nudged up to Luna's estate and stopped. The two griffins flew up, squawking alarm. The fish ignored them; to it they were like flies, beneath notice.

Orb walked up the hallway that was the throat. The mouth opened, and she stood looking down on the grounds. "It's all right!" she called.

The griffins recognized her, doing twin double-takes, then settled down.

The guitarist approached, took one look out the mouth, and backed away. "Maybe you can have it go down," he said.

"Oh. Yes," Orb agreed. She had been so intrigued by the situation that she hadn't thought of the obvious. "Down, Jonah, if you please."

The fish slowly sank, coming to rest in alignment with the lawn. They stopped out as Luna appeared.

"Well," Luna said. "You seem to have found your transportation."

"We seem to," Orb agreed. "Jonah, this is Luna; Luna, meet Jonah."

"So pleased to make your acquaintance," Luna said formally. The fish made the slightest wiggle of a fin; perhaps that was acknowledgement.

"The Gypsies told us about him," Orb explained. "He is looking for the Llano, too."

"Yes. I did some spot research when I realized how you were approaching. But you know this fish is not completely reliable."

"But not dangerous?"

"Not to you or those you accept. It's just that this is not a servant, but rather an ally, and sometimes your interests may not coincide. I wasn't able to ascertain more than that."

"Sometimes I wish our futures weren't clouded," Orb muttered. "Then we could read them for ourselves and avoid a lot of mischief."

"It is a necessary protection, I'm sure," Luna said. "My father seldom made errors in judgment about magical matters." She contemplated the huge fish a moment more. "Well, let's get your things moved in."

"Just like that?" Orb inquired, raising an eyebrow.

"Mrs. Glotch has bookings piling up; I told her to start scheduling them, because you have solved the problem of transportation."

"You have confidence in us, Moth!" Orb said, smiling.

"Of course I do, Eyeball!" Luna agreed. Then they exchanged a sisterly hug.

They moved Orb's things in. The big fish turned out to have a number of compartments separated by bony walls that served nicely as private rooms, and there was a lavatory region in the tail that had running water and a facility for the disposal of wastes. It seemed that somewhere along the way, someone had gone to some trouble to outfit Jonah for human comfort.

"But how does he eat?" Orb asked.

"It seems he doesn't need to eat. He is magically suspended, until he obtains his release and can die."

"Does that mean we had better not be inside him when we find the Llano?"

Luna laughed. "Perhaps so! But first find your song."

The boys moved in that evening, the fish moored beside their apartment complex. No outsiders seemed to notice the oddity of the procedure. They simply carried their bags and equipment into the mouth and returned for more, as if loading a moving van. They left it to Mrs. Glotch to settle their accounts with the renter; they were checking out.

Orb, fatigued, slept early. Her bed consisted of a section of her chamber floor that was marvelously soft and comfortable and tended to shape itself somewhat to her contours without being obsequious about it. There were some definite advantages to traveling in a living creature!

She woke in the night, hearing voices. Still dazed, she lay still and listened. The voices seemed to be close, yet there was no one in her room. Soon she realized that the bony structure of the fish was transmitting them, so that she could clearly hear what was said elsewhere. Yet that had not been the case before; the noise of the boys and Lou-Mae setting up their rooms had been blessedly muted.

"You *flew?*" the organist's voice demanded incredulously. "On her carpet?"

"I was scared stiff," the guitarist responded. "But like I said, those townsmen were after us, thinking we were the Gypsies, and the river—"

"But that carpet only holds one!"

"She sort of put me in front, and she got on behind, and put her arms around me, and her legs around me—"

"Man!" the drummer exclaimed. "You were between her legs?"

"I guess. I was so scared, I never noticed. That river—"

"Let's get this straight," the drummer said. "You were hunched up like this, and she was behind you like this, on that li'l carpet? Her boobs pressed up against your back, and her thighs—"

"Damn it, don't make it like that! She saved my stupid life! I was so far out of it, all I saw was that damn river, till she put her hands on my eyes and sort of calmed me down."

"Damn, if it'd been me—"

"Yeah?" the guitarist asked challengingly. "And what of your black chick?"

"Listen, man, don't call her no—"

"Well, don't make like there's any dirt between me and Orb!" the guitarist retorted. "She don't give a shi' for me, she just wanted to save my worthless life and maybe get me off the H. And you know, I was off it maybe three hours, cause I was just starting to feel the pang when I gave her the stuff, and it was a good hour after that. But I couldn't do it; I couldn't get the shakes outta my hands, and I had to play. 'Cause she had to dance, and . . ."

"She danced?"

"And how! I never saw the like! Seems she had to prove she was a Gypsy, for the fish, and this Gypsy dance—whew! I never saw a porno tape better'n that! The way she threw that stuff around, I like to've busted a string!"

"Her?" the drummer said derisively. "She'd spook if she even knew how her skirt hikes up when she's on the harp, showing her gams. She thinks sex appeal's a crime!"

"Just don't forget," the organist said, "we need her. Without her, we're nothing. Forget her skirt!"

"*You* forget her skirt!" the drummer retorted. "I sit right opposite her when we practice. She's got the best damn legs—"

"She's got the best damn everything," the organist said. "Think I'm blind? I'm half behind her, and sometimes I see down her blouse, and you think I don't drool? But it's ten times all the luck we ever deserved that she joined us, and we don't none of us want to do anything at all to sour her. Keep your hot eyes on your music."

"Yeh," the drummer agreed. "But my point is, we know she'd never do that kind of dance. She's got the body for it, no doubt at all, but not the mind."

"But she did it," the guitarist insisted. "I tell you, I was on a new sniff, so maybe you think I saw more'n there was, but—"

"On a sniff? H don't pack much punch that way!"

"You think I was going to shoot up in front of her? It got the edge off, anyway, so I could feel my strings and play. I tell you, she may be dowdy with us, but when she lets go with it, hang on to the moon! I've seen some real hot dances, but that one she did—if they could bottle that stuff, man of a hundred and ten could have the potency of—"

"So our beautiful prude ain't so prudish somewhere else," the drummer said thoughtfully. "I wonder why she wants the Llano? I mean, *we* need it to get off the H, but she's already got everythin' any man or woman'd want. What's she need it for?"

"Just be glad she does want it," the organist said. "She's one good woman, and we're sludge. Just let her be."

"One good woman," the guitarist echoed. "I'd be dead now if she weren't."

"So are we going to get this room shaped up, or not?" the drummer demanded.

The last comment was fading, and thereafter there was nothing. Orb could hear the bustle of their labors when she concentrated, but their voices no longer come through to her.

She lay awake, wondering about that. What a coincidence that the reception had been so good, just when they were talking about her! The sound of their voices had awakened her; perhaps they had been talking for some time before she listened. Yet it had faded when their subject changed.

Coincidence? She wished she had the little snake ring again, to squeeze yes or no to that question. She was in another magical creature, and maybe—

There was a quiet knock at her portal. "You up, Orb?"

"Awake, anyway," Orb said. "Come in, Lou-Mae."

"I hate to bother you," the girl said. "But something funny happened, and—"

"You heard voices?"

"How'd you know? I was lying there, drifting off, and then clear as day I heard the words 'black chick.' I knew it was me, and them talking about me. But all they said was—"

"Not to call you that," Orb finished.

"You heard, too? After that I listened, but I couldn't hear anything. But it—I mean, if I wasn't dreaming—"

"I think we have just learned another property of the big fish," Orb said. "When anybody talks about anybody, the other person hears. They mentioned you in the course of a conversation about me. So I heard somewhat more than you did."

"Then I'm not crazy!" Lou-Mae said, relieved.

"And neither am I. But it occurs to me that we had best be quite careful what we say about others, while we are here."

Lou-Mae smiled knowingly. "Meanwhile, we sure can listen!"

Orb returned the smile. She liked Lou-Mae. "But tell me—is it true that my skirt shows too much leg when I play the harp?"

The girl considered. "I never thought about it, but you know, when you set cross-legged, I guess it could. You mean they were peeking?"

"Just noticing. I'd better change to slacks."

"Then they'd know you had caught on."

"Um. But if I don't—"

Lou-Mae brightened. "I'll give you a pair of slacks! Then you'll have to wear them, so's not to hurt my feelings, at least for practice."

"I would certainly not want to hurt your feelings, Lou-Mae," Orb said gravely.

"I wonder how long it'll be before they catch on?"

"That may depend on us," Orb said. Then they were silent, lest even that reference reach the appropriate ears and give it away.

Lou-Mae returned to her chamber. Orb lay awake for a time,

pondering this and that. She had mixed feelings about the boys' assessment of her. Any woman, she realized, liked being considered beautiful, but not crudely. They saw "boobs" and "gams" while she would have preferred some more esthetic and less specific image. Still . . .

Meanwhile, she had learned something new about Jonah. She liked the big fish very well and was liking him better as she got to know his qualities.

In the morning the girls were up first, while the boys slept late. "You know, if we don't watch it, we're liable to wind up as cooks and housekeepers," Lou-Mae remarked. "Who's going to do the cooking?"

"Oopsy!" Orb exclaimed. "That never crossed my mind. We'd better hire a maid."

"We can do that the same time we go shopping."

"Shopping?"

"For slacks."

Orb laughed, remembering. That overheard dialogue did embarrass her; the notion that her thighs were being ogled while she played—she knew she should shrug it off, but she found she couldn't. She wanted to embarrass the boys the way they had embarrassed her, uncharitable as that attitude might be. But of course she couldn't.

Actually, they had no supplies for breakfast, so had to leave Jonah for it. The fish remained moored by Luna's estate. He descended at their behest, and they disembarked. Then Jonah slowly ascended to rooftop height again.

"But why don't people stare?" Lou-Mae asked.

"They can't see him, dear," Luna said. "He allows only selected people to see him. You are invisible inside him."

The girl shook her head. "That's hard to believe."

"Jonah," Luna called. "Would you show them how it works?"

The fish slowly faded from view. Then there was nothing but sky.

"That's easier to believe," Lou-Mae said.

Luna served them breakfast. Then Lou-Mae went shopping, and Orb went to the employment agency. Luna's connections helped her here, too; the man had a list of prospects waiting when she arrived.

"But you don't even know what I want!" she protested.

"A female cook and housekeeper, competent, discreet, and unattractive."

Orb paused, taken aback. That *was* what she had in mind, her pique at the boys making her want to bring in someone whose legs they would not ogle. She was abruptly ashamed of herself, but not enough to change the specifications. "I will talk to them."

"There is only one present at the moment," he said. "Interest fell off when the applicants were advised that an indefinite period of travel with young musicians was entailed."

"I can't think of why," Orb muttered with irony. "Well, let me see that one."

The woman was about fifty years old and looked worn. Her hair was straggly and her enthusiasm minimal. "Can you cook?" Orb asked.

"Fantastically."

"Keep house?"

"Perfectly."

"What kind of salary are you looking for?"

"Nominal."

"You know that we are traveling with three young musicians?"

"So?"

"And don't know our precise route, or when we will return here?"

"Yes."

All the answers were right, but Orb felt somewhat out of sorts. Why was this woman so obliging?

"You know that we will fire you if your representations prove to be untrue?"

"Yes."

"Why do you want this job?"

"I don't."

"What?"

"I don't."

"Then why did you apply?"

"It's better than nothing."

Such enthusiasm! Orb decided to try to jolt the woman into some more revealing statement. "We're looking for the Llano."

"Yes."

"You knew that?"

"Jonah wouldn't take you otherwise."

"How do you know of Jonah?"

The woman sighed. "If you ask me, I have to answer. But you won't like it."

"All the same, I think I'd better know." The complexion of this interview had changed entirely.

"I am of demon breed. I seek the Llano. When Jonah moved, I came. I can't find it myself, but maybe someone else could. I doubt you find it, but I have to look."

"Demon breed!" Orb exclaimed. "You are from Hell?"

"No. Some demons are earthbound. Cursed. The Llano can abate my curse."

"What is your curse?"

"You will not like my answer."

"Do you intend to harm me, or any of us?"

"No. I can not harm any mortal person."

"Then I can handle the answer."

"I must have relations with a man every hour of the night. Every hour adds an hour to my age."

"Relations?" Orb was amazed. "You mean—?"

"I am a succubus. I have no choice."

A fifty-year-old succubus! "You don't want to do it?"

"I hate it."

"Then why don't you stop?"

"The curse compels me."

Orb remembered the guitarist's attempt to stop taking H. For those afflicted, there was no way to stop. "Frankly, I'm not certain you would make a suitable employee."

"I do not sleep. I do exactly what I say. I am a perfect employee by day. By night my curse manifests. In the morning I am ten or twelve hours older. In another century I will be a hundred years old and still immortal, unless I find the Llano."

Orb experienced a stirring of sympathy. "How long have you been at this?"

"One century. By day I seem to age at half the mortal rate, because of the penalty of the night—but I can not die. You mortals can not know what a blessing death is."

Orb found that she believed this. "You are fifty years old, in your body, but still you must seduce a man every hour of the night?''

"I revert to my original form during those hours. All my aging is then—but it shows only by day.''

Orb found her feelings mixed. She felt genuine sympathy for this creature, but was appalled by her nature. What would the three boys do, if—''

Delicious malice took over. "You're hired," she said. "What is your name?''

"Jezebel.''

The boys were up and hungry by the time Orb returned with Jezebel. For some reason they had not disembarked to go to a fast-food station. "I can take care of that," Jezebel said. She snapped her fingers and a junk-food container appeared in her crooked arm. She handed it to the drummer. "Gorge," she said.

The three opened the package. Inside were hamburgers and bottles of cola: the ideal breakfast by their definition.

The drummer glanced at Orb. "How'd she know?''

"Jezebel understands musicians," Orb said. "She is to be our cook and housekeeper for the tour.''

"She housekeeps, too?''

"I suspect you have not experienced her manner of keeping house," Orb said with a straight face.

The boys departed with their breakfast. Orb showed Jezebel to her chamber. "Or do you need one?''

"Certainly." Jezebel gestured, and a shelf of books appeared. "My library. I do a lot of reading in the off hours. I admit it's escapism, but it certainly beats the dull routine of my curse.''

Orb glanced at the titles. They ran the gamut from the classics to the latest junk romance. A succubus read romance for escape? Well, why not? A succubus was a creature of sex, not romance. Like any woman, she was apt to find the former more readily than the latter, and less satisfying.

Lou-Mae returned with a package—slacks for Orb, her gift. "Why thank you, Lou-Mae!" Orb said, as if surprised. "I shall be sure to wear them!''

Mrs. Glotch showed up with an itinerary; she had set up a tour that circled the entire nation with reasonable dispatch. Every three to five days they had an engagement in a new location.

Mrs. Glotch had not before encountered the fish. Only with difficulty was she persuaded to visit Jonah even briefly. She glanced about the interior with vague disapproval and hastened back to her office in the normal world.

They commenced their tour. Orb bid farewell to Luna, saddened in much the manner she had been when they parted in Ireland, and entered Jonah. The great fish lifted high, oriented, and swam vigorously through the air toward the first city on the list.

Orb was about to go to her room for a rest when the guitarist intercepted her. "Yes?" she inquired.

"I just wanted to say, uh, well maybe it's not . . . " he faltered.

"Is something the matter?"

"You know about the H."

"Of course. You know how I feel about that."

"Well, I'm trying to get off it, but—you know."

"I know." What was he trying to say?

"I haven't taken any since I got on the fish," he blurted.

That brought her up short. "I thought you had to take it every few hours. It has been a full day. Isn't that unusual?"

"Yeh. And the others haven't touched it either. We don't take it unless we have to, and . . . " He shrugged.

"Jonah!" she exclaimed. "Could it be—?"

"That's what I was thinking. Big magic fish, maybe he don't go for that sh—that stuff in him, you know?"

"If so, Jonah is an unmitigated blessing!" Orb exclaimed.

"That's why we didn't go out this morning. 'Cause if it's true, when we go out—"

"The craving will return," Orb finished. "I don't blame you. Fortunately we can remain within Jonah until—"

"Until we gotta perform," he said. "That scares me."

"Still, to be free of your addiction for all the rest of the time— I am very happy for you!"

He nodded. "And—I just wanted to say—to thank you for saving my life. I guess I owe you. I guess that's a bad debt, 'cause there's nothing I have or can do that you need, but—" He shrugged.

"I appreciate your thanks," Orb said, touched. "I am sure you will prove worthy. Give it time."

"Well, if we find the Llano—"

"Complete freedom," she agreed.

He left. Then she suffered a wave of doubt and regret. She had knowingly hired the succubus. When night came, what would become of the Sludge? At first they might take it as a blessing, but after a few hours . . .

But what could she do, now? She had hired; she did not feel free to fire. She should never have allowed her private pique over a remark about her legs to influence her this way!

Jezebel produced an excellent afternoon meal, wholesome and balanced. She set it up on the table-bone of the area they had designated as the dining room, requiring everyone to clean up and eat together formally. The boys had to go to the bathroom to comb their hair and clean their fingernails and change to better clothing.

Orb refrained from smiling; it seemed that the housekeeper had old-fashioned values, and they were not out of place here.

The boys stared at the food disapprovingly. "Potatoes?" the drummer inquired distastefully. "*Milk?*"

"And a fresh salad," Jezebel said. "Rule of the house while I'm here—one meal a day is going to be done right. The others you can have as you please."

Lou-Mae took the drummer's arm. She was fetching in a bright green knitted dress. "You can handle it, Danny."

He brightened. "You want it, baby, you got it. In fact, if you want to housekeep for me—"

"First you get off the H," she said firmly.

"I *am* off the H!"

"Off the fish, off the H."

"Yeh," he said, looking crestfallen.

News spread quickly! Already Lou-Mae knew the effect Jonah had on addiction and was not deceived by it. The drummer had in his fashion just proposed to her, and she had responded with her condition—kick the habit first.

The guitarist's willingness to take to the air in Jonah—that could also be the magic of the big fish! No more phobia.

They proceeded to their repast. Indeed, it was an excellent

meal. They were becoming a family, thanks to what Orb would have deemed to be the most unlikely agency.

But when night came . . .

Before night came evening—and a storm loomed ahead. Suddenly Jonah lurched, changing course. "What's the matter?" Orb cried, as spent dishes slid to the floor. But then she remembered what Luna had told her: the fish was cursed to swim through every element but his own. Jonah could not handle water.

The storm was expanding, and new cells were forming to the sides and behind. Jonah would soon be trapped in rain. But the great fish had an answer: he dived. He threshed powerfully down through the air, entering the ground without pause, and darkness closed outside.

Darkness! Luna looked at Jezebel, who was washing glasses. But the woman was unchanged. Evidently it was night, not darkness, that did it. Which made sense; otherwise the simple expedient of keeping the lights on would eliminate the threat of the succubus.

But night was nevertheless approaching. Orb was increasingly uncomfortable. She knew she had done wrong and felt guilty. Still, she saw no way out.

The boys had a television set. They set it up in the main chamber and tuned in on their favorite programs, which to Orb seemed to consist of unremitting violence and eroticism with a smidgeon of humor thrown in. Well, maybe they were about to get what they deserved, after all.

Except that Lou-Mae was with them. If she were present when . . .

Orb looked at Jezebel—and her worst concern was verified. One moment the woman had been dowdy and fifty; the next, as the sun officially set at this spot of the globe, she was a sultry creature of twenty, in a provocative gown. The succubus had manifested.

But Jezebel continued washing glasses. Then she started in on the dishes. Her appearance had changed, but not her activity.

Orb joined her, drying the dishes and putting them away on the herringbone shelving that was part of Jonah's architecture. "Ah, Jezebel—" she began.

"Yes?"

Orb lost her nerve. She was liable to get her answer all too soon. "Where did all the food and dishes come from? Did you just conjure them?"

"I conjured the dishes from my collection," Jezebel said. "You're welcome to use them. The food has to be new, though, so that comes from local establishments."

"But—but then are we stealing from—?"

"No, Mrs. Glotch gets billed for it. I leave a receipt in place of the food, and they know where to get the money. Modern electronics is wonderful!"

They continued talking while they finished up the job. Then Jezebel paused, glancing down at herself. "Oops—I've changed! Night's here. I never noticed."

"You changed about half an hour ago," Orb said.

"Oh, I couldn't have! The curse—" She looked at her watch. "But it *is*! How can that be?"

"You mean you don't have to—?"

"No compulsion at all," Jezebel said wonderingly. "That never happened before."

"Jonah!" Orb exclaimed. "He nulls the H addiction! He must null other curses, too!"

"You mean I can actually relax at night? No added hours? No grimy men?"

"So it seems."

"I knew the big fish was a rare one, but I never knew that! What a—" She cut off abruptly, choking.

"What's the matter?" Orb asked, alarmed.

"Just certain words I can't say. I get associating with mortal folk, sometimes I forget. I tried to say, you know, that word you use for something good from a certain party."

"A blessing?"

"That's it. I guess the fish can null the involuntary stuff, but not the voluntary. I mean, I can choose what to say, so I don't *have* to say that word, so I still can't. Still, that's a little thing. The big thing is wonderful!"

Orb felt similarly relieved, albeit for different reason. She liked Jonah better yet.

Lou-Mae came out for a glass of water. She paused as she spied Jezebel. "Who are you?"

"This is Jezebel," Orb said. "Her appearance changes at night."

The girl's eyes narrowed. Evidently Jezebel reminded her of something other than a cook.

"I am a succubus," Jezebel said. "Recently retired. I have no interest in your man."

Lou-Mae's gaze flicked back toward the room where the boys were. She didn't trust this. "What's a creature like you want here?"

"I want the Llano. It will free me forever."

"I thought you said you were retired."

"By courtesy of Jonah. Outside I fear that is not the case. As with your man's problem."

The girl assessed that. "Then when we perform, you stay here."

"Gladly."

Lou-Mae thawed somewhat. "Why don't you come and watch the TV?"

"Is it worth watching?"

"Hardly."

"Good. That's the kind I like."

They went to the other room. Orb hesitated, then shrugged and joined them.

The drummer turned to look at Lou-Mae and spied Jezebel. His mouth fell open. The other two turned and stared.

"This is Jezebel," Lou-Mae said. "What are you staring at? Never seen a cook before?"

The drummer put his face back together and returned to the television. The organist and guitarist hesitated, then did the same. Jezebel paid them no attention at all; she was definitely not interested.

The night was quiet. In the morning Jezebel was back at age fifty, and breakfast was cooking.

"Say, Ms. Kaftan—" the succubus began.

"Orb."

"Very well. Have you noticed—"

"About the sounds here?" Orb finished. "I gather the boys were talking about you when they were alone."

"For an hour, it seemed! I was reading *War and Peace* since

I don't sleep anyway; first time in my life I had the night to myself, and it was strange. Then these voices—those kids have some big ideas!''

"Are you sorry that your situation changed?"

"Never! *All* kids have big ideas, but none keep them long with me, and they aren't very original anyway. It was just that I couldn't understand why they said them in my hearing."

"Jonah lets the subject hear," Orb explained. "The boys didn't know you could hear."

"Nobody told them about this effect?"

"Now who would want to do a thing like that?"

Jezebel smiled. "All I wanted was the Llano. But this tour is beginning to be fun."

"Just don't talk about anybody," Orb said. "We're lucky they sleep soundly in the morning, or they would have heard this dialogue."

The succubus nodded, touching her finger to her lips.

The storm had passed, and Jonah was swimming in the sky again. He seemed to be doing about fifty kilometers per hour, which would get them to their first booking in plenty of time.

In midmorning they staged a rehearsal. Jezebel listened raptly from the rear of the room, obviously impressed. The group really got into it, running through their entire repertoire before pausing to consider new additions. They now had songs of every type, making it a variety show, with a number of them acted out in the manner of "Danny Boy." It seemed to Orb that the magic was getting stronger, though she cautioned herself that she might be imagining that.

Then Lou-Mae glanced out a window-scale. "It's dark!" she exclaimed.

Orb looked. "We're back underground!"

It took some time to verify it, but it seemed that Jonah had been listening, too, and had simply tuned out the outer world and sank blissfully down until they were horrendously deep under the earth. Yet there was no harm done; when they stopped their performance, the big fish forged back to the surface and resumed his travel toward their destination city.

"I suppose a person or creature has to be able to appreciate music in order to have any interest in the Llano," Orb said. That seemed to sum it up.

– 9 –

LLANO

They arrived at the site of their first regular booking. The hall had a fair audience, but was not filled. It seemed that the news of their talent had not filtered all the way down to the larger paying public. Still, it was the largest audience they had faced, and Orb was sure they had drawn a better crowd than ordinarily attended.

Many of the people seemed bored or cynical, as if refusing to believe that this out-of-town group could be worthwhile. Perhaps some were critics expecting to give indifferent ratings.

Orb smiled privately. She expected that to change.

The performance started—and indeed it changed. The numbers ranged across the musical horizon, but all were imbued with the magic, and the magic held the audience rapt. The truth was that even poor music would have sufficed with the magic, and good music would not have without it. But the music was good and getting better as they refined it.

They gave a second performance the following evening. This one was a sell-out.

So it went, as they settled into the routine of the tour. Half a dozen cities into it, the Livin' Sludge had become the hottest group on the circuit. Mrs. Glotch reported that at the rate they were going, every member of the group would be wealthy by the time the tour concluded.

Recording companies approached them for albums. They discussed it and decided not to record, because they weren't sure the magic would come through. Indeed, that seemed to be the case, because an illicit recording was made of one of their performances, and later reports were that it was deemed a fake because it lacked the impact of the live act.

They traveled the eastern part of the nation, then the southern, and then the southwestern. They had little need of maps, because Jonah simply swam to each city requested. Nevertheless, Jezebel liked to know where she was, so she obtained a map.

"Say!" she exclaimed. "Here's Llano!"

Orb almost dropped her harp. "What?"

"Right here," the woman said, showing the map.

Suddenly everyone was there. They found a region, and a river, and even a town by that name. "Do you think that's where—?" Jezebel asked.

"I wonder," Orb said. "It never occurred to me that it would be on a map! I suppose it could be coincidence."

"Not much coincidence in this world," Jezebel said. "Not when you fathom how things operate."

"We've got a gig near there," the drummer said eagerly. "Geez, if we could find that song, and if it works . . . " He looked at Lou-Mae.

The others nodded. They all knew that that romance had become more serious with every performance of "Danny Boy," and that only the black girl's adamance about H prevented it from going further. She would not commit herself to a drug addict; that was absolute. This only increased the drummer's desire to get off it, but he could not.

They had their performance in the nearby city, then directed Jonah to swim to the Llano. He set forth, and they slept.

In the morning they found the fish hovering over a broad, flat, treeless plain.

"Did he get lost?" the drummer asked. "Not a town or river in sight!"

"Cursed immortal creatures don't get lost," Jezebel said. "I know."

The drummer shrugged. By this time everyone knew Jezebel's nature, and that she was as totally uninterested in obliging any of their big notions as was Orb. The boys regarded it as a phenomenal loss, though it didn't seem to bother them by day. By night, however, their frustrated conversations were a source of continuing amusement to all three women. It seemed to be the consensus that never in history had three such attractive and virile young men been so intimately housed with three such beautiful women with so little significant action. What a ghastly loss! Lou-Mae was shocked by some of their notions, Orb was disgusted, and Jezebel bored. But not one of them ever hinted to the boys about this aspect of Jonah's nature; it was too much fun to listen. In fact, they discovered that they could talk freely to each other, from their individual chambers, simply by doing it; it seemed that by Jonah's definition, talking to a person was the same as talking about a person. It was convenient.

They rechecked the map, and found that Jonah had brought them to the Llano Estacado, or Staked Plain, instead of to the county, town, or river.

"But maybe he's right," the guitarist said. "Maybe this is the real place."

"I don't know," Lou-Mae said, teasing him. "See how all the little counties are real squares, here, straight up and down. But down next to the County of Llano they're all jumbled, as if God just took them and shoved them over to make room for Llano."

He contemplated the map. "Maybe you're right."

"I'm not sure that human boundaries have any meaning for this," Orb said, though she, too, was struck by the manner that a large section of the counties had been skewed, as if riding a tectonic plate that had rotated forty-five degrees. *Could* that relate?

They decided to accept Jonah's verdict: that the plain was the correct Llano. The fish descended, and they disembarked.

Orb walked out on the plain, seeking the song. She did not know what she was looking for, but she hoped that if she made herself receptive it would come to her. If this truly was the place for it. She had been disappointed in India; the source of the Gypsies had not been the source of the Llano.

The Gypsies. It made no obvious sense, but maybe—

She looked around. The others were far removed, looking in their own fashions. No one would see.

She began to dance the *tanana*, hoping that it would somehow attract the song to it. She moved her body in the ways that were calculated to inflame men's minds, and assumed the poses that no decent girl should know. She was dancing for neither man nor fish, but for the song. Would it work?

She got into it, the spirit of the dance hauling her body and mind into it, making her wanton. Then it seemed that a melody began to come, very faint but evocative. Its theme was lovely, prettier than any mortal tune, but underneath was a richness and power that was to any ordinary song what the ocean was to a lake. The essence of it reached into the very heart of her, reshaping that heart to its own likeness, changing her being in an ineffable manner. Ah, the song, the song . . . !

Then it faded, and she found herself exhausted, standing alone. Had she tuned in on the Llano? Had she imagined it? She could not be sure of its source, but there was something; she felt it within her, like the onset of a pregnancy.

A pregnancy. What had happened to her baby, Orlene? Would she ever know?

Disheartened, she walked back to the floating fish. She was not sure whether she had accomplished anything.

The tour continued. They played to larger and larger halls, always filled to capacity. It seemed that the whole world now knew of the Livin' Sludge; news items manufactured from nothing appeared daily in the media. But they were bound to their quest, telling no one else about it. The Llano—where was it?

Orb's power of music was growing; there was no longer any doubt. She could tell this not so much by the way the Sludge performances mesmerized ever-larger audiences, but by the way the other members of the group performed. She no longer had to sing or play; she merely had to be there. That had not been the case at the outset of the tour. Now Lou-Mae could sing alone, and the magic reached out; the drummer could play a solo, and the magic was there. But the others informed her that when they practiced while she was out of the fish, it didn't work. They could play well enough, but there was no magic; they all felt the difference. "When you're with us, it's in three-dee color," the drummer explained. "Otherwise, two-dee black/white. Without you, we're just another nobody group."

"Well, we *are* a group," she responded, trying not to feel flattered, knowing that her talent was from no virtue of hers; she owed it to heredity. "We will always perform together."

But she spoke prematurely. They were looping north, now, and it was winter; storms and snow interrupted communications and transportation. A few days before Christmas the weather was so threatening at the city of their engagement that they decided to set up at the hall early. Jonah nudged up to the building, and they unloaded the instruments. They no longer needed the mikes and amplifiers and speakers, because the magic reached the members of the audience more effectively. That was another evidence of Orb's increased power. The drummer and Lou-Mae and the organist remained there to warm up, while Orb and Jezebel elected to fit in some Christmas shopping. The guitarist hesitated, then decided to return to the fish with them. Orb knew why; away from Jonah, he was subject to the call of the H and he preferred to avoid that.

They boarded the fish, and Jonah swam up over the city. They went downtown, where Orb and Jezebel got off. The wind cut cruelly along the streets, driving them quickly into the stores. That was all right; shopping was what they had come for. Orb intended to get token gifts for all the members of the group, and Jezebel was interested in new books for her library.

They forgot the time and were late finishing. Dusk was closing when they stood on the street with their arms full of packages, and Orb mentally called Jonah.

Normally the fish arrived promptly, but this time he didn't. They waited somewhat impatiently, the wind seeming to become more cutting. Orb's cloak automatically thickened, keeping her warm, and Jezebel was immune to temperature, but they didn't like getting their hair mussed. Finally they backed into an alcove for shelter—and found themselves in the company of several shivering musicians of another kind. They were of the Salvation Army, and it was evident that their effort to raise funds had been practically blotted out by the weather.

Orb set down her armful and reached into her purse—only to

discover that she had spent all her available cash. She looked at Jezebel, who shook her head in negation. "They wouldn't care for demon-offering," she muttered.

"Oh, I don't know," Orb said. "Isn't it the spirit that counts?"

Jezebel shrugged and brought out a golden coin. She tossed it in the kettle—and the moment it touched, it burst into flame, taking with it whatever paper money had already been there. "Damned money!" the succubus exclaimed, meaning it literally. "Now look what I've done!"

Appalled, Orb looked at the musicians. How could she apologize for this? She knew that Jezebel had not intended evil, but the evil attached to her without her choice.

"I—I'll try to make it up to you," Orb said. She borrowed a book from the hands of the nearest musician, and opened it, and began to sing:

"Onward Christian Soldiers, marching as to war,
With the Cross of Jesus going on before."

She did not have her harp with her, knowing that it was quite safe in Jonah. But the magic was present, and the melody rang out across the street. Jezebel shrank away, but the others joined in. The magic spread out to touch them, too, the effect amplifying.

People hurrying by paused to listen. Others emerged from the stores. By the time the song was finished, there was a crowd—and offerings were pouring into the kettle, far more than enough to make up for what had been lost.

Then Orb saw Jonah nudging in. She hurried to pick up her packages. "Bless you, soldiers!" she cried. "Come on, Jez!"

Jonah opened his mouth and they stepped in. No one seemed to notice. The crowd was beginning to dissipate, but money was still coming into the kettle. The musicians seemed bewildered, but pleased.

They had boarded just in time, for now the sun was setting, and Jezebel became her nocturnal self. "I was afraid I'd get caught out there too late!" she said. "But you know, Orb, if you don't have the Llano, you surely have something like it. What you did was what the Llano does."

Orb paused, surprised. "I never saw it that way," she said. "But I suppose—"

"We got to get moving!" the guitarist said, hurrying up the throat. "It's almost time for the show!"

"I know!" Orb exclaimed, sweeping on toward her chamber. "We forgot the time, then Jonah delayed. Where were you going, so far away?"

"Nowhere," he protested. "Jonah was just sitting there waiting; it only took him a minute, once he started moving. You mean you called him before?"

"Certainly I called him!" Orb snapped as she picked up her harp. "A good ten minutes before he came!"

"Maybe he didn't hear you."

"He must have, because he did come—eventually."

Jonah was swimming down again. Orb and the guitarist stood just inside the piscine lips, ready to jump out the moment the mouth opened. "I'll have cocoa waiting for you," Jezebel said, standing behind them. They had discovered by experimentation that no drug, alcohol included, had any effect within the fish, so the boys had gravitated to the more wholesome snacks that the girls preferred. Even the caffeine in coffee was nulled. Clean living was the order of the day and night, in Jonah.

The mouth opened. The tongue flipped, and abruptly they were out.

"Hey!" Jezebel exclaimed.

Orb looked at her, startled. "But I thought you were staying in!"

"That's what *I* thought!" the succubus replied.

"Jonah spat us all out," the guitarist said.

Orb turned to face the fish. "Jonah, she wasn't supposed to—" But she broke off, for Jonah was gone.

"Where are we?" the guitarist asked.

"Why, at the auditorium for—" Orb broke off again. For that was not where they were. Instead they stood before the city hospital.

"Jonah got the wrong address!" the guitarist cried. "He never did that before!"

"Did he?" Jezebel asked. "Then why did he spit me out? You

have to watch these demonic types; I know. I think he wanted to clear us all out of him.''

"I can't believe that!" Orb said, flustered. "All he had to do was make known his wish, and we would have left."

"Listen, we can't worry 'bout that right now," the guitarist said. "We got a show to make!"

"But the hospital is all the way across the city from the engagement hall!" Orb said, upset. "The program is set to begin now; we can't possibly get there on time."

"What about me?" Jezebel asked. "You know what's going to happen within my hour?"

Orb put her hands to her head. "I don't know what to *do*!"

"Call the hall, call a taxi," the guitarist said. "I'll do it."

But there was no phone on the street, and no taxies in sight, and the blustering wind was buffeting them. "Inside, there must be a phone," Orb said.

They piled into the hospital. But they had entered by a side door, and there was no desk and no phone. They moved down an endlessly long series of halls.

A white-gowned doctor emerged from a side hall, almost colliding with the guitarist. "Ah, there you are!" the doctor said. "Not a moment too soon! We ran out an hour ago, and our replacement can't get through till tomorrow."

"This is a misunderstanding," Orb said quickly. "We don't belong here; we're just looking for a phone."

"You don't have the medication?" the doctor asked, appalled. "The message said an entertainment group was bringing it. We have terminal patients in pain; we don't know how we're going to tide them through the night! Listen."

They listened. Now they heard a low groaning that seemed to come from several rooms, punctuated by a sudden scream. "They are beyond ordinary drugs," the doctor said. "The pain reaches through and it doesn't stop."

The guitarist swallowed. "Could you use spelled H?"

The doctor looked at him with renewed hope. "You *are* the courier!"

The guitarist brought out his packet. "Guess so."

The doctor took it eagerly, weighing it by heft. "This is potent?"

"Strongest H on the market."

"Excellent! This amount should tide us through the night.
What's the charge?"

The guitarist gulped again. "No charge. It's—you know, gray
market."

The doctor nodded. "We certainly appreciate this! A dozen
patients will bless you, sir!" He hurried off.

"You gave away your H?" Orb asked, still hardly believing it.

"Well, it's, you know, good for killing pain, when the legal
stuff don't work."

"But how will you get through?"

"It was them or me, and what am I worth?"

"About what I am," Jezebel said glumly. "Damn, I hate what
I'm going to do!"

Orb made as if to tear her hair. "Why did Jonah do this to us?
Everything we have had is going to fall apart tonight!"

Jezebel looked at her. "You know, when you sing, your magic
touches everyone near. I wonder—if Jonah can do it—"

"Yeah!" the guitarist agreed as if grasping at a straw. "You
make us more than we are! Maybe if you sing now—"

Suddenly Orb remembered her experience in the Llano Estacado. That feeling of wholeness, of power. Was it possible?

"Take my hands," she said.

They took her hands, standing there in the hospital hall. Orb
sang the song that came to her, heedless whether it was relevant.

"You must walk that lonesome valley
You have to walk it by yourself . . . "

The magic came, spreading through her body slowly, as if encountering resistance. She fixed the image of the plain in her
mind, seeing it as the valley of the fate of those with desperate
compulsions. She walked that valley, not by herself, but with and
for those who could not otherwise get through it.

"Oh, nobody else can walk it for you . . . "

But somebody else could walk it *with* them, and that was what
she was doing. They walked for themselves, but buttressed by

her song, that was spreading slowly to their bodies. It was not the Llano, but it suggested it, as the magic suggested that of Jonah, stabilizing them. She became a conduit for a hint of the enormous power she sought, the power to put a hold on a curse. The walk of life itself, through lonesome territory, but *not* alone. Sustained by the strength of friendship and commitment.

Orb became aware that the song was over when they disengaged their hands. "It's backing off!" the guitarist said. "I think I can fight it, now!"

"Yes," Jezebel agreed. "Not as far off as it is in Jonah, but distanced just enough."

Orb wasn't sure what she had accomplished, or whether they had merely convinced themselves that she had helped. She decided not to question it. Certainly something had passed through her.

They resumed their walk down the hall. Now they came to a desk. "Ah, you must be the entertainers," a nurse said. "That ward's about to burst at the seams! We promised them their kind of music, but with this weather we were afraid you wouldn't get through. Right this way."

"Their kind of music?" Orb asked. "What is that?"

"They call it 'rusty iron'," the nurse said. "It's horrible." She paused, glancing back at them. "Uh, no offense, of course. To each his own peculiar taste."

"You know that kind?" Orb asked the guitarist.

"Some," he admitted. "But listen, that stuff is bad! We used to try it once in a while, before we got with you, but, well, that's part of what got our other singer out of her head. You have to be insane to go for it."

"Here we are," the nurse said. "The psycho ward. Go right in."

"Suddenly it makes sense!" Jezebel said.

"Wait!" Orb protested. "We can't do this! We—"

"You have to," the nurse said, looking harried. "They'll riot if we renege now! We had to promise—"

"You don't understand," Orb said. "I'm the only one here with an instrument, and I have no knowledge of—"

"*You* don't understand," the nurse said. "The season and the storm have brought the inmates to the point where any trifling thing can set them off. We're shorthanded for the same reason. Once things get out of control, there will be absolute mayhem!" She unlocked the door and drew it open.

The sound hit them like the roar of ocean breakers. It was bedlam. Patients were running around, some in dishabille, some screaming unintelligibly, some banging against the furniture. Harried aides were trying to attend to the needs of individuals, but it was evident that they were so tired that they were hardly better off than the patients. This might once have been an orderly ward; now it was at the verge of chaos.

"They're here!" the nurse screamed. "Find your places!"

The effect was magical. "Rusty iron!" a patient cried jubilantly, and suddenly every person was scrambling for his chair. This was evidently intended to be a social setting, with comfortable chairs and television and assorted board games, cards, and books; the cards and books were scattered across the floor, and the television screen was filled with an interference signal, appropriately. Live entertainment was what was required.

"We've got to do it, somehow," the guitarist said. "But you know I can't sing a note, and without my strings—"

"I'm not part of this at all," Jezebel reminded them. "Cooking's the only mundane skill I ever tackled."

"But I couldn't possibly do this—this rusty iron," Orb said. "The best I can do is support someone else who performs it. All I can do alone is my kind of song."

"Do what you have to do!" an aide cried urgently. "Maybe they'll buy it!"

"A skit!" the guitarist said. "Like Danny-Boy and Lou-Mae! We could act the parts, and you sing."

"Let's get it going!" a patient exclaimed, banging his fist against the wall beside him. There was a clamor of agreement.

"Anything!" the nurse hissed.

"I'm no actress," Jezebel protested. "At night I only do one thing well and I'm damned if I'll do that here."

"Come on," the guitarist said, taking the succubus by the arm. "You can do this much. Just stand here and look at me, and I'll look at you, and Orb will sing, and we'll just follow when we hear. With her magic it can work!"

"Get it on!" the patient cried. He began to stamp his feet on the floor. This was quickly echoed by the others.

"Shut up, you freaks!" the guitarist yelled. "How can we do anything with all this noise, and no amp system? Get it quiet; then we'll perform!"

The stamping subsided. Quiet came to the ward.

"Okay, Orb," the guitarist said. "Make it come to life."

Orb had her harp in place, her fingers poised. She was ready— except that her mind had suddenly gone blank. "I—can't think of any song!" she whispered, horrified.

"Any of the ones we do!" he whispered back. "Maybe they'll buy it!"

But Orb's mind remained blank; she could not remember any of their regular numbers. She seemed to have been struck by a kind of stage fright that depleted her entire store of music. Too much had happened; Jonah had undermined her security by stranding them like this, and her effort of song and will to stabilize her two companions had seemed to have used up her magic. She was powerless.

"Believe me, if all these—" the nurse said, her gaze scanning the assembled patients nervously. Already the feet were preparing to resume their stomping. From there it would surely lead to worse things, for these were not sane people.

Believe me, if all these— Orb thought, as if reading the words on a sheet of music.

Then her fingers moved on the strings of the harp, and she began to sing.

> "Believe me if all these endearing young charms
> Which I gaze on so fondly today,
> Were to fade by tomorrow and fleet in my arms
> Like fairy gifts fading away . . . "

Orb heard herself with new horror. She was launching into one of the oldest and staidest of the mundane favorites, totally alien to the craving of this audience! Yet it was all she had, suggested by the chance words of the nurse. All she could do was throw herself into it and hope that the magic helped.

But the patients weren't stamping; they were listening, perhaps in amazement at the irrelevance of this effort. The guitarist was gazing at the succubus as if she were the most innocent of lovely young maidens, and she was gazing back at him as if it were true. How long could this hold?

She continued singing, aware of the audience as if apart from herself. Their astonishment was turning to something else as the song progressed; every pair of eyes were fixed on the two standing figures, who continued to look only at each other. They seemed impossibly young, untried, unsure, yet loving.

"No, the heart that has truly loved never forgets,
But as truly loves on to the close,
As the sunflower turns on her God when he sets,
The same face which she turned when he rose."

It ended, but no one moved. The audience seemed locked in stasis, looking at the pair on stage, who continued to gaze at each other. It was as it had been the first time they acted out "Danny Boy," but more general; every face was a sunflower. The guitarist looked devoted and handsome, animated by his loyalty to his love; Jezebel looked radiant, as if she had never before received such a look, and was animated by it.

Jezebel turned. Now Orb saw her eyes. Tears were streaming down her cheeks. Then, silently, she collapsed.

Startled, the guitarist grabbed, catching her before she struck the floor.

Then the monstrous nose of Jonah came through the wall. The mouth opened. The guitarist picked Jezebel up in his arms and stepped in. Orb scrambled up with her harp and followed. The audience remained frozen.

Jonah closed his mouth and swam strongly on through the hospital, passing rooms and people as if they were illusions, and emerging from the upper level. The fish was on his way— somewhere.

The guitarist carried Jezebel on down the throat and to her chamber, where he set her carefully on her bed-region. "Is she all right?" he asked worriedly.

Orb knelt down and checked the woman as well as she could.

"I think so. She's not mortal, you know; I don't think she can be killed. She must have fainted. But I can't think why."

"Look at her face," he said. "She was crying . . . "

"I didn't think that demons could cry," Orb said.

"She just looked at me when you sang, and the tears started." He shook his head. "God, she's beautiful! I guess I love her."

"But she's a succubus!" Orb protested. "She's a century old!"

"I'm going to kiss her."

Somewhat dazed, Orb backed away. The guitarist knelt down beside the unconscious woman, leaned over, and kissed her on the lips.

Jezebel stirred. Her arms came up to embrace the young man, then stiffened. "No!" she said. "I have no right!"

"No right?" the guitarist asked.

"To play such a role. I am not, was never, never can be—oh!" She turned her face to the side, the tears flowing again.

The guitarist looked at Orb, baffled. "What does she mean?"

Now Orb understood. "The song—took her. But she's a demoness, sullied by a century of her nature. She believes she has no right to pretend to be what you saw in her."

"I *know* what she is!" he said. "Look at what *I* am! God, when you sang—"

"I think demons *can* weep—when they experience true emotion," Orb said, working it out. "She may never have experienced it before, and it overwhelmed her."

"Then she—?"

"Loves you," Orb finished. "To whatever extent such a creature can. But she feels unworthy."

"She'd have to be a hell of a lot lower than that to be unworthy of *me*!" he exclaimed.

Then the fish nudged down. They were at the hall where the engagement was supposed to be. In fact they were *in* the hall; Jonah was delivering them right to the stage. Orb could see the others there, gazing up.

"We have to go," Orb said.

"Yeh." The guitarist got up. But he pointed a finger at Jezebel. "This isn't over," he said.

She just looked sadly at him.

Orb and the guitarist hurried on out, stepping from the mouth directly onto the stage. They took their normal places, and the show went on.

In a few days there was an item in the local newspaper describing the mysterious manner in which a contingent from the Livin' Sludge had pacified the psychotic ward with a single song. The patients had shown much improvement, and many had taken to painting pictures of sunflowers.

Similarly the scheduled concert had started off uncertainly, but developed into a rousing success when the absent members reappeared. Only two of the early numbers had the magic, but all of the later ones. The reviewers were uncertain why, but Orb and the others worked it out when they compared notes.

Orb had sung twice in that period: once to stave off the awful hungers of her companions, and once for the psycho ward. At the times she had done that, the remaining Sludge had come alive. The magic had reached out to them, too, enabling them to thrill the audience.

She also had private conversations with Jezebel and the guitarist. Nothing had been said to the others about that aspect of recent developments.

"This is ridiculous," the succubus said. "Demons can't love!"

"And you do?"

"Even if I were mortal, I'd be four or five times his age!"

"And it makes no difference?"

"I've always hated my nature! I did it because I had to. When I got free of that, here in Jonah, I knew I'd never do it again, as long as I had any choice!"

"And now you want to?"

"Not by day. But by night it's driving me crazy! Not the—that hasn't changed. But I just want to be with him, to please him, and if that pleases him . . . "

Orb remembered how it had been with Mym. "Then why don't you go to him?"

"And corrupt him? I'd rather die! Anyway, what future can there be in it? How could I face him by day, with the others knowing?"

Orb shook her head. She didn't know.

But when she talked with the guitarist, the answer came clearer.

"I know she swore off that stuff the moment she could, but God, I wish I could be with her, you know, just—I mean I wouldn't have to touch her, I don't want to make her hate it, but if I could just be with her at night . . . "

"What about the day?" Orb inquired.

"Yeh. That's rough, too. I wish it could be like now. I mean, nobody knowing. She's just the cook. But at night—you know, secret love. Nobody knowing that either."

Orb took a deep breath. She felt responsible, because her song had triggered this. "Go to her at night. She will keep your secret."

"But she doesn't want—I mean—"

"Yes she does. She feels about you as you feel about her, the awkwardness and everything. Secret love—that seems best."

"You mean it?" he asked incredulously.

"You did a very nice thing, when you gave away your H. Perhaps this is your reward."

"But—"

"Go to her," Orb said firmly.

He looked as if he had just received news of a phenomenal inheritance. "If you're sure—"

"Just remember her nature. We won't be in Jonah forever, and then she will revert to her normal state. What I did was only temporary. Even if you stay with her then, you will have to share her, in her fashion."

He nodded soberly. "Better a little time than none," he said. "I do know her nature."

Orb was left to her own thoughts. Back in Ireland, she would never have thought she would send any man to a succubus, not even a drug addict. But she had learned something of the ways of life and love and had become less judgmental. Every person was caught in the web of circumstance, and right and wrong became matters of opinion. If a man who thought himself worthless had found someone who thought otherwise, and if a creature who had been a slave to sex now was discovering the positive side of it, where was the evil?

Evil. That reminded her of the prophecy—she might marry Evil. Others had taken that to mean she would be the bride of Satan. Orb doubted that; as far as she knew, Satan had never married, and certainly she would never do such a thing. So the obvious interpretation had to be wrong, and some more devious one would eventually manifest.

And what would that be? That she would marry an evil man? Why would she do that? She was getting over her loss of Mym; time had passed, after all, and she had another life now. But he set the standard for her; she could not get interested in a lesser man.

Ah, but interest had not been specified. Suppose she married for some reason other than love? Yet what could that be? She would not do it for money, certainly!

But perhaps she would do it for good. If she discovered that she could do a great deal of good in the world by making a token marriage with an evil man—

She shook off the notion. The prophecy simply didn't make much sense, so the sensible thing to do was to dismiss it. What would be, would be, and surely the truth would turn out to be other than the implication.

Already there were strange aspects, though. She was a musician, utilizing her natural talent of magic projection to amplify her trained talent of music. But now her magic was spreading to the whole group she was with, and sometimes even when she was not close by. This most recent series of events, where she had seemingly put a hold on both the succubus' nature and the drug addict's craving—that was more than music! She knew, in a way, what she had done; she had borrowed from Jonah, copying the manner he held those urges in abeyance. She didn't understand the mechanism, but somehow her magic had read it and brought it to them. Still, that was a power she either had not had before or had not known she had.

Jonah—why had the big fish deserted them for that period? He had spit them out at the wrong place, then come for them later. Could that be coincidence?

Hardly! That session had put Orb on the spot and forced her to extend herself, drawing on her magic. The fish's lateness in picking them up from their shopping trip had had a similar effect; she had done some good for those who were trying to collect money for a good purpose. Jonah must have known!

Was the big fish trying to guide her? Why?

Then, perhaps, she understood—the Llano. They all wanted

to find that magical song. There must be some way to do that, which Orb could use—if she first mastered the full powers of her own magic. If she found the Llano, so would Jonah.

"Very well, Jonah," she murmured. "I will seek to explore and develop my full potential. You help me when you can."

There was no response by the big fish, but Orb knew she had in him an ally and perhaps a friend. She needed that support, for though she was back in a group, with constant activity, she was lonely. If only Mym had been able to—

Orb found herself crying, for no apparent reason.

Some months later Orb happened to see a picture on a page of a newspaper. She froze. *That was Mym!*

She read the caption. PRINCE AND PRINCESS OF INDIA VISIT, it said.

Now she looked at the woman in the picture. She was indeed a princess, regal and stunningly beautiful.

This was the marriage they had arranged for her beloved. Orb forced herself to read the article and learned that the Princess was his betrothed, called a complex Indian name that translated to "Rapture of Malachite," and indeed she wore malachite, costly green stones. The Prince had a speech affectation, so the Princess did most of the talking, eloquently expressing the sentiments that he unobtrusively signaled to her. They had come to negotiate a loan for their nations, and their prospects were very good, for the Prince was forceful and clever despite his affectation, and the Princess most persuasive. When she leaned forward to make one of the Prince's points, even the most cynical official paid close attention.

Orb noted the woman's evident cleavage. Of course the official paid attention!

But this was a showcase liaison, intended to appeal to westerners. Was there any genuine feeling involved?

Orb stared at the picture and into the picture, feeling her magic reach through it and to the reality beyond. The picture was old; she felt that now; it was a dated newspaper. But still she felt the reality behind it. There was love there. Mym did love her, and she loved him.

Orb felt something breaking in her. Of course she was happy

for Mym, she told herself. She wanted him happy, whatever his situation. The woman was blameless and good; no fault in her. But oh, the hurt, even after all this time!

She had to get away from here for a time, to be by herself. Far away!

Her vision blurred. Her mind seemed to blur, too. Somewhere in the far distance she heard a melody, and she knew it was a fragment of the Llano. She tuned in on it and felt her whole body blurring.

She seemed to expand, diffusing across the chamber, then across the giant body of the fish. She remained herself, but larger, and her substance thinned as her dimensions increased. She seemed to be no more than fog, now as large as Jonah, now larger.

She continued to diffuse, becoming so large that Jonah was only an object intersecting her torso. There was no discomfort; she seemed to occupy a different plane, able to overlap without contact. There was wind, but it did not bother her either. There were clouds, and her substance phased through them without resistance. Simultaneously it extended down to the ground and beneath it, completing a phenomenal sphere. No, not a sphere— a shaped representation of herself. She grew and grew, and thinned and thinned, yet her identity remained. She was the most monstrous of invisible giants!

Her center remained within the fish, but the fish was now a minnow, entirely contained within her body. Near her geographic center, which was—never mind! Still she expanded, her legs plunging down through the globe that was the world, her head reaching up beyond the sky. She was increasing at a greater rate, a geometric rate, doubling her size every second or so, as fast as she might want.

She became so vast that the globe itself began to seem confining. Her feet poked out through the bottom of it, and she stood with it slowly turning around her legs and getting smaller, casting its shadow into space. She was larger than all the world!

But she had been in quest of something—a sound, a melody. Where was it? She bent to peer down, cocked her ear, and tuned it in, faintly. It was from the surface of the great Pacific Ocean, a spot just within her right thigh. She put her finger on it. "Here," she said.

Her word did not sound, for her head was beyond the effective atmosphere, but it had meaning, for it was backed by her will. She began to shrink, but not as she had grown. Her center of awareness was at her finger now, and she was coalescing about that. The world expanded much faster than it had shrunk, and she closed precipitously on the spot.

Then, abruptly, she was there. She stood on a tiny isle in the sea, beside an inlet, and in the inlet was a single lovely sponge, growing just beneath the water's surface. It was from it that the evocative sound came.

Orb squatted. A musical sponge?

Then she came to her senses. What was she doing here, and how had she come? She was alone on a Pacific isle, with no other land in sight, no civilization. She might have imagined her diffusion and condensation, but this was real!

She walked around the island, finding only sand and rocks. Wind blew back her hair. The sun shone down. She picked up a stone and tossed it into the water. It splashed. Reality.

Well, she had wanted to be alone. The melody had come from an alone-place. She had sought it and found it. Now what was she to do?

What had caused her to seek isolation? Oh, yes—the picture of Mym. But already that jolt was passing; he was happy with his new life, and she was no part of it, and that was the way it had to be. The little snake-ring had informed her truly; she had seen him again, but not as before. That aspect of her existence was done.

It was amazing how quickly she found herself accepting that. She must have been ready for it, merely awaiting the signal. She was free of Mym, to the extent she needed to be; she could now seek other romance.

With Satan? She kicked the sand with sudden anger. No! That prophecy could have no validity! She would seek her own, and to Hell with Satan!

Well. So nice to have decided. Now how did she get back home to Jonah?

She came again to the inlet. She peered into the calm water. There was the sponge, its faint music continuing.

"That music brought me here," she said aloud. "It must be part of the Llano. Magic. But how do I return?"

She tried to remember what she had done before, but could not. She had just, somehow, expanded—and contracted here. Thus she had in a few seconds traveled thousands of kilometers.

Now she was stuck here, no longer wishing to be alone. The wind was picking up, stirring the waves. Clouds were shaping overhead, possibly considering a storm. She had no shelter, no umbrella, no mackintosh. No food, no company. Except for the sponge.

She peered down at it. The water was becoming turbulent here as the wind whipped the waves across. "What are you going to do when your water starts frothing?" she asked it.

The music of the sponge intensified. It began to grow.

"You!" Orb exclaimed. "I emulated that technique from you!"

The sponge continued to grow, fading as it did so. It became an expanding shadow of itself, projecting a gauzy portion above the water. Soon it enlarged itself out of sight; there was only thinning mist where it had been, and then nothing.

"Wait for me!" Orb cried. She concentrated, tuning in on the music, joining it, becoming part of it.

She expanded. This time the process was much faster than before. In a moment she was towering invisibly over the isle, shooting out in all directions. She grew to encompass the world.

Where was Jonah? She reoriented and found him, cruising along over the continent. This time she did not need to put her finger on the target; she merely coalesced about that portion of her that included the big fish. She could solidify at any site within her expanded body; all it required was the melody and her attention.

Soon she was back inside Jonah. Her targeting was imperfect, and she solidified within the wrong chamber.

Jezebel and the guitarist were locked in a most passionate embrace.

Embarrassed, Orb puffed into whale size, then recoalesced about her own chamber. She was glad that things had worked out so well for that couple, but she had never intended to snoop on them!

Then, solid, she marveled at what she had done. Just like that, she had enlarged, then contracted, changing her location silently and efficiently.

She had caught a part of the Llano and traveled across the world!

But her exploration of the fragments of the Llano was far from complete. Perhaps her most significant progress occurred because of a deceptively irrelevant item.

The drummer and Lou-Mae were, as they put it, an item; the guitarist had his secret love to sustain him, and that continued to be the way he wanted it. The organist had a girl friend with whom he communed via a tiny magic mirror he had bought for the purpose. She had been a Livin' Sludge fan and had sent her picture, nude to the waist. That had been enough for him; their correspondence had intensified. But she declined his frequent invitations to join the tour; her family needed her on the farm, she said.

The organist had discussed the matter freely with his companions, Orb and Jezebel included. Was Betsy stringing him along? Was her picture faked up, so that her assets were not as represented? Did she just want a distant association with him for the purpose of notoriety? She seemed like a really nice girl—and that led to another question. What would a nice girl want with a creep like him?

"Sometimes a nice girl can get to like a creep, if he has redeeming qualities," Lou-Mae said, looking at the drummer.

"Gee, thanks," the drummer said, smiling. He was poring over fan mail, methodically working his way through a monstrous pile of it. "How about getting a nice girl to answer some of these for me?"

"I've got my own pile to answer!" Lou-Mae protested. "They never told me that success would bring so many letters!"

"We need a damned secretary," the guitarist said.

"Don't look at me!" Jezebel said. "I've got all I can do to keep up with the housework!"

"An undamned secretary," the guitarist amended himself, smiling.

"I wonder," Orb mused. "Does Betsy do that sort of work?"

The organist looked at her. "You mean—?"

"Why don't you visit her," Jezebel said, "and take Orb along, and sing your girl a song? Then she'll come here."

The organist nodded. He looked at Orb.

"If she is as represented . . . " Orb agreed. "But I have one question: does she know about the H?"

"What I thought," the organist said, abashed, "was if she came here to Jonah, there wouldn't be any problem about that. I know she wouldn't go for H, but maybe when we find the Llano that won't matter any more."

"But if we don't find the Llano, you may have trouble trying to fit into her world."

"We've got to find the Llano!" he said fervently.

They happened to be within range of Betsy's farm, though there was an engagement scheduled for the following day. "We'll do it now," Orb said. "Jonah can drop us off, then take the rest of you to the city, where you can set up. Then Jonah can come back for us in plenty of time."

"Uh, remember what happened last time," Jezebel reminded her. "Sometimes Jonah doesn't come on call."

"He seems to have reason when he doesn't," Orb replied. "If he strands us this time, it will surely be for the best." But she hoped they would not be stranded; that had been an uncomfortable adventure, despite its net benefit.

Jonah obligingly deposited the two of them at the farm. Orb had her knapsack with her harp and her carpet, just in case. When they were safely on the ground, the big fish swam away, quickly disappearing.

The farm did not look healthy. Rows and rows of plants were wilting in the baking heat. There were channels for irrigation, but they were dry.

They approached the house. A young woman in coveralls was cleaning manure out of stalls. The horses did not look well fed.

"It's *her!*" the organist whispered, terrified.

"Then let's introduce ourselves," Orb said, taking the initiative. She strode forward, and the organist had to follow.

The girl paused as she spied them coming. She was grimy and sweaty, and her hair was matted against her head, but she had an excellent superstructure. It seemed that her picture had been an honest representation. "What can I do for you?" she inquired tiredly. "You come to buy a horse?"

"Not exactly," Orb said. "I am Orb, a singer for the touring group called the Livin' Sludge, and this is—"

"It's *you*!" Betsy exclaimed, recognizing the organist. "Oh, I'm a sight!"

"You're beautiful!" he said.

She paused as if straight-armed. "You think so *now*?"

"Sure! I mean, I never knew a girl before who really worked."

She flushed, flattered. "I'm not really working, I'm just filling in. I need to get out on my own. But—"

"But not on some freak show," he said.

"I didn't say that!" she protested.

"I thought maybe you were some groupie, you know, or maybe just stringing me along. Why'd you send your picture like that?"

She grimaced. "Well, I guess it was more or less of a joke. Farm life—it's like this. I wanted to seem different. And I really like your music. And when I got to know you—" she shrugged. "I didn't think you were serious. I mean you musicians have a girl in every city, don't you?"

"No," Orb said. "You're the only one he's kept in contact with. He asked me to help convince you to join us on the tour."

"But I can't sing or play!" she protested. "All I know is farm life, and not a lot of that."

"We need a secretary," Orb explained. "It really isn't professional work. It's just that there is a lot of mail coming in, and we'd like to answer it, but with the rehearsals there just isn't time to do it properly. We need someone who can go through it on a full-time basis, and sort it out, and call our attention to the important letters, and—do you type?"

"Oh, sure, I do that. But—"

"We could pay you, of course. We have a housekeeper already. But you would have to travel with us."

"Now wait!" Betsy said. "I sent that picture, sure, but I'm not that kind of—"

"We can see that you aren't," Orb said. "This is a legitimate offer. It is true that this man would like to have you with him, but there would be no commitment apart from that of the job."

Betsy looked at her. "You know, I don't think I'd believe him, even though I like him a lot. But you—you I believe."

"Then you'll do it?" the organist asked, hardly daring to believe it.

"I don't know. It would be like a dream come true, to travel with the Livin' Sludge and see the whole country. But with the farm drying up like this, I'd sure feel guilty about walking out."

"I saw that you had irrigation ditches," Orb said. "But why aren't you running water in them?"

"What water? They're taking it all for the poison gas plant, drying up our river. If we don't get rain soon, we're finished! Us and every other farm in this area!"

"For what kind of plant?" Orb asked, appalled.

"Well, they claim it's a chemical plant. But there was a leak—I mean a news leak, not the other kind, thank God!—and we found out it's making poison gas for the next war. And it uses an awful lot of water—something about the refinement process. We got up a petition to close it down, but they went to court and they had the money, and now they've got first call on the water. In this drought—" She shrugged. "Nothing anyone can do. If only it would rain!"

"A poison gas plant!" the organist exclaimed, horrified. "I wish we could get rid of that!"

"Oh, enough rain would do it," Betsy said. "Enough to wash right down that channel of theirs and flood the thing out! That would do us some good, too."

"Rain," Orb said, a farfetched idea coming to her.

"Bring us a deluge, and I'll go anywhere with you!" Betsy said, laughing somewhat bitterly.

The organist spread his hands. "I wish we could! But that's not the kind of magic we're into."

But Orb was tuning in on what she believed to be another fragment of the Llano. She concentrated, seeking it out. It was similar to the melody for traveling, but different, too; it involved expansion, but not of her own body. Contraction, of something else. A summoning and intensification—

"Say, Ms. Orb, are you all right?" Betsy inquired.

"Hey, wait!" the organist cautioned her. "I think she's caught a piece of the Llano."

"The what?"

"It's the magic song we're all looking for, to get us off the— I mean, it's like nothing you ever heard. It—she got some of it a few months back, and—" He faltered, not wanting to speak of either H or the succubus.

"Is there something I ought to know about?" Betsy asked alertly. "Just what's going *on* on your tour?"

Orb was concentrating on the elusive melody of summoning, ferreting it out, strengthening it in her mind. But it wasn't enough. "Get—harp," she gasped, not looking at him.

The organist scrambled to obey. In a moment Orb's harp was in her hands. Still she clung to the tail of the melody, resonating to its enormous power without quite being able to grasp it. "Set me up!" she snapped, unable to spare the attention to do this for herself.

They took her by the arms and guided her to the ground. They drew up her legs—she felt the organist's hands on her knees, but knew he was not being familiar. The harp came back into her hands.

"She epileptic?" Betsy asked, worried.

"No. It's the song. It—"

"Tell her the truth!" Orb said, as her fingers sought the proper strings. She couldn't start playing until she found the precise place, but she had to be ready.

"We're into H," the organist said reluctantly. "We want the Llano to get us off it."

"You're all drug addicts?" Betsy asked, shocked.

"Not her. Just us, the original Sludge. Once she sang my friend free of it for a while. But she can do it only a little; she needs the Llano to do it all. Meanwhile, Jonah holds it down."

"Who?"

The organist went into his answer, but Orb tuned out. She had zeroed in on enough of the melody to amplify! Her fingers moved, playing chords on the harp, and its magic amplified the effect. It was strange music, unlike anything she had played before, but its power manifested increasingly as she grasped it, the feedback providing her more and more of it. It was the melody of the operating system of the Elements! With it she was moving the Element of Air, stirring it—but not enough. All she could generate was a light breeze; the leverage simply wasn't there.

She needed something else. And she thought she found it, in a distant variation of the theme. The Element of Air related to what she had done when traveling: diffusion and concentration. This other related to heat. In fact, it was the Element of Fire. She pursued this melody, her fingers dancing over the strings of her harp. More quickly than before, she caught it; she was learning how.

She tuned in on Fire, juxtaposing it with Air, at the site she watched with her mundane eyes. The air was now being heated. But it was already hot; she was doing only what the sun was doing—and doing no good for the parched crops. It was water she needed, not fire.

She quested for the Element of Water, scenting its melody. More quickly yet, she traced it down, caught hold of it, tuned it in. Using it, she summoned water. She knew the humidity was rising.

But that was not enough for rain. The air would simply drift onward, retaining its moisture. She needed to make it yield that water, to precipitate it. To do that, she had to cool it—but all she had was heat, not cold. She had the melody of intensification, but not of alleviation. Should she quest for the rest? She risked losing what she had, for her mind was already overflowing with these vast and potent new themes. How long could she retain them?

No—she could do it with the tools she had acquired! Air— Fire—Water. She concentrated her attention, fixing it on a large region of air. Then she summoned water into it, raising the humidity. Then she summoned the heat, heating the moist air. This increased its capacity to support water. So she summoned more water.

The process accelerated as she became conversant with the separate themes. She was, indeed, tuning in on the Llano: the great processes of nature, the wind and sun and moisture, that together shaped the weather. She continued the intensification, building up an enormous mass of hot, moist air above the parched fields. Something would soon have to give!

It did. The heated air was less dense than the cooler air surrounding it, and began to rise. Air swept in from the great geographic torus, displacing the heated mass, squeezing under it. Orb continued to heat the region, so that the incoming air warmed and followed the prior air up.

The process accelerated further. The outer air swept in with greater authority, and the warm mass rose faster. The original mass expanded as it achieved elevation, and cooled as it did so, bringing itself to the dew point. Precipitation occurred; the air now carried too much water to support, and the water emerged as tiny droplets. The circulation of the air carried positive and negative charges into the cloud, mostly positive above, mostly negative below, and so the droplets became charged in positive and negative layers. These charges built up, until intra-cloud lightning occurred to nullify the disparity. But the process was constant, so more lightning was needed, and more. The lightning, instead of causing the precipitation to ease off, increased it a thousandfold.

Now Orb could relax. The storm had become self-sufficient, drawing in its own air and water and ionized particles. It would continue until it dropped some of its water on the parched ground.

Betsy and the organist were staring at the thickening storm. What Orb had done at the start had been invisible to ordinary senses, but now there was no doubting the effect. A phenomenal deluge was in the making.

Soon the rain came. Quickly Orb put away her harp. The three of them stood there, getting soaked.

Betsy, her clothing plastered to her body, was nevertheless radiant. "I think our farm is saved," she said and turned to embrace the organist.

So it was that the last of the Sludge got his woman. But Orb realized that she had stepped into a new dimension of potential. She had used her music and the power of a fragment of the Llano to influence the course of nature itself. She realized that this was just the beginning. If a poorly grasped fragment could do this, what could the full melody do? Suddenly her reasons for pursuing this song seemed trivial; she might as well have gone naked into the jungle to pursue a tiger.

– 10 –

NATASHA

The Sludge continued to tour, and Orb continued to explore the powers of the melodies that had come to her. They rehearsed while traveling in Jonah and discussed her discoveries, for they were all interested. They knew that, if she mastered the Llano, she could do for them permanently what she had done temporarily—abate their addictions to H, abate the curse on Jezebel so that she could be faithful to the one man she cared for, and bring regular rain to Betsy's farm.

In fact, if she mastered the Llano, she could abolish all addiction and compulsion and vagaries of weather, immensely improving the world wherever she went. They could continue their tour, but in addition to bringing music to the masses, they could bring all manner of other good things. They were dedicated, now, to this aspiration. They realized that only Orb had the capacity to find the Llano, but that her success would benefit them all in both selfish and unselfish ways. They had sought personal gains, but had found a higher mission.

Orb tried to perfect the powers of the music, but all she had were fragments. She could keep the boys free of H while she was with them, but not when apart from them, unless they were in Jonah. She could keep the intolerable lust of night from Jezebel on a similar basis. There had been a mix-up once, and the succubus had gotten separated from Orb's vicinity for an hour. Jezebel had barely made it to the guitarist in time, abating that hour with such dispatch that there could be no doubt of her demonic drive. He never complained about the episode, but agreed emphatically that they should never allow such an accident to happen again.

There was better success on the matter of traveling. Orb practiced and in due course was able to make her way to any spot of the globe in seconds, by expanding to world size and contracting swiftly at the new site. The travel was silent, almost unnoticeable to others; she simply faded gradually from view and reappeared when she returned. She visited Luna, who seemed only moderately surprised, and even her old home in Ireland, but her mother had disappeared. That brought her quickly back to Luna; what had happened?

"She has found another occupation," Luna said. "Don't worry; she's satisfied."

"And didn't tell me?" Orb demanded. "Didn't even bid farewell?"

"She felt it better to leave you out of it," Luna said.

Orb's temper frayed. "She told *you* and not her daughter?"

"She meant to tell you herself, at the proper time." But Luna saw the way Orb was reacting and relented. "I suppose it won't hurt if I tell you. Do you remember how she used to be an aspect of Fate, before she fell in love with Pace?"

"Well, that was a bit before my time—" Orb stiffened. "You mean—?"

"She went back. She's Fate again."

"But she couldn't—I mean, Clotho is young and—"

"As Lachesis."

"The middle Aspect!" Orb exclaimed. "But why?"

Luna shrugged. "If you had a chance to be an Incarnation, wouldn't you take it? Especially if you'd had a few decades' experience in a similar role? Her Earthly life was over."

Orb cooled as abruptly as she heated. "Yes, I suppose it was. I'm glad for her. I will be seeing her again?"

"Yes. At the proper time. I gather that a certain party has been as active as ever, so she's been really hopping to keep down the mischief. She doesn't want his attention to focus on you—you know why—so she's been staying clear for now."

Now Orb understood. That prophecy! That she might marry Evil! Naturally her mother wanted to avoid that if at all possible. So she was staying away from Orb, hoping that Satan would never think of her. It made sense.

They agreed not to discuss the matter further, because even the mention of Satan's name could attract his attention and bring him visiting. Orb departed, expanding and contracting back to Jonah. She had much to think about!

She also visited Tinka, the blind Gypsy girl in the Basque country. Tinka could not see Orb's form, but was aware of her in a moment. "Orb!" she exclaimed gladly.

They hugged. "I thought of you and thought I'd drop in," Orb explained in Calo, and that seemed sufficient. "How are you doing?"

"I did as you asked," Tinka said quickly. "I gave Orlene and the ring to a nice American tourist couple. I know they are taking good care of her."

"I'm sure they are," Orb agreed, feeling a pang for her lost baby girl.

"If only I could have my own . . . "

Orb pondered. She had abated addiction and passion in others; could she—? "One moment," she said.

She expanded back to Jonah, picked up her harp, and expanded back to France. "Let me sing for you," she said, setting up the harp. "I can't promise, but there is a chance—perhaps a small, foolish one—that—"

"That I could have my own?" Tinka asked, catching on immediately.

"If this works," Orb agreed.

Then she played and sang, seeking another fragment of the Llano. Need seemed to enhance her chances, and she saw this as legitimate need. Tinka deserved her own.

She sensed an aspect of the melody, tuned it in, overtook it, caught it, and made it her own. She sang it, serenading her blind friend, and the music permeated Tinka's body, working its subtle magic.

"Oh! I feel it!" the Gypsy exclaimed.

Orb concluded her song. "Of course it can't be certain," she warned. "Your husband has his part to do—"

"He'll do it! He'll do it!" Tinka exclaimed. "If I have to dance the *tanana* on his belly, he'll do it!"

Orb smiled. Tinka was an attractive woman, and the Gypsies were lusty folk. She would probably come on like a succubus, with equal success.

They talked, embraced, and parted. "But I will visit you again, often," Orb promised. "I have ready means of transport, now."

But the most challenging aspect of her approach to the Llano was the storm. She had generated a spot thunderstorm; periodically she duplicated that, expanding to Betsy's farm and causing more rain there. But the power she drew on was far more massive and complex, and she knew that she grasped only a tiny part of it. The melody of the fragment of the Llano gave her the ability to manipulate the fundamental processes of the Elements, but it was like riding a dragon—could she really control it?

She learned. Bit by bit, with many errors, she increased her command of the weather, until she was able to generate a broad, gentle rain or a tight, small storm. But those errors could be critical; once she let one get away from her, and a tornado formed and ravaged a farmstead. She was lucky no one was seriously hurt. When she traveled, she affected only herself, harmlessly; when she focused on a person, she affected only that person. Her ability to protect the boys from their hunger for H was growing; similarly, Jezebel was able to range farther from Orb's immediate vicinity, and Tinka did indeed get pregnant after enticing her husband to appropriate labors. But the weather could kill, and that risk haunted her. She had to understand it better—and to do that, she had to continue experimenting, though this entailed increasing risk.

In due course, the tour brought them again to the Llano region of the country. Here was where she had had her first true encounter with the magic song, she believed in retrospect. Thereafter she had been able to do things through her music that had been impossible before, to become a sorceress of sorts. She had dreamed of finding the Llano, as if it were a simple tune she could hear and understand at one sitting; now she knew that it was phenomenally more complex than that. Even if the whole of it were spread out before her at once, she would not be able to assimilate more than a tiny bit of it. She had to master it bit by bit; there was no easy way.

Jonah settled to the plain, and Orb stepped out on it, as she had the year before. She walked alone, seeking a greater understanding. Her quest for the Llano had not eased as she approached it; it had intensified, until now the tour and the shows they gave were of peripheral interest to her. She craved the Llano in much the manner she might have craved a lover; indeed her interest in men had not been great after she lost Mym, while the magic song promised things she could hardly imagine.

She walked, carrying her harp and opening her awareness to whatever offered. In this manner she had found that first vital suggestion of the magic; could she find more?

A spider appeared, dangling from an invisible thread. Orb paused, admiring it. The spider expanded, becoming fist-sized, then soccer-ball-sized, and finally medicine-ball-sized. It changed its form, two legs extending and thickening to reach the ground, two more becoming human arms, and the rest shrinking until they disappeared. In a moment the spider had become a human being, a middle-aged woman.

"Mother!" Orb cried, abruptly recognizing her.

The two hugged. "I thought it time to visit you," Niobe said.

"Luna said you had become Lachesis!" Orb said. "That you would come to me when the time was appropriate."

"True. Matters have been complex, but now we must talk."

"I never expected to see you here now," Orb said. "I was— did Luna tell you of my quest for the Llano?"

"She did, dear," Niobe said. "And your quest is good. But there are pitfalls along the way—"

"So I have found!" Orb agreed. "An imperfect mastery is dangerous! This song—it enables me to change the weather, to travel—"

"Yes, of course. The Llano is the most potent theme of this realm. But I was thinking of one particular danger that you may not have anticipated. Do you remember the prophecy?"

"How could I forget it! That Luna might marry Death, and I might marry Evil. When I saw Luna associating with Thanatos—"

"Exactly, dear. I had a concern about that, but I discovered that Thanatos is a good man, firmly on the side of good and, I think, worthy of my granddaughter. But the same can not be said for Satan—and it seems it is Satan whom you are destined to encounter.''

"I would never associate with Satan, let alone marry him!" Orb exclaimed.

"But he is the master of deception and treachery," Niobe said worriedly. "Remember when I took you and Luna to the Hall of the Mountain King, and a demon almost got us wiped out?"

"I remember," Orb agreed. "If you had not been with us—"

"I can't always be with you now," Niobe said. "In fact, the requirements of my present office are such that I can seldom be with you at all. Important matters must soon claim my attention again; I have only a few minutes now to give you warning."

"Warning of what?"

"Satan has set a trap for you. He means to complete the prophecy and marry you, regardless of your will."

"But he can hardly marry me against my will!" Orb protested.

"My dear, you underestimate the power of the Llano. You have employed it to change the nature of others, nullifying compulsions they can not overcome themselves. The Llano has similar power over you, if used against you—and he means to use it. He will stun your will, so that you must acquiesce to the marriage and be his love-slave. This is the trap."

"I don't believe it!" Orb exclaimed. "I would never—"

Niobe cut her off with a sad headshake. "You always were headstrong, Orb! Don't let it lead you into this disastrous mischief! Accept my warning, so that you may escape the trap."

Orb stifled her outrage. "How can I escape it?"

"I wish I knew. But I know who does know. I must go now, but I will send Gaea to you. Listen to her, Orb!"

Then Niobe metamorphosed back to the huge spider, shrank, climbed up her thread, and disappeared.

Orb walked on, troubled. Could Satan really enslave her by using an aspect of the Llano against her? She had indeed seen its power over others; why should she be immune? Her mother would not mislead her; she had to play it safe and learn how to nullify this trap before she fell into it.

A mist formed before her. It coalesced into human form, becoming a stately woman. "I am Gaea," the woman said.

So Niobe had sent the Incarnation of Nature, as promised! Orb had never met a female Incarnation before and now suddenly was meeting two, one of them her own mother! "Mother said—"

"That I would tell you how to deal with Satan's ploy," Gaea finished. "I shall indeed! None of us can afford to have Satan complete the prophecy. If he means to use the Llano on you— and if Lachesis believes that is so, it must be so!—your only recourse is to nullify it with another aspect of the Llano. Every function of the Llano has its counter, if you can but find it."

"You don't know the counter?" Orb asked, worried.

"Child, I know it, but I am uncertain how much it will help you. I will do what I can, but there is risk."

"Risk in avoiding the trap?"

"The Llano is no children's plaything, girl! When you invoke it, you are starting a fire that can do much damage, if mismanaged. Satan can not be harmed by it; he is already damned. But you—" She shook her head.

"But if I do not invoke it, I became a slave to Satan!" Orb protested. "What could be worse than that?"

"Madness," Gaea said succinctly. "Satan would use you and forget you in due course; you might not even be damned, if you never submitted in your heart. Once the prophecy was fulfilled, he would have little further concern for you. But if you try the counter and fail, there would be no end to the madness."

"Are you suggesting that I should—should submit?" Orb asked, appalled.

"Of course not! But you must be aware of the risk entailed in the tool you use. Only then can you make the proper decision."

Orb thought of being made subject to Satan's will, a love-slave. "I'll take the risk! How can I escape?"

"He will sing the will-null aspect of the Llano. It is the only aspect of it he has mastered; such magic does not come easily to him, for he is the Prince of Lies, with no true power. You must counter it with the will-null-null aspect. I can teach you part of this."

"Part of it?"

"It is a duet. Satan, being supernatural, can sing both parts together; you, being natural, can not. I can teach you one part; the other must come from another."

"Someone else knows the Llano?" Orb asked, interested on another level. "Who?"

"His name is Natasha. He—"

"*He?* Isn't that a female name?"

"Evidently not. Natasha may be the finest mortal singer, if it is not yourself. If he joins you and sings the complementary theme, then you can escape Satan's trap. But if he does not— the single theme, unsupported, will destroy your mind."

Orb did not like the sound of that. "How do I know he will sing the duet? Or that he is even near?"

"He need not be near; he can use the Llano to travel, as you do. He will hear you sing. But as to whether he will join you— that no one can say. He may, if he chooses. But he may not."

"Is there no other to fill that role?" Orb asked despairingly.

"Few can sing any part of the Llano," Gaea said gravely. "Fewer can sing it well. Only Natasha can sing it well enough to counter Satan's rendition."

"This Natasha—what kind of man is he?"

"The best of men," Gaea said. "But he has been questing for the Llano so long and finding aspects of it, that he may not take your recitation seriously. He might take it to be a trap of Satan's— a trap for him. Satan has tried that sort of thing before."

"I think I'll just avoid the whole issue," Orb said, turning abruptly about.

"You can not, child. Satan was not truly aware of you before, but now he is. He will seek you wherever you go and spring his trap there. It is better to tackle it at a time of your choosing than at a time of his."

"I can choose the time?"

"You can, now—by moving it up. Satan seems to be not quite ready. But soon, in days or perhaps hours, he will be."

"How can I choose it?"

"By starting to sing and play the Llano. He will fear that you are mastering the countertheme and be prompted to act immediately."

Orb sighed. "Teach me that theme, then."

"I can not sing it," Gaea said. "But I can write the music." She raised her left hand, and a parchment appeared in it; her right hand now held a quill pen. She wrote the music, swiftly, with sureness and elegance, and handed the parchment to Orb.

Orb took it. Then Gaea faded. Orb was alone.

She looked at the music. It was clear enough, an unusual

melody, but singable. There were paused written into it to accommodate the companion voice. She was sure it would be beautiful when properly done, but she saw no particular magic in it.

She brought out her harp, settled down on the ground, and propped the music against a tree before her. It would take her only a short time to memorize this; the parts of the melody seemed to follow naturally from each other, so that there was no problem here. She began to play it, but did not sing, heeding Gaea's warning.

The song took her, its magic manifesting. There was indeed power here; the theme shook her to the core. If she were to sing it—

The scene changed. Instead of the bare plain, there was now a kind of church, except that, instead of religious symbols, there were demonic ones; and instead of comforting or esthetic stained-glass scenes, there were depictions of torture and misery.

Satan appeared. He was red, with small flames playing about his limbs, and glowing horns and tail. He turned to gaze at Orb, and his eyes were windows to Hell, flickering with passion and violence. "Now you will marry Me!" he proclaimed.

"Never!" Orb retorted as bravely as she could manage, though fear washed through her. Her mother's warning had been all too true!

Satan sang. It was indeed the Llano; Orb felt its devastating power immediately. Her will left her; she sat and listened, overcome by its compulsion.

Satan gestured, without breaking his song. The second part sounded, complementing the first, as if two men were singing, but there was only one. It added a dimension; now Orb could hardly even think of resisting. The harmony, dreadful and beautiful, governed her will.

Satan beckoned. She got up and walked toward him. Her clothing shifted, becoming a bridal gown, with a train and veil. His aspect changed; a tuxedo now clothed him. He was uncannily handsome despite his color and his horns. Still he sang, and she was aware of almost nothing besides that sound.

She joined him at the altar in the front. He put out his hand, taking her elbow, turning her with him as he turned. Now a demonic shape surmounted the altar: the infernal priest that would marry them. Its arm moved, and something glinted—a sacrificial knife. Orb did not need to ask what was about to happen; she knew. The thing would cut her arm, and cut Satan's arm, to mingle their blood, and they would then be married by the law of this framework.

Satan took her arm, stripping back the white sleeve. He stripped his own sleeve. He grasped her hand and carried her arm forward. The demon brought the blade close.

Orb, horrified, finally broke out of her trance enough to make a sound. She sang the countertheme she had just learned. At first it was faint and unsteady, but in a moment the power of its theme emerged.

Satan was singing, casting about her a web of submission. Orb was singing, fending off that web. She succeeded in freeing her head and arms, so that the demon could not cut her, but she could not free the rest of her body. It was as if she were in a cocoon, able to move within it just a little, but not to escape it. She needed more than she had.

But her song was proceeding, staving off the marriage. Until the first pause. Here she required a response—and there was no one to make that response.

Abruptly all was silent. Satan had ceased his song, but her confinement did not abate. The spell had been set in place. If she did not escape it now, she would never be able to.

There was no answer. She tried to sing again, but her throat locked; she could not resume until appropriately answered. Satan waited, slowly smiling, knowing that the victory was about to be his; her one hope was fading. She felt the surge of madness rising in her as the incomplete theme turned against the one who had invoked it.

Orb focused her will, trying to project whatever magic she had out to the corners of the globe, the curvature of the plain. She felt it going out, carrying the fading melody. Would there be an answer?

Satan nodded. He signaled the demon; the prey had not escaped. The demon brought the knife forward as Satan took Orb's bare arm again. She tried to fight it, but could not; the scant protection made by her song had seeped away. Only her eyes remained free—free to weep.

The knife touched Satan's red arm, and a thin streak of blood appeared. It crossed to Orb's arm.

Then, faintly, she heard it. Was it, could it be—?

Yes! It was the companion theme! Natasha was answering! The barely audible melody caused the walls and floor to resonate, animating with the suggestion of its potency.

That answering passage freed her to resume. She sang her own part, and the infernal church began to waver. Infused by the countertheme, it was losing its power over her.

Satan resumed his song, but now its compulsion was diminished. Orb felt its horrible tug at her being, making her weak and despairing, but she was able to resist it.

She stepped unsteadily away from the altar, out of reach of the demon's knife. She retreated to the spot where her harp was lying and picked it up, never pausing in her singing. She knew she was on the way to her escape, but she felt the looming of the madness, too; if Natasha did not respond again, she would still be lost.

Her passage ended—but the distant voice of Natasha was louder now, and it brought her renewed strength. She marched resolutely to the wall and through it, out to the landscape beyond, while Satan's song faded behind.

From beyond the crest of the low hill ahead came Natasha's voice, singing the alternate theme. She walked toward it, singing in her turn. At the crest she encountered him as he came up from the other side.

He was a well-knit man, sturdy rather than tall, wearing a bright plaid shirt and green denims. His hair was fair, long and wavy, in the fashion of the ancient knights, and his features were ruggedly even. He would not have seemed outstanding in a crowd, except for one thing—his voice.

Not since her father had died had Orb heard the magic by a man. The Gypsy girl Tinka had the magic, but not as strongly, and it wasn't the same. Her father's voice had been passable, but when he touched her, the music of the mighty orchestra had manifested and transformed his voice and her world to splendor.

Natasha had the magic—and his voice alone was as fine as any Orb had heard. Satan had sung at her with a rough bass, both parts; Natasha was a honeyed tenor, of perfect timbre and volume, surely a joy even without the magic. But the magic that he had was potent; it reached out to move her from a greater distance than her own magic could. The combination thrilled her; she felt almost as if she were treading on clouds as she approached him.

They stopped singing and stood for a moment facing each other. There was no sound from behind.

Orb turned and looked back. The obscene church was gone; there was only open field.

"You play a dangerous game," Natasha remarked.

"I didn't choose it," Orb said. "Satan tried to—to marry me."

Natasha pursed his lips. "Then you must be the damsel of the prophecy."

"What has my reputation become!" Orb exclaimed with mock dismay.

He laughed. "When I set out in quest of the Llano, I learned that there was a woman who would sing it as well as I, but that Satan had his eye on her and would try to take her before I met her. When I heard your melody I had forgotten that; I answered only because it had to be answered, lest madness come. I did not know it was you, or that you would be beautiful, or that your voice and magic be so wonderful. I think I had no call for my jealousy."

"Jealousy?" Orb was still adjusting to this abruptly changed situation.

"I was always the most respected singer of my group," he said. "In my pride, I thought that none could be my equal. When I learned that a mere woman . . ." He shrugged, smiling. "How can I resent one as stunning in every respect as you? I think I never truly understood why it was that others listened so raptly to me, until I approached you just now and was stirred by your voice and your magic. Truly, singing with you has been the high moment of my life—and I do not even know you!"

"I am Orb Kaftan, of Ireland," Orb said, discovering that the thrill he described applied as readily to her. Never before had she encountered her equal in this type of music, and it was indeed a transcendent experience.

"Natasha, of this country," he said.

"If I may inquire—"

He laughed, as he seemed to do readily. "My father wanted a girl. My mother wanted a boy. My mother was victorious, but my father had his revenge. He named me after the girl he had desired—in fact, after a woman he had desired, before he married my mother." He grimaced. "You may call me Nat, if you prefer."

Orb found herself liking him and suspected that she would have, even if he had not just rescued her from a fate or two worse than death. "I am most grateful to you for saving me from Satan," she said.

"I am most grateful to myself for doing it," he said. "There are few better things than earning the gratitude of a woman such as you."

It seemed best to skirt that subject. "What if Satan approaches me again, when you are gone?"

"Have no fear of that!" Nat exclaimed. "It is the easiest thing to thwart him, when you know the key. I learned it by accident, serendipitously, in a bypath of my quest for the Llano."

"Easy? I was unable to resist! What is this key?"

"Simply sing his alternate part," Nat said. "That nullifies the effect, instead of completing it. When you preempt half of the theme he requires to bind you, you render the whole harmless. I can quickly teach you that part; you need never fear Satan again. He made his play and lost, and for that I am thankful."

He was hardly the only one! "Teach me!" Orb said.

"What, now?"

"I shall not feel safe until I know Satan can not touch me! I knew the prophecy, but thought I could resist it; now I know that I could not. Not by myself."

He held up both hands in a gesture of surrender. "How can I refuse? I will sing it for you now."

He sang it, his voice rising so fine and clear and full that Orb felt a wash of joy flow through her. She recognized the second theme that Satan had sung, but this time it was beautiful instead of grim. She could have picked it up before, if she had realized how she could use it. As it was, she had been terrified, too desperate to escape to make proper note of such a thing.

Nat finished, and Orb settled down with her harp, improvising an accompaniment, and sang it. She could feel the partial power of it as she did so; this was definitely an aspect of the Llano!

When she was done, he sat beside her. "I had thought your magic was a bit less than mine, but with that instrument it is more. How came you by that harp?"

"It was given me by the Mountain King," she said. "It enhances my magic, so that I can enchant an audience."

"You have enchanted me," he agreed. "How is it possible that you, hearing a theme once, can sing such a compelling rendition? I required many rehearsals to master it.''

Orb shrugged, flattered. "It is my nature."

"I think I am glad I rescued you," he said. "Tell me, if this is not too forward—"

"I am unmarried," Orb said, flushing. "Otherwise I think Satan would not have—"

"Of course," he agreed immediately. "I should have realized. You need never marry until you wish to, now. Let me say candidly that all I know about you now is your appearance and your voice, but that these are sufficient to provoke my interest. May I court you?"

Orb was startled, but held her composure. After all, she had been approached by men before as abruptly. Her reaction was less because of the expressed interest, or the courtly manner of its expression, than because of her realization that she was more than casually receptive. It was true that Nat had just saved her from a horrible fate and perhaps nullified a long-time prophecy: "One may marry Evil." How important that word "may" was! The issue had been in doubt, and the doubt had been resolved. Yet it would be safer to be married, so that Satan had no ready route to that objective. Even if that were not the case, Nat was an extremely interesting and talented man. "You may," she breathed.

"I thank you for that permission, Orb," he said. "Considering that, let me sing you the Song of Awakening."

"I don't think I know that one," she said.

"It is another aspect of the Llano that I have discovered in my questing. I must warn you that, like all the aspects of that song, it is potent."

"I want to learn all of the Llano," Orb said.

"I don't know whether any single person has learned all the parts of it, let alone mastered them," he said seriously. "I understand that its entirety is as complex and varied as life itself. Few are even capable of singing the least of it, though some in moments of special inspiration or need do rise to the occasion."

"So I understand," Orb agreed. "Yet what a challenge!"

"What a challenge!" he echoed, his voice suffused with longing. "If the parts can do what they do, what might the whole accomplish? I have dedicated my life to that pursuit."

"So have I," Orb said.

"Then I will sing you the Song of Awakening, and may the consequence be on our heads," he said with a smile. "I did warn you."

"You did," she agreed.

He stood, took two steps forward, and turned to face down the hill. He breathed deeply, setting himself. Then he sang.

From the first note, the magic manifested, holding her almost breathless, stunned by its beauty and anticipation. She had never heard a finer voice or finer theme! She seemed to become one with the environment, breathing its melody.

The sound spread out like a living blanket, and the world went dark. Orb was surprised, but not alarmed; the feeling was good and more than good. She felt the magic surrounding her, suffusing her, filling all the world about her, building up for what she knew would be a thrilling culmination. She knew already that every story ever told about the Llano was true; its power now seemed infinite.

There was a gleam of light to the side. It broadened and brightened, turning red. It illumined the nether sides of dark clouds, and rays passed between them to touch other clouds, causing them to glow like stately hanging embers. The red became orange, and amber, and the surrounding light spread out to animate the ground. It was the sunrise.

Now Orb recognized the melody; it was the Song of the Morning! The music she had first heard as a child, that had brought her out to the field and the forest and the river for her adventure with the water sprites. She had heard it often thereafter, but in recent years she had been caught up in other matters and didn't go out to the natural country at dawn. What a delight this was, to discover her old friend in this new guise! Of course it was an aspect of the Llano; she had always known that, but had never thought it could be evoked by human voice. Nat had brought her a treasure!

The sunrise broadened to light the landscape, the rays of the slowly lifting sun spearing out past the bank of clouds they heated to touch the ground. At each touch, a secondary glow manifested, the turf and rock developing preternatural clarity and colors, seeming more real than before. Dew glistened, striking delicate fire, forming a field of sparkling gems, seemingly more precious in its transience than any stone could be. Tiny spider webs became chains of miniature beads.

The great, brilliant ball of the sun appeared, that transcendent orb after whose pale sister Orb herself had been named. It was too bright to look at; yet in this vision, she could do so without pain, appreciating its might while shielded from its harm.

A ray came down and touched her directly, illuminating a circle about her. She was bathed in its warm brightness, becoming more colorful herself, feeling more beautiful. It was as if she had come into existence at this moment, or had been renewed in better form. She was—awakening.

The song continued, harmonizing in its fashion with the natural things within its ambiance. The ground stirred before Orb; she watched closely and saw new shoots coming up, breaking through the turf. The stems spread, branching, thickening, reaching, taking in the strengthening beam of the sun, putting out leaves that broadened and angled themselves to catch the slanting light.

Buds formed, expanded, and opened into flowers of all colors. Some suggested roses, some tulips, and some orchids, but they were not; they were simply the magic flowers of the morning, their loveliness for her eyes alone.

Orb looked around. The entire landscape had turned verdant, thickly grown with flowers. She was in a garden, the massed fragrance of the flowers adding to her joy.

Then at last the song ended. It had not been long, objectively; her experience of it had dilated her awareness and delight.

She gazed at Natasha, the source of this wondrous experience. She had not realized how handsome he was! "I never knew it could be sung," she murmured.

"I will teach it to you," he said.

"I think—not now." she said. "I—have had enough experience for one day. I think I had better return home."

"Of course," he said, coming to her and extending his hand to help her stand.

As she stood, the flowers faded. The relatively barren landscape returned. Even the hill was gone; they were standing in the featureless plain of the Llano. Far away, near the horizon, she spied Jonah swimming toward her.

"But I will see you again," she told Nat.

"Certainly," he agreed.

She walked toward the big fish. When she paused to look back, Natasha was gone.

– 11 –

SONG OF DAY

She told the others, of course, for the pursuit of the Llano was
their common mission. Even Betsy, who had known nothing of
it at first, had become interested as she realized what it could do
for the organist and her folks' farm.

They were also interested in Natasha. "You're the only loose
cog aboard, you know," the drummer remarked. "Everyone else
has paired off, one way or another. But maybe we should meet
this guy, just to be sure he's right for you."

"You have no authority over my social life!" Orb exclaimed
indignantly.

"Yes we do," Lou-Mae said. "Because we care."

That undermined her righteous ire. "I really don't know much
about him, except that he's the finest singer I ever met and he
knows aspects of the Llano."

"And he saved you from Satan," Jezebel added. "That's
enough to recommend him by itself. Only—"

"Only what?" Orb asked, aware that the succubus might have
an important qualification.

"Well, you know I'm a demon. I didn't ask to be, any more
than the rest of you asked to be human. I'm not of Satan's camp;

demons come in many varieties, just as mortal creatures do. But some things—are more demonic than others."

"Whatcha saying, woman?" the guitarist asked. "You think Nat's a demon?"

"It is possible," she said. "If I could meet him, I could tell."

"I hadn't thought of that," Orb said, dismayed. "A demon?"

"Demons can do things that mortals can't. Like singing—you know how we can change our forms. Well, some of us can change our voices, too. Our substance is more malleable; and, of course, eternity allows us to perfect something, if we work at it."

"But not all demons are bad," the guitarist said, evidently sensitive about this matter.

Jezebel smiled. It was night now, and she was in her sultry stage. "That depends on how you see it. To some, I am the most evil of creatures, because—"

"Well, they don't know anything!" he said. "You just never had a chance, before you got aboard Jonah."

"True. But still, it is not wise to trust a demon before you know him well. We don't know what motivates this Natasha, and if anything happened to Orb—"

"But it's only speculation that he's a demon!" Orb protested.

"Still, maybe it would be better to be sure," the drummer said. "We don't want to interfere, but if we could just get to know him, maybe . . . " He trailed off.

"I will ask him to come and meet you, next time I see him," Orb promised, knowing there was justice in their doubt.

Meanwhile, she practiced the Song of Awakening, which she knew as the Song of the Morning. The others were awed as the miraculous sound filled the fish and caused the chamber to darken, then brought the beautiful dawn and the sprouting of plants and blooming of flowers. It was illusion, of course, that faded slowly after the song was done, but a marvelous one. As Orb perfected it, the effect intensified, so that it was hard not to believe in its reality.

"You know," Betsy said, "the time may come when you do it so well that it will become real, and dawn will come a second time in one morning." She was a farm girl and really appreciated nature.

Orb laughed, but privately she wondered. The Song of Awakening was the human version, while the Song of Morning was nature's version. There were surely ramifications that she did not know, but if she perfected them, so that her version more closely approached the natural one, it might indeed have that effect. After all, the Song of Travel enabled her to jump across the globe. The magic music did relate to real things, when properly executed.

She thought also about Natasha. It had not been coincidence that he had rescued her from Satan, for she had sung a portion of a fragment of the Llano, and he was attuned to the Llano. But it had been a most important event in her life, for Satan had indeed trapped her and almost completed the prophecy. She had a common interest with Natasha in the Llano, as she did with the members of the Livin' Sludge and with Jezebel and Betsy—and with Jonah. That interest bound them all together, however diverse their origins and natures. But it was more than that, for Nat was a handsome and talented man, and she was without a man. She had not felt deprived, but now her interest was quickening. His Song of Awakening, presented as courtship, had indeed moved her.

Now she remembered her childhood vision. A wedding! She had never thought of it in the excitement and horror of Satan's attempted forced ceremony; and indeed, that had not been the wedding of the dream. Mym had not been there to conduct her down the aisle. But if she—with Natasha—could it be? Then what of the other part of the dream, the devastated world?

And if Natasha were nonhuman—what then? She could not dismiss Jezebel's warning. The succubus was in a position to know. A demon was a creature of a different order from the human. The sprites were of the demon kind, and the dryads, different phyla of the Demon Kingdom. They varied as widely as did the creatures of the Animal Kingdom, or the plants of the Vegetable Kingdom, or the stones of the Mineral Kingdom. Just as she could love a pretty flower or a sparkling gem, she could love a demon like the hamadryad of the water oak. No, demons were not by definition evil! But to develop a romantic relationship with one—that was another matter.

Was she prejudiced, she asked herself. The guitarist had a romantic relation with the succubus, and Orb could not fault it; Jezebel was a good woman in every human sense of the word, as long as her passions were under control. Why should Orb feel that the kind of relationship that was good for a fellow human being should be bad for her? She couldn't answer that, except to acknowledge that she could not accept it for herself with equanimity. Perhaps a relationship was possible, but she would first have to know for certain exactly what Nat was. If human, fine; if demon, she would have to consider longer before deciding how or whether to proceed.

Yet when he had sung the Song of Awakening—ah, what a stirring there had been in her breast! There had been a seeming dawn within her awareness, as well as in the world. Who could say where this day might lead?

"Mrs. Glotch has scheduled us for Hawaii," Betsy announced brightly, looking up from the pile of correspondence she was handling. "I've always wanted to see their pineapple farms."

Orb pursed her lips. "I'm not sure that's wise. Jonah doesn't like to pass over large bodies of water."

"Oh? Why not?"

"He is cursed. He can not swim in water, and if anything should happen over the ocean, he would be in terrible trouble."

Betsy's brow wrinkled. "Why? What could happen to him?"

"Well—" But Orb found herself stumped. "What *could* happen to a creature cursed to be immortal until his punishment was terminated?"

"Probably a lot of pain," Lou-Mae said.

Orb nodded. That would be enough. "I suppose we'll just have to see whether Jonah will take us," she said. "If not, it's understandable, and we'll simply have to cancel the engagement."

When the time came, they asked the big fish to go. Jonah hesitated at the verge of the ocean, then lifted high and braved it. They were on their way.

At first it was intriguing, swimming above the great ocean, for they had never done this before. But it was a long swim, and soon the novelty dulled. They settled down to the routine of rehearsing, eating, talking, and sleeping.

Lou-Mae came to wake Orb. "Something's wrong," she whispered urgently.

Orb rubbed her eyes. "You quarreled with—?"

"No, I mean with Jonah!"

Now Orb was alert. "Jonah! How do you mean?"

"He's swimming crazy. I think he's sick."

What would it mean to be inside a sick fish? "Oh, I hope not!" Orb said sincerely. She flung on a housecoat and dug her toes into her slippers.

Now it was evident: the big fish's course was erratic. He seemed uncertain where to go and kept changing course.

"I wish we could talk to him!" Lou-Mae said nervously. "Ask him what's wrong . . . "

But Orb had discovered it. "There's a storm out there; I can see the lightning flashes through his scales," she said.

"He don't much like storms!" Lou-Mae said.

"He's trying to avoid the rain," Orb said. "But it has closed in all around. He's cornered, as it were."

"But he can dive down underground and—oops, we're over the ocean!"

"Now we know why he doesn't like to swim over the ocean," Orb said.

"What happens if he gets rained on?"

"I don't know. He is cursed to avoid water. I suppose it would be a violation of the terms of his curse. But what that means in a practical sense . . . " She shrugged.

Jezebel appeared, in her ravishing nocturnal aspect. "I have a notion. It strikes me that Jonah is much like a demon, during his curse. Demons don't die, but they can hurt. Probably every drop burns like fire. A mortal would die pretty soon and be out of his pain, but for a demon it goes on and on."

"How would that affect us?" Orb asked.

"Well, he's sure to thrash around. You would, too, if someone kept poking you with a red-hot poker. It won't be too comfortable in here."

The guitarist showed up, looking green. "Can't we get this tub out of the rollers?" he asked plaintively. "I get seasick."

"Cheer up, lover, the worst is yet to come," Jezebel informed him maliciously. The news of their liaison had of course circulated quickly enough; the secret was only maintained against outsiders.

"You're a demon!" he said.

"I had noticed. Can I help you?"

"Just pull out your blouse so I have somewhere to vomit," he said miserably.

"Mortals have odd tastes," the succubus remarked as she pulled out her blouse, showing her full breasts. Others laughed appreciatively, but the guitarist for once had no interest. "Come on, sailor." She herded him off toward a bathroom.

Orb gazed out through the scales. "We've got to do something," she said. "It's our fault Jonah got caught here."

The organist appeared, with Betsy. "You conjured rain, Orb; can you make it go away?"

"I could try. But I don't know the proper theme. I might just make things worse."

"Better not risk it," he agreed. Then he had another notion. "You can keep us off the H when you have to; can you get Jonah off his problem with water? So he can swim in it again?"

"Again, I could try, if I knew the theme. But if I got it wrong—"

"Well, it's the Llano he's looking for, same's us. Maybe if you—I mean we could all try the Song of Morning, and maybe—"

"I don't know," Orb said. Then the fish lurched, throwing her against the wall. "But then again—"

They tried it. The guitarist was too sick to participate, but the drummer and Lou-Mae and the organist joined. Orb sang the Song of Awakening, and Lou-Mae made a harmony, and the others accompanied. The magic spread out strongly, animating them all, and it developed into the best rendition yet, with the darkness closing in so absolutely that stars appeared above.

Jonah's lurching stopped. He relaxed, slowly sinking down through the turbulent atmosphere.

But what would happen when he touched the restless surface of the ocean?

Orb peered through the scales as the magic sunrise formed. She could see that it was raining now, outside, and the rain was washing across Jonah's surface. That meant that their song was enabling the fish to tolerate water. Perhaps the sea would be tolerable, too.

They completed the rendition. Flowers bloomed across the floor, and the chamber was fragrant.

"Sheez, we should do this number on the tour!" the drummer exclaimed.

Lou-Mae considered. "Why not? So it's a piece of the Llano; it's the greatest music we know. Everybody should hear it."

Orb nodded. "I suppose we could try it." She walked to the wall, to get a better view of the exterior.

Jonah made a shudder. "Maybe we better sing it again," Lou-Mae said.

"Try it without me," Orb said. "I'll try to help you with the magic. If we can do it in relays, maybe we can keep him quiet without wearing ourselves out."

Lou-Mae and the drummer and the organist tried it by themselves. it wasn't as good as before, but it did quiet the fish.

Orb watched as Jonah sank slowly toward the heaving ocean. The key point would be when he touched. If he could do that without damage, they would be all right.

The fish shivered. They felt it as if it were an earth tremor: minor motion, but significant alarm.

Jezebel reappeared. "Jonah's afraid," she said.

Orb pointed down. "Of that?"

"I don't think so. The song's calming him. It doesn't seem that he can't touch water, just that he's afraid to. The Llano helps quell his fear, but not all the way."

"What could a creature like him be afraid of?"

"I don't know, but I think we'd better not dismiss it till we know what it is."

Jonah settled onto the water. His nervousness increased despite their music. Yet the water did not seem to be hurting him. He floated like a ship, rocking gently to the swells.

Then the big fish jerked into motion. His side fins raked through the water like oars, and the bottom portion of his tail threshed the liquid into foam. He was not swimming, so much as stroking across the water.

"Something's out there!" Jezebel said. "I'd better take a look." She strode to the wall and through it, startling Orb. But of course she was a demoness, able to dematerialize and walk through walls so she could reach her prey. She just hadn't done it openly before.

Almost immediately the succubus reappeared. "There's something ugly out there,'' she reported. "There's a glow, and what look like ghosts, and Jonah's trying to get away from them. You'd better look."

"I can't go out there," Orb protested. "I'd drown!"

"I can take you to the top of the fish," Jezebel said. "It's pretty flat there, and you can hold on to a fin. I really think you should go."

Orb trusted the succubus' judgment. She took Jezebel's hand, and they walked through the wall and up, coming out on the fish's broad back. The rain was pelting down, but the skin was rough, offering good traction, and Orb had no trouble keeping her feet.

"There," Jezebel said, pointing.

Orb looked. She saw the glow, and it was not a healthy illumination. Grotesque shapes moved within it. She squinted, brushing the spray from her face. "What *is* it?"

"I think it's demonic," Jezebel said. "But there are different kinds of demons, as you know, and some in-between forms like zombies that—"

"Zombies?"

"Well, I'm not sure. What do they look like to you?"

Orb continued peering. The fish was slowing, and the shapes were gaining, spreading their unhealthy light. "Skeletons."

"Same thing, maybe. Do you think that's what Jonah's afraid of? Looks to me he can handle water, maybe not to swim in, but to float on, but those things are walking on it, which means they're supernatural, and I'd guess they're after him. If he knew it, he'd stay well clear if he could."

"We've got to stop them!" Orb exclaimed.

"The supernatural's hard to stop, when it's in its element. I don't want to scare you but—"

"With the Llano!" Orb cried. "I've got to try!"

The succubus shrugged. "I'd help you if I could, but you know my talent isn't singing."

Orb started singing herself, trying the Song of the Morning, the only significant fragment of the Llano she knew.

The skeletons marched right on, their bone legs walking across the water, their skulls facing Jonah. The song had no effect.

"Worse," Jezebel murmured. "Now I see why he slowed. There're more on the other side."

"Maybe if I had my harp," Orb said doubtfully.

"I can fetch it for you."

"Thank you." Orb was too distracted to say more. The dancing skeletons closed in inexorably. Jonah's shuddering became more violent. Orb had no reasonable doubt, now; this was the menace the big fish feared. "Jonah, I will try to protect you," she said aloud.

The shuddering eased. Jonah had heard and understood.

But could she do it? The Song of the Morning hadn't worked; what would? Sometimes the magic had worked with other songs—but what applied to skeletons?

Their forms were coming clearer as they approached. They were not simply dancing; they were doing a crazy sort of jig. She would have thought it random, if they were not all doing it together, perfectly synchronized. Their bone legs moved this way and that, and their bone bodies seemed to lose balance and almost fall over before abruptly snapping back to the vertical. The effect would have been eerie, even if performed by fully fleshed folk.

Jezebel reappeared, leading the drummer by the hand. Orb realized that she had done an absent-minded doubletake when the succubus chuckled. "No, I'm not two-timing my man," Jezebel said. "We figured you could use help, and there's no way to plug in the organ up here, so I brought the drummer instead." She handed Orb her harp.

"But the rain will ruin the drums!" Orb protested.

"No more than it will your harp," the drummer said. "What use will either be, if Jonah gets wiped out?"

Orb acknowledged the validity of that. "I tried the Song of the Morning, but it didn't work."

The drummer stared at the advancing horde. "Know any songs about skeletons?" he asked with a certain bravado.

"Just one my father used to sing me," Orb said. "A joke, a Halloween kind of round."

"Try it," he said, setting up his drums.

"This is ridiculous!" Orb muttered as she took up her harp. But then, so were the dancing skeletons.

"Say, isn't that the Drunken Sailor's Hornpipe?" Jezebel asked, gazing at the dancers.

"The what?" the drummer asked.

"It's a dance. I learned it about fifty years ago, when I worked a dancing group."

"You were a dancer?"

"I didn't say that."

"Oh." He was disgruntled.

Orb started to sing and play, and the drummer picked up the beat and amplified it powerfully. "Have you seen the ghost of Tom? Round white bones with no skin on!" It was a humorously grisly song, but it held nostalgia for her, taking her back to the years of her childhood when Pacian held her and tickled her and sang to her, and the orchestra of his magic presence filled her limited universe. Oh, she loved her father! Now he was gone, and if there were skeletons where he was, surely he was singing to them, too, and making them laugh.

Orb was uncertain how much of the wetness on her face was rain and how much was tears.

But the song wasn't stopping the skeletons. They were coming quite close, in seeming phalanxes, and the first phalanx was now quite near Jonah's huge tail.

Orb tried another song, one from their repertoire, with no better effect. Music simply wasn't doing it.

One skeleton separated from the lead phalanx. It danced crazily forward, toward the tail, its bone feet treading the water as if it were completely solid.

"That *is* the Drunken Sailor's Hornpipe!" Jezebel said. "See, it's one of the few dances I can do." She went into the jig, and it was the same motion, lean and lurch as the skeletons were doing. "You step here and here, around and back, and that off-balances you, so you switch feet, so," she explained as she did it, her flesh heaving dynamically.

The closest skeleton paused, its skull facing the succubus.

"Hey!" the drummer said. "They're dancers! So they tune into dancing!"

The skeleton resumed its forward motion. It came to the tail and reached out to embrace it. But at the touch, Jonah jumped as if receiving an electric shock, and indeed there was a flash at the point of contact.

Then the skeleton was gone—and one section of Jonah's tail had become skeletal.

"Geez," the drummer said.

"I told you he'd have reason to fear demons," Jezebel said. "They want to make him one of them—and I'll bet there are enough of them to do it."

Another skeleton detached itself from the phalanx and danced forward.

"I've got to stop this!" Orb said, handing the succubus her harp and striding along the back of the fish. Part of her mind remarked on the confidence with which she gave her invaluable harp to a demoness—but she knew the harp would not tolerate the touch of a deceitful or evil creature, and Jezebel was neither, despite being of demonic stock.

"Hey, don't!" Jezebel cried, following. "It'd only take one skeleton to convert you! I think they take out their own mass!"

Orb paused. Obviously there was justice in this notion. What could she accomplish, if she became an instant skeleton? Yet how could she let this horror proceed without even challenging it? She was afraid and angry.

"They're dancers," the drummer called, coming up behind them. "Orb, you know a dance that'd stop anything in its tracks."

Orb stiffened. But now a realization came: the huge fish had accepted her after she had danced the *tanana* for him. Was this the reason? Insurance against these awful dancers?

The second skeleton was approaching the tail. "Beat the cadence for the Song of the Morning," Orb said tersely to the drummer. "I'm going to dance to it."

"Got it," he said, scrambling to set up his drums again.

"I'll tell the others," Jezebel said, stepping down through the fish's flesh.

He started the beat, and it was good, but not good enough. "With the magic," Orb said, touching his shoulder.

As she did so, the magic came, her power transferring to him. "Got it," he repeated.

The beat took hold, and there was indeed magic to it, creating the semblance of the song. Orb began to dance. She was conscious now of her housecoat plastered to her body, and dragging at her legs. Impatiently she struggled out of it and threw it aside, wearing only her nightie. She was aware that this was clinging to her torso like a wrinkled second skin, worse in its fashion than nakedness, but she had no choice; she had to have freedom of motion.

She danced the *tanana* to the beat, addressing the skeleton. The thing paused, then matched her, switching from its hornpipe to the *tanana*. It coordinated with her motions, completing the dance. It leaped and spun and gazed sidelong at her with its bony sockets. There was no doubt that she had found the key to making the skeletons react. But where could this lead?

Well, if the others did not advance until this one was through, and she distracted it long enough, the storm might clear, and Jonah would be free to swim back into the sky, escaping the skeletons.

The beat of the drums intensified, seeming to pound against the entire universe. *Boom, boom, BOOM, BOOM!* The skeleton danced more wildly, matching the increasing emphasis—and then began to fall apart. The violence of this dance was becoming too much for it, and it was self-destructing!

The bones flew off randomly, leaving the skeleton without part of one arm, then part of the other, then its skull. Finally the rest of it collapsed and fell into the water, sinking out of sight.

Orb breathed a panting sigh of relief. They had done it! They had stopped the skeleton from touching Jonah!

A new skeleton detached itself from the phalanx and danced toward the tail.

Oops! The job wasn't finished! Orb set herself, the drumbeat resumed, and she began to dance again. She addressed the second skeleton, and it reacted as had the first. They danced together, and the skeleton was a marvelously fine dancer; she found herself picturing it as a handsome Gypsy man, strutting and posturing and turning on in the timeless manner.

Then the beat intensified; the man flew apart, and his pieces sank into the rain-wet waves, his magic gone.

But the storm had not abated, and the skeletons had massed until they were closing in on every side. Another emerged from the phalanx near the tail, but now others were stepping out from other phalanxes, to approach the large fins on either side and the head. Jonah's nervousness increased.

"We're in trouble," the drummer said. "You can't dance forever, and you can't go one-to-one with three or four at once."

Jezebel emerged with Lou-Mae on one hand and the organist on the other. "Maybe each of us can address one skeleton, and hold them off each section," she suggested.

They tried it, but the others did not know the *tanana* and the skeletons responded to nothing else well enough to make a difference. There was not time to teach them; it had taken Orb hours of practice, many days in succession, to perfect it. Even had there been time, she doubted that Lou-Mae could learn it; the dance appeared indecent to outsiders. Meanwhile, the skeletons were marching in on every side.

"We have to have stronger medicine," Lou-Mae said. "You said your friend Nat knew strong songs—"

"Natasha!" Orb called, hoping he could hear. The skeletons were about to touch on every side; if the man did not come—

There was the distant sound of a sustained note, as of someone singing an extraordinarily powerful melody. The very surface of the ocean seemed to quiet as the music stroked it. The skeletons paused in their dancing, exactly as they were, canted to one side. Natasha had heard!

The note became a melody, growing louder. The song spread out to fill the region, beautiful and resonant and profoundly moving. "That man can *sing*!" Jezebel murmured. There was no response; the others were mesmerized by the song, human beings and skeletons alike, listening.

Natasha approached, still singing, his voice holding the horde in stasis. He appeared on the surface of the water, walking on it in the manner the skeletons did. He passed by them and stepped onto the skin of the fish, climbing the steep side until he reached the relatively flat back where Orb and the others stood.

He paused in his singing, standing before them. The skeletons resumed their dancing and advancing.

"They're trying to make a skeleton of Jonah!" Orb exclaimed. "Can you stop them?"

"With the Song of Power," Nat replied. "You may know it as the Song of Day."

"Quick, before they touch!" Orb urged.

"Give me a beat," he said, spotting the drummer.

The drummer settled down to his drums and started the beat. It was a standard pattern, as he did not know what was wanted.

Natasha resumed his singing. It was the same song as before, but more forceful; the sound seemed to make the very atmosphere reverberate. The night lightened, then became day, the sun riding high and striking through the mass of the storm cloud, vaporizing it and turning the black waves green. The light became intense, causing the white bones of the skeletons to shine.

Nat gestured to the drummer, and the beat picked up. The song became louder, the feeling in it so intense that Orb felt as if she were riding a muscular stallion through an endless fire. Her nightie dried and became diaphanous.

The skeletons felt it, too. They started to move, but not in their dance. They were trying to escape, but could not; the sun's beams bore pitilessly on them. They were rocking to the drum beats, as if shaken by some invisible hand. Then they were falling apart, their bones disassociating and dropping into the water with little splashes. In a moment, all the skeletons were gone.

Nat brought his song to a close. As he did so, the day faded, and the night of reality returned. But the storm was gone, and so were the skeletons; those abolitions had not been illusions.

Orb flung her arms around him and kissed him on the cheek. "You rescued me again!" she exclaimed.

"It was my pleasure," he said gallantly.

Then Orb remembered her situation. She was in her scant nightie, on the back of a monstrous fish, and her friends were watching. She let go and drew back a little.

Somewhat awkwardly, she performed introductions. "Nat, this is Lou-Mae . . ." She went through the names; Natasha acknowledged gracefully, and the others were polite.

"Maybe we should go inside and let Jonah swim back into the sky where he likes it," Jezebel suggested.

Nat looked about. "Just how did you get up here?" he inquired.

"Jezebel brought us," Orb said. "She—"

"No secret," Jezebel cut in. "I'm a demoness. Take my hand; I'll lead you in."

Orb, knowing the succubus' suspicion about Natasha, kept quiet. Nat took her hand, and Orb took the other, and they walked down through the flesh and into the fish's comfortable interior.

Jezebel turned them loose and went back for the others.

"Not to appear unduly critical," Nat said, "but are you sure you can trust a demon?"

"This one, yes. Demons vary as widely as do living creatures; they fit no single mold."

He shrugged. "I wouldn't know."

Abruptly, the scene froze. All sound and motion ceased, leaving Orb alone untouched. Natasha stood like a statue, three-quarters of the way through his shrug.

Then two new figures appeared. They did not enter; they simply became present. One was cloaked in black, the other in white.

"Let me guess," Orb said. She glanced at the black figure, then at the white. "Thanatos—and Chronos." Of course it was no guess for Thanatos; she had interacted with him before, when he put her together with the Livin' Sludge.

"Even so," the Incarnation of Death agreed, with a hideous smile on his skull-face. This time he did not lay back his hood, so the effect continued, but Orb now had no concern about it. Any person Luna trusted was worthwhile. "Chronos has stopped time so that we may converse. We fear you are being deceived."

"I hate being deceived," Orb said. "My mother warned me of a trap before, and even with that warning I barely escaped it. Is there more trouble coming?"

"There may be," Thanatos said. "It is our concern that this individual may be demonic, perhaps an agent of Satan. It is not safe for you to be involved with him if this is the case."

"Involved!" Orb exclaimed. But of course she was, in the general sense; for the second time, Natasha had saved her from a very bad situation. "What gives you the notion that Nat could be demonic? He was just saying that—"

"We believe that your objectivity is vital to certain future events," Thanatos said. "Satan is aware of this and may be trying to influence you by sending a minion. The realms of time on Earth and of the Afterlife may be subject to compromise. We would not want your future to be distorted by any agent of Satan."

"My future? If one of you is the Incarnation of Time, surely you can readily check my future and satisfy yourselves as to its adequacy!"

"Not readily," Chronos said, speaking for the first time. He looked like a normal living man, once allowance was made for his office. "The future is not fixed; it is multiple, and it is constantly changing. There are variants covering a spectrum of alternatives, some of which are positive, some negative. It is our interest to encourage the positive."

"But surely you can see whether Satan has any influence on many of those variants, and whether Natasha has any involvement," Orb protested. "In fact, you can follow Nat's life forward and back, and discover whether he is human or demon, can't you?"

"Not readily," Chronos said. "Satan is adept in his manipulations and can clothe reality with illusion so cleverly that it becomes almost impossible to separate the two. The real Natasha could have been replaced by a demon who emulates him perfectly, and I would have to devote far more of my attention to tracing this down than I can spare from my duties."

"Needle in the haystack," Orb said, seeing the problem. It had not occurred to her that a real man could be replaced by a demon, but of course it was possible. "In that case, you, Thanatos, should be able to test this man and verify his nature directly. After all, you can read souls, and demons don't have souls, do they?"

"It is true that they don't," Thanatos agreed. "But for a deception of this nature, it would be relatively simple for Satan to provide a demon with the simulation of a soul. My tools for measuring souls are relatively crude; I am not God." He smiled grimly.

"You are saying that with all the powers the two of you possess, you can not tell whether a given entity is human or demon?" Orb asked incredulously.

"Ordinarily it would be no problem," Thanatos said. "In this case, it may be."

Orb whistled internally. Obviously she had overrated the powers of the Incarnations! "How then should I tell whether Natasha is human or demon?"

"I suspect you will have to fall back on the old-fashioned devices," Thanatos said. "Demons are not subject to certain limitations of human beings, such as their fixed forms, but do have limitations of their actions that living people lack, such as what they may touch or say."

"You mean the Christian Cross? A demon can't touch it?"

"And holy water, or any sanctified relic. Neither can a demon say the name of God or sing a hymn. He may undertake enormous convolutions to avoid exposure by such means, to divert the subject, perhaps to ridicule the necessity, but when directly challenged, he can not do these things."

"But not all demons are creatures of Satan!" Orb protested. "Some can be quite decent folk."

"The limits do not reflect decency," Thanatos said. "They reflect origin. We concede that a good demon may be a better friend than a bad human being—but the bad human can touch the Cross, while the good demon can not. The barrier is absolute. That is why such tests have been established; it is not possible to cheat such identification."

"So you want me to test Natasha? To see whether he is of human or demonic stock?"

"Correct," Thanatos said.

"And if I do, and he turns out to be a demon—what does that prove? As you said, a good demon may be better than a bad human being—and a bad man could be an agent of Satan, too."

"Unlikely, in this case," Thanatos said. "The original Natasha is a good man; Chronos has already checked his timeline and verified this. He would never align with Satan; indeed, he would oppose Satan with all his power. Only Satan could arrange to replace such a man with a demon simulacrum. Therefore, if this is a demon, it has to be Satan's minion. We hope this is not the case, but we believe it must be tested."

Orb sighed. Their logic seemed tight. "Very well; I will test him—in my own time. If he should turn out to be a demon, I certainly shall have nothing to do with him. But I'm sure this is not the case; after all, he has twice rescued me from severe distress and he has taught me part of the Llano."

"What he claims is the Llano," Chronos said, gesturing with his left hand.

Orb saw that there was a ring on one of his fingers. It looked just like the one Mym had given her: a tiny coiled snake.

"That ring!" she said. "How did you come by it, Chronos?"

He glanced at it, as if startled. "Oh, this charm? It is of demonic nature, but aligned with the forces of good. There are many of them, all very similar."

"Luna has some," Thanatos said. "I'm sure she would give you one, if you asked."

Disgruntled by this revelation of the commonness of a charm she had thought unique, Orb retreated. "No, of course not; I was just curious." For an instant she had almost had a bad vision of someone stealing the ring from her baby; but of course, that was impossible; the ring could not be stolen or taken by force; it had to be honestly given. Her daughter would keep her ring until reaching the age of discretion; then she could do with it as she chose.

Unless Tinka had not put it on Orlene's finger, but instead had sold it . . .

No! Orb knew her friend would never have done such a thing. She adjusted her emotion and addressed the present situation. They had been talking about the Llano—and there was another body blow to her certainty. "You mean that was not part of the Llano Natasha taught me? The Song of the Morning?"

The two Incarnations exchanged glances. Both shook their heads in perplexity. "I'm afraid neither of us knows that song," Thanatos said after a moment. "The Llano is a different kind of magic from that we utilize. Perhaps what he has taught you is valid. That would not necessarily exonerate him; if it is not a religious piece . . ."

"It's a—a natural piece," she said, lacking a proper description. "It makes the dawn come, and the day brighten, and it destroyed the dancing skeletons that threatened us. Would an emissary from Satan sing such a song?"

"That does seem doubtful," Thanatos admitted. "You say it actually banished demonic creatures?"

"It actually did."

"I don't see how a creature of Satan's would do that." Thanatos shrugged. "But of course that is not my specialty. Mars would know the answer; he is the expert in combat, especially against demonic forces."

"Well, at such time as I encounter Mars, I will ask him," Orb said. "Meanwhile, I can certainly make the other tests; that should make the matter academic."

"We appreciate your cooperation," Thanatos said. Then Chronos lifted his other hand, which now held a large, glowing hourglass, started to tilt it—and abruptly the two were gone, and Natasha resumed animation.

Orb scrambled feverishly amidst her thoughts. What had they been talking about, before the stasis? She hated deceiving the man, but until she was sure of his nature—

Ah—about demons. They had agreed that not all demons were evil. That seemed ironic, in view of the timing of the arrival of the visitors.

"I can show you how nice Jezebel is," Orb said.

Then Jezebel reappeared, with Lou-Mae and the drummer at her hands.

"Jez, would you mind very much if I performed a test on you?" Orb asked, feeling embarrassed.

"Welcome," the succubus said. "Just let me fetch in the last pair." She disappeared through the wall and soon returned with Betsy and the organist.

They assembled in the main chamber. "What was this test?" Jezebel inquired.

"Well, I have been warned that—" Orb hesitated, but saw no diplomatic way to say it. "—that Natasha might be of demonic origin. So—"

Nat straightened. "How's that?"

"So I need to run a test," Orb continued doggedly. "But I need a—a control person, to verify that the indications are valid. That the test works."

"Who made such a suggestion?" Nat asked, becoming nettled.

Orb forced herself to face him. "Chronos and Thanatos. They told me that—well, never mind that. I hope you're willing to—"

"I hardly expected a reception of this nature," Nat said. "It would seem to me that—" But now he broke off, for the others were gazing at him.

"You know," Jezebel said, "if there is one thing that demon skeletons would respect, it would be an agent of Satan's."

Nat stared at her angrily. "You ought to know, demoness."

"They told me that my—my destiny was important," Orb said. "That Satan might try to influence me. So I really have no choice."

Nat grimaced. "You insist on this—this trial?"

"I'm afraid I do," Orb said miserably.

"Then let's have the test," he snapped. "What do you have in mind?"

Orb addressed Jezebel. "Please repeat after me the words I say." The succubus nodded. The others were silent; they were embarrassed by this scene.

"Demon," Orb said.

Jezebel smiled. "Demon."

"Person."

"Person."

"Angel."

Jezebel shook her head. "You know I won't say that."

"But could you if you wanted to?"

"Want to? I wish I could! But it's impossible."

"Hell," Orb said.

Betsy jumped. Jezebel smiled. "She's not swearing," she explained. "Hell."

"Earth."

"Earth."

"Heaven."

Jezebel balked. "If only . . . " she said sadly.

"Satan."

"Satan."

"God."

Jezebel spread her hands, defeated.

"Thank you," Orb said. She turned to Natasha.

"Angel. Heaven. God," he said, disgusted.

Orb felt guilty. "Does someone have a cross?"

"I do," Lou-Mae said quickly. She drew on a thin gold chain at her neck and brought up a fine silver cross.

"Give it to Jezebel," Orb said.

"Please, no," Jezebel said. "Its approach would damage me."

"I'll take it," Nat said. He extended his hand and took the cross. He glanced at Orb. "Satisfied?"

"Almost," Orb said, wishing she had never gotten into this. "I would like to sing a hymn."

"Let's spare the demoness the pain of attempting that," Nat said grimly. He handed back the cross, then inhaled, and sang:

"I'm just a poor wayfaring stranger,
A-traveling through this world of woe;
But there's no sickness, toil nor danger,
In that bright world to which I go."

As he sang, the walls of the chamber faded, and the gloom of the exterior night developed. The darkness was not total; rather, it was the murk of a dismal twilight, through which the man seemed to be trudging. The world of woe.

He proceeded through it, concluding:

"I'm going there to meet my Savior,
To sing his praise for evermore,
I'm just a going over Jordan,
I'm just a going over home."

As he did, the light increased, as from the overflowing brilliance of a transcendent realm ahead. Then, at the seeming point of realization, the effect faded, and the walls of the chamber reappeared.

Natasha glanced once more at Orb, then faced about, and stalked toward the wall.

"Wait!" Orb cried. "I had no choice—"

But already he was fading out. She picked up the harmonies of the traveling theme and knew he was going to some other point on the globe. She tried to match it, but could not. He was gone, and she had no way of telling where.

"I guess I'd be mad, too, if someone accused me of being a demon, and I wasn't," Jezebel said.

"Especially after he helped someone out of a jam," the drummer added.

"You're not helping much, you know," Lou-Mae said.

Orb fled to her bedroom, where she flung herself down sobbing. She was hardly aware as the big fish resumed swimming, moving up through the air, reorienting on the original destination.

What else could she have done?

– 12 –

SONG OF EVENING

Time passed, but Natasha did not return. The Livin' Sludge completed its engagement in Hawaii and made it safely back across the ocean. Now that Orb knew the Song of Day, she had no fear of the dancing skeletons; indeed, she was not certain they existed any more. She was grateful to Nat for teaching it to her, wanted to thank him, and could not. Oh, if only she had not affronted him by testing him! Yet still she did not see what else she could have done, given the warning of Thanatos and Chronos.

Lou-Mae shook her head. "You had better go to him, Orb," she said. "We've got a few days off now; why don't we stop at the Llano plain, and you can look for him?"

"I think he would have appeared by this time, if he wanted to," Orb said sadly.

"He's a man. He has his foolish pride. He wants you to make the first move. Go out and sing for him, and he'll hear."

Orb felt hope. "You think so?"

"I don't know a lot about men, but Jezebel does, and she makes a lot of sense. She says they think they're superior. They really believe that their animal lust is nature's highest calling. Pretend you can't live without him."

"I don't think I have to pretend," Orb said forlornly.

Lou-Mae smiled ruefully. "I know how it is. Pretend you're pretending. There's not a man alive and not too many dead who would turn away from you if you sang and danced and pleaded."

"But I don't want to plead! I have my own pride!"

"What's your pride worth, without him? Same as mine without Danny-Boy?"

"Very little," Orb admitted. "He asked to court me, and I thought it was just opportunism, but every time I hear him sing—"She shook her head. "I just want to be with him."

"That man certainly can sing," Lou-Mae agreed. "I thought no one could match you, but he—" She shrugged.

"He can sing," Orb repeated. "I think I live, now, to sing with him."

Jezebel entered the chamber. "Someone sings as well as Orb? That I don't believe."

"You don't?" Lou-Mae asked. "You were there. You didn't like it?"

"I was where?"

"Down on the ocean, when Orb danced with the skeletons."

"Orb did what?"

Both Lou-Mae and Orb looked at her askance. "You don't remember?" Orb asked.

"I certainly don't! What are you talking about?"

Orb glanced at Lou-Mae. Did the demoness have a short memory? How could an episode like that have escaped her so soon?

"Maybe it was a dream," Lou-Mae said diplomatically.

Jezebel shrugged. "Demons don't dream."

The guitarist wandered in, fuzzy-eyed, for it was still before noon. "Hey, big momma," he mumbled, embracing Jezebel.

"'Sokay, kid," the demoness said, stroking his head.

Orb almost choked. *By day?* When the succubus was middle-aged?

Then she realized that their relationship had become more than a nocturnal thing. The guitarist, deeply insecure, had emotional need for a luscious, adoring woman by night—and for a mature, supportive mother figure by day. Jezebel was serving both needs. Orb realized that she had no call to feel disgusted; it was better that she understand, just as it was better that she comprehend her own nature.

So it was that Jonah swam to the region of the Llano, and Orb got out and took another walk by herself. It was summer now, and the air was nice.

She sang the Song of the Morning, and the dawn came magically, and the flowers bloomed, but Natasha did not appear. She sang the Song of Day, but it wasn't the same without him.

Then she experimented with a combination—some of the travel theme merged with some of the storm-generation theme and some of the Song of the Morning. The result was strange.

The night closed, as it did at the onset of the Song of the Morning, but when the dawn came it was inverted. The land was redorange, the sky green, and the sunrise blue. The illuminated clouds were bright, while the sun was a dark ball. The bright region seemed to be the coldest, while the shadows were warm.

When the flowers bloomed, they started as blossoms and budded stems and roots. Startled, Orb focused more closely on them, and they came apart into separating circles and ovals and lines, as if reduced to their composites, which were mathematical. A larger pattern formed as the parts of the flowers intersected each other, extending their network into the sky and the ground. The ground became translucent, then lost its remaining cohesion.

Orb found herself standing on a pattern whose reality was shifting. The ground had become the lines of the pattern, and her feet were sliding down between the lines. Her orientation changed, so that she was no longer vertical, but it didn't seem to matter. She was as she was, and reality was around her.

Reality? This was no variant of the reality she had known all her life! The pattern fragments of strange flowers were everywhere, filling her world, displacing what she had known. It was pretty in its fashion, but she preferred the normal values.

She had stopped singing, but the pattern remained. It seemed she could not simply revert to normality.

She sang again, the straight Song of the Morning, with no admixture of other aspects of the Llano. The fabric of the inverted flowers tore, and curled to either side as if it were paper, and disappered.

She stood in a kind of channel that contained a single ridge whose cross section was triangular. It seemed to be made of firm plastic, bright yellow. It was high enough for her to sit on. Beyond the channel there seemed to be nothing, no wall, no landscape, just emptiness.

She sighted along the ridge. To one side it narrowed in the distance until it disappeared. To the other, it broadened until it filled everything.

Perspective? No, it was literal; the size of the ridge really did change with its location; only the convention of her prior experience had made it seem to be even.

Then she saw something moving. It seemed to be a spindle or double cone, rolling along the ridge. But as it moved toward her, it expanded in diameter and evidently in mass, for the ridge was vibrating increasingly. It came toward her, gathering velocity.

She remembered her geometry classes, where much effort had been expended in the analysis of conic sections. One formula defined a slice of the cone, with the size and shape of the slice determined by the parameters of the equation. Some sections were perfect circles, others were ovals, and others looped through on the inside but never closed on the outside. If a knife were taken to a physical cone, so that it sliced through the cone at different angles, these were the shapes it could make.

Now, it seemed, she had encountered the original cone. Size was one of its variables; as it changed its location, it expanded to fill the universe as it existed at that site. That meant that there was no room left for Orb; she was an intruder on its space. What would happen when it reached the spot where she stood?

The thing was coming at her with logarithmic acceleration. She was about to find out! Growing rapidly enormous, it rolled upon her. She would be crushed!

She sang again, the start of the Song of the Morning. The fabric of the ridge and double cone tore and curled, exposing the reality beyond.

It was green. A thought gave her momentary hope: the Green Mother, Nature—could she be here? But it faded.

This was a forest, with huge, quiet trees. Moss and ferns grew up their dusky trunks. Vines descended from their branches. Thick foliage grew at their bases.

But it was poison foliage. The surfaces of the leaves glistened with exudation. Orb knew it would be disaster for her to allow that to touch any part of her.

Yet the foliage grew all around. She could not take a step without encountering it. As she watched, it extended visibly, the branches closing in.

This was not the reality she desired! She sang again, and it tore across as the others had, peeling back to reveal what lay beyond.

It was a city, with many tall buildings. Highways cut through it, separating the sections, and walks crisscrossed, reuniting the sections. She was standing in the center of a broad street.

A truck came down that street, its tires squealing. It bore down on her. She ran to the side, but the truck corrected its course to intercept her. Now she knew that she was no detached spectator; these settings were trying to eradicate her!

She sang again, and the street curled up, more paper, taking the truck with it. The new reality was revealed below.

This was a plush chamber, evidently an ornate boudoir, with a huge round bed piled with pillows.

In fact, she was in the bed, clad in a sheer nightrobe, the type calculated to drive any man who saw any women in it to a madness of lust.

A door burst open, and a man entered. No, not a man—he had goat's horns and goat's feet and a caprine beard. His body was furry, his ears were pointed, and his nose projected into a snout. He had one other attribute that was both obvious and shocking. He was a satyr—the original creature of lust.

The satyr's blazing eye fell on her. He gave a bleat of anticipation and leaped toward her, his salient characteristic leading. There could be absolutely no question of his intent; it was manifest in his nature and his action.

Orb whammed him in the snoot with a pillow. She rolled off the bed and fled across the floor toward the door. But as she reached it, it closed, merging seamlessly with the wall. She scraped her fingernails across it, trying to gain purchase, but there was nothing.

The satyr made a grunt of urgency and leaped again. He was incredibly agile. Orb dodged to the side, but one hooflike hand caught her robe. The material stretched like hot cheese but did not tear; in a moment he was hauling her in, hand over hand, the material molding itself to her backside while it stretched out in a tent before her, bringing her forward in a state worse than nakedness.

She raised a foot to push him away, but he caught her leg and hauled on it, his hoof-fingers hot on her flesh. Drool spilled from his mouth as he brought that salient characteristic into position.

Orb finally remembered her only weapon here, her voice. She sang, and the fabric of the setting tore and curled, the satyr's expression of lust converting to rage as he saw her escaping him.

How had she gotten into this? Could she really have found herself raped by a vision conjured by a modification in the Llano?

Now she stood near the peak of a snowy mountain, the wind cutting cruelly. She still wore the sheer material of the robe; it bagged in front, clung behind, and offered no protection at all from the wind. Already her bare feet were slipping on the icy slope, causing her to lurch toward a clifflike descent.

She sang, and the scene tore away. Now she was in deep night, with stars in their myriads surrounding her. In fact she seemed to be in space, for the stars were in every direction. One was larger than the others, closer, hotter; it drew on her body, hauling her in to itself. Its sphere seemed to expand enormously, its fires reaching out like tentacles. Her gown burst into flame.

She sang—and the scene tore. She stood naked at a shell-covered beach, the waves of a restless ocean surging against it. One wave developed far out, hunching itself into greater mass, looming high and savage as it crashed toward her. She turned and ran from it—but the beach was a narrow island, with no high ground at all, no protection. The wave loomed over her, a white crest broadening at its fringe as its devastating descent commenced.

She sang, and the white crest became a tear. The wave was paper, disintegrating as the tear spread.

She was in a great, dimly illuminated cave, with stalactites extending from the ceiling in toothlike points. All the hues of precious onyx shone from them; lovely swirls and patterns manifested in the dripping stone.

This setting, at least, seemed to offer no immediate threat. Orb cast about for some natural exit, knowing that if she sang again, the scene would tear and thrust her into a new one that might be worse. She had to find some better way out!

She remained naked. It seemed that whatever she lost on one

setting remained in that setting; she could not recover it in the next. But perhaps she could find new clothing here and keep it with her.

She walked between the stalactites, finding a path through the cave. The light was brighter downslope; maybe that was the exit to the surface.

It turned out to be the light of a fire. Creatures squatted beside it. She walked toward them, glad for this sign of civilization. "Do you have—?" she began.

The creatures looked up, then leaped up. They were demons, huge and shaggy!

Orb opened her mouth to sing, but paused. The demons seemed afraid rather than aggressive. One of their number remained down, evidently wounded or ill.

"I will—trade you," Orb said, poised to sing herself into another setting if attacked. "Some clothing—for some healing. Do you understand?"

The demons watched noncommittally.

"I—I know a demon," Orb continued. "A succubus. Once I helped her overcome her curse. I think if I sang a regular song— it might help your friend."

Still they stood. They did not seem to comprehend her words. But as long as they did not attack . . .

She moved slowly toward the sick one. What could she sing that was not the Llano and that might help? Did the song matter, as long as her intent was to help? Why not use one of her old favorites, then?

"By yon bonnie banks and by yon bonnie braes,
Where the sun shines bright on Loch Lomond . . . "

She did not have her harp with her, but the magic came, and it touched the sick demon. The demon stirred, and a light seemed to play about it. It lifted one arm, its paw hesitating in the air.

Orb reached out and caught the paw. With direct physical contact, the channel of magic intensified. She felt the illness in the creature, but already the malaise was retreating before the healing she was making. By the time the song was done, the creature was much improved.

She let go its paw. "I think the tide has turned," she said. "It may take a few days yet."

One of the standing demons moved. It tramped to a pile of furs in an alcove. It lifted one and held it out.

They had understood! Gratefully, Orb took the fur. She draped it about her shoulders. It was heavy but warm, reaching down to her knees. It would do.

"Thank you," she said. "Do you know a way out? A way to reach my kind?"

They shrugged. Then there was a rumble. The floor shook, and a stalactite fell. It was a cave-in!

Orb started to sing the Llano, but paused again. She could escape—but what would happen to these demons if she did? Would they be crushed in the fall of rock? Some threat always manifested when she came into a scene; if she had brought this destruction with her, she was responsible.

She could not risk it. "Touch me!" she cried. "Make a chain!" She grabbed at the paw of the ill one and reached for one of the standing ones. "Everyone must touch!"

Confused, they linked paws, as the shaking of the cave increased. Orb sang the Song of the Morning again, and the setting tore apart. A new setting was revealed behind it—and she and the demons were in it, standing on a cloud.

Their cloud was floating above a tranquil landscape of crosshatched fields and trees. But the land was far below, and there seemed to be no safe way down. Meanwhile, their feet were sinking into the stuff of the cloud: it would not support them long.

"Must try again," Orb said, linking hands. She sang, and once again the fabric tore.

They were in what seemed to be giant intestines. Fluids pulsed through the flexing walls, and substances oozed. Thick fluid coursed along the base. Some of it touched the foot of one demon, and the creature jerked its foot away. Digestive acid, evidently!

Orb linked and sang again. The intestines tore. They emerged into a landscape of garbage.

Cans, banana peels, coffee grounds, automobile bumpers, and soiled sheets formed a mountain of refuse. The smell was terrible. Even the demons shied away from it.

Orb grabbed their paws and sang again. The garbage tore, and a new scene started to form—but this time she did not stop singing. She knew she had to break the endless cycle of settings somehow; perhaps this would do it.

The new setting tore even as it formed, and the one after that. Now they were in a mixture of settings, as parts of partly formed scenes overlapped other parts. It was like the pages of a picture book being flipped; by the time one scene could be glimpsed, it was gone.

Then Orb saw a castle. She stopped singing, trying to catch that scene, and succeeded. They stood in a lush garden replete with statuary, and ahead was a large stone castle. "Maybe we can get help here," she said. The demons, bemused, shrugged and shuffled after her as she marched toward the castle.

They came across three people near the back entrance. Two women and a man had evidently been relaxing on a stone patio. Both women were supremely beautiful, and the man—

Orb made a little scream of astonishment. "Mym!" she cried.

"Orb!" he replied. He rose gracefully to his feet and, in a moment, was embracing her. "How did you come here?"

"That's a complicated story," she said. "Just where are we?"

"In Purgatory. Didn't you know?" Then he stiffened. "Don't tell me you're dead!"

"Dead? Why should I be dead?"

"Very few living folk come here."

Then she absorbed what he had said. "This is Purgatory? Where the dead get sorted? What are *you* doing here?"

He gestured to the demons to make themselves comfortable, then led her to a chair. "I live here, now. I am Mars."

"Mars?" she repeated blankly.

"The Incarnation of War. I assumed the office, after—oh, we have much to catch up on!"

"I should think so," she agreed. "Perhaps you should introduce me to your friends."

"Oh, yes, of course," he said. "But first I must explain that—"He spread his hands, looking embarrassed.

"That our romance is over," Orb said. "Of course." Then she did a double-take. "You aren't stuttering or singing!"

"The Green Mother took my stutter," he said. "We—Incarnations do things for each other." He turned to the beautiful fair young woman. "This is Ligeia, my beloved. She is a dead princess; I met her in Hell." He smiled, realizing how that sounded. "Li, this is Orb, my first love."

Ligeia extended her hand. "He has told me much about you," she said graciously.

"And this is Lila, my mistress," Mym said, turning to the dusky woman. "She is a demoness, who can assume any form."

Lila extended her hand. "I can see why he loved you," she said huskily.

Orb's mouth worked twice before she connected it to her voice. "A demon mistress? Do I misunderstand?"

Ligeia laughed. "A prince can not be satisfied by a single woman," she explained. "He is best off with a harem. Since Lila can assume any form, she serves in lieu of a harem. But only when I am indisposed."

"You have been indisposed rather often, Li," the demoness remarked. "Do you think I don't realize that you are releasing him to me when you don't have to?"

"It becomes a princess to be generous, Li," the dead woman replied. "It is also known that no decent woman can match the performance of a damned creature." Both smiled; evidently no insult was intended.

"In my day, it seemed that one was enough," Orb said, deciding to take this lightly.

"After you, no single woman sufficed," Ligeia said.

"You know I didn't leave you voluntarily," Mym said. "I was kept under palace arrest until I agreed to spend a month with the princess selected for a political marriage. She was Rapture of Malachite, and she was no better pleased with the notion than I was."

"I saw a picture," Orb said. "Evidently you worked it out."

"I did not want to love her, but I did," Mym admitted. "Then I became Mars and brought her with me, but this existence wasn't right for her, and she left me. Now I love Ligeia. It is no affront to you, Orb. Had things been otherwise—"

"I understand," Orb said, beginning to. As a prince, Mym had been subject to the peculiar discipline of his office. Now he was filling the role of a prince in the form of an Incarnation, and women were indeed part of it.

"But now you must tell us how you came here in the company of demons," Mym said.

"I was looking for someone, and I sang the Llano incorrectly and got locked into a mélange of settings," Orb said. "Each had some threat for me, but I could escape it by singing for the next. The demons were in one; their cave was collapsing, so I brought them along. Now I need to find them a place to be."

Lila rose. "I will see to that," she said. "I know their kind."

"Another demon is my friend," Orb said. "I know you aren't necessarily bad folk."

"Not when we come under the influence of good human beings," Lila said. She approached the other demons and spoke to them in gutterals.

They clustered about her. At last someone spoke their language!

"Who were you looking for?" Mym inquired.

Orb feared she was starting a blush. "Like you, I have found other company. But we had a—a difference, and he left. So I was looking for him."

"I have no jealousy of your friend," Mym said. "I can have no further relationship with you. Ligeia knows that no demoness could ever replace her in my life, but you—I think I never stopped loving you, but now it must be the love of friendship. So it is best that you have your own companion. Tell me his name, and I will try to find him for you."

"Natasha," she said.

He cocked his head. "It *is* a man? I never thought—"

It was Orb's turn to laugh. "He is a man. He sings—as well as I do, with the same magic."

"Now I *am* jealous," Mym said, smiling. "Of course you must love him."

Lila returned. "They will take up residence in our garden," she said. "There is a cave that resembles the one they knew. They say Orb healed one of them."

"He was ill," Orb said.

"I heard you mention Natasha," Lila said.

"Yes. He is the one I—"

"I knew one by that name once," the demoness said. "Before I departed Hell."

"A demon of Hell?" Orb asked. "Surely a coincidence of names."

"I hope so. This was no demon. He was a pseudonym of Satan himself."

Orb's breath caught. Speechless, she stared at the demoness. "Orb would not have any interest in Satan!" Mym said.

"I realize that. But I have known Satan for millennia. It is hard for any living person to appreciate the levels of his deviousness. If he wished to make an impression on Orb—"

"He does," Orb said. "He tried to marry me. Natasha saved me."

"I would not trust that," Lila said. "Such a scene could readily have been staged."

"But I tested him," Orb protested. "I made him touch the cross, sing a hymn—that's why he was angry."

Ligeia nodded. "Those are good tests. Surely, then, this is a legitimate man."

"Not necessarily," Lila said. "While it is true that no creature of Hell, including Satan, can do these things, Satan can *seem* to do them when he chooses to. He could devise a cross from infernal material—"

"It was a silver cross, worn by a pure-minded friend," Orb said.

"That would be very hard for him to get around," Lila admitted. "Still, he might wear a glove, or even generate an illusory hand, so that he only appeared to touch it. There are ways and ways, and Satan knows them all."

Orb was becoming increasingly upset. "I—I think I am close to loving this man. I can not bear to think that he could be—"

"Surely he is not," Ligeia said.

But Mym remained doubtful. "It would be better to be absolutely sure," he said. "Is there any way we can set Orb's mind at ease? The notion of her being with Satan is appalling."

"He can generate an illusion for any purpose," Lila said. "Only through his actions can you know him absolutely, for he is the Incarnation of Evil."

"What action could Satan never take?" Mym asked.

"He could never do genuine good or side with right against

wrong. Evil must do evil, though he may try to clothe it in a semblance of good."

"Then can we arrange one more test?" Mym asked. "It has become doubly important to me to set Orb's mind at ease. I would not have her hurt in any way, for she was my first love and my salvation. Also, I would not give Satan any satisfaction of any nature whatsoever; he is my absolute enemy."

"I don't want any more tests!" Orb said. "I can't even find Nat now, and if—"

"This is for me more than for you," Mym said "I must be assured that you are in good company, on a personal and professional level."

"Professional level?"

"I am the Incarnation of War," he reminded her. "If Satan is trying to subvert you, we may be sure it is for nefarious purpose, and it behooves me to prevent it."

Orb was swayed. She knew that Mym would not play her false, even if their romance was over. Lila's words had instilled in her a new doubt, and it was indeed best to have it laid to rest. She did feel guilty, yet still could not see a better course.

She temporized. "I don't even know where he is, now," she said. "Or exactly how I got here. If I sing again, this reality may tear across, and I'll be lost again."

"The Llano is a dangerous tool," Lila said. "You have to use it properly, or reality does get compromised."

"You know of it?" Mym asked her. "I have heard of it, but never had experience with it."

"The Llano can move a person in and out of Hell itself," the demoness said. "It is one of the fundamental tools of magic. The tiniest portion of it can work what some call miracles. When she misapplied it, naturally she was in trouble. But all she has to do is neutralize the imperfection, and the problem will end."

"You know how to do that?" Orb asked, excited.

"That much, yes," Lila said. "Of course it won't work for me, because of my origin, and I don't know the rest of it, but that much I picked up from a former lover, some centuries back. It's just an elementary countertheme that resets things at their nominal values."

"Will you teach it to me?"

"Certainly. It goes like this." She paused. "Just a moment while I assume my singing form." She shimmered, and was abruptly in the form of a stout opera singer, complete with medieval robe.

She sang a rather simple melody that nevertheless had an eerie quality. It lasted only a few bars.

"That's it?" Orb asked.

"That's it," the demoness said, shifting back to her sultry, sexy format. "As I said, it can have no effect when I sing it, but you should be able to make it work. It's the same theme the Purgatory Computer now uses to cancel its own glitches, but it long predates the computer."

Orb sang it, exactly as she heard it. She felt the magic operating, subtly adjusting what was around her, as if something that had been unseated was now settling into its proper place.

"I felt it!" Lila said. "Now you can travel under control."

"You mean I can use the same mechanism to change voluntarily?" Orb asked. "I can go to any of those settings?"

"Of course. Wasn't that what you intended to do before?"

"No. I just got caught up in it."

"That must have been a harrowing experience," Ligeia said sympathetically.

"It was. If I hadn't happened to land here, there's no telling where I would have finished."

"Oh, you would have been all right," the demoness said. "You were just skipping randomly about the globe. You would have come to somewhere you recognized, eventually."

"But there was danger everywhere I went!" Orb said. "Bad waves, cave-ins, or satyrs chasing me in a bedroom—" Now, belatedly, she became aware of her attire: the demons' fur draped somewhat haphazardly across her bare body. She must be a sight!

"Probably because of the error in the Llano," Lila said. "It tended to put you at the dangerous fringe of reality. This site is no exception: Purgatory is the brink of Hell for many souls."

"Do you—I'm not properly dressed—" Orb said, embarrassed.

"Of course, my dear," Ligeia said immediately. "I have many suitable gowns. Except—"

"They won't hold up beyond Purgatory," Lila finished. "Because they are of supernatural stuff. Let me make her present material into an outfit." She approached.

"But I can't take it off!" Orb protested, glancing at Mym.

"No need," Lila said. "He's gotten quite enough ogling for this hour." She touched the fur, and it writhed, changing shape on Orb, becoming a snugly fitting sleeveless dress. "You are a well-formed woman."

"Mym's taste runs to that," Orb said, glancing at each of the other females significantly.

"But only your flesh is mortal," Ligeia said. "Therein lies its special appeal."

"Yours is mortal!" Mym told her.

Ligeia put her hand to her mouth. "Oh, so it is, now! I forgot! I animated a mortal body for you." She turned to him. "So why *were* you ogling her, dear?"

"She didn't realize what she was showing," he said, shamefacedly.

"And there we have the voyeuristic truth of the male nature," Ligeia said. "Always seeking the illicit thrill. I'm sure he never stared like that when you offered it to him openly, Orb." She frowned. "Do you realize what this means?"

"I'm banished to the harem," Mym said, chastened.

Ligeia turned to Lila. "Can you assume the form of a zombie?"

"Of course," the demoness agreed. "Exactly how rotten did you have in mind?"

Then, seeing Mym's look of horror, all three women burst out laughing. "Actually, I can play the role perfectly well myself," Ligeia said. "I was dead a long time before he rescued me from Hell."

Obviously Ligeia was very sure of her man. Orb envied her the relationship, and not just because it was with Mym.

"If I may change the subject," Mym said determinedly, "we do have a test to run. Let me look up this man Natasha." He turned and walked into the castle.

"I tease him, but he is a good man," Ligeia said.

"I know," Orb agreed.

"Is it true you had his baby?"

"It is true," Orb said, surprised. "How did you know?"

"I looked you up in the record, of course. I thought it best to learn his past history. It was terrible, what happened to you."

"I suppose I can't object, since my mother is Fate."

"Do you know why Satan should be interested in you?"

"There was an old prophecy, dating from before my birth, that indicated I might marry Evil," Orb said. "I suppose that attracted his attention."

"It could simply be the challenge of it," Lila said. "Satan has no shortage of women, demon, dead, and mortal alike. But like our Incarnation here, he prefers what is forbidden. A lovely mortal woman, daughter of an Incarnation, forewarned against him—there, perhaps, is the ultimate challenge."

"And so it can remain," Orb said hotly. "I have absolutely no interest in the Prince of Evil!"

"Of course you don't," Ligeia agreed.

Mym emerged from the castle. "I found a listing for a male singer named Natasha," he said. "That must be him. I noted his summoning theme, so Orb can reach him."

"Summoning theme?" Orb asked.

"Every person has one," Mym explained. "That's how we Incarnations locate individuals accurately and quickly. I'm sure Thanatos and Fate couldn't operate without that tool."

"And what of the test, dear?" Ligeia inquired.

"There is an action coming up now," he said. "An encroachment on a reservation that could escalate into bloodshed. I was going to squelch it outright, but it should do for this purpose. The sides of good and evil are solidly established. Satan is unable to associate with good, so if he's involved, it will be clear enough."

"A possible escalation into war—and you wish to suppress it?" Orb asked, surprised.

"An irony," he responded. "As Mars, I try to control war, not incite it. Otherwise much evil would accrue, as Satan well knows."

"And you say I can summon Nat?" Orb asked, not at ease about this.

"Yes. I suggest you bring him to the site and ask him for help in righting wrong. A true mortal will be able to do that; Satan will not."

"But if I test him again—"

"I will intercede," Mym said. "He will listen to me."

She sighed. "I hope so. I don't want another man taken from me in the manner of the first."

"I think your mother would not do that to you again," he said. "Actually, she was not in the office when it happened. Now take my hand."

She took his hand. A great red sword appeared in his free hand, glowing. Then the scene was moving around them, with blurred rapidity. Suddenly they were standing at the fringe of an American Indian village. Women and children were packing dried herbs, evidently preparing them for sale.

"They are magic herbs," Mym explained. "The native Indian magic remains the most potent; they have had many generations to perfect it. Those herbs are extraordinarily valuable and represent the major source of income for the tribe."

"Why aren't they reacting to us?" Orb asked.

"We are invisible and inaudible. You will become evident to them when you lose physical contact with me; my sword does it. But first I must give you the summoning theme. The action is just about to break."

"But isn't there danger, then?"

He brought out a colored stone. "Hold this; it will protect you from physical harm."

She took it. "It looks like one of the Magician's charms that Luna inherited."

"It relates," he agreed. "Now here is the theme." He hummed a brief melody.

"That will summon Natasha?" she asked doubtfully.

"It will," he assured her. "Be ready; the raiders are on their way." He turned loose her hand.

Orb walked toward the Indians. "Hello," she called. "May I see your wares?"

The Indians turned to her, surprised, for they had not seen her arrive.

Then a carpet sailed in, one of the large utility models, supporting four rough-looking men. They carried rifles and pistols. One of them fired into the air. "That stuff is ours!" he cried.

The Indians were stunned. Their braves were not present; the packing was women's work. They had no weapons.

The carpet landed beside the table. The men began grabbing at the bags of herbs.

A young woman approached them. "Please," she said. "Those herbs—we have labored all season to grow and harvest and prepare them, so their magic would be strong. Our tribe will starve if—"

One of the men whirled on her. "Shut up, squaw!" he said, tossing a bag into a bin on the carpet. Then he took a second look. The woman was lovely, the very picture of the Indian maiden, her black hair braided with bright beads. "Second thought, I'll take you, too."

The maiden screamed, but the man produced a rope and trussed her up and tossed her onto the carpet. "You're going to be a lot of fun, breaking in, before I put you on the slave market," he grunted.

Another man spotted Orb. "Hey, there's one for me!" he exclaimed, stepping toward her.

But Orb had seen more than enough. She sang the summoning melody.

Suddenly Natasha was there, looking startled. "Who—why—?"

"I did it," Orb said. "These men are stealing these Indians' livelihood, and their women, too. We must stop them!"

"But—"

"It's a plain case of good against evil," Orb said. "Don't you agree?"

"Hey, who's this character?" the first woman-stealing man demanded.

"Is she right?" Nat demanded in return. "Are you stealing what belongs to these Indians?"

"Yeah," the man said, drawing his pistol. "You object?"

Nat looked at Orb, then at the bound Indian woman. "What do you plan to do with the captive?"

The man laughed. "Hey, you a pansy? Whatcha *think* I'm going to do with the squaw?" He brought the gun to bear.

"Then I must ask you to desist," Nat said. "What you are doing is wrong."

"Bye-bye, pansy," the man said, and pulled the trigger.

But as he did so, Natasha started to sing. It sounded like another aspect of the Song of Day, but it had more of an edge to it.

The effect was electric. The man froze in place, his finger not quite completing its pull on the trigger. The others also stood where they were, not moving. The sound mesmerized them, as it did Orb; it was impossible to act while it dominated.

Then it intensified. Nat's voice seemed to fill the universe with its power, making the trees shiver and the ground reverberate. He faced the men, and the men crumpled and fell, their eyes staring unblinkingly into the sky. The effect was directed, for Orb did not fall, and neither did the Indian women and children.

Then Nat eased off and finally let the song expire. The four raiders were unconscious, sprawled around the carpet.

"Let's get this trash out," Nat said. He grabbed a man by sleeve and foot and heaved him onto the carpet.

Orb went to the bound woman, quickly untying her. Then the two of them unloaded the bags of herbs, while Nat attended to the other men. Soon all the bags were back on the table, and all the men were piled ignominiously on the carpet.

Then Nat stood on the carpet and sang again. This time it was a variant of the travel theme. The outlines of all of them and the carpet fuzzed and then were gone.

The Indians stared. "I think he's taking them somewhere," Orb said.

Mym appeared. "I apologize for my suspicion," he said. "That man acted for good." He shook his head. "I thought you were being generous when you said he could sing as well as you could, but though his voice is different, it is hardly inferior. He is surely a proper match for you."

Natasha reappeared, coalescing at the spot he had left. He was now alone. "I deposited them in Siberia, the Russian steppe," he said with satisfaction. "They will have a very difficult time getting free of that! Over there, they don't coddle criminals—" He broke off, spotting Mym.

"This is Mars," Orb said quickly.

"The Incarnation of War?" Nat asked, seeming not entirely pleased. "Aren't you a trifle late?"

"He—I knew him before," Orb said.

"You were involved in war?"

"We were lovers," Mym said.

Nat's mouth hardened. "I never inquired into her past history," he said. "It wasn't my business."

Orb saw any possible reconciliation going up in smoke. "Nat, please, let me explain! It was years ago, before I knew you, and it's over! He—he has a princess consort and a mistress now."

Nat's grimness did not abate. "You, an Incarnation, dazzled an innocent mortal woman, then threw her over for a princess?"

"He wasn't an Incarnation then," Orb said desperately. "He didn't throw me over! He was a prince in hiding, and he stuttered, and I had his baby—"

Nat turned to her. "That seems more than a passing flirtation."

Mym nodded. "It was love. I would have died for her. But my father would have had her killed; I had to leave, though I wronged her grievously. Now, as she said, it is over."

"It doesn't *look* over," Nat said.

"Nat, please!" Orb repeated.

Mym's giant red sword reappeared in his hand. "Do you call me liar, sir?" The Sword brightened ominously, and a trace of blood appeared at his lip.

"No, Mym, no!" Orb cried, knowing what the blood portended. He was a berserker!

Nat considered for an awful moment. "I would not call an Incarnation a liar," he said at last.

Mym relaxed. "Allow me to clarify. I will never stop loving Orb; she is the finest mortal woman I have known. But what was an affair has become a deep friendship, and I have no romantic designs on her, nor she on me. We each have developed other interests. I want only what is best for her."

"I appreciate the clarification," Nat said.

"Can't you see she loves you?" Mym flared.

"No!" Orb cried, appalled.

"No?" Nat asked, turning again to her.

A gulf of sorts opened around her. "Please . . ." she whispered.

"I shouldn't have spoken," Mym said. "I shall depart." He disappeared.

"I thought you thought I was a demon," Nat said.

"I wronged you," Orb said. "I was looking for you, and got lost, and found Mym, and—oh, please, don't go again!"

"I suppose a person has to be more careful about love than about mere acquaintance, especially when a prior relationship has been destroyed."

Orb stood there, feeling naked, feeling the tears on her face. "Nat, you once asked to court me. . . . "

Abruptly he smiled. "And shall again!" he said. "I shall sing you the Song of Evening." Without further preamble he broke into song.

It was a theme like the Song of the Morning, and like the Song of Day, but warmer than either and more tender. The melody of it spread out, bringing a kind of twilight that intensified the scene. The Indian women stood rapt, becoming beautiful, the beads in their hair glowing. The trees of the nearby grove were preternaturally green and clear. The sand was golden. The hues of early sunset spread across the sky.

Orb had never experienced a song like this. It lifted her up, warmed her, suffused her with its tender emotion, and made her an utterly feeling creature. Her gaze fixed on Nat as he sang, and he seemed to glow like the sun, so handsome that the pleasure of his visage coursed through and through her. He had called it the Song of Evening, but she recognized its other identification: the Song of Love.

She moved toward him as if floating on a cloud, her arms spread. The doubt in her faded, banished by the delightful fire that was spreading from her heart to her bosom and to her whole being. As the song finished, the seeming night closed in, and she came into his arms.

She did love him.

– 13 –

GREEN MOTHER

"You found him," Jezebel said as Orb coalesced into the kitchen.

"How did you know?" Orb asked, facetiously, looking at the middle-aged woman.

"The whole fish brightened by two magnitudes when you arrived," the succubus said.

"I'm in love."

"What else is new? Can you eat?"

"Of course not!"

"Try, anyway." And the woman set about the poaching of two eggs in the air, not bothering with stove or pot. Orb found that she could, after all, eat.

The others came in. "When's the wedding?" Lou-Mae inquired.

Orb choked on her egg.

Betsy laughed. "Not this afternoon, then."

"Am I wearing a sign?" Orb demanded. "I just discovered my own feelings, and here all of you—"

"We're teasing," Lou-Mae explained. "You were the only one of the party hunting, and we're so glad it's over."

"Tell us everything," Betsy said eagerly.

Orb raised her hands in surrender. She told them everything. "And now I must tell my mother," she said as she concluded.

A spider appeared, growing as it slid down its thread, transforming into Niobe. "She already knows," she said.

"Oops! I forgot your office! You were watching my thread!"

"Only passingly, dear; it is only one of millions." Niobe smiled. "But a special one."

"Nat's not a demon," Orb said.

Niobe paused, as if something odd had happened. Then she regrouped. "I really came on other business. You see, your thread is now taking a significant direction, and I think it is time for you to be aware of this."

"Is this something that is not our business?" Lou-Mae asked. "We can leave."

"No, my dear," Niobe said. "It may be your business." She shimmered, and her grandmotherly form appeared: a large black woman. "You bet, honey," this figure agreed. Then she changed into a young and very pretty oriental girl. "Yes, true," she said. "We know of youth and love, too."

Lou-Mae took this in stride, having encountered Fate before, as did the three males, but Betsy's eyes grew round.

Orb touched her hand. "My mother is an Aspect of Fate," she explained. "There are three Aspects: Clotho, Lachesis, and Atropos. They spin the threads of life, measure them, and cut them; they also partake of the different ages of life. It seems that this is a business visit."

Niobe reappeared. "You see, Orb, you are destined to assume the office of the most powerful of the Earthly Incarnations— Nature. You may have noticed your powers increasing."

Now it was Orb's turn to be astonished. "An Incarnation— me?"

"Some come to their office almost randomly, as with Death, who kills his predecessor, or Time, who simply takes the Hourglass. But some are destined for their office because of what they are. Gaea is ready to retire, and you are the one with the capacity to take her place. Your magic operates through music; as you approach the office, your power increases. Already you are able to do much of what the Green Mother does; and soon you will do more."

"But it's the Llano!" Orb protested. "The song is the mechanism; without it I have no special abilities."

"True only to a degree," Niobe said. "The Llano is one of the world's most versatile and potent tools, but only a few possess the ability to use it. You have shown that ability. You can use it, but you can also go beyond it, as you perfect your skill, and apply the principles of natural magic more directly. The song is merely a useful guideline during your learning stage. You are the candidate."

"But I never sought—never imagined—"

"Neither did I, dear. But now it has become plain. You are very near the point of decision; if you choose not to assume the office, you will have to guide your course accordingly."

"But I'm in love with a mortal man!"

Niobe nodded. "Nor do I for a moment disparage that. I was an Incarnation and I came to love a mortal man; I left my office in order to marry him, and you were the result. I have never regretted that decision. But I made it when I was well informed. Now it is necessary for you to be similarly informed, as you make your decision."

"You mean I can't—can't marry and be an Incarnation?"

"Oh, it is possible for an Incarnation to marry," Niobe said. "But there are considerations. An Incarnation is frozen at her present level; she never ages, never dies—and can't have children."

"No children," Orb repeated numbly.

"While her mortal spouse does age and die and could sire offspring—with a mortal woman. That is why I stepped down, dear. I could have married your father and kept my office, but I could never have given him the attention he deserved, and you would not have come into being. Of course I had already borne a child; still—"

And Orb had borne a child. But to be denied the ability to bear another, one she could keep and raise as part of a family—that horrified her. "Are you saying that I must turn down the office?"

"By no means, dear. I am merely trying to impress on you the gravity of your decision. You can marry, you can become Nature, you can do both, or do neither—but the distinctions between the four situations are significant. I believe you should discuss these matters with your friends and take all the time you need to come to your best understanding of the alternatives."

"We don't know anything about this!" Lou-Mae protested. "We would not presume to—"

The grandmotherly Aspect, Atropos, reappeared. "You going to marry your man while he's on H, child?"

"No!" Lou-Mae said, her lip trembling. "But—"

Atropos pointed at Orb. "As Nature, she can take him off H, permanently. That's why this is your business."

Lou-Mae looked at the drummer. "Oh, Danny-Boy!" she exclaimed. "If she could do that—"

The pretty oriental girl, Clotho, appeared. "And you," she said, looking at Jezebel. "As Nature, she could abate your curse permanently and give you control over your form by day and night."

The succubus reeled as if struck. "I would sell my soul, if I had one, for that!"

Niobe, the Lachesis Aspect, returned. "And you, dear," she said to Betsy, "could have ideal weather at your farm, permanently, if she chose it—as well as a man free of addiction."

"But I have not been able to do these things!" Orb said. "Anything I do is only temporary."

"The fact that you can do them even on a temporary basis is indicative," Niobe said. "As Nature, your powers would be enormously increased. You could restore sight to the blind, mortality to those cursed with immortality, and youth to an old tree. Anything within the scope of your office—and that is a great deal indeed. It is no minor position you contemplate."

Orb sat back, her thoughts whirling. Such power!

"Consider well, my child," Niobe said. Then she became the spider, and the spider climbed up the thread and disappeared.

"I guess it *is* our business!" Lou-Mae said. "All those dreams, for all of us! We thought the Llano, but it's you who can do it."

"I've got to think!" Orb exclaimed, tormented. "It's so easy to misuse power, and I know so little about it! I never realized when I sought the Llano—!" She sang the travel theme, and in a moment was on the far, deserted island where she had encountered the traveling sponge.

But in another moment Natasha was there. She flung herself

into his embrace. "Oh, Nat, suddenly it's so complicated!" she exclaimed. "I thought the world was mine, when I loved you, but now—"

"I sensed your disquiet," he said. "That's why I came."

"I am to be an Incarnation, like my mother—if I choose. But then I could not have a family and would not age."

"Would not age?" he asked, hardly displeased. "You would always be as you are now?"

Orb had to flush. He was of course a man, much concerned with a woman's form. "But I could not have another baby," she reminded him.

He frowned. "Could you perhaps have the baby, then assume the office?"

"No!" Orb cried in sudden anguish, remembering how she had to give away Orlene. "I want a real family! I want to devote myself to my baby, to raise it to maturity, as my mother raised me!"

"Of course," he said, chastened.

"But oh, there is so much good I might do, if I assume the office!"

"I will love you as a mortal or as an Incarnation," Nat said. "I can not make this choice for you. But I wonder—"

"Yes? You have a notion?"

"It seems to me that you already can do a great deal. Perhaps you can accomplish much of the good you wish, without giving up your mortality."

Orb thought about that. "I suppose I could try. But you know, the Llano gives you similar powers. I wonder—"

"I am not destined for the office of Nature!" he exclaimed, laughing. "I have quested for the Llano since childhood and rehearsed every fragment of it I have found, over and over. I have done all I can with it; progress is always slower than before. I am at my limit. But you—you hear a theme once, and it works for you as well as it ever has for me! Your potential is much greater than mine. I would be jealous, if you weren't so beautiful." Then he sobered. "Or are you saying that you have outgrown me already? I would not try to hold you, if—"

"Oh, no, Nat, no!" she cried, kissing him.

"Then you might try the things you wish to, and that will give you a clearer notion of your choices. I will abide your decision, whatever it may be."

"You are most kind, Nat," she said. "I will try."

She returned to Jonah. "My powers have been increasing," she announced. "Now I know what they are leading toward. I was not able to do some things before, but maybe now I can. Are you willing to experiment?"

The drummer stepped forward. "You know what I want," he said. "If you want to try, I sure do."

Lou-Mae glanced sidelong at him. "You *are* talking about H?" she inquired archly, and the others laughed.

Jonah swam to ground, and they debarked. The experiment had to be conducted outside of Jonah, to ensure that it was not the big fish's magic operating.

Orb tried the Song of Evening, that she had just learned. The sound of it had confirmed her burgeoning love for Natasha; could it abate the dread addiction, for the sake of love? She willed the craving for H to be banished from her subject, the drummer.

The twilight came, and the beauty of the nocturnal vision. Clouds became orange. She remembered Nat's comment about the facility with which she picked up the new themes. She had not considered this before, but it was true that she had always learned music at a rate others could not match. Certainly the parts of the Llano worked for her as they had for him, and she had not rehearsed them.

The drummer screamed.

Startled, Orb cut short her song.

"No, go on!" he gasped. "It's working!"

She resumed the song. Now she saw that the drummer was gyrating in an unnatural way, as if opposing forces were drawing at him. He screamed again, but this time she did not pause. It seemed that a temporary nullification of the craving was painless, but that a complete cure was another matter.

From him something came. It looked like a ghostly snake, its head rocking back and forth as if seeking something to strike at. But the melody hauled it forth, drawing it on out of the body. It was the H addiction, struggling all the way, inflicting the punishment of its withdrawal. It glared balefully around, remaining hooked in by its tail, like a moray eel. Then the theme became too much for it, and it let go and puffed into smoke. The drummer fell to the ground.

Lou-Mae ran to him, cradling his head in her arms, as Orb's song ended. "Is it—?"

"It's gone!" he panted. "It was hell letting go, but it's gone!"

"We can't be sure of that," Orb warned him. "Only time will tell—time away from Jonah."

"I tell you, I *know!*" he said. "H has let go!"

"I hope so," Lou-Mae said. "Why don't you and I stay out here, and if you can go the day and night without H . . ."

He brightened. "Yeh! No more unicorns!"

"Shut your mouth!" But she was smiling.

Orb and the others retreated to the big fish. "If it really is so—" she began.

"You can do me next!" the guitarist and the organist said together.

"And me," Jezebel said.

"Meanwhile, I believe I'll rest," Orb said. She went to her room and lay down. But she found she could not truly relax; she was too excited.

"Nat, where are you?" she whispered.

He coalesced beside her bed. "Did you speak my name?"

She sat up and wrapped her arms around his waist. "How did you hear me?"

"Once I knew that I loved you, I invoked that aspect of the Llano that attunes to your speaking my name. It is akin to Jonah's relaying of talking to the object of the discussion. Thus I heard you immediately."

"You know about Jonah? How is that?"

"He is one of the special creatures of this world. I discovered his nature on one of the bypaths of my search for the Llano. But he would not help me on my quest; he knew that I was not destined to complete it."

"But he's helping me!" Orb said.

"Because you have the potential I lack."

"Or because I danced the *tanana* for him."

Nat pursed his lips. "Yes, I had forgotten you know that dance! Some time you must dance it with me! But beware; it—"

"Drives men mad with desire," she concluded, laughing. "I

will save it for some suitable occasion.'' One of the things she liked about Nat was his conduct; he never tried to take advantage of her, either by the straying of his hands or by suggestion. She knew he desired her, but he was too disciplined to allow it to show aggressively. He reminded her of Mym in that respect; that seemed to make Mym's endorsement more significant.

"I should not remain here," he said, confirming her assessment.

"I thought I was tired, but I can't rest," she said. "Is there somewhere we can go?"

"There is all the world. Perhaps you should visit your friends."

"I'd like that," she agreed. "But it gets so complicated, expanding to the size of the globe, then orienting on the tiny mote that is my destination. I don't know where all my friends are and wouldn't want to intrude uninvited."

"But you don't need to expand, or to intrude," he said. "The Llano provides many ways to locate folk and to travel."

"It does? All I know is the expansion and the tear-sheet settings that occurred when I misused it."

"I'm sorry, I thought you knew, and traveled as you did from preference. I will show you the other mechanisms."

"Oh, will you?" Orb clapped her hands in little-girl style, thrilled.

"For example, the theme I just used to hear you speak my name. You must think of the person to whom you wish to attune, then sing this melody." He sang a brief, strange, evocative tune. "Thereafter you will hear if that person speaks your name or even thinks of you with more than passing interest. Then—"

"Wait, let me master that first!" Orb exclaimed. "Let me see— on whom shall I orient? I know—my Gypsy friend Tinka!" She focused on the lovely blind girl and sang the melody. She felt the peculiar action of it reaching out, attuning, linking the two of them in a passive bond.

Nat shook his head. "You never cease to amaze me! It took me a year to perfect that application!"

"Does it work for nonhuman folk, too?"

"It works for anyone who cares for you. The bond is already there; the Llano merely activates it."

"Then I could attune to Jonah, so that I could always return to him without having to search."

"Indeed—if he cares for you. I'm sure he does, or he would not be serving you now."

Orb sang the theme again, focusing on the big fish. She felt the reaching, and the body of Jonah shuddered. He was aware!

"Oh, this is fun!" Orb exclaimed. "I'd better attune to Lou-Mae, so I will know if they need me." She did so.

Nat shook his head. "Three attunations in hardly as many minutes. One at a time is all I can manage!"

"Oh, I didn't mean to embarrass you! I didn't realize—"

"You did not embarrass me, you please me more than ever. I see how much greater your potential is than mine; I never before encountered such a woman. But perhaps you will tire of me."

She turned and kissed him. "I doubt it, Nat. I do not sing better than you; it is merely the magic that is in my nature, no virtue in me. You have done what you have done the hard way, and I respect that."

She continued attuning, reveling in this wonderful new power he had shown her. Then she paused, startled.

"Someone's thinking of me!"

"Focus on it; you should be able to recognize the person."

Orb concentrated. "It—it's Tinka! She wants to see me!"

"Then I must show you the quick-travel theme," Nat said. "Maintain your focus on her and sing this melody." He sang another, similarly evocative.

Orb held her focus, and sang—and it was as if a page were turning, not tearing, but simply moving aside to reveal the new location. This was the true application of the mechanism she had misused before! She had used the Song of Morning, which was marvelous for its purpose, but ill-suited for travel. Now she had the correct application.

The new page was Tinka's home. The blind girl stood there, gazing out the window though she could not see the view. Here it was dawn, the rays of the sun struggling to crest the high outline of the mountain range.

"Hello," Orb said in Calo, the Gypsy language.

Tinka turned as if unsurprised. She was fuller in the body than she had been, quite buxom. "I wanted to show you my baby."

Her baby! Orb had forgotten. She had perhaps enabled the girl to become fertile; of course she should meet the baby!

Tinka showed her to the crib. There was a healthy baby boy, sleeping. Orb realized that the woman's increase in bosom was because she was nursing.

"If you could tell me what he looks like—" Tinka said wistfully.

"He's beautiful!" Orb exclaimed. But she felt a siege of her heart, abruptly reminded of her own baby, Orlene. To have been able to keep her, to raise her . . .

"I never really missed my sight, until . . ."

Orb banished her own discomfort. "You must have it!" she exclaimed. She took Tinka's hands and sang the Song of Morning, willing the Gypsy to see what she was seeing.

The room grew dark. Then the dawn came, with its lovely colors and effects. Tinka shivered as the magic coursed through her. The morning clouds brightened, becoming gray and white and red and orange, their edges blazing. The beams of the sun spread out in a semicircular splay, illuminating the sky, then dropping down to touch the land, warming it.

Tinka made an exclamation of wonder. She was seeing it!

Orb held on to her and kept on singing. The plants sprouted, and grew, and budded, and flowered. Beauty surrounded them.

Then the song ended. Tinka was breathing hard. "I saw the dawn!" she whispered.

"What do you see now?"

"It is dark again. But for a while—"

"You have the magic," Orb said. "Sing with me." She held on to Tinka's hands and began the Song of Morning again.

Tinka joined her, for she did have the magic and could pick up any melody immediately. The strength of the pulse going through them doubled, the magic reaching out and in, permeating their bodies. The sunrise manifested with greater intensity, and the flowers seemed real.

As the song ended, Orb let go of her friend and reached down to pluck one flower. She brought it up before Tinka's face. "What do you see?"

Tinka blinked. Her eyes focused. "All pretty, with petals—" she said, reaching for it. "Fuzzy—"

"Sing again!" Orb said. She took hold of the girl's wrist below the flower and sang the Song of Morning a third time. Tinka joined her, and the magic intensified even more than before.

When it was done, the flower in Tinka's hand had grown into a bouquet, and her eyes were fixed on it. "Now it is clear," she said.

"Look at your son," Orb said.

They turned to the crib and looked down. "He is beautiful!" Tinka said. Then she began to cry.

Orb held her, knowing that she had found another aspect of her developing power. Nature controlled vision; nature could remove it or restore it. The Llano was only a tool; Orb's will and Tinka's readiness had shaped it.

Then the baby awoke and began to fuss. Tinka picked him up.

"I will return often, until I am sure you can see always," Orb said. "Call me when you want me." Then she thought the new travel theme and turned the page to her room in Jonah.

Nat was gone, but she thought his name, and he appeared. "Oh, Nat, I went to her and I saw her baby and I cured her blindness!" Orb exclaimed. "I used a power of Nature!"

"I am glad for you."

"I really should rest now."

"Yes, you should."

"Let's go somewhere."

"Anywhere you wish."

Orb considered. "I—I wish I could see my baby. Orlene. Not to interfere. Just—" She shrugged. "But I don't know how to tune in on someone who doesn't think of me."

"It can be done," he said. "This variant of the theme." He sang again, and it was similar to the attuning melody, but distinct.

Orb thought of Orlene and sang the variant. She felt the magic questing out in a search pattern, traversing the world at its own rate. Then it fastened on its object, and the connection had been invoked.

"But can I really go to her?" Orb asked uncertainly.

"Exactly as you just did."

"But I don't want to disturb her life. I just want to see."

Nat smiled. "If you use the expansion-travel theme, but do not coalesce completely, you will be invisible and inaudible, like a ghost. In fact, that is how ghosts do it, but they are capable of no more, generally. This way." He sang and faded out.

Orb tried it. Instead of expanding, she simply lost mass, until she stood with too little substance to be visible. Now that she was in this state, she was able to perceive Nat, similarly diffuse. "Oh, there are so many things to learn!" she exclaimed. Her voice was a mere shadow.

"But you learn them so readily," he said. He was not whispering, but she knew that only she could hear him. They were on a slightly different plane of existence.

"Come with me to see my daughter," she invited him.

"As you wish."

Orb moved into the page-turning theme, orienting on Orlene, and in a moment was there. Nat stood beside her.

The little girl was in nursery school, waiting her turn on a swing. She was about three years old, wearing a smudged dress and comfortable little shoes. Her hair was tied back in a ponytail, its buckwheat-honey hue matching Orb's hair exactly. She was well fed and seemed contented.

Then the child raised her hand. Orb saw the serpent-ring on one finger. Evidently the ring was squeezing, telling her something. She looked at Orb, her eyes unfocused.

"She knows I'm here!" Orb exclaimed. "The ring told her!" Hastily she turned the page, back to Jonah.

Nat reappeared beside her. "That is a good protective charm your daughter has," he remarked.

"I can't visit her again," Orb said, upset. "If she knows I'm there, then I'm interfering in her life."

"But she is your child."

"Not any more. I must let her have her own life. I can see she is well cared for; Tinka gave her to a good family. No, I must leave her alone."

Then Orb turned to Nat, put her head into his shoulder, and cried. She could be the Green Mother, but she could not be a mother to her child.

The tour of the Livin' Sludge continued, and its success continued. The magic enchanted audiences of every type. But the group knew that their association was coming to a conclusion, because Orb had found the Llano and would in due course be assuming the office for which she was destined.

The abatement of the drummer's addiction held; he was free of H. Orb did the others similarly. Their quest was finished, and they made plans for marriage and regular employment in the future. She sang to Jonah, enabling him to swim in water again; his curse, too, was done. He continued to serve the group, but it was understood that, after the tour, he would go his own way. She sang for Jezebel, making permanent the state that Jonah had enabled on a temporary basis, and giving her the power to control her form by day or night. The guitarist knew that she would never age naturally—but now she could age unnaturally, as desired. After he died of old age, she would go her way, but would never need to indulge men indiscriminately.

Orb visited the old water oak. The hamadryad recognized her, but would not approach. Then Orb sang a song of renewal to the tree, and the deadwood revivified and the leaves brightened. She had contributed perhaps a century to its life and strengthened the hamadryad accordingly. Then the dryad came down and touched Orb's hand fleetingly in gratitude. It was enough.

Orb spent much time with Natasha, and her devotion to him became broader and deeper and more intense. He was everything she had wanted in a man, without realizing it until encountering him. He was always there when she needed him, but he never made demands. They visited far places and sang together, and the very heavens seemed to brighten and assume new significance. It had been a long time since she had loved a man, and she was glad that the interim was over.

Meanwhile, her powers of magic grew. She could make the weather change with little more than the thought of a given melody; a more involved effort had caused the pattern of the climate in the neighborhood of Betsy's farm to become regular, so that there were neither droughts nor floods to destroy the crops. But once she had done favors for her friends, she became dissatisfied; there was too much grief and hunger and mysery in the world. The problem of drug addiction was not limited to the Livin' Sludge, and the problem of physical impairment not limited to Tinka's blindness. How could she deal with these things on a spot basis, while neglecting their far worse aspects on the global basis?

So it was that as the tour came to an end, she arrived at her decision. She was going to take the office of Nature.

She told her friends aboard Jonah. They congratulated her, unsurprised. "You can still drop in on us, when you have time," Lou-Mae said, giving her a hug. "We'll always be your friends."

"But have you told Natasha?" Jezebel asked.

"He said he could accept whatever I decided."

"Men do say that, but they don't always mean it. Better tell him soon."

"I will tell him now," Orb said. She turned the page and was beside Nat, where he waited for her on a tiny tropical island.

He smiled at her. "You have decided."

"I have decided. I will give up the family and will assume the office of Nature. I will be the Green Mother."

"Then I will have something to ask you, and something to tell you," he said gravely.

"Ask me now, and tell me now," she invited him.

He smiled. "These are not minor matters. Assume your office; then I will say what I must say."

"But you said you could accept my decision!" she said, alarmed.

"And so I can and will. But I think you must make your decision on me after you make it on the other matter."

"If you don't want me to be Nature—"

"Please, I must not discuss that now. There is a thing I may tell you only when you have the office."

Troubled, she gazed at him. "Suddenly I don't understand you, Natasha!"

"I may say no more at this time," he said apologetically.

"Then I will say more," she said. "I love you and want to marry you. If you can not accept marriage to an Incarnation—"

"I think we shall have the proof of that soon enough."

"If only you would tell me what is bothering you, before I—before it is too late to change my mind!"

He simply shrugged.

Nettled, she turned the page to a far place, the snowy top of the mountain she had visited when her travels had been uncontrolled. There she spread her arms and opened her desire; she would be Gaea.

She felt herself expanding, not physically but psychically. Her awareness came to encompass all the world, every living thing in it, and every unliving thing. She permeated the globe, partaking of its nature everywhere. She *became* its nature.

Now the hunger in Africa was not a concept to her; it was part of her. The cold weather near the poles and the hot weather near the equator were aspects of her being. All the happiness of the world was hers, and all the suffering.

Now she knew why the prior Gaea had been ready to let the office go. It was such an enormous burden of responsibility! Suddenly the power she had acquired seemed inadequate to the job she had to do. How could one person oversee all the activities of the world? She was overwhelmed.

She felt herself tugged. She went where summoned and came to her residence in Purgatory. It most resembled a giant tree, but its appearance was malleable; it could be whatever she wanted. The prior Gaea had left it for her.

A young man was by the entrance. "I represent your staff," he said. "I am a lesser Incarnation; we thought it best that I handle the transition, until you are comfortable in the office. The staff consists of souls trained to serve you; they will continue to serve, or will retire in favor of replacements you may choose."

"Who are you?" she asked, surprised. "You look familiar."

"I should; I have just interacted with you. I am Eros."

"Eros! The—?"

"Incarnation of Love," he agreed.

Orb decided to set aside the implications for the moment. "You know how this office is run?"

"I know how it has been run. All decisions are yours, but we will help in whatever way you require. Perhaps you will want to interview the other lesser Incarnations who work with you, such as Phobos, Deimos, Hope—"

"In due course," Orb said. "I have one matter to settle before I get into it. Can you keep things on an even course for now?"

"If you direct, Gaea."

"Do so. I will return shortly." Orb knew she should get on into the mastery of her office, for it was important, but she simply couldn't wait to settle with Natasha.

She turned the page back to the isle. He was there. "I am Gaea," she said. "Now talk to me."

"Now there must be truth between us," he said.

"There has not been before?" she asked archly.

"There has not. I will explain. You must withhold your answer until you have heard the explanation."

"I will withhold my answer," she agreed.

"Gaea, I am asking you to marry me."

Orb relaxed. She had grown afraid he had changed his mind! But, heeding his caution, she did not answer.

"Now I must tell you that our relationship has been based on a lie. I am not the man I have represented to you. The testing of the prophecy is now upon us."

"The prophecy?" she asked blankly.

"That you might marry Evil."

"But—"

"Spell my name backwards."

Orb pieced it out. "Natasha. AHSATAN."

"And punctuate it. Ah, Satan. That is the realization of the truth. I am an Incarnation, as you are now. The Incarnation of Evil."

Appalled, Orb stared at him. Her worst horror was facing her— in the aspect of the man she loved.

– 14 –

FORBIDDEN SONG

"You are naturally confused," Nat said. "That is why you must hear my explanation. The attempt to void a valid prophecy can be a treacherous thing. When the Incarnations ascertained that the prophecy relating to Luna's relationship with Death and your relationship with Evil was valid, they were of course horrified. But it was not an absolute. It contained the qualifier 'may.' That meant there was doubt—and therefore room for negotiation."

"Negotiation!" Orb snorted.

"In the course of protecting Luna from My interference, your mother compromised her position on you. She promised to guide your thread away from politics, and I promised never to harm you. It was understood that this represented her acquiescence to My interest in you."

"Mother wouldn't—!"

"Of course, upon reconsideration, she regretted this, as did the other Incarnations, especially Mars, when he learned of it."

"Mars? Mym said you were a good man!"

"Not exactly. At any rate, I naturally inspected you more closely thereafter—and perceived your destiny as the Incarnation of Nature. Then My interest increased. I saw, too, that you were very like your mother, in her prior session as an Incarnation. She was the most beautiful woman of her generation, a terrible thorn in My side, but I confess to becoming somewhat smitten with her along the way."

"Niobe would never—!"

He nodded. "True, true. She would have nothing to do with Me. But when I saw how you resembled her, in appearance and mannerism, I knew I could be attracted to you as I was to her. Then it occurred to Me that a union between the Incarnations of Evil and Nature—"

"No!"

"Would give dominance of the mortal realm to Me. At last I had the opportunity to defeat Mine ancient antagonist. Therefore—"

"No! No!" Orb cried, understanding.

"Naturally the Incarnations opposed this suit. But Niobe had already compromised your thread, and there was the prophecy, whose application had suddenly clarified. Thus it was we negotiated. We set up a compromise, whereby I would be permitted to court you without interference from any other Incarnation—"

"They would *never*—"

"My dear, they thought I would fail. Because I agreed to court you wholly by lies, which are of course My specialty. I was required to lie to you at every turn, until the end. The end is now, and for the first time I am telling you the truth. I am Satan, the Incarnation of Evil, and I love you and want to marry you."

Orb was unable to accept this. Was Nat testing her love for him by making an impossible claim? How should she deal with this? All she could think of at the moment was to accept his statement as a starting place and explore it until the flaw was revealed.

"You say you are Satan and you lied to me throughout. But the aspects of the Llano you taught me are valid; they do work. I have been healing people, traveling in new ways—"

"I must clarify the levels of deceit I have employed. It is of course impossible to make every aspect of a situation a lie; there would be conflicts and paradoxes that would quickly render it nonsense. A lie has to be structured, internally consistent, so as to have the greatest final impact. Thus a lie is mostly truth, ironically. When the parts of a lie are verifiable as truth, it lends credence to the lie and gives it far more power than it would otherwise have. You might think of it as a mathematical analogy: negative numbers cancel each other out, but a structure of positive numbers that is then assigned a negative value is negative. Lies cancel out, while truth augments itself, but a structure of truth given a false value is the most potent lie of all.''

"I think you are leaving me behind,'' Orb said.

"What I told you of the Llano is true. But my purpose in telling you those truths was false. By showing you spot truths, I was deceiving you in a far more fundamental fashion. For one thing, I was encouraging you to believe that I was not Satan. Thus those minor truths were contributing to the greater lie.''

"But I tested you! I proved that you could not be a demon or Satan!''

"It was no valid test; it only deceived you.''

"Now that I can't accept! I had you touch a silver cross, sing a hymn—''

Nat nodded. "I realize how difficult this is for you, but I must make you understand the truth now. I used a device the Incarnations had not anticipated. I took you into three extensive visions, and the visions were lies though their parts were true. Little within those visions was valid in the real world.''

"You are confusing me again!'' she said hotly. This was evidently some sort of game, and she liked it not at all, but she had to play it through. "What were these visions?''

"Each was associated with a song: the Song of Awakening, the Song of Power, and the Song of Love. Three of the five major themes of the Llano, the Song of Songs, if you care to call it that. I lied to you when I said I knew only fragments of the Llano; I know all of it, but I can only *use* fragments.''

"Five themes?'' Orb asked, distracted for the moment by this information. "What are the other two?''

"The Songs of Loss and Dissolution. You would call them Night and Chaos. But you would not want to sing them.''

"Why not?''

"Orb, this is straying from the subject. It is my duty now to make you understand and believe the deceit I have practiced upon you, so that—''

"Teach me those songs," Orb said abruptly.

He looked flustered. "Gaea, I am trying to tell you the truth, and those themes are only mischief! I am the Lord of Mischief; I know! The themes of the Llano equate roughly to the five Elements, or the five Kingdoms, and as you know, some of those are dangerous. There may come an occasion when you have use for the Song of Night, but never for the Song of Chaos, and I would be deceiving you anew if I—"

"Five Elements?" Again the detail distracted her from the main thrust, as her mind sought relief from the awful truth that was encroaching on it.

"And five Kingdoms. But—"

"Animal, Vegetable, Mineral . . ."

"Demon and Spirit," he finished. "But the correspondence is only apparent, not substantive. Actually, every theme of the Llano aligns with every Element and Kingdom, forming the basis of the enormous power of Nature, once you learn to use it. That will take years, decades, but—"

"You say you are telling me the truth now," she said grimly. "Teach me those songs, then."

He sighed. "How hard it is for Satan to do good even by indirection! If it must be—"

"It must." Orb knew she was grasping at something irrelevant to the main issue, but her need now was to establish some basis for belief, to feel at least partly in control. To make Nat do her bidding, instead of telling her what she abhorred.

"Then I will teach them to you. But I beg of you, consult with the other Incarnations before you invoke Night, and never invoke Chaos, for it is forbidden."

"Then why does it exist?"

"Because it is the ultimate weapon against Me," he said reluctantly. "When all else fails—but believe Me, the cost is too great! I love you, Gaea, and—"

"Get on with it."

He sang the Song of Night. Darkness closed about them, like the gloom of absolute negation; nothing was visible or audible, and there seemed to be no sensation of any other kind. Only when he finished did the sensations of existence return.

"But if you sang it, it would not be mere illusion," he said. "It would—"

"And the other?"

He sang the song of Chaos. This time there was no effect; it was just a melody that bore an evident affiliation with the Songs of Morning, Day, Evening, and Night, but had a broken beat that gave it an uncanny awkwardness. Orb did not like it at all, but it was certainly no horror.

"That's it?" she asked, disappointed.

"It has no power for me. Or for anyone. Only for Gaea. Each Incarnation has one weapon against which no other Incarnation can stand, not even Me, not even Mine ancient rival. The Song of Chaos is the Green Mother's weapon. But I urge you, I plead with you, I beg you, Gaea—never invoke it! You have already made a captive of Me."

"But if what you say is true, you are my ultimate enemy!" she exclaimed. "And if it is not—"

"It is true. Every experience you had in association with the learning of the first three songs was part of their visions, and so each was a lie, but this is the truth."

"But the songs worked for me when I wasn't with you! I cured Tinka's blindness, got the Sludge off H—"

"The aspects of the Llano are valid. That lent verisimilitude to the visions. Not much else was true."

Orb felt as if her head were being compressed by the pressure of unwelcome information, and her heart was slowly turning cold. Still she fought the concept. "You are saying that when I first met you, when you helped save me from Satan's forced marriage—"

"That was not Satan. It was a demon playing the role. But the vision began before that."

"Before—" Orb considered. "You can't mean—when I talked to the Incarnations? To Mother and Gaea?"

"They were demons in the semblance of Incarnations."

"But they warned me of the trap and told me how to escape it!"

"By singing a duet with Natasha," he agreed. "A script to introduce Me in a form you could accept. Then there was the vision of the dancing skeletons—"

"A vision? That?" She was appalled anew.

"From the time you woke in the storm, until the time you resumed the trip to Hawaii. There was no storm; it was all the vision."

"But Thanatos and Chronos warned me about you—"

"Demons in their semblance. The real Incarnations would never have served Me in such fashion. The tests were mock; in the vision, My rules govern. In reality, I could not have accommodated those tests."

"You were so angry at me—"

"No. I merely seemed so. The vision had accomplished its purpose."

"And when I sought you—the mixed up Llano—"

"All vision, scripted by Me. In reality, your former lover Mym is Mars, and he has consort and mistress as represented, but you encountered none of these. When I sang, I accomplished no good, for there was no evil other than that of the script."

Belief was forcing itself upon her. "All—"

"All part of the courtship," he concluded. "To cause you to fall in love with Satan, so that you would marry Me, completing the prophecy."

"I—how could the Incarnations have gone along with this?"

"As I said, it was a compromise. They thought that I could not succeed in winning you through any tissue of lies—especially since I had to tell you the truth before I married you. It was their belief that you would at this point turn violently against Me."

Orb's head seemed to be whirling. "I can't believe this!" But she feared she could.

"I shall be glad to show you My domain. I think you will be convinced. Or you can ask any of the Incarnations."

"But—*why?* What do you care about the validity of an old prophecy?"

"You believe that I am lying now when I say I love you?" He seemed so earnest and was so handsome that she found herself wanting to believe.

She fought the desire off. "If you are Satan, you are made of lies! I must not believe you!"

"Then I will merely remind you of the power I stand to gain, if allied with the Incarnation of Nature. You and I together can swing the balance toward evil, and Mine antagonist will not prevail in the end. The crisis of power that Luna is to mediate will never occur; My victory will already have occurred."

"Luna! You expect me to betray her?"

"Join with Me, and I will see that no evil comes to her or any other you wish to protect."

"But Satan can not be believed!"

He held out his arm. "Scratch Me. Bind Me by blood. I will take any oath you wish. That you can believe."

She stared at him, becoming convinced. "Then you really are Satan, doing this for power?"

"For love and power, yes."

"Get away from me," she said dully.

He faded out.

For a long time she sat on the isle, staring out across the water. Slowly the sky clouded, and an unnatural stillness developed. The surface of the ocean became like glass. There was a grayness throughout.

At last she reacted. She began to sing the song of Night, and isle, sky, and ocean vibrated to the magic of it. Darkness closed, Stygian, impalpable, oppressive. As she sang, she expanded and discovered that the gloom enfolded all the globe; no one on Earth could see. Even so was the mood of her heart.

But it wasn't enough. She had suffered the loss of her love in the worst possible way, by being completely duped, and grief was not the appropriate emotion. The way those visions had been crafted so artfully to play on her innocence—'Can't you see she loves you?' demanded of Natasha by the pseudo-Mym while she protested that her affair with Mym was over, *protested this to Satan!*—leading her on, meddling freely with her deepest feelings! No, grief was not what was called for! *Rage* was the appropriate emotion! And what could she do about it?

Her being reached out and found the heart of the Llano, its most potent aspect—the Song of Chaos, the forbidden theme. Now in her fury she invoked it, starting a reaction that spread throughout the world. Her passion gave it maximum force, though she did not understand its implications. Her shock at the revelation Satan had made was finding its expression.

Ponderous and subtle forces had been invoked; the elements

of Water, Air, Fire, Earth, and Void were in motion. But the initial effects were slight. Some animation returned to the surface of the ocean, and the sun shone down more brightly. The day was warming.

Orb was disappointed. She had vented her outrage in the most effective way she knew, and it seemed to have fallen flat. What use was it to rail at what Satan had done to her, if nothing happened?

The heat increased. Vapor rose from the water. Orb became uncomfortable on the isle, because of the humidity, so turned the page to her tree-house in Purgatory.

Eros was there, looking grim. "What's the matter?" Orb asked.

"I wish you hadn't invoked the Song of Chaos," the youth said. "There is apt to be Hell to pay."

"To Hell with Hell!" Orb exclaimed. "Satan played a hell of a trick on me; I have a right to be angry!"

"To be angry, yes; to unleash Chaos on Earth, no. This is the one process that cannot be abated."

"Good! I don't want it abated! I want a real show!"

"That is irresponsible—" he started to say, but she turned a page and was back aboard Jonah.

The tour had been finished; the others were waiting only for Orb to get settled in her office, before dispersing to their new lives. Jezebel was the first to spot her. "You're back! How'd it go?"

Orb sighed. "I assumed the office and told Nat—but it was a disaster. He—"

Then she was crying, and Jezebel was holding her. Orb hardly cared about the anomaly of a demoness comforting the Incarnation of Nature; she simply needed support.

When she lifted her head, the others were there. Brokenly, she told them: "Natasha—is Satan. All his proofs of mortality were false. He wants me to join him in evil."

"But he touched my cross!" Betsy protested.

"It was a vision. He didn't really touch your cross; we all dreamed it happened."

"But I don't dream!" Jezebel said.

Suddenly something clicked. "It was a dream—the skeletons and touching the cross and singing the hymn and everything!"

Orb exclaimed. "And Jezebel doesn't dream! No wonder she
didn't remember it! If only we had taken the warning!"

"You mean—she wasn't really there?"

"Of course I wasn't there!" Jezebel said. "Since then I've
picked up what you're talking about; all of you had an experience
I didn't. But I never thought of Satan—I mean, that he could
have arranged it. I let you down!"

"No, Jez, no!" Orb exclaimed. "I let myself down! I was too
eager to believe the false proofs he offered. I should have questioned you!"

"There really wasn't time to get it straight," Lou-Mae said.
"Satan is clever, I'll say that for him."

"Fiendishly clever," Orb agreed bitterly.

"But what has happened to the weather?" Betsy asked. "It
seems so steamy out, all of a sudden."

"I'm afraid I did it," Orb said. "I was angry and I sang a new
aspect of the Llano, the Song of Night, and then it seems I invoked
Chaos."

"Chaos!" Jezebel exclaimed. "That dates from before the time
of H—of the good place, or of Hell, or mortality. Chaos hates
all of it!"

"But Chaos has no power now," Orb said.

"Not unless allowed it," the succubus said darkly. "You know
how it is when an evil demon gets summoned? If there isn't proper
protection, that demon can't be banished, and a whole lot of mischief can result. If Chaos takes hold—"

"I think I'd better get some advice," Orb said.

She turned the page to her mother, Niobe.

Niobe was at her residence in Purgatory. It resembled a monstrous spider web, with a home fashioned of silk.

"It's real trouble," Niobe said. "I queried the Purgatory Computer, and it says there is no telling what can result when Chaos
starts operating. It could cancel itself out, because there is a lot
of randomness in its nature, but it's more likely to run a pretty
rough course." She glanced askance at Orb. "Why did you
choose to start off your office by invoking such a dangerous
thing?"

"You know my temper," Orb said ruefully. "When I discovered that everything I had known of Natasha was false—" She

paused. "You did not come to me on the plain of the Llano to warn me of Satan's trap?"

Niobe shook her head. "We had agreed not to interfere."

"So it is true that you made a deal with Satan?"

"It is true. We were caught by the interpretation of the prophecy; no one knew the outcome except perhaps Chronos, and he would not talk. So we concluded that it was better to get the matter settled one way or the other. I had to trust that you would not be deceived."

"I was deceived," Orb said heavily. "I—fell in love with a simulacrum, in part because of challenges made by what I took to be the Incarnations, you included. Then I learned that it was Satan. What was I to do?"

Niobe shook her head. "Every Incarnation has to deal with Satan, and it is always difficult. I had to make a small tour of Hell to find the Magician before I could find the way to stop the threat Satan posed. Mars had to bring the world to the very verge of extinction by war before he could stop the threat Satan posed for him. Now it is your turn. I can not tell you what to do."

"It was Mym—Mars—the facsimile of Mars who finally convinced me that the man I know was not—what he was. All a vision!" Orb sighed. "Does he really have a consort and a demon mistress?"

"He really does," Niobe agreed. "But he would never have led you to Satan!"

"I was completely credulous," Orb said. "When Satan revealed himself, I couldn't believe it. When I did, I just wanted to strike back at something. So I sang. The most potent song I could. I suppose I was motivated by the fact that Satan himself urged me not to do it. Now I don't quite know what I've done."

"No one can know for certain, dear. But Chronos can probably make it right, if—"

"You mean by manipulating time? Isn't that dangerous?"

"Yes. But that may not be the problem in this instance."

"What *is* the problem?"

"We promised not to interfere until this matter has been decided. If Chronos took action now, it would constitute interference."

"The matter *has* been decided!" Orb said. "Now that I know the situation, I'll never deal with Satan!"

"It is not decided until Satan concedes defeat," Niobe said. "That is always the way it is in these tests of will."

"What does it take to make him concede defeat?" Orb asked irately.

Niobe spread her hands. "Each case is different. We'll simply have to wait and see."

"Does that mean we can't do anything to stop Chaos?"

"I fear it does. It is like an illness that must run its course. But it might be best to keep a close eye on that course."

"I'll try," Orb said.

She hugged her mother, then turned the page back to Jonah. And was appalled.

The big fish was rocking in a storm. The water no longer hurt him, but the winds were buffeting him back and forth, and the Sludge were hanging on to whatever offered.

"Why doesn't Jonah swim away from the storm?" Orb asked, grabbing hold herself.

"He's been trying to, but it keeps getting worse," Jezebel said. "Never seen weather like this before! It was all the big fish could do to drop Betsy and the organist off at her farm. They left their regards for you."

Orb looked out the transparent scales. It was hard to tell whether there was cloud or water outside, but certainly there was turbulence. She wished that Betsy and the organist had remained with Jonah.

"I'll find out how far it extends," she said. "Meanwhile, it may be uncomfortable here, but safe; weather can't really hurt Jonah." She expanded, becoming swiftly huge and diffuse, searching for the limit of the storm.

There seemed to be no limit, only confused patches of lesser intensity. Rain and swirl were everywhere. It was like a giant sauna. Evidently the rising heat and humidity were responsible.

But if the effect was global, what of the cold poles? Orb expanded to globe-size so she could investigate.

It was hot at the poles. Meltwater was pouring from the icecaps at such a rate that she knew that in a few days no ice would remain.

What would that do to the level of the ocean?

What of the seacoast cities? What of the lowlands? The great valleys that could flood?

She oriented on the traveling show in India, where she had first met Mym. She coalesced, assuming her natural form beside a wagon.

The rain of the monsoon was pouring down. But was it monsoon season here? She wasn't sure, and feared that this was an atypical phenomenon. The wagons were parked, for travel was impossible; the road was awash.

Drenched, she forged to the closest wagon. It looked like— yes, it was the mermaid's wagon.

Orb pounded on the door, announcing the presence of a visitor, then pushed it open and climbed inside.

"Orb!" the mermaid exclaimed. "It has been years!"

And what was she to say now? That she had started a process that represented danger for everyone here? That the water level could rise and flood them out?

But if she didn't give warning, what then?

"A lot has happened," Orb said. "There may be danger. I have come to warn you. This rain—it may get worse. I think you should get the wagons to higher ground."

The mermaid shook her head. "There is no road we can travel. We must wait it out here."

"But there may be flooding!"

The mermaid smiled. "That doesn't really frighten me, you know. I won't drown. But I suppose it could be bad for the others and the animals. Still, the wheels are already mired; we'll simply have to sit it out."

Orb saw that she was right. The show would not be moving. "I hope it's all right," she said, taking the mermaid's hand for a parting squeeze.

Outside she had another notion. She concentrated, trying to invoke the elements, so that she could bring coolth and dryness and abate the rain. But she could not; that aspect of her power had been pre-empted by the developing Chaos. She was helpless before the weather.

She turned the page to Ireland, to the place that retained its nostalgia for her: the water oak in the swamp. This time the hamadryad came down to greet her, still grateful for the rejuvenation. But the rain was blasting down here, too, and the wind was tearing at the foliage of the tree.

"I'm afraid it may flood," Orb said.

The hamadryad agreed; she was quite concerned. Already the level of the swamp water was high.

"And it is my fault," Orb continued unhappily. "I—I fell in love with an illusion and, when I learned, I was angry and I invoked a theme I should not have."

The hamadryad touched her hand, briefly, understanding. That did not make Orb feel better.

"I hope it is not too bad here," Orb said.

The dryad smiled encouragingly.

Orb turned another page, to Tinka's house in France.

Here, too, the rain was pouring. The roof was not tight; water was dripping down inside. Tinka had set out pans to catch it, but was obviously unhappy. Her baby was crying; she was trying to comfort him by singing, but the howl of the wind drowned out her voice.

She smiled gladly when she saw Orb. She was so glad for her sight! But Orb was glum. "I'm afraid there will be worse coming," she said. "Perhaps flooding; can you move to higher ground?"

"No, I must wait here for my husband to return," Tinka said. "Perhaps then we can go."

"I hope it will be all right." But Orb was sickly uncertain that it would be.

She traveled around the globe, finding the rain everywhere. Still the temperature increased; there seemed to be a hothouse effect. The polar ice was diminishing at an alarming rate. The flooding was occurring at coastal cities in the high-tide regions. There was hardly any distinction between day and night; the swirling rain was everywhere.

She returned to Jonah. He had finally given up the battle and swum belowground, where it was calm.

"The same all over?" Jezebel asked.

"All over," Orb agreed grimly. "The polar ice is melting, the sea level is rising, and the rain just keeps coming down. And I can't do anything to stop it; I have lost my control over the elements."

"Then you must rest," Lou-Mae said solicitously.

"And eat," Jezebel added. "I just happen to have some blueberry pie here."

Orb tried, but her appetite was small and her rest tormented by thought of the possible consequences of her indiscretion. Before long she was turning the pages again, traveling the globe.

The hamadryad's tree was standing in water; all the swamp was flooded. The nymph was perched in the branches, staring at the coursing muddy water. "The roots—they can't breathe," she said, feeling the pain of her tree.

There was nothing Orb could say. She moved on to India.

Flooding was well advanced now. The wagons stood in water up to their hubs, and the rain continued. Was the world to experience another deluge like that described in the Bible? No, surely there wasn't enough water available to do that.

She entered the mermaid's wagon. "I think the wagons must be left," she told the mermaid. "They will be submerged, and the others will drown. But you could help them now, guiding them to higher ground."

"Well, I really don't enjoy brackish water," the mermaid said. "But I think there is no need. The wagons will float."

"They'll float!" Orb exclaimed. "I never thought of that!" But then she reconsidered. "But they'll separate, and some could overturn in the storm."

The mermaid nodded. "You're right. We'd better take precautionary measures now. We can tie them together and build stabilizing outriggers. I'll have to spread the word. If you will carry me outside—"

Orb reached over the tank and put her left arm around the mermaid's upper torso. The mermaid heaved her tail up, and Orb caught it above the flukes. Staggering, she carried the mermaid down and out, almost falling as she set her in the swirling water.

"Ugh!" the mermaid said, grimacing. "Filthy stuff! But I can handle it." She spun about, testing it for depth, then swam with facility toward the lead wagon.

Orb smiled. The mermaid complained, but she was happy. Not only was she free of her tank, she was serving a useful purpose.

Orb waited long enough to be sure that the mermaid could get the attention of the occupants of the wagons, then turned the page to France.

The flooding was proceeding here, too. The main street of the village had disappeared. Tinka was peering worriedly out; her husband had not yet returned.

"You must get to higher ground!" Orb told her. "While you can. For the sake of your baby."

"For the baby," Tinka agreed, shaken.

"Maybe I can locate your husband. How can I identify him?"

Tinka described the man in sufficient detail. Orb expanded to encompass the region, orienting on the pertinent characteristics, and found them. She coalesced.

The man was in the mountains, but the treacherous conditions had caused his wagon to slide off the trail and break a wheel. He was unable to proceed until he got it fixed, and the job was difficult.

Orb introduced herself. "Ah, you are Tinka's friend, the one I never met!" he exclaimed. "I thought she invented you—a fantasy to divert herself!"

"The village is flooding. I will bring her here to you."

"She should not be out in this weather with the baby!" he protested. "She is not used to the outside, for her sight has not long been restored; she would get lost."

"I said I would bring her," Orb said. "No walking."

"Are you some magic creature, that you can do this?"

"Yes." Orb turned the page back to Tinka. "He broke a wheel," she reported. "He is fixing it. I will take you to him. Is there anything you need to take with you? I think you will not be returning here soon."

"Things for the baby!" Tinka exclaimed, dashing about the room. In a moment she had made a bundle of supplies and had donned a waterproof shawl to cover herself and the baby.

Then Orb put a hand on Tinka's shoulder and turned the page to the wagon.

Tinka handed Orb the baby and bundle and went to help her husband. Orb was impressed again at the efficiency of Gypsies when there was a task to be done. She was also struck by the presence of the baby in her arms. If only she could have kept Orlene! But even if she had not had to give up her daughter before, how could she have kept a child while assuming the office of Nature?

She couldn't have, of course. When she had given her decision to Natasha, she had affirmed that conclusion; she had chosen the office rather than the family.

Natasha—ah, Satan! How could she have missed that, before? She had been blinded by love. But oh, if only it could have been real! Her heart felt leaden; it craved the illusion, when the reality was the worst horror she had dreamed of. To marry Satan—

She stood in the rain, holding the baby and the bag of belongings, glad for the moment that the incessant rain masked the tears on her face. What a colossal fool she had been!

The Gypsy team labored on the wheel. They lacked the proper tools, but were clever with makeshift; in due course the wheel had been jury-rigged into serviceability.

Tinka, bedraggled and dirty, returned to take her baby. "I thank you, Orb," she said.

"It was my pleasure," Orb responded miserably. She found that she hated giving up the baby; he had become a symbol of what she had thrown away.

"For everything."

But if Orb had not yielded to her anger, this hot rain would not have occurred. She was owed no thanks, just condemnation. But she knew that Tinka would not listen to that. "Go uphill," she said. "Until the rain stops."

The man nodded.

They boarded the wagon, and the horse resumed hauling. Orb waved, then turned the page back to Jonah.

The Sludge were sleeping, except for Jezebel. She was in her luscious form, evidently having been sharing with the guitarist. Since she never slept, she emerged to join Orb. "What can I fix you?" the succubus inquired.

"Some piece of mind," Orb said. She found it easy to relate to the demoness, perhaps because she was feeling somewhat damned herself.

"The rain has to stop some time," Jezebel said.

But it did not stop. It went on and on, and the heat continued. Soon Orb was out in the world again, turning pages from one region to another, helpless to reverse the ongoing disaster.

The coastal cities were being flooded out. The water impeded the exodus of the people; highways had been submerged and roads washed out. Most people seemed to have retreated to the taller buildings, moving to the higher floors as the water rose.

But the heat was causing the air to expand and rise; winds were stiffening and with them the waves. Breakers smashed at the buildings, wearing them down relentlessly. Orb saw some buildings that had collapsed; if there had been people in them, they were there no longer.

The wreckage of boats was being tossed about. This was no safe sea for sailing! But what other way did trapped people have to escape?

Could she take any of them and turn the page to higher ground? There were so many in trouble that she could help only a few, but she had to try.

She expanded, searching for the need, and found a building that was being overwhelmed by the waves. She coalesced to it. A woman and two children were standing on the roof, hanging on to the aeration pipes as the wind howled through. "I will help you!" Orb cried. "Take my hands!"

Numbly, the woman and children obeyed, clasping their hands about hers. They did not question her arrival.

Orb turned a page—and found herself alone. She had not been able to carry them with her!

She turned the page back. The three were there, staring, not knowing what had happened. "Maybe one at a time," Orb said, taking the hand of the little girl.

She turned the page—but the child was not with her. She could no longer take people with her! She had done it with Tinka and her baby, but now her magic seemed to have been drained. Maybe the Chaos was absorbing it, drawing on any magic available for its vast effort of demolition.

She turned the page back, determined to find some way to succeed. But this time she found only a massive wave crashing across the top of the building. She expanded and thinned out, so that it did not affect her—but when it receded, the woman and children were gone.

Orb knew that similar tragedies were occurring all over the world. She had merely sampled the horror of it.

What had she wrought?

With fading hope, she turned the page to the water oak in Ireland. The water was now halfway up its trunk, and the hamadryad was perched in the foliage at the top, very much like the woman and children of the building.

Orb joined her. "I can't move human folk any more, but maybe I can move you," she said. "Take my hand, and I will try to take you to higher ground."

"I cannot leave my tree!" the dryad cried, distraught.

Of course that was true. A hamadryad was a creature of her tree, perhaps even the soul of the tree; she could not leave it. "I hope the water stops soon," Orb said, grief-stricken.

The dryad gazed at her without expression.

Orb turned the page to India.

The wagons were floating, but precariously. The occupants were bailing them out, but the constant fall of water was refilling them. A stiff wind was carrying the caravan out toward the widening sea.

Would these good folk survive? Orb, ashamed, did not make her presence known.

She returned to Jonah, who remained deep below ground. "The whole world is being flooded," she reported to the succubus. "I have lost my power to transport other people; I can only watch them perish."

"It can't rain forever," Jezebel said. "There isn't enough water."

Orb, helpless, retired to her chamber and lay down, not expecting to sleep. She did not feel tired and concluded that this was because of her new status as an Incarnation. But she dropped off almost immediately.

When she woke, the situation seemed unchanged—but she realized that this was deceptive, because of the ambiance of Jonah. She turned a page to the water oak—and was appalled, for it was gone. Evidently the waves had undermined it and carried it away, hamadryad and all. An old friend had been lost, and what could Orb do?

She went to India. The lowlands had been replaced by a turbulent ocean, and there was no sign of the floating wagons. The winds were so violent that it was obvious that full-fledged ships could have foundered; the wagons had not had any chance. More old friends were gone.

But the mermaid—she should have survived! Where was she?

Orb expanded, spreading throughout the region, questing for the mermaid. She found her, swimming deep down, where the water was quieter. But she could not greet the mermaid down here, and she worried about the threat of large sea creatures. Suppose one decided that the mermaid was prey?

However, no large predators seemed to be feeding now. The rain and melt that was causing the ocean level to rise was also diluting the salinity of the water at the upper reaches, and that seemed to be distracting the creatures. The mermaid had been making do with fresh water for so long that she had no problem. Perhaps she would be all right.

Orb turned the page to southern France, orienting on Tinka. She found the wagon sloughing through muck, ascending the mountain, its wheel holding. No danger of flooding here, at least.

She was about to return to Jonah, when she paused, noticing something. The mountain slope seemed to have changed its complexion. The ground was furred. So were the trunks of the trees, and even the leaves.

Orb reached out and broke off a twig. She felt a little tug inside her and realized that she was Nature, now, and related intimately to every living thing, including the twig she had just severed from its tree.

She inspected the twig. It seemed to have sprouted new life. It was covered with something like algae.

Algae were growing on everything, and fungus sprouted, too. The humid, hot ambiance was encouraging the growth of such things. It seemed to be one of the harmless consequences of this weather.

She returned to Jonah—and found him in motion, swimming through the rock. "Where to?" she inquired.

"Oh, good," Lou-Mae exclaimed. "I wanted to say good-bye to you. We—Miami is pretty low, and my folks—I've got to be with them now."

"And I've got to be with her," the drummer said. "So we're getting off and see what we can do."

Orb wanted to caution them about the condition of the coastal cities, but realized that they could hardly save themselves while letting friends and relatives be threatened. "Get them to high ground as fast as you can," she said. But how much high ground was there in Florida?

Not enough, she knew. The entire state would soon be submerged. The relatives would be lost—and Lou-Mae and the drummer.

She had to do something! But what? She had lost her power to transport other people, and in any event, a whole city was threatened, and all the other coastal cities of the world. What could she do to save them?

She was the Incarnation of Nature, wasn't she? She *should* be able to do something! And she had to!

She turned the page to Purgatory. There was Eros, as if waiting for her. "Just tell me one thing," she snapped. "What powers can I invoke, as Gaea?"

"Any power of Nature," he replied. "To any degree. But you have to know how, and only long experience can make you perfect. I can't help you there; I only know about love."

"Where were you when Satan was corrupting me?" she asked fiercely.

"I did not interfere in that; a lesser Incarnation can not affect a greater one. You came to love him on your own, and I had to accede."

Surely so. "Where can I get the information I need to master my office?" she asked tightly.

"There is no written text, if that's what you mean. You have to master it on your own."

"I don't have time for that! I need instruction! Who can provide it?"

He shrugged. "Only the former Gaea, I suspect."

"But she's in Heaven!"

"No, she's on Earth. She still has some of her natural life to live out."

So the former Gaea remained among the mortals! Orb expanded, orienting on her, found her, and coalesced beside her.

"Why, hello, Gaea," the woman said. She looked exactly as she had before—as Satan's emulation of her had looked.

"Why did you give up your office to me?"

"Nothing lasts forever," the woman said. "I was becoming fatigued, trying to keep natural order throughout the world. Any error, and such consequences! It is a nervous business. So when I saw one who had the potential to replace me, I encouraged it."

"You encouraged it? You mean you could have prevented it?"

"Oh, certainly! Not all Incarnations step down involuntarily. When you expanded, I contracted, until finally you expanded all the way and assumed the whole of it, and I let myself slide back into mortality. When you tire of it, and a successor offers, you may do the same and finish out your mortal life in the situation you helped generate."

"But I am making a mess of it!" Orb protested. "I sang the wrong theme, and now Chaos is loosed upon the land!"

"We all make errors at the outset," the woman said calmly. "How well I remember the Black Plague! It was all I could do to prevent it from wiping out the remaining population, but after that I certainly knew more about my office!"

"But I sang the Song of Chaos!"

The woman nodded. "I really didn't think you were ready for that one. But if you can master it, you will have an extremely powerful tool."

"That's why I came to see you! I have no idea how to stop it from destroying the world. If you can tell me—"

"I can and I can't," the woman said. "You see, I did not use music for my command process. So I do not know how that applies. I suspect you would not be able to use the command process I am familiar with."

"What is that?"

"Pseudo gestures."

"What?"

"Gestures that do not reach the level of performance. Patterns of muscle tension. The body has many muscles and many more combinations."

"I know nothing about that! I sing the themes—"

"Which I know nothing about. Therefore I can not provide you with specifics. But I can tell you what I would do, if my system remained operative. I would hasten the cycle of the pattern of

Chaos you have invoked, hoping to clear it before its havoc was total."

"Can't I simply nullify it?"

"If there is a way, I do not know it. Other things can be neutralized, but Chaos is different. It has to complete whatever course it runs—which can not be predicted. But the less time it exists, the less damage it is likely to do. It is a calculated risk—but of course there can be no certainties, with Chaos."

Orb was hardly reassured. "How can I use my music to hasten the cycle?"

"You should be able to use the same theme that invoked the cycle, and invoke it again, and again. Each invocation should translate it to a new application. Of course that is dangerous, because it is apt to accelerate its power as well as its velocity. It is possible that you would be best off leaving it alone."

"But people are dying!"

"I realize that. But when you go for double or nothing, or triple or nothing, the result is not always what you prefer."

Orb sighed. She knew the former Gaea was right. A gamble was a gamble. "I thank you for your comment," she said and turned the page back to Jonah.

"I don't think you will be able to save your folks," she said to Lou-Mae. "It is my fault; I set in motion a pattern I can not control. But I may be able to change it. The risk is that I will only make it worse. How do you feel?"

Lou-Mae hardly seemed to consider. "Let's try to save them first. If we can't, then you gamble."

"Then I gamble," Orb agreed, relieved to have the basis for the decision clarified.

– 15 –

CHAOS

The level of the ocean had risen fifteen feet. The runoff from the rain across the state of Florida made it worse. Much of Miami was under water, the buildings poking out of the great new lake. The inhabitants were crowding into the diminishing islands of high ground and into the upper stories of the sturdier buildings. Still the rain washed down.

Orb shook her head. Most of the city's population might be alive now, but the continuing rise of water doomed them. Whatever boats had been serviceable had already gone, and it would be impossible for most of the people to swim what might turn out to be hundreds of miles to truly secure ground.

Jonah taxied to Lou-Mae's home section. It was under water; the people were gone. Rubble made islands where buildings had collapsed, and garbage floated around them. Lou-Mae stared, her face expressionless.

"They went to high ground," the drummer said quickly. "They had time; the water rose slowly."

"Yes . . ." she agreed, her shock easing.

"I can find them," Orb said. "Give me a description of a friend or relative, and I will orient."

Lou-Mae described her mother. Orb expanded, and when she

intersected the woman, she coalesced to that spot. It was in a large building being used as a refuge. People were crowded on the upper floors. A number were injured; a makeshift infirmary section had been cordoned off for them.

Orb saw with horror that the same furry growth she had seen in France was appearing here. The walls were covered with it, and the ceiling, and it was even on some of the clothing of the people. The heat and humidity fostered it, and it was encroaching everywhere. The air itself seemed to taste of it.

Lou-Mae's mother was a massive woman, but she just about jumped off the floor when Orb materialized before her. Orb was the only white person in the room.

"I am a friend of Lou-Mae's," Orb said. "She wants to join you here, to try to help you. The rest of her family, her friends— are they all right?"

"Most—for now," the woman said grimly. "You got a way out of here?"

"Not for this number of people," Orb said. She wasn't sure that Jonah would admit any person who wasn't part of the Sludge, and certainly not hundreds.

"Then tell Lou-Mae to stay clear, because she's better off where she is."

"She won't do that," Orb said. "She wants to be with you. I will have to bring her."

The woman nodded, understanding. Orb turned the page to Jonah. "I found her," she announced. "She's all right, but she wishes you would stay clear."

"I know," Lou-Mae said. "I won't."

"She knows." Orb directed Jonah, and he swam to the building.

Lou-Mae had a tearful reunion with her mother, introduced the drummer, and caught up on the status of other family members. Then she turned to Orb. "They're never going to get out of here. Go back to the fish. Take the gamble. We'll ride it out with them."

Orb sighed. Lou-Mae knew the risk. But it was obvious that the risk of allowing the present situation to continue was worse. She returned to Jonah.

Only Jezebel and the guitarist remained there. "I'm going to try it," Orb said.

"That's all you can do," Jezebel said. "Maybe the guitar can help?"

The guitarist fetched his instrument. "Just tell me what you want."

"It's like the Song of the Morning or the Song of Day, but different," Orb said. "Start with that and modify as seems right." He nodded.

Orb set herself, then sang. The Song of Chaos reached out beyond them, beyond Jonah, expanding in the manner of her diffusion traveling, embracing the turbulent world. The chamber faded, and it was as if they were in the rain, becoming part of it, part of the moving air and water. The song took hold of that ambience and stirred it, intensifying it. Darkness came, and light, but the darkness was vast and strong, while the light was limited and weak. Chaos was awakening to new power.

Orb felt a chill as she sang, not of the body. She was playing with a force she hardly understood. Her first invocation of it had led the world to this watery horror; what would follow now?

She completed the song, the part of it she could. The rest of it would complete itself in its own fashion.

"The power of that thing!" Jezebel murmured. "I'm not even human, but I felt it. It would shake Hell itself!"

"It is a gamble," Orb repeated. "I don't know whether I am doing right or wrong."

Outside, the rain was easing. Orb expanded and found that this was happening all around the globe. The temperature had stopped rising, and the weather was slowly clearing.

She coalesced. "I think we have turned the corner," she said, with immense relief. Then she went to her room and collapsed into sleep.

She woke somewhat refreshed. Jezebel fixed her breakfast. She didn't know what time of the day or night it was, but breakfast seemed appropriate. Jonah was under the ground again, and everything was quiet.

Belatedly, Orb considered that. "Why is Jonah down?" she asked.

"He generally has reason," Jezebel said.

"I'd better look."

Orb turned the page to Miami. It was quiet, and the temperature had dropped a little. The water still stood around the buildings, but the worst seemed to be over.

Still, she checked on Lou-Mae. She remained in the island building with her mother and the others. They had food from the supplies of a restaurant that had been on the lower floor; the flooding and lack of electric power would cause the food to spoil soon, so they were only cutting down on the waste.

The algae grew everywhere. Someone had evidently tried to scrub down a section of the wall, but already the stuff was growing back. The scent of it in the air was stronger; it was impossible to inhale without breathing it.

Lou-Mae and her mother were all right, but the drummer lay under a blanket. "He has a fever," Lou-Mae explained worriedly. "Several others have it. One of us is a doctor, but he says it's impossible to tell what it is yet; it doesn't act like the flu."

"I could take him back aboard Jonah," Orb said.

"No, he says he wants to stay here with me. I'll take care of him."

"Maybe I can sing him well," Orb said.

"Oh, has your power returned?" Lou-Mae inquired, brightening.

"I don't know." Orb went to the drummer, took his burning hand, and sang the Song of the Morning. The effect of night came, and then dawn, amazing the others in the room, but Orb knew that there was no healing effect. That aspect of her power remained pre-empted by the Song of Chaos.

"He'll be all right," Lou-Mae said, putting a brave face on it.

"I'll keep in touch," Orb said. Her heart was heavy, but there was nothing more she could do.

Then she thought of something. Quickly she removed the necklace she wore, with the moonstone amulet the Magician had given her as a child. As an Incarnation, she no longer needed it. She turned back to Lou-Mae. "Please wear this," she said, putting the chain over Lou-Mae's head.

"What is it, Orb?"

"A charm. It will protect you from harm."

"But—"

"Please, I want you to have it. Never take it off. Promise."

Lou-Mae hugged her. "I promise, Orb!"

Back aboard Jonah, she decided to check quickly on the others. She turned pages, verifying that the calm extended to all the world. Tinka's wagon was safely ensconced on a high slope, the mermaid had found herself a grotto near the new shore, and the fields of Betsy's farm were draining. Much damage had been done everywhere, and many lives had been lost, but the carnage had stopped.

Could it really be so easy? Orb distrusted this, so she turned the page to Purgatory. This time she went to the castle of War, having a certain female curiosity about aspects of her former lover's situation.

She was met at the front gate by a hooded figure. "Mym?" she inquired hesitantly.

The figure drew back its hood. Its head was a writhing mass of maggots.

Orb screamed.

"Thank you," the figure said. "What is your business?"

Orb realized that this was not Mym. "I—I wish to see Mars."

"And who are you?" The maggots writhed as it spoke, forming a mouth and shaping the words.

"I—just say a friend." She felt uneasy about revealing her nature or her business to this thing.

The gruesome figure turned about and moved into the castle. Orb was satisfied to wait outside. What kind of company was Mym keeping, these days?

Soon a lovely young woman appeared. That was literal; she simply manifested where there had been no one before.

"Lilith," Orb said, recognizing her.

The demoness was taken aback. "Have we met before?"

"Not directly. You are Mym's demon mistress."

"True. But who are you?"

"His former lover," Orb said with a certain satisfaction.

"You are not Rapture of Malachite."

"Before that."

Lilith made the connection. "The one who had his baby! I should have recognized you; I have emulated you in the past!"

"Emulated me?"

"Assumed your likeness." The demoness abruptly shifted to

a mirrorlike image of Orb. "Mym never stopped loving you, you know, so sometimes I—never mind. I simply wasn't expecting you here. Come in; I know he will want to see you."

Orb complied. "The figure who—with the worms—?"

"Oh, that's Pestilence, one of the handmaidens of War, as it were; a lesser Incarnation. He's on duty now, so he answered the door. It takes a while to appreciate him."

"He's—on duty?" Orb was starting to make a connection of her own.

"Supervising the breeding of the vermin and diseases and fungi, now that conditions for them are ideal."

"The mold—the algae—"

"That, too," the demoness agreed. "Harmless, but the microscopic fungi aren't. There'll be a plague like none seen before, as those new spores infest the human systems. Pest is very proud of his effort."

The drummer was running a fever, as were a number of others. Now Orb knew that the change in the weather had come too late; the worst damage was invisible. Spores in their trillions, infiltrating every part of the environment, taking hold in animals and people, generating illness that would be tough to fight off even with modern medication, and hellish in the present situation.

Another woman arrived. "Ligeia," Orb said. "Or should I say Princess?"

"I'll dispense with your title, Gaea, if you will dispense with mine," Ligeia said. "I can see why Mym loves you."

"That's past," Orb said, embarrassed. "I came only to talk with him."

"Of course. Incarnations consult with each other frequently. I have sent a messenger; Mym will be with us shortly. Meanwhile, you must have tea with us."

"I—yes," Orb said, out of sorts. Ligeia was so poised and gracious!

They went to the patio in the rear garden. It was exactly like the one Orb had seen before.

"How is it that you know us?" Ligeia inquired as a servant took care of the details.

"I met you—in emulation," Orb said. "Satan—"

"How well we understand!" Ligeia said. "I was captive in Hell, and Lilith was a creature of Hell, before Mym freed us. The deceptions of Satan are myriad and intricate. The emulations gave you false information?"

"Mixed. Yet they were so like your reality and were so persuasive—it is as if I have been through this scene before. I—" Orb paused, beset by the notion that this could be another vision. How could she tell the difference between vision and reality, when the emulation was so accurate?

"And now you are not sure of us," Lilith finished.

"Would—would you object if I verified—?"

"Please do," Ligeia said. "We *do* understand, Orb."

Orb turned the page to Jonah, fetched her harp, and turned the page back to the castle. "A deceiver may not touch my instrument," Orb explained. "It was a gift of the Mountain King. If you would . . ."

Ligeia smiled. She not only touched the harp, she set herself and played a chord on it.

"You know the harp?" Orb asked, amazed.

"Not well. But as a mortal princess, I was expected to be able to make an impression on a prince, and music is one way. This is a beautiful instrument."

Lilith approached. "I am crafted largely of deception," she said. "So this may not—" She reached out and touched the harp. Nothing happened.

"You are not deceiving anyone now," Orb said.

"I have practiced none since Mars saved me," Lilith said, still touching the harp.

"What, not even when you emulated me that night?" Ligeia inquired with pretend malice.

"He wanted you, but you were indisposed," the demoness said. "So he asked me to—"

Ligeia laughed. "I knew it, Li! I was teasing you."

"But for your tolerance, I would not exist, Li," the demoness replied.

Orb shook her head. "This is as it was in the vision. Consort and mistress—friends! I think I would not have understood this before I came to know Jezebel."

"You know Jezebel?" Lilith asked with interest. "The succubus?"

−263−

"She retired."

"That isn't possible!"

Ligeia put her hand on the demoness' arm. "You forget whom you address."

"My apology, Gaea," Lilith said, abashed. "Of course you, alone of all folk, could enable her to change!"

Ligeia intercepted whatever awkwardness was developing. "Orb, I'm sure Mym is about to arrive. Would it be too much to ask you to sing for us, since you have your harp with you? I understand there is not your match in all this realm."

"There is one," Orb said, a shadow crossing her soul.

"Who might that be?"

"Satan."

"Satan? I never realized—"

"It is true," Lilith said. "He seldom indulges, but I knew him before he assumed his office. As a mortal he was the most moving male singer humanity has produced and knew it. I think that made him easier to corrupt."

Orb and Ligeia both turned to the demoness. "You corrupted him—as a mortal?"

"On orders of his predecessor. It was an irony. Satan feared the potential for good inherent in this mortal singer, so he sent me to foster evil in his heart. I succeeded too well. The mortal became corrupted and displaced the one who had sent me. Thereafter I loved the new Satan—until he sent me to corrupt Mars. Now I love Mars."

"Mars is easy to love," Ligeia said.

"Amen," Orb said.

"So glad to find you in such agreement," Mym said from the doorway, startling all three women.

Ligeia recovered first. "Orb was about to sing for us," she said. "Then she must talk with you."

"No."

Again all three were startled. Again, Ligeia recovered. "She came to consult as an Incarnation, Mym. You can not deny her that."

"That, no," he said. "It is the song I may not hear."

"You used to like my singing," Orb remarked, perplexed.

"My love for you never died," he said seriously. "It was

-264-

superseded, but it remains. I know the power of your music. If I heard it again, I would desire you above this woman and this creature, and that would prejudice our relationship. Talk with me; do not sing to me."

"I think he is making sense," Lilith said to Ligeia. "She was his first love, and now she is more than she was."

"We shall leave them to talk," Ligeia agreed.

"No need," Orb said quickly. "I wanted only to consult about my present situation. I invoked the Song of Chaos, and when it threatened to drown the world, I invoked it again, hoping to cause it to pass more swiftly. It seemed to end, and that worries me; I can not believe that Chaos can be abated simply by reinvocation. Can Chaos cancel itself out?"

"I doubt it," Mym said. "But I may know whom to ask."

"Who?" Orb asked, hardly daring to believe that there was a ready source of the information she needed.

"The Purgatory computer. It knows everything; the only problem is getting it to respond relevantly."

"I have not had much experience with computers," Orb said doubtfully.

"It seems to be a demonic device. Lilith should be able to make it behave."

"I can try," the demoness agreed.

"I would take you myself, but it is too difficult to be close to you for long," Mym said. "What is past must remain past."

"Yes," Orb said, flattered. She had embraced the pseudo-Mym of the vision, but this reality left her with a better self-image.

"This way," Lilith said. "We can walk; it is close by."

Orb remembered something. "You emulated me—for him?"

"He is not joking about the effect you have on him," the demoness said. "He would never have left you if he had been given any choice. I emulate any woman he asks me to, but when I did you, he just looked at me with such longing and sadness that even I, who have no true human emotions, was discomfited. He did not touch me then, afraid of what passion might resurge in him that could never be truly gratified."

"Thank you for telling me," Orb said.

They entered an impressive building and made their way to the computer room. Lilith activated the machine.

BY WHAT AUTHORITY DO YOU TOY WITH ME, REFUGEE FROM HELL? the screen printed.

"I'm helping an Incarnation," Lilith retorted with satisfaction. "The new Gaea."

AH, THE DAUGHTER OF FATE. WHAT A MESS YOU ARE MAKING OF THE MORTAL REALM!

Orb found it strange, addressing a screen of print, but she had to respond to this. "I am coming to you for help to alleviate that mess."

ONLY CHRONOS CAN ALLEVIATE IT, IF HE WILL.

So there was a way to stop this! "Why wouldn't he?"

HE HAS A PERSONAL REASON.

"What is that?"

A MACHINE DOES NOT PROPERLY COMPREHEND HUMAN MOTIVATIONS.

"Well, then, I'll just go and ask Chronos to help."

LOTS OF LUCK, the screen printed sardonically.

"Ligeia was right," Orb muttered. "It *is* a demonic device."

"I'm sure it would do well in Hell," Lilith said.

LOOK WHO'S TALKING. Then the machine clicked off.

"Now how do I locate Chronos?" Orb asked. "I presume he has a castle or something here in Purgatory."

"He does, but others don't go to it unless invited. It is best to put out a call for him and wait until he answers. We can do that for you; I'm sure he will come to you in due course."

Orb sighed. "At least I know that someone can help. I thank you and Ligeia for your assistance."

"We remain in your debt," the demoness said. "You helped make Mym what he is, and he is our—" She paused, evidently trying to say a word.

"Salvation?"

Lilith nodded. "Sometimes I almost forget my origin. There are words I can not utter."

"I understand. Another demoness is my friend; perhaps you will be, too."

"I can see why Mym loves you."

Orb gave her a hug, and the demoness clung to her for a moment as a lost child might. Then Orb turned the page back to Nature's Abode.

This time she decided to explore it more thoroughly. She still felt most at home in Jonah, but knew that she would have to get used to her Purgatory residence. Unfortunately the tree-shape of it reminded her of the hamadryad's tree in the swamp in Ireland, and that grieved her. Abruptly she turned another page, to Jonah.

He was back underground. "The weather is picking up again," Jezebel said.

Orb went to Miami. The weather was worsening; there was no rain, and the water level had receded somewhat; the ambient temperature was down, but gale-force winds were battering the buildings. The water had eroded the foundations of a number of buildings, and more rubble was in evidence. The city was still in serious trouble.

She checked Lou-Mae. The room was a disaster area. Most of the occupants, including both the drummer and Lou-Mae's mother, were down with the fever, sprawled across the floor. Lou-Mae herself was unaffected and was working valiantly to attend to those who could not help themselves. Orb suspected that it was not natural immunity, but the Magician's amulet that was protecting her from the ravages of the pestilence.

There was an odor. The building's sanitary facilities had evidently failed with the loss of power, and this surely fostered the pestilence. But until the water receded and left the building dry, there was nowhere for the people to go. Those who had sought the high ground had retreated to whatever buildings were there, in the face of the rising winds.

There seemed to be nothing she could do. She knew that Lou-Mae would not desert her mother or the others and she could not transport the group of them to another place. She could only hope that the winds died down before the waves became too violent.

She turned a page to France. Here, too, the winds were increasing and the temperature was dropping. Tinka and her husband seemed to be all right.

The level of the sea around India was dropping. This eased the plight of those whose land had been inundated, but the mermaid's grotto was being uncovered. The mermaid would soon be in trouble if she didn't move to deeper water before being isolated.

The storms were developing all around the world, battering the limited shelters of the people suffering from the plague. Orb understood now that the Chaos had not ended; it had only been changing course. Now the new course was progressing, and the storms might be the result of that change. Air that had been heating was now cooling, and ice that had been melting was reforming. The polar caps, almost depleted, were growing again. The winds were the result of the developing inversions of temperature, as air masses tried to equalize and could not.

The seacoast cities of the world were getting battered. Buildings that had withstood the rising waters now were collapsing as the wind drove the waves across with new force.

Orb turned a page back to Miami. The city was like a battle zone. Monstrous waves crashed across, even though the water level was down. The sea was doing more damage to the foundations now than before, because the constant surging and retreating of the waves tore at the ground in ways that the standing water had not. Several fragments of concrete were being thrown into the melee, gouging out more of itself.

She went to the building where Lou-Mae and her mother and the drummer were. The situation was worse; a number of the patients were dead. Efforts to help the sick had ceased; too few well people remained. In fact, the only one completely free of the malady was Lou-Mae. She was holding the drummer, trying to comfort him, but Orb could see that he had lapsed into unconsciousness or worse. His skin was discolored, his face was swollen so badly that he could not have opened his eyes, and there was blood on his shirt where he had been coughing. The others were no better off.

Meanwhile, the wind buffeted the building. Every time a wave struck, the room shook. There were sounds of things falling, and Orb experienced the sickening feeling of settling. This building was about to go!

"Lou-Mae, you have to get out of here!" Orb exclaimed.

"I can't! Mama's dead, and Danny-Boy's dying! I can't leave them!"

"But you can't help them! The plague—"

Lou-Mae just held the drummer, as if she could infuse health back into him. Orb could make no further impression on her.

A larger wave crashed outside—and the building went. It shuddered, and the floor tilted. The steel supports groaned as they twisted out of place; the ceiling tore from its moorings and sagged down. Things fell down from the story above—things like bodies.

The bodies on this floor started sliding, the drummer with them. Lou-Mae tried to hold him, but only started sliding down herself. The wall buckled and a panel sprang loose; suddenly there was nothing between the interior and the drop-off to the raging ocean several stories below.

Orb tried to hold the woman, tried to turn the page, but found herself alone; she still could not take anyone with her. She turned back, rejoining Lou-Mae. "Jonah!" she cried. "Here to me!" Then she hung on to Lou-Mae as they all slid down the increasing slope. The bodies were funneling in toward the open panel, jamming against each other; this slowed progress, but not enough.

Then the head of the big fish appeared, poking through the building. Orb hauled Lou-Mae up physically—she could still do that!—and dragged her into the mouth. When the woman was safely on inside, Orb tried to go back for the drummer, but it was too late; the upper stories were collapsing, and everything was going down in stages.

"Danny-Boy!" Lou-Mae cried, trying to launch herself back out, but Jonah had closed his mouth. She clawed at the flesh, screaming, but could not get through.

Meanwhile the building was settling into rubble. Orb watched it through the transparent scales. Another wave crashed through, accelerating the process. Even had the occupants been well, few could have survived this. The drummer was gone.

Jezebel appeared. "Take Lou-Mae to her chamber and try to get her to sleep," Orb said. "She—the others are dead." She sounded cold to herself, but it was horror inside.

The succubus put her arm around Lou-Mae. "I wish I could feel what you feel," she said.

"You wouldn't like it," Orb replied, and turned the page to Betsy's farm.

Her worst fear was realized. The storms were raging here, too. Something very like a hurricane was blasting across the plain, lifting the drying soil and hurling it in clouds against anything that offered. The day was dusky because of it. Orb had to brace herself against the fierce wind and squint to keep out the particles of grit.

Betsy's farm was taking a beating. Whatever remained of the

crop after the flood was now being swept away by the wind. The house was under siege, as the wind tore at its edges. The gusts were so strong that Orb found herself blown along. She wasn't hurt, as her office made her invulnerable to physical harm, but any other person would have been at risk.

She made her way awkwardly to the house and knocked on the door. Such was the noise of the storm that she could hardly hear the knock herself; she was sure the occupants couldn't hear it. So she expanded until she was diffuse enough to pass through the wall, then coalesced inside.

No one was there. Surprised, then alarmed, Orb looked around. Where could they have gone? Surely they hadn't been caught outside by surprise!

Then she realized that farms on the plains were accustomed to handling storms. There should be a safe place to hide.

Betsy and the organist and her family were there, waiting out the storm in a small cellar designed for this purpose. There was still water standing on its floor, but this was a small penalty for the security it provided. They seemed to have escaped the plague; this region had not been as good for the multiplication of the spores.

"I don't know how bad it's going to get," Orb said. "But I'm afraid it will be very bad."

"We'll ride it out," Betsy said bravely. "How are the others doing?"

This was the question Orb had dreaded, but she had to answer it. "Miami—is gone. The waves—"

Both Betsy and the organist were stricken. "Lou-Mae—" Betsy whispered.

"I got her back to Jonah. But the others—"

"Oh, damn," the organist muttered, knowing his friend was dead.

The wind intensified, howling past with frightening force. It seemed to be trying to lift the house off its foundation.

"You had better get clear," Betsy said to Orb. "Thanks for stopping by." It was evident that she had no intention of leaving, though she knew there was a place for her and the drummer in Jonah. This was the family farm; there might have been a time when Betsy wanted to leave it, but now she would stay here.

Orb turned the page to France. Here the situation was worse; trees were down, and the wind had blown the wagon away. Tinka and her husband and baby were huddled against a firm face of rock, covered by a blanket. The force of the wind was diminished here; the bulk of the mountain intercepted it.

Orb decided to leave them alone; they were as well off as anyone. She went on to India.

Here the wind had hastened the outflow of water, and the land all around the mermaid's grotto was dry. Evidently it had happened too swiftly for the mermaid to escape; she was stranded. At first Orb feared she was dead, but she was only avoiding the fierce wind by lying flat.

"I will help you reach a better place," Orb screamed over the wind. "The sea—"

"The sea is too turbulent above," the mermaid screamed back. "And too cold below. I need a pool!"

"I'll find a pool!" Orb agreed. She expanded, searching for one reasonably close by.

She found it: a deep one used by a wealthy estate, now deserted. The buildings of the estate were battered, but the pool had suffered only the accumulation of debris. Orb fished out what she could, then turned the page back to the mermaid.

"I will carry you there," she cried. She got her arms around the mermaid's body and heaved her up. She staggered toward the estate.

What had taken only a moment by magic means was a wearing trek with a physical burden while being buffeted by the wind. Orb had to put the mermaid down and rest frequently, and it required over an hour to traverse the distance. When they finally got there, Orb was so fatigued she fell into the pool herself. Now the roles were reversed, as the mermaid caught her and bore her to the edge, keeping her head above water.

"Oh, it's good to get back!" the mermaid exclaimed. "Let me fill my gills!" She dived under, expelling the air from her lungs, so that her gills could function.

Orb, satisfied that she was all right, foraged in the main building of the estate for some food, which she brought to the pool. The mermaid grabbed it eagerly. "I'll check on you every so often," Orb promised, and turned the page back to Jonah.

"Maybe you should rest," Jezebel said. "It's too bad that your meeting with Chronos didn't work out better; you should save your strength for what may come."

"Chronos? I haven't met with Chronos yet," Orb said.

"But you said—"

Orb glanced at her sharply. "Has there been another vision, a dream-sequence?"

"Demons don't dream," Jezebel said. "I remember clearly what you said just half an hour ago—"

"I have just spent at least an hour helping a mermaid reach a pool. I'm bedraggled and tired now, and am quite sure I haven't spoken to you about Chronos recently."

The demoness didn't answer.

"It's getting worse," the guitarist said. "We can feel the rumbling, even through the rock."

"The winds were gale force and rising in India," Orb said. "But I'm afraid to sing the Song of Chaos again. How is Lou-Mae?"

"Sleeping," Jezebel said. "I think Jonah is helping. But you know she's not going to be happy when she wakes."

"If only I hadn't started this!" Orb lamented.

"I think Satan started it. He led you on, knowing how mad you'd be when he told you the truth. He's collecting souls by the millions now."

"*Damn* Satan!" Orb swore, hating the logic of the plot.

"They say he works over each new Incarnation," Jezebel continued. "He taught you that evil Song, didn't he? He saw you coming, and really—"

Orb, unable to listen, turned the page to Ireland—and regretted it. The water had receded, but the swamp was a tangled mass of roots and mud, with few trees standing. The hamadryad's water oak was gone.

Orb stood there in the savage wind and cried. She wished passionately that she could undo the damage she had done, but knew she could not. She had to carry through, but knew that she had already failed so grossly as the Incarnation of Nature that she would have to resign the office the moment things stabilized. She couldn't resign now, because this disaster was not the responsibility of her successor, assuming any successor existed; Orb had to face it herself.

After a time she turned the page to Betsy's farm.

And blinked. The house was gone.

The wind was so savage here that it was impossible to see more than a hundred feet, but there was no question: the house had been blown away. Orb expanded, questing for the cellar, and found it.

It was empty. In fact, it was simply a gouged-out hole, much larger than the original cellar. It was evident that the storm had spawned a tornado and torn the very stones and timbers out of the ground and scattered them across the landscape. Betsy and the organist and Betsy's family were gone.

Orb gazed around the horizon. A tornado? By the sound, there was another coming. She expanded and confirmed it; three of them tearing across the plain, spewing out sand and debris, their terrible tails whipping back and forth as if searching for anything not yet destroyed. Farther out were two more, orbiting each other. Indeed, they were everywhere, growing like monstrous trees. Some were so twisted that they seemed to be rolling like elongated barrels along the ground, their funnels impinging on the territory of neighboring tornadoes. Hell had arrived on earth, here.

She returned to Jonah. "The farm—gone," she said dully. The individual tragedies were losing their impact; they were only samples of what the whole world was suffering.

Jezebel didn't comment. What was there she could say?

Orb knew now that it was not going to stop. The flood had been replaced by the storm. If she sang again, what worse could happen?

She fetched her harp and sang the Song of Chaos a third time. But this time she tried a variation, intuitively; she modified it with the error-nullification theme. If straight repetitions didn't do it, maybe a null repetition would.

Again she felt it taking hold. But even if it stopped all the trouble this instant, too many lives had been sacrificed.

When the song was done, she moved to the surface, apprehensive about the result.

The wind was dying.

But did this mean an end to Chaos, or only the onset of another aspect of it?

Where was Chronos? He was the one who was supposed to be able to help! Why hadn't he contacted her before this?

Orb turned the page to Purgatory, then sought Chronos' mansion. She would brace him directly!

A maid met her at the door. "The Incarnation isn't in," the woman said.

"I'll wait," Orb said, pushing past her. She was beyond the point of politeness.

"It isn't wise," the maid protested.

"Just send him a signal, or whatever. Tell him Gaea is here. I won't leave until I talk with him."

The maid spread her hands. "No one can reach Chronos when he's out. He isn't like other Incarnations."

Orb picked a comfortable couch in the front room and lay down as for sleep. The maid departed.

To her surprise, Orb did sleep. She woke abruptly when Chronos entered the room. He was a handsome figure in a white cloak. "Ah, Gaea," he said. "In your lovely stage. Had I known you were coming, I would have been here to greet you."

"I left a message," Orb said curtly. "Why didn't you answer?"

"What message?"

"Hours ago! They said it would reach you!"

Chronos nodded. "Ah, I understand. You are early in your tenure, and do not properly appreciate my nature."

"The Purgatory computer says that you are the only one who can help me. The world is being demolished by my error, and I have to stop the disaster!"

"Let me explain," Chronos said. "I exist backwards. The message you left remains in my future, your past. Probably this visit of yours has nullified it, so I have no news of it in my past, your future."

"Backwards," Orb repeated. "Yes, of course. I didn't realize—"

"However I'm sure we shall be reconciled, because we have had a long and beneficial association."

"That can't be. I'm going to resign as soon as I can somehow stabilize the Chaos I invoked."

"Chaos?"

"If you live backwards, you have to know all about it, don't you?"

"Not necessarily. Your future, and therefore my past, is malleable. What you foresee occurring may differ from my experience."

"But if you have lived through it—"

"I have lived through a single track of it—one of an infinite number available. I try to avoid interfering with my own track, but sometimes it does change. This is of course an uneasy business for me, though I am immune from paradox."

"Well, I have an uneasy business outside!" Orb retorted. "Are you going to help me or aren't you?"

"I would be inclined to help you, for the sake of your beauty and the long association we have had. However—"

"For the sake of what?" Orb asked sharply.

Chronos smiled. "I suppose that was not an honest answer. But I do not believe it would be wise for you to know either the source of my inclination or my reason for denying it."

"You would do something for an attractive woman that you would not for an unattractive one?" Orb demanded. Her frustration and fatigue were telling, and she knew it, but she hardly cared.

"Well, men do," he said reasonably. "It depends on the relationship. But your case is special. You have generally met me in your assumed guise of age and maturity; to encounter you now in your beauty is—"

"I suspect that if I understood what you were getting at, I wouldn't like it," Orb said. "So much for the source of your inclination; what is your reason for denying it?"

"They are linked. Perhaps you had better simply accept my statement that I do not wish to interfere with the present course of history."

"Even though life on Earth is being wiped out?"

"Well of course it didn't—won't come to that, exactly."

"Are you being deliberately perverse? I am not making much sense of this."

Chronos sighed. "I suppose I had better explain. But I must warn you that to prevent this explanation from changing the very matter of which I speak, I shall have to erase this particular line after experiencing it."

"Erase it?"

"I shall set the time back to this point, and our discussion will not have happened in your reality."

Orb realized that such was the power of this Incarnation, that he was not bluffing. "No! I forbid that! If you have a legitimate rationale for your action or inaction, and it concerns me, I believe I have a right not only to know it, but to remember it. I want you to tell me exactly what is on your mind, and why you seem to be refusing to help me undo the damage I have done."

"But you see, Gaea, your knowledge would almost certainly change the matter that I relate! Therefore it would become meaningless, and perhaps much worse."

Orb stifled a sharp retort. She reminded herself that her impetuous meddling with an aspect of the Llano had gotten her into trouble more than once, this time quite seriously. There could be merit in his caution. "Then tell me, and let me judge whether it is proper for me to remember. But you must promise to let me decide."

"I suppose you do have that right," Chronos said unhappily. "But—would you mind changing to your other form?"

"My other form?"

"The mature one. You—I prefer that you change."

"I hardly know what you're talking about. This is the form I have had since maturity; I know of no other."

"Again, my vantage betrays me. In your future I have known you in the other guise. The reason for my concern will be apparent when I have explained."

"Then you had better tell me what form you are asking me to assume and how I should do it."

"I really don't know how you do it. It is just one of the powers of your office, as it is for Fate."

"One moment," Orb said. She turned the page to Fate's Abode. The young oriental woman was there. "Could I speak to my mother for a moment?" Orb asked.

"I'll wake her." There was a pause, then Niobe appeared.

"What is my other form, and how do I achieve it?" Orb asked.

"Why I don't know, dear; the prior Gaea had many forms, and I'm sure you will, too. I think you just—choose it."

"But I have no idea how!"

"Perhaps if you imagine a progression in your appearance similar to mine," Niobe said. "In my youth I looked like this." She changed to a young and startlingly beautiful woman.

"Oh, mother, I had almost forgotten!" Orb exclaimed. "You were such a creature!"

"But I didn't take care of myself," Niobe said, reverting to her middle-aged spread. "I suspect something similar would have happened to you in time, if you had not assumed your office. If you will just imagine it—"

Orb concentrated, trying to picture herself when she became her mother's age.

"Yes, that's it," Niobe said.

"You mean I changed?"

"Come to the mirror, dear." She led Orb to a full-length mirror.

Orb was astonished. She was now a solid, middle-aged woman, perhaps twice her normal mass, her hair starting to gray. "Oh, ugh!" she exclaimed.

"No, it is very good," Niobe said. "You look very much the part of Mother Nature now." She contemplated Orb critically. "Except for the green hair."

"My hair is not green!"

"Precisely. The Green Mother traditionally has a green tinge about her."

Orb concentrated. "Like this?" Now her hair showed greenish in the mirror.

"Yes, dear. That is very nice."

Orb realized that she must have chosen—in Chronos' futuristic past—this form for much of her official activity. "I suppose it will have to do. Thank you, mother."

"Do be careful, dear."

"It's late for that!" Orb turned the page back to Chronos' domicile.

"Yes, much better," Chronos said. "You are your familiar self."

Orb was not completely pleased, but elected to pass over the matter. "Now tell me everything I need to know."

"It began about fifteen years hence, in your framework," he said. "Perhaps a few more. I was—well, I met a ghost."

"A ghost! There are millions of them being made right now!"

Chronos shrugged. "This ghost had an unusual proposition. He wanted me to impregnate his wife. This was a thing he could not do himself, of course."

Orb realized that this was a highly unusual story. She resolved not to interrupt until it was complete.

"I met his wife and fell in love with her. I could not marry her, of course, but I lived with her like a husband, and she bore my child, though it was legally the child of the ghost. Unfortunately, the baby had a malady and died, and she committed suicide because of her grief. She was the perfect woman and the perfect mother and she felt she had no life without her baby."

How well Orb could understand that! If only she had been able to keep her own baby!

"That left my own life meaningless. With the ghost's help, I assumed the office of Chronos and have held it until this time. As you can appreciate, I would not have come to this had I not met the woman, and had she not died. I think I would give it all up, to live out my life with her, but I can not, and I believe I am a competent officeholder and that my input is beneficial. This is the past that I feel I should not change, the future that you will come to know."

"I am sorry for your tragedy, of course," Orb said. "But I do not see how it relates to me. Meanwhile, I have a most pressing problem in my present, not my future."

"But your present affects your future, and therefore my past. The woman I loved, and will always love, is alive today, as a child. Her name is Orlene."

It was as if cold water had been dashed on her. "Who?"

"Your daughter—who in her adulthood rather resembles you as you are now. That is why I find your natural appearance so disconcerting."

Orb thought of her reaction to her encounters with Mym, both real and in emulation. "I understand. But—my daughter?" This was such a surprising development that she was still assimilating it.

"As a woman of twenty. Old enough to know her mind. She had a magic talent, the ability to perceive the best matches in people, as if the people glowed. I glowed, for her." He leaned over and put his face in his hands. "Forgive me," he said, his voice muffled by his fingers. "It has been long since I have spoken of her."

Orb gazed at him with a certain compassion. Her baby girl— as a woman this man had loved! Now at last she knew Orlene's future!

And Orlene had died—would die prematurely, in tragedy. That was the second shock. Her death precipitating this man's assumption of his present office. No wonder he was concerned about Orb's reaction! If she acted to save Orlene, by diverting her from the ghost marriage, Chronos might never become Chronos!

Her eye fell on the ring on Chronos' finger. The one that looked like the ring Mym had given Orb and that she had given to her daughter. Orlene had given it to him, as a signal of her love for him!

Or was it another imitation? Beset by a sudden intense curiosity, Orb extended her hand to touch the ring.

It came to life immediately, uncurling and sliding from Chronos' hand to hers. It coiled about her finger.

"Is it really you?" she asked.

The ring squeezed once.

Of course it could be lying—another ring of the type, pretending to be the one she had owned. But she doubted it.

"What he says is true?"

Squeeze.

"You could not help my daughter?"

Squeeze.

Orb put her own face in her hands, sobbing silently. For a time she remained thus. When she recovered, the ring was back on Chronos' finger. It was his, now, by the right of the chain of love.

She found Chronos looking at her. "Now you understand," he said. "I dare not change her future; therein lies paradox."

"But she *has* no future, if the weather continues!" Orb protested. "She may already be dead!"

"That need not be final."

"Not final! What is more final than death?"

"Time."

"But if she dies, your paradox is already upon you! You must save her."

"No, I may not interfere with the natural order where it concerns my own past. That would risk a disaster worse than we can
know."

"But—but if you have experienced the future—how can this
present holocaust be reconciled with that?"

"It can't."

"You are talking riddles! You can't meet and love a woman
who was killed in her childhood!"

"There is a way through. That is what I must accept."

"You live backwards! You have already experienced it! What
happens? How can this be undone?"

"There is no problem about the how. I can act at a later time—
an earlier time, for you—and nullify this particular path. The problem is the why. Only with the advice and consent of the other
Incarnations will I take such an action, for it affects us all."

"You don't know whether you did it? Will do it?"

"Because the action I will take affects my own past, I can not
be sure what has happened in my past. There is a region of un-
certainty, where the lines of history diverge and tangle. Nothing
is absolutely fixed. In one of those lines the decision will be made,
and it will guide what I will do in your past."

"You have no notion at all what is going to happen?"

"Only that the ultimate decision was yours. I acted as the Incarnations agreed, after you decided. I believe it was the correct
decision."

"So I can save the world?"

"So it seems."

Orb realized that this was as much of an answer as she was
going to receive. "If I can save it, I will save it," she declared.
"No matter what."

"I am not sure of that," he replied.

"Not sure—!" But she decided not to react further in his presence. She turned the page back to Jonah.

Jezebel was there. "Who are you?" she asked, startled.

"What do you mean, who am I?" Orb said. Then she realized
that she was still in her new, mature form. Hastily she willed
herself back to normal.

"You have learned a new trick," Jezebel remarked.

"Yes, it seems I have."

"You look tired. Let me fix you something to eat, and you can rest."

"I don't know whether I'm tired or not, now," Orb said. "After that meeting with Chronos, my mind is spinning!"

"Chronos is going to help?"

"He won't commit himself! He says that I will be the one to decide. But—oh, it's all so frustrating!"

"Well, eat," Jezebel said, setting some toast before her.

Orb looked at the watch on the wrist of the demoness. Surprised, she looked at her own. "I think your watch has stopped," she said. "It's two hours behind mine."

"Oh?" Jezebel compared the two, then went for a desk clock. The clock agreed with Jezebel's watch. "I think yours has gained."

"Gained? How could it?"

Jezebel shrugged. "You have been traveling all around the world. Perhaps it got jogged."

"I suppose," Orb agreed. She reset her watch.

She discovered that she had gulped down her toast in short order. "I can't sit here while that's out there," she muttered, and turned the page to Fate's Abode.

The oriental woman was there, as before. "May I talk to my mother again?" Orb asked.

"Again?"

"Yes, she helped me an hour ago."

Niobe appeared. "An hour ago? No."

"What do you mean, no? You showed me how to assume a mature aspect." Orb shifted into it, then back.

Niobe considered. "You were visiting with Chronos?"

"You know I was, Mother! And what he told me—my daughter, your granddaughter—"

"Let me tell you something about Chronos, dear. His mansion reflects his lifestyle. Anyone who enters it lives backwards. I have experienced the effect many times. A visitor emerges earlier than she enters. On occasion I have even met myself arriving. How long were you there?"

"How long—" Orb repeated, realizing. "You mean—an hour earlier than—?"

"You are now in your own past, as it were, by that amount.

Don't worry, it clears automatically after you catch up. It is like a string that loops back on itself; it may not reach as far, but it's all there.''

"Jezebel!" Orb exclaimed. "She said I'd talked with Chronos—before I did! Only I was in *my* time, and—oh, it's all confused!"

"These things happen," Niobe said. "I suggest you go off by yourself until it clears, then proceed normally. I was about to take a nap; Clotho will alert me when you arrive, in your past. But after this—"

"I'll be more careful with Chronos!" Orb finished.

"Yes. I'm surprised his staff didn't warn you."

"I think they tried to, but I—you know how I am."

Niobe kissed her. "Of course, dear. I will not speak of this, when you arrive again. You understand."

"So as not to confuse me further," Orb said, already confused enough.

"Yes. We all have to make accommodations, when dealing with Chronos."

Orb turned the page to the isle where she had talked with Natasha. She sat on the sand, trying to make sense of it all. Intellectually, now, she understood, but emotionally she remained confused. She had in effect traveled backwards in time, without realizing it! She could appreciate why Chronos was uncertain on some details; she had done it only once, and her confusion was great.

What was she to do? She had brought on this disaster, so was responsible. Chronos said that he could help, but only if she decided what should be done, some time in her future. So perhaps what she needed to do now was to decide her proper course. She did not want to make any more mistakes!

The wind blew past the isle, gouging sand from the beach and hurling it into the ocean. She saw waterspouts all around. If she had not assumed physical immunity from harm with her office, she would be in trouble now! What had happened to the calm brought about by her third singing of the Song of Chaos?

Then she realized that she was still in her own past! She had lost about one hour, going backwards in Chronos' mansion instead of forward. That meant that her life was two hours behind where it should be—the one she had retreated; and the one she had failed to go forward. She had labored to India to help the mermaid, then returned to Jonah, then gone to see Chronos—and returned to Jonah an hour earlier, for about half an hour of food and talk. Jezebel had remembered that, when Orb seemed to return half an hour later. Now she was here at the isle, and the moment of her singing must be incipient.

She remained on the beach, watching. How fortunate it would be, if the Chaos finally abated!

She considered turning the page to Luna's mansion. How desperately she needed the company of someone who truly understood! But surely Luna had problems of her own, dealing with the storm; better to leave her alone. "Ah, Moth," she murmured. "When I really need you, I dare not go to you!"

The time came. The wind died. The waterspouts lost momentum, shriveled, and withdrew into their clouds, which in turn thinned. The sun emerged, and the savage waves sank back into placidity. Her song had really cooled things off!

Cooled? Now she was aware how much it was cooling. Despite the sun, the air was cold.

She watched, hesitant to travel again until she had a clearer notion what was developing. The air chilled until she knew that the normal person would have had to don heavy clothing. The sky clouded again; ice crystals were forming as the upper reaches chilled and the dew point was reached.

Now she traveled. She turned the page to India.

The mermaid's pool was cooling, too. Water was slower to yield its heat than the air, but it was obvious that the mermaid would need some protection before the pool froze. Already she was huddled and shivering. What could Orb do?

She considered starting a fire. But that would be of only limited value and dangerous; how could the mermaid properly tend it? What would happen when the fuel gave out?

Yet what else offered? Orb couldn't carry her magically to a better place, and there was nowhere to go physically.

Luna! Luna could help, by lending one of her many amulets. Just as Orb's own had protected Lou-Mae, another could protect the mermaid. She turned the page to Luna's house, glad of the pretext to go there.

And stood in shock. The house was a mass of embers. It had been burned down! In fact, all this section had been razed; smoke was still rising from neighboring blocks. What had happened?

But she knew what had happened. Crazed people had run amok and torched the neighborhood—just part of the savagery unleashed as the natural order broke down.

Where was Luna? She couldn't have—no, of course not; Thanatos would have protected her. He had probably taken her to his mansion in Purgatory for the duration. Luna was the key to so much of this; she was the one Satan really wanted to eliminate. Thanatos knew that and guarded her constantly; there was no need for Orb to be concerned.

But oh, the sheer waste of this! Any chance for anyone to take shelter from the cold in this neighborhood was gone, carelessly destroyed. Luna's beautiful house, all her paintings, the two handsome griffins . . .

Orb knew that if she allowed herself to dwell on this, she would dissolve into useless tears. All of it, ultimately, was her own fault. But now she had to hold her emotion in check and do what she had come to do.

She walked through the ashes, stirring them up with her feet. Where had those amulets been? Unable to locate them, she expanded, orienting on what she wanted, and found it—a warming stone. It was the only one remaining; the others had either been removed or had lost their magic in the fire. She coalesced and bent to fish it out of the rubble—a red, rubylike gem.

She turned the page back to India. "Take this stone," she told the mermaid. "It will keep you warm."

The mermaid reached a hand turning blue to take the amulet. As she touched it, its effect manifested. "Oh, it's warm!"

"It's warm. As long as you hold it, you will be warm, too. This is the best I can do for you, until this weather changes."

"It's enough," the mermaid said gratefully. She dived below the surface, expelling the air from her lungs so that she could use her gills. Now she would survive, even if the surface froze over.

Orb turned the page to France. Here on the mountain the cold was worse; snow was falling, and Tinka and her husband and baby had insufficient protection—

What could she do? She had given the only warming charm to the mermaid. Then she knew.

"Tinka," she said in Calo.

The blanket stirred. Tinka looked out, her breath fogging. "Orb!"

Orb drew off her own cloak. "Take this. It will become whatever you need to wear, even a thick, heavy blanket."

"I know," Tinka said. "I saw its magic many times. But you—what will you do without it?"

"I have no further need of it," Orb said, pushing the cloak forward.

Doubtfully, Tinka took it. Then she stared. "But you have nothing else on!"

Indeed, Orb was now standing naked in the snow. "As I said, I have no need. But you do. Take it, use it, keep it."

The mound stirred. "What?" the man's muffled voice came.

Tinka snatched the blanket down over his head. "Nothing out there for you!" Then she focused on the cloak, and it became an enormous furry poncho that settled over the existing blanket. That would keep them all warm, both by its form and its magic!

The mound heaved. Tinka squeaked and disappeared below. Orb, satisfied, turned the page to Ireland.

She had forgotten that the water oak was gone. The site was covered with ice and snow. She expanded and found that all of Ireland was slowly freezing. Indeed, all the world; the people who had survived the storms were now squeezing into what structures remained, shoring them against the creeping cold, burning wood salvaged from wreckage, and hoarding blankets. There was no electricity, no oil delivery; the world had been reduced to a relatively primitive status.

It was better than the storm, Orb told herself. But she wasn't sure. How cold would it get?

She returned to Jonah. Jezebel eyed her somewhat warily. Orb laughed, experiencing a temporary relief from the horror she felt. "Jez, I owe you an apology. You did hear me talk about Chronos. Let me explain." She explained. "So you see, I wasn't being crazy or perverse. I'm under tension, but it hasn't cracked my mind quite yet."

"I'm glad to hear it," the succubus said seriously. "Now why don't you put something on, before my man wanders in here."

Oops! She remained naked, as she had gotten out of the habit of wearing anything but the magic cloak. She had felt no discomfort in the snow, but Jezebel was right; she needed to be clothed. Hastily she donned the blouse and skirt the succubus produced— one of Betsy's outfits.

Betsy, of course, had no further need of it. Now, abruptly, Orb burst into tears.

The demoness comforted her. She was good at it, perhaps because of her experience with the guitarist. Soon Orb got a new grip on herself. "Thank you. I'm all right now."

"That's good. We're in enough trouble as it is."

"Oh? Has something else happened?"

"Nothing new. We're running short of food. I can get more, but the economic system has broken down, so I can't arrange for proper payment of it."

"I see your point. I think I can get by without it, now, and so can you, but the guitarist and Lou-Mae—"

"Yes. And she isn't doing all that well."

"She has reason. Jez, it's my fault; I started this when I invoked magic I didn't understand. I have tried twice to change it, but each time more people have suffered. Should I try it again?"

"When I went out last time, it looked pretty cold," the demoness said. "How bad—?"

"I don't know—but I fear it will just keep going."

"Then maybe it's better to gamble again."

"I suppose so. Chronos says I will make the final decision. Maybe one of my attempts will succeed, though I don't see how it can help those who have already died."

"It seems best to gamble on the living."

"Yes." Orb fetched her harp and sang the Song of Chaos a fourth time. This time she didn't bother with the null-theme; it hadn't helped.

She knew the moment she finished that it was taking hold. Jonah shook. It wasn't the big fish; something was happening outside. Orb expanded and found that the rock through which Jonah swam was heaving. She expanded further, so as to survey the globe, and found that the effect was global. The whole world was changing.

What was happening? There seemed to be enormous stresses developing in the crust of the Earth, causing it to quiver in its effort to release tension. Those stresses were building rapidly; what would be their result?

All too soon she saw it. Huge sections of the ground buckled under the pressure, the tectonic plates being jammed together. Elsewhere new fissures opened up, and lava spewed out. Long-dormant volcanoes came suddenly to life, and new ones erupted. The geology of the world was going crazy!

Orb quickly coalesced on India, on the mermaid's pool. She was already too late; there was nothing but a fold of lava there. She turned the page to France and saw the mountain toppling over a vast new void beneath it. Tinka and her family were gone.

She expanded again, distraught. All the world was going, as earthquakes leveled every remaining building and volcanoes buried the rubble in ash and lava. The crust of the Earth was wrinkling like the skin of an elephant, turning over and over, and the smoke and ash was so voluminous that day had become night everywhere. There was no longer any air to breath; the fumes of the convulsion had replaced it.

She turned the page to Jonah—and found only lava. The huge fish had been crushed and obliterated by the titanic forces of the earth, and all the occupants were gone. Jezebel should have survived it, but perhaps was lost in the Chaos. Orb was alone.

She hovered in stasis, unable even to decide how she should feel. The calamity was so complete! She had reacted in pique and destroyed the world. What remained for her?

– 16 –

WEDDING

After an indeterminate time, Orb became aware of company. A spider was hovering before her.

"Mother!" she exclaimed, knowing that no mortal spiders existed anymore.

Niobe manifested in her natural form. "I think we should talk, dear," she said.

"Isn't it late for that?" Orb asked dully. "I've ruined everything."

"Not necessarily. Chronos can help."

"Chronos said I would have to decide for myself."

"And so you shall, dear. Come with me."

Orb suffered herself to be guided, and found herself in Chronos' mansion, along with the other Incarnations.

"We are at a critical pass," Mym said without preamble. "The war between good and evil hangs in the balance. As I see it, Gaea has three choices. She can allow the present condition of the mortal world to remain—"

"No!" Orb cried. "I killed everyone! I want only to undo as much of the damage as can be arranged and retire in shame from this office."

"Or she can sing the final copy of the Song of Chaos," he continued as if she hadn't spoken.

"Each repetition is worse than the prior one!" Orb said. "What will the final one do?"

Thanatos leaned forward, his skull-face showing beneath his hood. "You invoked the Elements of Chaos, each rendition turning it to another form. First Water, then Air, then Fire—"

"Elements!" Orb said. "Water—when the flooding came! Air—when the storms came! I never realized! But Fire—I never invoked that!"

"Nulled," Thanatos explained. "That brought chill rather than flame."

"Oh." Now Orb remembered what she had learned before: that every Song of the Llano interacted with any of the Elements or Kingdoms. She had tried to negate the Song of Chaos, but had only reversed the invocation of Fire. "Then I invoked Earth, and it destroyed everything. What can the fifth Element do, worse than that?"

"That is the Void," Thanatos said. "It will reset the universe to its original state, without form and void."

"Total Chaos," Niobe said. "Destiny reversed."

"So that God and Satan have to start their eternal war again, from scratch?" Orb asked, appalled anew. "All of what has happened before counts for nothing? All of what all of you have done—undone? How could I let that happen?" Now she understood why Satan had said this was the ultimate weapon against him—but that its cost was too great.

"Or she can vote to allow me to reverse the course of recent time, restoring the world to its state just before she started the Song of Chaos," Chronos concluded.

"Yes!" Orb exclaimed. "If you can do that—"

"There is a catch, dear," Niobe cautioned her.

"It doesn't matter! If all the damage I have done can be undone that simply, of course that's what I want! Then I can retire without singing and let someone more balanced and competent assume the office."

Mym shook his head. "You can not retire, Orb. That is a condition of the reversal. You must carry through your office."

Orb spread her hands. "Then I will! Whatever is required to bring my friends back, to restore everyone—"

"What is required is the agreement of all the Incarnations," Thanatos said. "That is the only manner a situation of this gravity can be resolved."

"But don't you all agree? How can any of you deny this?"

"We are not the only Incarnations, dear," Niobe said.

"Oh, of course there are lesser Incarnations, like Eros and Pestilence—none of them would object, would they?"

"None of them do," Mym agreed. "But there are two major Incarnations. One of them can be presumed to agree; He never interferes in the affairs of the mortals, no matter how tempting it may be."

"Oh—God," Orb said. "The Incarnation of Good. Of course. But—"

"But the other is the Incarnation of Evil."

"Satan!" Orb said, understanding. "Who opposes all good of any kind!"

"I heard My name?" a new voice said. Natasha stood there, smiling.

Orb turned her face away, her emotions abruptly raging in contrasts seemingly as savage as those she had loosed upon the world. What he had done—!

"I think you know the situation," Mars said to Satan. "Do you accede to the course we propose?"

"I could be persuaded," Satan said.

Orb was determined not to speak to him at all, but the words came from her before she knew. "How can we believe anything you say? You only want the destruction of man!"

"Not so," Satan said smoothly. "I only want to tilt the balance of power My way, relegating Mine ancient adversary to the lesser role. It hardly behooves Me to allow mankind to be consigned to the Afterlife when the balance is inappropriate."

"And it favors God now?" Orb asked, knowing it was true. "So that if everyone dies now, He wins?"

"Even so."

"Then you have to agree to revert the world!" she exclaimed to Satan. "Because you don't want to lose!"

"No."

She gazed at him, not knowing what to make of this. "But if you have no chance to win, this way—"

"I lose," he said slowly. "But so do you. Do you want your friends, and all the other innocent people of the world, to die, just to spite Me?"

Orb thought of Tinka, of Lou-Mae, of the Livin' Sludge, the mermaid, and all the others of the world. They were surely bound for Heaven, but their lives on Earth were incomplete. Her daughter Orlene was still just a child. "No," she admitted, tears stinging her eyes.

"So you are prepared to compromise, to save your friends."

"I would do anything to undo the damage I have done," Orb said brokenly.

"You would even promote My welfare?"

"What are you getting at?" she snapped.

"I have proposed marriage to you. The offer stands. Do you accede?"

"Oh, God," she breathed. "Your price for letting the world return!"

"True."

"Gaea's power allied with yours, tilting the balance to you."

"In time, that will be the case. This is My object."

Now at last the full significance of her childhood vision was clear. A wedding—or a devastated world. Her choice.

Orb looked desperately around at the others. "What am I to do? If I align with him, God loses! But if I don't—"

"This is the nature of the decision you must make," Chronos said. "None of us can make it for you."

"But the world loses either way! Is this what you have lived through?"

"No," Chronos said. "But as I intend to explain to you later, my past is malleable. It may be that I will be required to divert it to another course."

"What am I to do?" Orb repeated, distraught.

"We can not advise you, dear," Niobe said. "But perhaps one question will suffice to clarify your thinking."

"What question?" Orb asked hopelessly.

"You now know Satan for who and what he is. Do you love him?"

The implication struck Orb with stunning force. She put the back of her hand to her forehead, reeling. With all her being she tried to deny it, but could not.

"God help me," she whispered brokenly, "for I do love Satan."

"And I love you," Satan said. "I offer you the world."

"But what I say is the truth," Orb protested weakly. "What you say is a lie."

"Perhaps," he agreed. He extended his hand to her. "I ask you again, Gaea: will you marry Me?"

Orb fought, but her heart had betrayed her. She knew Natasha for what he was, for the Incarnation of Evil, but she did love him and wanted to be with him in all the ways that love might dictate.

Slowly her hand moved out to meet his. "I will," she breathed, half sobbing. Was she doing this for the benefit of the world or from selfishness? Was she already moving into his orbit of evil?

Satan held the hand, captive to his success, and faced the others. "Does anyone object to our marriage?"

No other Incarnation spoke.

"Then we shall hold the wedding at this moment, in Hell," Satan said. "All of you are invited, as honored guests and witnesses, together with any others who wish to attend. I welcome your participation and support. There shall be no question about the legitimacy of this union."

"This moment will not occur for several days, considering my action," Chronos said.

"Precisely," Satan said. "We shall all return to the time just before Gaea invoked the Theme of Chaos. None of this will have happened, and our memories of it will fade. But the agreement has been made, and all of you are party to it. It will be honored."

"It will be honored," Chronos agreed.

"My objection to your action is withdrawn," Satan said. "We are now unanimous. The world shall be spared the ravage of the Theme of Chaos. Proceed with your action."

Chronos raised his hand, and the Hourglass appeared in it, expanding to greater prominence. The sand within it brightened, flowing in its thin stream between the chambers.

The sand turned blue.

Orb was alone on the isle, mulling her situation. Her anger and grief and confusion prompted her to do what she knew she should not: sing the Song of Chaos.

Chronos appeared. His shining Hourglass held a fine ribbon of sand that was turning from blue to red. "Gaea, you must not do it," he said.

Orb was startled. "What?"

"Do not invoke the Theme of Chaos," he said. "It will destroy the world. Do you remember?"

Orb remembered. "The next few days—all my friends, all the world—gone! Is it a vision?"

"A vision, now," he agreed. "A reality that has been abrogated. Instead, you must marry Satan."

"Marry Satan!" she repeated, outraged. But then she remembered that, too. "I—agreed," she said. "I love him."

"You agreed to marry him so that the world could be saved. Now you must carry through the agreement you made. Only because of this am I permitted to change the course of history. Do you understand?"

"Everything is undone?" she asked. "My friends—?"

"The world is untouched."

The relief was immense. "I must marry Satan," she said.

Chronos nodded. He disappeared.

Orb gazed again across the sea. She sighed. "Satan," she whispered.

He appeared. "You have decided?"

"I will marry you."

"You remember?"

"As in a vision. But it stands. You gave me back the world, and I will marry you."

"Is that all?"

She looked at him. He was tall and fair and comely, the picture of the man she had known as Natasha. "How is it that you have no horns or tail, now that your masquerade is off?"

"This is My true form," he said. "My true mortal form, fixed as it was when I assumed the office. My true form as the Incarnation of Evil is as you describe. Both are valid. But this is the one I prefer to use with you. Is that the extent of what you have to say to Me?"

"I love you." He might be the creature of lies, but she had to tell the truth.

Satan smiled. "This is what I wished to hear, Gaea. May I embrace you?"

"You have to ask?"

"Yes, this first time. There must be no coercion."

No coercion! But how could she protest? "You may embrace me, Satan."

He took her in his arms, and she thrilled to his touch, even knowing him for what he was.

"May I kiss you?"

She wished she could claim that she detested this, that she was only acting a necessary part, but she could not. She desired Satan's kiss. "You may."

He kissed her, and she felt the same passion for him she had before, despite her self-reproval.

"May I—"

"Not until after the wedding," she said.

He laughed, she laughed, and it was good, in spite of everything. She did want to marry him, heedless of all that portended.

"Am I damned, Satan?" she asked.

"An Incarnation cannot be damned. But even if you remained mortal, your damnation is determined only by your motives and your actions. Are you marrying Me for the good of the world?"

"Yes. But also because I love you."

"Neither the good of the world nor love will damn you."

"But my power added to yours—I am contributing to your capacity for evil!"

"Would you love Me less if I exercised that increased capacity?"

"I—I think I would have to."

"Then I will not exercise it."

"But how can I believe you?"

"You can not trust My words, but you can see My actions. Through them you will know that I love you."

"How I wish it could be so!"

"You shall believe," he said. "In time."

She was afraid he was right.

The wedding was a phenomenal production. This section of

Hell was like a monstrous cathedral, with a domed ceiling that reached up so high that there seemed to be clouds drifting within it. Great arches enclosed the main chamber, ornamentally carved with exquisite taste. Stained glass was prevalent, its pictures illustrating scenes from earthly mythologies.

There was a dais in front, with seven elaborate chairs in a semicircle, each of carven ebony invoking aspects of the office of a particular Incarnation. One was in the likeness of a skeleton, with the legs shaped into the seat and arms into armrests and the skull into a headrest. Another was like a large wicker hourglass. A third was fashioned like a spider, the legs paired to form the enclosure for the occupant. Another seemed to be a huge red sword and scabbard. Another was like a tree, its branches twining about to form the appropriate shape.

At the ends of the semicircle were two larger chairs. One was decorated with representations of pitchforks and the faces of demons; the other with halos and angel faces.

Orb noted these details with a certain detachment; she was standing at the back in her wedding gown, awaiting the onset of the ceremony.

Suddenly the benches in the main section were filled: all the people Orb had known in life were there, including many who had died long ago. Childhood playmates, teachers and casual acquaintances; adult associates, friends, relatives, and those she had interacted with in however minor a manner. Everyone she had encountered, ever.

She wanted to go out and talk with them, for she saw her father Pacian and others who had been long gone from her life. But she could not; she was the Bride, and had to play her part in the ceremony. Probably many were illusion, anyway; would God release her father from Heaven to visit a function in Hell?

The Incarnations entered and took their seats: Thanatos, Chronos, Niobe as Fate, Mym as Mars, and Satan. The seat for Gaea was empty; Orb could not be in two places at once, on this occasion.

The seat reserved for God remained vacant. He had been invited, but did not intervene in the affairs of mortals or immortals. In any event, He was unlikely to support the merger that would

shift the balance of power away from Him. Orb found herself
feeling sorry for God. If only, just this once, He would—

Would what? Rain fire down on this ceremony, preventing the
marriage? That certainly was not His way! Yet if he did not act,
all else would become academic; the final power would no longer
be His.

And if He did act, where would Orb be? She had agreed to this,
knowing the consequence.

The great chair sat mute. Was God even paying attention? If
only He would give some sign!

Mym rose from his chair and walked down along the side of
the chamber.

It began. A choir appeared, children—no, small demons—arranged by height, each in a white robe and holding a songbook.
They sang—and the sound in any other setting would have been
deemed angelic. Orb had never heard a mortal choir sing so perfectly; every note was precise, every part perfect.

There was a motion in the choir. Something odd was occurring.
Orb peered down the aisle and saw what it was: Individual demons
were fading out and being replaced by others, who sang as perfectly, so that the song was not interrupted.

Mym appeared. "Are you ready, Orb?" he asked.

"The usual. Butterflies in stomach," she said, smiling bravely.
"What is happening with the choir?"

"They are singing angelically," Mym explained. "That is not
healthy for demons."

"They are being abolished?" she asked, horrified despite her
lack of sympathy for the creatures of Hell. "For singing well?"

"Ordinarily a demonic creature cannot be angelic in any sense.
But for this occasion there is a special dispensation. When they
perform in a manner that is better than their limit, they cease
being demons and become the next stage up: damned souls. They
fade out, being unable to remain in the demon choir. Others come
in, eager for their chance."

"So Satan really *is* being decent?"

"So it seems," Mym said. "Everything has been absolutely
straight. He doesn't want any objection to this wedding, no quibble, no technicality that might invalidate it."

"Why are you participating, if you don't approve?"

"We did make a deal, and you deserve any support we can provide."

She laughed, somewhat shakily. "I suppose we should get on with it." She took his arm.

They walked down the aisle, exactly as in her early vision. The music swelled, but not into the conventional bridal melody. They had decided on a different approach.

Satan walked in from the side and turned to await her arrival. Light shone down on him. He was the most handsome figure of a man she had ever seen. Whatever coercion he had used to bring her acquiescence to this union—and her memory of that and everything else that had occurred during the vision-interim was fading—had been largely unnecessary. She loved him and wanted to marry him.

When she reached the dais, Satan took her hand. Mym went to take the chair reserved for Mars. They turned together to face the guests.

"Gaea and I have elected to make our vows in song," Satan said. He smiled. "There has been a question which of us is the better singer. That question shall now be resolved. The superior singer will be the one whose love for the other is greater. You will be the judges."

He turned to Orb. Her harp appeared in his hand. He bowed to her and held it out. "I yield the first performance to you, the first woman I have truly loved."

Orb took the harp—and almost dropped it. It was her own; she could not mistake that. But how had Satan, the Prince of Lies, been able to handle it? Not only that, he had said he loved her, while holding it. Satan was of course far too powerful an entity for the harp to hurt, but the conflict should have destroyed the harp—if Satan were lying.

She could not pause to consider this at this moment; it was her turn to sing. Satan had gone to his chair. She had the stage.

She sat on the floor, bridal gown and all, and set up the little harp. No problem now about how much leg might be showing; the gown was so voluminous it covered everything and more! She played a chord, then started.

She sang the Song of Evening, the aspect of the Llano concerning love. There were no words to it, but they hardly mattered: the theme itself was the statement.

The sunset came to the cathedral, bringing out the preternatural color of dusk and the grandeur of the sun behind clouds. She saw the members of the audience staring raptly and knew that they had never in their lives heard a more evocative song than this. The power of love infused the assembly and transformed this section of Hell itself with its delight, comfort, and passion. Orb was truly in love, however unwisely, and this was the expression of that love.

There was a hush when she finished like that of fulfilled love. Orb had not done this in any competitive spirit, but as the most honest expression of her feeling, but she knew that there was no way that even Satan could match it.

She got up and went to the chair reserved for Gaea. Satan rose and came forward. He had no instrument; all he had ever used was his voice.

He sang, *a cappella*—and Orb received another shock. *He was singing a hymn!* How could that be? It was one of the few things Satan could not do.

> "Amazing grace, how sweet the sound,
> That saves a wretch like Me.
> I once was lost, but now am found
> Was blind, but now I see."

Orb listened, mesmerized. This was the hymn "Amazing Grace," exquisitely rendered. She had thought that there was no way Satan could match her presentation of the Song of Love, but he was going into a type of song that exceeded it: a song of the love of God. Yet this was impossible, by definition.

He began the second stanza—and now the demon choir joined in as background. What had been beautiful became transcendent. Orb suspected that no angels in Heaven could have sung more angelically than this. Indeed, the flickering in the choir intensified, indicating that the strain was too much; no demon could sing this way for more than a moment without losing its definition.

As he sang, Satan turned to face Orb. His gaze sent shivers of heat and chill running through her; his aspect and his voice were totally persuasive.

> "'Twas grace that taught My heart to fear,
> And grace My fears relieved;
> How precious did that grace appear
> The hour I first believed."

Satan was a liar, indeed the Prince of Lies. The truth was not in him. Yet Orb found herself unable to doubt his sincerity now; he was addressing her, and when he sang "grace" she heard also "love." He did love her as she loved him; there was no other way it could be.

How could the Lord of Hate love anyone or anything except power? Perhaps that was the explanation: it was the power inherent in the office of the Incarnation of Nature that Satan truly loved. She was fool enough to love him, and he loved what he stood to gain by his alliance.

Satan turned back to the guests as he sang the next stanza, and they seemed as rapt as was Orb herself. What Satan was doing was impossible, yet he was doing it. The demon choir was flickering so rapidly that it seemed unreal. Satan himself seemed to be developing a glow.

Could this be another vision? That would account for the effects; Satan was not really singing a hymn, not really uttering words that were forbidden to him. It was all a dream, crafted for maximum effect.

But if this were the case, the wedding was not valid. That was where the notion foundered. Satan might fool her into believing she had married him and, in that manner, have his will of her in any way he chose. But he could not fool the other Incarnations: not Chronos, who had lived through future history; not Fate, who was her mother; not Mars, who had loved her. They would not accept the marriage unless it was real; and if they did not accept it, the alliance was suspect. It *had* to be real for Satan to achieve his purpose.

This ran through her mind as she listened, entranced. Satan was doing what he could not do, and she believed it, and the guests and other Incarnations believed it. Perhaps there was no proper explanation. Meanwhile, her doubts had run their course and faded like mist; she believed the Prince of Lies and she loved the Lord of Hate.

The choir flickered into nonexistence; all the available demons had been upgraded to the status of damned souls. For the final stanza, Satan sang alone. He turned again to Orb, and the glow about him intensified. He had become godlike in the nobility of his countenance. He met her gaze and sang with an earnestness that transfixed her.

> "Must Jesus bear the cross alone
> And all the world go free?"

The light about him became so bright that it resembled flame. Orb's eyes were smarting from the effort of looking at him. What was happening to him?

> "No, there's a cross for everyone
> And there's a cross for Me."

As Satan concluded the hymn, the light turned blinding. Orb squinted, then blinked—and he was gone!

She lurched to her feet. "Satan, my love!" she cried. "Where are you?"

Mym stood. "He is gone, Gaea," he said.

"But—"

"He was doomed the moment he took up his cross. He knew it, but he had to do it. He has left you at the altar and given you back the world."

"What cross?" she asked, horrified.

Niobe stood and walked toward Orb. "The cross of his true love for you," she explained.

"Then he wasn't lying," Orb said. "He really did—"

"He really did, dear. He knew he could never truly marry you, but he had to come as close as it was possible to do. To love you, to have your love in return, and to complete the vows of marriage. But you are now a widow."

"The glow—" Orb said, numbed.

"It was the brightness of the redeemed souls being released

from Hell. He could no longer hold them, once he invoked the forbidden song. He truly loved you, as he had never loved before, and he gave up everything for you."

Orb looked at the empty chair that had been reserved for God. Had God really elected not to attend? Surely He had known . . .

Then the magnitude of her own loss struck Orb. She fell into her mother's arms and sobbed with her private heartbreak.

"Not too much, dear," Niobe murmured. "When you cry, Gaea, the world cries with you."

Indeed, it was raining throughout the world. But no damage was being done, and in time the sunshine would return. Now it was time for her to learn the office she had assumed and so far neglected—to concentrate on being a Green Mother.

AUTHOR'S NOTE

As I wrote each of the prior novels of this series, their themes tended to impinge on my own life. Thus Death became prominent during *Pale Horse* and Time during *Hourglass* and Fate during *Tangled Skein* and War during *Red Sword*. Perhaps it is a matter of interpretation as much as of reality; you can be the judge. *Green Mother* concerns Nature, and I was indeed aware of the things of Nature.

To begin with, as I completed the prior novel in this series, my shoulder began to hurt. It worsened over the months, and finally the pain cut off all my exercises except running. I had been doing about thirty chins on my study rafter, and 75 Japanese push-ups in under four minutes, but the pain took no note of physical condition. When it began to manifest as I reached for my keyboard, I saw the doctor; I can live without the exercises, but this affected my livelihood.

It turned out to be tenonitis. Not "tendonitis"; there is no such word, contrary to public belief. It is an inflammation of the tendon that manifested, in my case, when I tried to stretch out my arm. When I was bitten by a deerfly and swatted it, the pain of the effort was so sudden and intense it had me reeling. I could not reach my back pocket or lift my hand above my head. I learned

-302-

how to be left-handed in most respects; fortunately I am already left-handed in a number of ways, such as eating. Sleeping was a problem because there was no position in which my right arm remained comfortable; I had to undertake contortions to avoid being awakened by a jolt of pain. Sometimes by day I would simply pick up my right arm with my left hand and put it where it needed to be. I'd rather not discuss the effect this ailment had on my love life.

Pills had no effect. Finally the doctor gave me a shot in the tendon, and that turned the corner. The inflammation gave ground as slowly as it had advanced; six months later it hardly bothers me, and in a few more months it should be gone entirely. I don't know whether I'll resume my arm exercises then; after about a year's layoff, I have lost what it took me ten years to develop, and I suspect I'll call it a day. The truth is, those exercises were pretty grueling, and I feel more relaxed in their absence. Thus I learn about my own nature; now that I am on the downhill side of 50, I'm more inclined to relax a bit.

In this period I also learned more about equine nature. We moved to the forest when my daughter Penny reached horse-craze age, and each daughter got a horse. I liked Penny's horse Sky-Blue from the start; she was a registered Hackney, a former racer, then twenty years old, which would be something like sixty in a person. Blue had raised her former owner from age ten to fifteen, and had raised Penny through the same range. The former owner is now married, and Penny is in college, so you can see how well Blue did her job.

Cheryl's horse Misty was another matter. She was arrogant, not acceding readily to the directives of her rider, and taking any feed she could get at. We had to fence Blue off during feeding time so that she could eat in peace; otherwise Misty would take it all. That is why Blue became the model for two of my creatures in other series, while Misty was unrepresented. I knew which kind of horse was better.

But in this period Misty developed severe foot problems. She saw the vet more times than I saw the doctor. The essence is that the bones in her front feet warped, so that she could no longer stand normally; she had to bend her legs just above the hooves back at a thirty degree angle when she stood, and was in obvious discomfort. She lay down for most of the day. This is the stage at which horses are shot, but we are not a horse-shooting family. We accommodated her as well as we could, bringing her food and water to her.

Blue, however, had a different notion. Realizing that the mighty had fallen, she took to stealing Misty's food. Now I had to fence Blue off to protect Misty. At one point I brought some hay to Misty that Blue hadn't deigned to touch, and opened the gate, figuring Blue wouldn't try to steal that. I was wrong; Blue charged in so determinedly that Misty lurched to her feet to avoid her. Blue bit at her anyway and stood outraged guard over that hay until Misty had hobbled far away and lain down again, hungry. Then Blue left the hay—still untouched. She had never wanted it; she wanted only to establish her dominance. We had wondered why Misty was losing weight, while Blue got fat; now we knew. My illness was reversible; Misty's will be terminal.

Thereafter I fenced them apart for the full day, opening the gate only at night. I had seen to my regret that horses are no better than people; when the underdog finally gets power, he can be just as mean as the overdog was. Might makes right. Human beings, at least, can sometimes rise above their instincts and act in a more generous manner—but I think not often enough. This is the nature of creatures of whatever kind.

Another aspect of nature is the weather. Here around Florida the summers get hot and humid—on occasion our high temperature for a day has been two degrees above the high for the nation for that day—and those who have read this novel know how that can lead to trouble. There has been tremendous overbuilding along the shoreline by those who apparently assume that hurricanes are a myth. It was time for a warning blow. It came in the form of storm #4 for the season, at the end of AwGhost—Hurricane Elena. She was just passing by, heading for Alabama or Louisiana; when she was safely by our latitude, I relaxed and turned in for the night.

I should not have. Elena took that opportunity to make a right-angle turn and headed straight for us. Now hurricanes are allowed to go ashore where they choose, but not right where *I* live! I worked up some magic and straight-armed that storm, pushing her off. But it takes an awful lot of magic to stop a hurricane in full advance, and I had been caught off guard. Elena slowed, but wouldn't turn away. For two days she hovered there, building up strength; she had been a minimal blow of about 90-mile-per-hour winds, but she swelled to a hundred, then to a hundred ten, and finally became a major hurricane of a hundred twenty-five, still determined to land on our house. The entire Florida shoreline in this region was taking a beating. Then, finally, the magic prevailed and shoved her back on course toward Alabama. What a struggle! But of course I should have known better than to relax before the storm had actually landed elsewhere.

The season kept throwing storms at us, but none of the others got that close. One was called Juan (pronounced Wan), that wandered all over. I could have told them that would happen; it was predicted in the operetta *The Pirates of Penzance*, in the song "Poor Wandering Juan." The path of storms can be predicted; you merely have to know the proper key.

But these were just warm-ups for the coming novel. Once I got into the actual writing, things intensified. Not all can be lightly dismissed. For example, the person who arranged to buy this novel, Judy-Lynn del Rey, Publisher of DEL REY BOOKS, was on the phone in SapTimber, spending an hour talking with me in an effort to straighten out a problem that had come up between the publisher and me about this series. In OctOgre Judy-Lynn had a stroke that put her in a coma. In FeBlueberry she died. She and her husband Lester had put me on the map as a bestseller in fantasy, along with Steven Donaldson and David Eddings and Terry Brooks; they had done more to make fantasy a big-time operation than anyone else I know of. I fear that thus suddenly a golden age is waning. There were other deaths in this period: Theodore Sturgeon, perhaps the best writer the genre has seen; Frank Herbert, author of one of the most successful science-fiction novels ever, *Dune*; L. Ron Hubbard, who left the genre for thirty years to found Dianetics and then Scientology, then returned; I have no brief for Scientology, but Hubbard was certainly a figure to be reckoned with.

Let's move on to a gentler aspect of nature: the nature of women. This novel was delayed because I came down with a flulike illness, running a fever of a couple of degrees for a couple of days. Then it dropped to normal, the same day, FeBlueberry

4, that Blue drove Misty from the hay. I relaxed and turned in
with a book; I always read myself to sleep. I was out of paper-
backs at the moment, so I was in a hardcover: *The Gentle Art of
Verbal Self-Defense* by Suzette Hayden Elgin, who is also a genre
writer. The essence of the book is that you can defend yourself
from verbal abuse if you are alert. The first thing is to recognize
when you are under such attack; it is obvious if someone calls
you a @#$%&*!! of a Censored/Blank, but not if the person says
"I don't understand why you don't try to be fair." Beware of
words like "even" and "really," as for example "If you really
loved me, you wouldn't be such a jerk." Recognizing the state
of siege, you may then respond in a guarded or diversionary manner, so that you don't wind up feeling like a C/Blank. I found it
interesting; I took judo classes for three years and learned that
you can't throw a person who retains his balance; similarly, Suzette shows, you can't verbally damage a person who retains verbal
balance. I had a coughing fit that delayed my sleep for an hour
or so; then when I finally nodded off, the book fell from my hand
and smote me on the mouth, cornerwise.

Now this did not seem quite fair of Ms. Elgin, considering the
doctrine she was preaching. I would have continued reading her
book on the morrow, after all. Wide awake again, I resumed reading, and in another hour I nodded off a second time. Whap! Suzette smacked me again. What a temper! It took me yet another
hour to nod off, this time with the book propped so it couldn't
hit me, making four hours in all. Next day my fever shot up to
new heights, peaking at 102.5°. My mouth felt like bruised cheese
rind. Thus it was two more days before I could resume paying
work, and yes, I did finish reading the book. Suzette, dearest, if
you really loved me, you wouldn't even *want* to publish in
hardcover. . . .

The nature of computers and their programs also figured heavily in my life at this time. Those readers who object to this sort
of discussion are encouraged to skim on down the page until I
return to something interesting, if ever. The fact is, though I resisted getting computerized for a long time, just as I resisted getting involved with girls throughout high school, when I finally did
get into it, I fell in a big way. For me, being on the computer is
like starting a fine automobile or mounting a dynamic horse: it

seems alive and exciting, with limitless potential. But it can also be ornery, and the challenge, frustration, and joy of it was never more evident than when I wrote this novel.

You see, I got a new program in No-Remember. I like PTP, the text processor I was using, but it had two weaknesses: it could use only half my computer's memory, so that I had to keep chopping chapters in half because they wouldn't fit, and it had no windows, so I could look at only one file at a time. My wife spied this ad for a text processor named Edward that solved both these problems, so we sent for it, just in case. And Edward changed my life. It addressed all my computer's memory, so I no longer had to divide files, and it had fourteen buffers, or places where files could be called up, as it were, in parallel. I could call up Chapter 1, Chapter 2, Chapter 3, etc. without exiting Chapter 4, and flick back and forth between the buffers to compare, or I could move material from one file to the other, or make a change in one and save it and close down the buffer. I spent a week getting into it, not because it was that complicated, but because it opened up such new horizons for me and made me appreciate new qualities about the programs I already had. For example, Edward had a squintillion places to put macros, those keys that do simple or complicated chores with single keystrokes, such as typing out my entire address-block. I rechecked SmartKey, which is a macro program, and discovered it would put macros in those new places, too; I never realized! Thus I could set fifty macros if I wanted, instead of the twenty-two I had before. I could embed macros within macros, putting a SmartKey macro in an Edward macro. And Edward allowed me to move its functions about, putting them on any keys I want. That meant I could place them to match the equivalent functions on PTP and not have to retrain my reflexes. What fun!

But Edward had some horrendous holes, too. At one point it filled our hard disk with garbage; at other times it blew the memory, which was a frightening experience, rather like a pressure cooker exploding, only the effects were nonphysical. We had to figure out exactly where those holes were, because they were like mines waiting for someone to blunder into them. More hours I lost, defusing mines! There were also some formidable problems. Edward couldn't underline, and I use underlining frequently. The wonderful Edward macros could not be saved for future use: some glitch in the routine that was supposed to save them. Edward's printing program was of the "batch" type, which was so completely unsuitable to my need that I never even loaded it into my machine. I discovered by experimentation that PTP would print an Edward file, and that I could use "escape" codes to put in underlining. That saved Edward; I could use it after all. I decided to write a novel with Edward and see how I liked it. Yes, *this* novel.

Thus, on-schedule DisMember 1, I started writing on Edward. I had to use special escape codes to underline, and PTP to print, and to set up my macros each time. But before the month was out, I knew I wanted to stay with Edward. It was those buffers. I had worked things out with PTP to accommodate my [brackets] system of writing; with Edward I didn't have to do that, because I could set up an entire separate buffer for my ongoing notes. And another for an ongoing Table of Contents. And one for a list of characters, so I didn't have to search through past text for names I'd forgotten. Plus any temporary notefile for stray notions about other novels that occurred to me while working; I could write them and save them with no fuss. Thus everything changed; my --->arrow<--- macros disappeared, and my brackets. I had a better system. Just about the time I worked it out, we got hold of a collection of public-domain programs that do marvelous little things that the regular programs never thought of, such as unerasing a program you erased by accident that contains irreplaceable material, or scrambling a file so nobody else can read it without the code word—and these, too, had their glitches that could and did blow the memory. After much struggle I figured out how to debug the major glitch and sent a letter to the public domain folk, who evidently hadn't known; they did not respond. Glitchers never do; that's human nature.

No need to go into detail about the myriad little refinements I worked out to integrate PTP and SmartKey and Edward; suffice to say that the three programs now seem like one, overlapping marvelously. But the doing took time, much time, and that coupled with other interruptions such as horses and illness and correspondence—I wrote 1206 letters last year, and am doing over a hundred a month so far this year—have run this novel into overtime, putting me behind schedule. Aspects of the novel do reflect the nervousness and wonder of the computer experience, such as Orb's first traveling by turning the pages on reality, and the manner that mysterious codes or sequences can do truly remarkable things. Just getting the page number in the right place took us three months to figure out; PTP vindictively shoved the page numbers for Edward text so far to the right they sometimes went off the page. The breakthrough? I now put nonprinting symbols in the heading. The printer just eliminates them and closes up the line, sucking the page numbers in several columns, and PTP never even knows, heh, heh. It can take real cunning to outsmart a stupid machine, but what a satisfaction!

In the middle of it all, our hard disk crashed. The human equivalent would be complete amnesia; all our programs were lost when we replaced the unit. Except that we had been careful throughout to back up almost everything of value. But it was another harsh lesson in the nature of computers, and of course it cost its share of time.

I don't attend many fan conventions—maybe one a year—and the one for 1985 was Fall-Con (a pun on Falcon, I think) in Gainesville, Florida, in OctOgre. (The Ogre does tend to make public appearances in that month, of course.) These affairs typically have one Guest of Honor, plus appearances by a number of other genre writers, and are good places to meet writers, artists, and fans, and to shop for genre books and art and artifacts. I spent several hours autographing copies of my books and chatting with whoever was interested. I don't go public much, but when I do, I try to do it properly. Rumors to the contrary notwithstanding, I have never actually been an ogre at a convention, as anyone in the know will verify. My memory for names and faces is sievelike, but I do recall some of the other writers there. Martin Caiden, author of the story that became TV's "Six Million Dollar Man." Robert Lynn Asprin, of the punnish Myth-Begotten series. (His wife is also Lynn, and I have contributed an Elfquest story to their volume *Blood of Ten Chiefs*; if any trouble occurs, I'm tempted to say "Take two Asprin and call me in the morning.") David Palmer, author of *Emergence*, a finely crafted post-holocaust novel. There are two Haldemans, and I met one of them, and my daughters met his daughter. Robert Adams, of the

Horseclan series. Meredith Ann Pierce, author of the delightful Darkangel trilogy, who reminds me of Rapunzel because her hair reaches nearly to the floor. The following week, collecting a daughter or two from Tampa's Necronomicon, I renewed acquantance with Andre Norton, the Grand Dame of the genre, and Roger Zelazny, author of the Amber series, and met Robert Bloch—remember *Psycho*? Florida is not a complete backwoods region for the genre!

Thus went my life during this novel. It's a pretty mundane life, overall, and I'm a pretty ordinary character. I suffer increasingly from allergies that can turn my nose into a faucet for hours or days at a time, and slobs cut in front of me in lines, and the phone glitches when I try to make a call. I presume these things happen to every nonentity, in this world. That is surely a major reason I seek respite in the realms of fantasy, where I have the illusion of importance. Yet even the mundane life has its minor compensations. When I walk out around the grounds I see the little cedar trees we planted as seedlings; now some of them are my height, and some are taller. I have paths that go to them, for I love paths. I know the little wild flowers that grow nearby; there was a violet beside a cedar tree that came up just for me each year. Then, abruptly, it was gone; evidently a horse had stepped on it. That saddens me every time I pass that spot. Nature can be cruel. There was a little pine tree growing, just rising into adolescence, and then the wind took down a big old dead oak, and that oak caught the pine tree and snapped it off. That, too, I mourn, even years later, though we have thousands of pine trees growing.

In fact we set up a region for Penny with pines, called Penny's Pines, with one for each year of her life. Then when we fenced it for the horses it was less accessible, so we moved Penny's Pines to a new spot. Since that time no new pines have appeared at the old site, but a score of new little ones have seeded in the new one; they knew! Penny and I are special; I have short brown hair and she has long blond hair, but one day we discovered that we match exactly at a given length; if I wore mine as long as hers, I'd be blond, too. Which explains why my mother always thought I was blond, and I thought she was color-blind. Our eyes match, also; Penny's my daughter through and through. We live and learn constantly about nature; even the little things aren't always what they seem.

When we built the barn and stalls for the horses, two huge spiders moved in, one with about a four and a half inch legspan, the biggest web spinner ever seen, and the other was larger. Fine; they trapped the flies that bother the horses. Then the larger drove out the other and took over that site. Then one morning that one was hanging from its web, dead; I never found out what happened. Whole life histories are available for our consideration, in Nature, if we but watch.

Death is integral to Nature, of course. It was my preoccupation with death that started this series, and I have had many letters from readers who say they were helped over personal crises of death by that novel. I always read and respond to these with mixed emotions: glad to have been of help, however distantly, but sad that the crisis had to come at all. Meanwhile, the Deathwatch, which I bought at the time of that first novel, I finally retired during this novel; in four years its functions had declined to the point where it simply wasn't worthwhile to use it. I set it aside with a special sadness. I shouldn't personalize machines, I know; still . . .

Death can strike at the least expected times. In this period of *Green Mother* the Tylenol crisis redeveloped, causing the company to discontinue capsules, because some grisly joker was putting cyanide in them. I have little brief for big drug companies, but this one strikes me as a singularly upright one, paying a singularly unjustified penalty for someone else's misdeeds. We may thus have seen one of the new forms that world terrorism will take, bringing death and ruin to innocent parties.

There was also the case of a most foolish challenge of Nature that resulted in tragedy. A launch of the Challenger shuttle was set, but the night was cold. We live at the same latitude, and our morning low was the coldest of the winter, sixteen degrees Fahrenheit. It wasn't quite as cold on what in my lexicon is called the Isle of Illusion, but there were long icicles on the equipment. Engineers were worried about the ability of the sealing rings to function in cold weather, but the powers that be overruled them and fired off the rocket anyway. Thus seven lives and a billion dollars thrown away needlessly, and the space program severely damaged, because people did not yield to Nature. That horrifies me on several levels.

While delving through my old papers in search of something else, I came across material relating to my researches for *Macroscope*, one of my earlier novels. It was an article in a 1967 issue of *Saturday Review*, by John F. Wharton, and I had highlighted significant passages. Now I find those passages relevant to my present thinking. They describe the nature of man: his enormous capacity for self-delusion, and his propensity to bully others. Thus, in the name of a compassionate faith, fanatics slaughter those who have done them no harm, and we race recklessly toward destruction. Religion doesn't stop it, it merely finds ways to forgive sin. This explains part of my cynicism about that subject; I prefer prevention to forgiveness.

Which brings me to my conclusion. I make no claim to any special depth in these novels; they are entertainments that merely flirt with the deeper concepts that underlie our superficial reality. Just as the screen of the computer is a window to an aspect of its inner workings, so is the human eye a window to an aspect of mundane reality. Codings and buffers enable the computer to present portions of its content as if they were all of it, and if you don't know how to use those controls, you will never see the rest. I see this as an analogy to the deeper nature of our existence. We see only the superficial aspects, the skin of a person, the paint on the wall, and extrapolate to perceive the larger situation. But even so, do we grasp it all? Or are there entire worlds that we can not perceive, alternate realities that are present but beyond our ken unless we learn the keys to their revelation? So far, this concept has been evoked mostly in science fiction and fantasy, but now science is approaching it, suspecting that we perceive only a tenth of the mass of the universe. What about the other nine-tenths? What is the key to its perception? Can science devise some magic spell to reveal it? Is the universe, seen and unseen, truly random, or is there some higher organization, some ethic superior to what we practice?

This leads us to considerations of God, which I shall define as the source of that higher organization. Some readers send me letters of proselytization, assuming that I have somehow lived my life without becoming aware of Jesus. I had a report that a fundamentalist school was banning my books on the grounds that I was a Satanist. (I wrote them a stiff letter, reminding them that Jesus would not have lied like that. I am at this writing approaching my thirtieth anniversary of marriage to a minister's daughter.) One reader wrote at length arguing that either Jesus was a stark, blithering lunatic who should have been put away, or he was correct when he claimed to be the son of God, with all that implies. No; this is a fallacy of limited thinking. The world is not black/white, it embraces all the shades of gray in between. Jesus did not have to be one or the other; he could have been a man who felt a strong need to reform the evils of the world, and whose parables were misunderstood by those who took them literally instead of grasping their messages. What mischief is wrought by those who take Jesus' words in vain—without realizing it! Jesus claimed to be the son of God? Of course he was. *We are all children of God.*

ABOUT THE AUTHOR

Piers Anthony was born in August, 1934, in England, spent a year in Spain, and came to America at age six. He was naturalized American in 1958 while serving in the U.S. Army. He now lives in Florida with his wife Carol and their daughters Penny and Cheryl. His first story was submitted to a magazine in 1954, but he did not make his first story sale until 1962. Similarly, he submitted his first novel, which was also his thesis for his B.A. degree from college, in 1956, but did not sell a novel until 1966. In 1985 his 50th book was published. His firxt Xanth novel, *A Spell for Chameleon*, won the August Derleth Fantasy award for 1977. His novel *Ogre, Ogre* may have been the first original fantasy paperback ever to make the *New York Times* bestseller list, and all his fantasies since then have been bestsellers. He is currently writing three or four novels and answering twelve hundred letters a year. His house is hidden deep in the forest, almost impossible to find, and he now has a computer in the horse pasture.

9 5 1 5   7 9